CW00921594

HUNTERS

The Ballad of the Songbird
Book 1

Jon Ford

Tepris Press
UK

Hunters

The Ballad of the Songbird – Book 1

Jon Ford

This is a work of fiction. Unless otherwise indicated, all the names, characters, businesses, places, events, and incidents in this book are either the product of the author's imagination or used in a fictitious manner. Any resemblance to actual persons, living or dead, or actual events is wholly coincidental.

All rights reserved. This book or parts thereof may not be reproduced in any form—electronic, mechanical, photocopy, recording, or otherwise—without express prior written permission of the copyright owner.

All songs, song titles, and lyrics contained within this book are the property of the individual songwriters and copyright holders.

ISBN: 978-1-736-1950-0-0

Editing by NT Anderson
Cover art by Marlena Mozgawa
Formatting by Jon Ford

Copyright © 2021 Jon Ford

First edition first published by Jon Ford, 2021.

All rights reserved.

www.jonfordauthor.com

Mum & Dad

Thank you for indulging my reading habit
all those years ago.
It **finally** paid off!

Love Always

xXx

| Prologue |

HUNTED

– Kareena St. Claire –
– Friday – Mont Tremblant, Pack Nation –

She ran.

Willing already exhausted legs to keep moving, her heart drummed against her rib cage as the thumping sound reverberated in her ears. Her lungs burned. She was already as good as dead, so why was she delaying the inevitable?

Fear.

The primal instinct drove her onward even as her rational mind told her it was hopeless. She cursed at every thorn that snagged her delicate skirt or left ugly scratches on her exposed skin. The uneven ground worked against her, threatening to trip her every panicked footfall.

I should never have come out here.

Yet what choice had she been given after what happened at the commune? She fled to the forest because it had always been a place of safety for her before. Now she felt the keen sting of its unexpected betrayal.

Stupid, stupid, stupid!

Her fantasies of being a princess in a fairy-tale forest were cruelly exposed as a childish delusion. Ironically, as her terror played out in ragged gasps, she realized she *was* living a fairytale. The one with the Big Bad Wolf. But there was no woodcutter coming to rescue her.

Who *could* save her? The monster had killed everyone she had ever cared about. She alone had survived purely because she fled. However, the same escape that kept her alive also caused the panic that rendered her hopelessly lost. A moment was all she needed to get her bearings, but it was time she simply did not have.

A root grabbed at her foot, sending her sprawling into a small sunlit clearing. She twisted to survey the tree line behind her. Surely this was it? Surely, she was caught.

She waited, trembling, trying to control her breathing. The forest was deceptively quiet, yet she knew the monster was still out there. He wouldn't give up. Not now. Would he?

She choked on a fearful sob and slowly crawled backward, her eyes anxiously scouring the forest in front of her. A gentle breeze ruffled the leaves, but of her pursuer there was no sign. Hope blossomed.

Please...

Maybe she had lost him.

As she held her breath, she became aware of a throbbing pain in the palm of her hand.

No!

She sobbed; her flowering hope cruelly crushed by the crimson droplet gathering at the edge of her palm. It dripped to the floor of pine needles beneath her. Another bead of blood followed. Perhaps she could have gotten away with a scratch, but this...

Any glimmer of escape, however fleeting, was irrevocably gone.

She ran.

| 1 |

LONDON

– Gayle Knightley –
– Monday – London, England –

"Bollocks," she cursed under her breath.

Big Ben chimed the hour as Gayle snatched her phone from her coat pocket, glaring at the screen. It confirmed what the bells were already telling her. Noon.

Fuck!

A missed call message begged for her attention. Her father. He could wait – she was late as it was.

The rain was settling in hard, matting her hair against her face. Scowling skyward, she noted that the dark thunderclouds mirrored her current mood. The sharp beat of the heels she wore echoed loudly as she crossed a deserted Marlborough Road. Brushing an errant pink strand behind her ear, she checked for nonexistent traffic. London wasn't the city from the old movies she loved. Its days as a European hub of trade and culture were long over. Tourists no longer visited for its rich history, stunning architecture, and a glimpse of the Monarchy.

The United Kingdom's place in the global theater was now broadly defined by how it had contributed to the War and to the future security of the world. It was where the fight back had truly begun. The history books made it sound vaguely courageous, billed as the Battle for Britain. Heroic propaganda was created to make the survivors feel better, when in reality, it had not been a pleasant time through which to live.

The Rising had been terrifying, and The Hunts had been dreadful.

The Purification... Well, that had been pure hell. No one ever talked about that these days.

It had truly been the darkest of times.

As Gayle approached the Victoria Memorial, she contemplated the nature of the 'invitation.' Her optimism regarding a change of her operational status had been tempered over the last nine months, with inactivity driving her to a place of bitterness and anger.

Stepping off the curb to cross Constitution Hill, the stiletto heel of her right boot skidded on the wet road. She gritted her teeth as her surgically repaired knee gave a painful reminder of why she had been removed from active duty.

"I warned you years ago about your impractical choice of footwear, Knightley."

Gayle pursed her lips.

"You're just pissed you don't look this good in heels, Torbar," she retorted.

"How come you're walking the Mall anyway? Don't you live over in Chelsea?"

She didn't answer; getting into a personal conversation with him was not on the morning's agenda.

"Ah," he said after a beat. "Charing Cross...you've come from your parents place in Ely."

Evidently, he wasn't just going to leave her alone. With their history she shouldn't have expected anything else.

"What do you want, Torbar?"

"I thought you'd quit."

"Vicious rumor."

"Really?" Torbar said sarcastically. "That's not what I heard. A little bird told me that Admiral Hawkins wanted you drummed out of the Service. But that you beat him to the punch and resigned."

It was hard to argue since that *was* pretty much exactly

what happened. Except the resigned part. Not that she hadn't tried, but she had been persuaded that maybe a 'medical leave of absence' would be a healthier option until cooler heads prevailed.

She didn't look at Torbar. She didn't need to. They'd known each other for the better part of a decade, and had once been...intimate, for want of a better word.

Gayle straightened her leg, gingerly testing the knee, and winced.

Could this day get any worse?

"I thought I'd misread the security memo when it said you were coming back to the Academy," Torbar continued nonchalantly. "But here you are."

She knew what he was doing. Their shared history meant she could read him like a book. His face may be displaying the blank look of innocence, but he was actively trying to push her buttons. Probing to see what she knew. Attempting to prod her into a reaction with such a benign, yet leading statement.

"Security memo?" she asked against her better judgment.

"I thought perhaps they were warning us." His annoying grin informed her of his pleasure that she had taken the bait. He was enjoying this as much as she was hating it.

Bastard!

In the interest of trying to keep a low profile today, she resisted the ever-growing urge to punch him in his square-jawed face. Tuning out his continued prattle, she instead refocused on her destination — Buckingham Palace.

Shunting aside the pain in her knee as best she could, she quickened her pace, knowing from experience that Torbar would struggle to match her lengthier stride. She was approaching the guardhouse when something he said re-engaged her attention.

"Word is that they're starting up the program again. That they want you to teach the new cadets."

She came to an abrupt halt as the security guard stepped forward from the small hut that was sheltering him from the rain. As she searched her coat pockets for her long unused Human-Fae Alliance identification, she finally turned to look at

Torbar.

"Norbel's recruiting again?"

"I guess they're supposed to be your replacements," he said flatly.

Gayle's jaw tightened and she felt her nails bite into her palms. "Where did you hear that?"

"Is it true?"

It had better not be.

She assumed she was being summoned to receive a bollocking about something she had done. Or, more likely, something she had neglected to do. Gayle knew High Command considered her a maverick, and only her track record of getting results forced them to turn a blind eye to her often-unconventional tactics.

Until *Bloody Valletta.*

They couldn't ignore that.

She swallowed hard and shoved the memory aside.

"I highly fucking doubt it. Can you really see me teaching a bunch of bloody kids?"

"Maybe you're right." Torbar shrugged. "I thought they might ask *me* to teach the new up and coming generation. But then again, *my* team's still on active duty."

"Piss off!" she growled, her fist tightening further.

"Although, if *you* teach them, they'd also get free tuition on how to use profanity creatively."

"I'm sorry, princess. Am I hurting your delicate fucking ears?"

He ignored her sarcasm. "Just remember – you were one of those kids once…"

She flashed her security pass at the disinterested guard who waved her through with little more than a cursory examination. Her reputation apparently still preceded her.

"We both were," she said. "But you're right on one point. The last thing they need is to be taught the bad habits of the *Bitch*—"

"—*of Bulgaria,*" Torbar finished. "It always did have a ring to it."

"Smartest thing to come out of General Matthews' mouth."

"Credit where credit's due – that Sofia mission was impressive." Torbar's tone hinted at genuine sorrow. "The 137th...they were really something."

In his own way, Torbar was expressing his condolences for her loss. Gayle wasn't sure how to respond to his gesture. This was virgin territory for them.

"Well, General Matthews certainly didn't agree with you," she said softly before hardening again. "Anyway, I don't know anything about new recruits. All I know is that my orders are to report to General Norbel here at midday, a meeting I'm already late for, so be a darling and piss off."

Torbar shook his head. "One day I'll teach you how to make friends and influence people."

"What the fuck do I need friends for?"

"Everyone needs friends." Torbar turned, waving a casual farewell. "See you around, Captain."

Gayle didn't bother reciprocating his gesture as they parted company, heading down opposite corridors.

Her footsteps reverberated off the polished marble as she entered the Grand Hall. Gayle glanced around the empty room. Norbel kept time like a Swiss watch, so it seemed damn peculiar that, despite her tardiness, she arrived first. With a deep breath, she resolved herself to waiting, tapping her foot impatiently.

World leaders and royalty had been among the first casualties of The Rising. While The Purification brought a peace to the country again, and the stability of a government in the Palace of Westminster, the Royal Family were simply irreplaceable. An empty Buckingham Palace became a redundant landmark, albeit one with a sizable grounds near the seat of democratic power. It was perfect for the needs of the Fae.

They repurposed it to become the headquarters of the Human-Fae Alliance, incorporating the HFA Academy. These halls and corridors were seared into her memory, as it was where Gayle had learned how to harness her genetic gifts. A school for hybrids – special children with both Fae and Human parentage.

The focal point of the Grand Hall was the stone shield

prominently featured high on the wall. A fist with the wings of the Fae was centrally sculpted, the motto of the HFA engraved elegantly beneath it: *'Fortitudinem per unitatis.'*

'Strength through unity.'

Idealistic words that represented something she had once believed true. Now, she was no longer sure. Valletta taught her a tough lesson: unity only gets you so far.

Stylized glyphs representing Earth, Air, Fire, and Water surrounded the winged fist. The Fae could manipulate these elements and, by extension, so could their hybrid offspring. Gayle could burn this whole Palace to the ground or unleash a tornado powerful enough to rip it apart brick by brick if the mood moved her. She closed her eyes, and absently scratched her cheek with a bitten fingernail. She hadn't used her powers for months.

She had been the Hunter they all aspired to. Holding all the Academy records and setting all the benchmarks. A quirk of her birth, to be fair, but it had still been a perverse source of pride for her.

Pride, however, often preceded a fall.

Her tumble had been bloody, and brutal.

Valletta. Fucking Valletta.

It haunted her, never straying far from her thoughts. She was now a tarnished example of what happens when power corrupts you. Did she have regrets about Valletta?

Honestly?

"Captain Knightley." His utterly perfect baritone broke her train of thought.

"General," she acknowledged.

Seeing him triggered a conflict of emotion. Anger, but also guilt.

Settle down... Take a deep breath.

"I was truly sorry to hear about Vaylur. I...I should have said it sooner, but..."

Words ran dry. No, she didn't want to be there, but despite the resentment burning within her, General Norbel was family. Her mother's brother. On the day she shipped out to Valletta with the 137th, her uncle had been involved in a flyer accident with one fatality – his husband. She found out about it three weeks later...after she woke from her medically induced coma. She had *meant* to contact him, but somehow never got around to it.

Grief, anger, injury...she could blame many things, but as time passed, reaching out to express condolences felt too long overdue. Awkward.

Norbel's eyes flickered for a moment as an emotion she couldn't place crossed his perfect face. His hands drifted together unconsciously as he touched the platinum band on his ring finger, turning it slightly.

"No apology is required...or necessary. Vaylur is now at one with the River. I lost a husband; you lost a team. You had your own feelings to process. I understood that, and our first meeting after..." He paused for a moment before saying it. "...Valletta was not conducive to family business."

His magnanimity gave Gayle another tiny pang of guilt. A sliver of empathy that cracked her dark mood briefly. Yet, as she followed her uncle to his office, the seething cocktail of resentment and anger swiftly reestablished itself.

"I am very glad you accepted my invitation," Norbel said, making small talk to break the silence as they walked.

"I wasn't sure if it was an invitation...or an order." Even as she said it, she inwardly cursed herself for seeming so petulant.

But truth be told, these feelings had been bubbling away inside her for too long now. She'd always had a temper, but this level of fury was new. Valletta had fundamentally changed her. The rage felt like it had become an integral part of her now.

Norbel sighed, indicating he hoped that Gayle would be a little more compliant than she had been at their last meeting nine months ago. Her stare dared him to confront her directly about the reason she had been side-lined for so long, but as she looked into his eyes, she saw them harden to flints. He wasn't going to bring it up.

"Please. Come into my office. We should talk."

Gayle took a deep breath before heading through the impressive wooden doors, entering the room beyond.

| 2 |

ONE WAY OR ANOTHER

– Zarra Anderson –
– Monday – Havana, Cuba –

Why is there so much goddamn runnin' in this job?

The sun was fresh over the horizon. It cast long shadows across the deserted early morning streets, creating a thousand dark hiding places. Ample opportunity for her prey to conceal himself if she let him out of her sight. Fortunately, he seemed more interested in running. Still, time was against her. As the sun continued its inexorable rise, the city would begin to wake up. Civilians on the streets would complicate matters considerably.

Zarra had to admit, as much as she hated the running, she was physically built for the chase. Long legs made quick work of covering ground, while her brain instinctively evaluated her pursuit options, mentally cross-referencing them with her quarry's escape route and rejecting the options that didn't help her. If he was a local, then he would have the distinct advantage of familiarity with these streets and the possibilities they presented. Not an unusual set of circumstances...this was the nature of the job. It simply meant that she had to be smarter than him and predict the choices he would make.

Somehow, it always ended up with her running.

Dammit, he's fast.

The worn rubber soles of her objective's battered sneakers

kicked up dust from the road surface as he abruptly altered course, veering off the main street through an opening in a low brick wall. He disappeared down the side of a ramshackle-looking house and into the shadows of the alleyway. Even as he was making his turn, Zarra was already evaluating her options. She deviated sharply to the left, heading toward the closest point of the wall in a direct line to where he had vanished.

"You got him?" came the voice in her ear.

"Not yet!" she growled back, without breaking stride.

She paced her last pair of steps to the wall like a triple jumper, timing the push-off with her left leg to perfection. Planting her hand, she flicked her legs up and slid over the wall smoothly, brushing it almost imperceptibly. As her limbs cleared the dusty bricks, she pushed off with her hand to keep forward momentum. Hitting the ground on the other side, still sprinting, she passed the corner only a handful of seconds behind her prey.

She saw him, closer now. He threw a glance back at her and was startled to notice the diminished gap. Redoubling his efforts, he feverishly cast his head around looking for new avenues of escape.

"Getting slow, Zee!"

"Shut up, Becka. I'd get him quicker without your constant yammerin' in my ear!"

He was fast...but she was faster. She was built like an athlete, where he was built like a wrestler. Under these circumstances, his physique was working against him.

Her thoughts flicked momentarily to her split lip, and the lingering taste of her own blood.

Fuck him.

She had tried to do this the easy way – talk first – but he wasn't interested. That lucky shot was the only one he was going to get. She shouldn't have let him tag her at all, but he was quicker than he looked. In the moment it had taken her to shake off the hit, he had smartly seized advantage of her decidedly ungraceful sprawling fall to make his escape.

They always ran.

Fuck 'em all.

But she was gaining, and he knew it. Which meant that very soon things were inevitably going to get punchy again. Yes, they always ran, but the other truism of the job was that they also never went down without a fight.

He had shown no evidence of being armed in the bar where she found him, but just in case, she popped open the safety locks on her holsters, one on each hip. It was best to be prepared. She'd done this too many times to expect a peaceful resolution.

Her target repeated his previous maneuver, dodging desperately into another alleyway and disappearing momentarily from her view. However, while he was clearly acting on a base instinct to elude capture, *her* brain was already processing his possible getaway options.

Zarra was a master of the hunt. Her thought processes were similarly instinctual but guided by a veteran's savvy gained from the experience of hundreds of comparable pursuits. As she closed on the abrupt turn he had just taken, she glanced down the parallel alley immediately preceding it, swiftly evaluating its features – a dead end blocked by a wall too high for him to clear. Zarra smiled inwardly. If the passage he had chosen was comparable in construction, he was trapped. There was nowhere left to run.

If he's gonna stand and fight, then this is the time to do it!

She instantly calculated the time it would take her to cover the distance from her present footfall, to turning the corner that led to her prey – a handful of seconds at most. Yet, in that scant time he could easily come to a halt and be waiting for her. Even unarmed, Zarra knew he undoubtedly had the strength to quickly gain the upper hand if allowed the element of surprise.

In a smooth motion, she drew the gun on her left hip and hit the ground just before the alleyway, right shoulder first. She rolled and came up on one knee facing down the passage, weapon brandished in the direction of her prey's only way out. Her heart pounded and adrenaline surged as she waited for the expected attack.

Nothing happened.

Her eyes snapped to him instantly, further down the alleyway than she had expected and rapidly approaching the high wall at the end. The bigger surprise was that he wasn't Human anymore. As she watched, he finished smoothly shifting form into a dark feline shape and moments later, free of the remains of his clothing, bounded over the wall with animalistic ease.

She surged back into motion, legs pumping again as she gave renewed pursuit.

"Fuck!" she muttered. "Becka, he's a shifter. T-seven...possibly an eight."

The 'T' was MercNet code for 'therianthrope' – Humans that could shapeshift into animals. Werewolves and their ilk. The following number was a designation of their transformation speed – the higher the number, the faster their ability to shift forms.

"You can't tell?" her companion replied with a hint of incredulity.

"He was mid-shift when I clocked him, but he's damn fast."

She slid her weapon back into its holster, thumbing a setting on the grip as she did so. She approached the wall at top speed and, without slowing, leaped to grab the top, hoisting herself up and over in one fluid motion.

"That was *not* on the warrant." Becka was all business now. "Class?"

"Five," Zarra answered immediately.

Class four was your standard Werewolf-sized animal form; lower numbers were smaller beasts, higher numbers larger. This one was definitely bigger.

"Form?" Becka asked.

As Zarra hit the ground on the other side of the wall, she stopped. The alley opened onto a courtyard. She eased slowly forward, hands resting on gun grips, ready for any sign of aggression. The courtyard had three different exits, and no sign of her target.

"Some kinda really big cat. Like a lion, or a cougar, maybe..."

With his enhanced pace while in animal form, the smart

choice would have been to go for the furthest door to try and throw her off his scent. Zarra's gut, however, told her that while he was strong, he was not especially bright. He would likely choose the shortest path.

She took off running toward the closest door, leading into an apartment building to her right. As she approached it, her hunch was confirmed by the splintered wood lying on the floor from the broken frame where he had used brute force to smash through it. She lowered her own shoulder and followed suit into the narrow corridor beyond.

"There are no cougars in Cuba, Zee."

"I ain't no expert on big cats, Becka. I'm just tellin' you what I saw," she growled. "Just get me somethin.' Anything. Check the goddamn 'paedia!"

"I'll check... Doesn't ring any bells, though."

"I just need to know what I'm dealin' with here ASAP!"

"Okay, keep your knickers on. I'm working on it..." As usual, Becka was unflappably British.

Zarra dashed along the tight corridor as fast as she could, thinking that the narrow space surely would have impacted his speed

Ahead of her, the doors to each apartment seemed undisturbed. The corridor turned left at the end, and if she was going to catch him, another shortcut was required.

"Becka, pinpoint my GPS – apartment...3A. I'm about to ruin someone's day..."

Skidding to a halt, she braced herself against the right-hand wall and lashed out quickly with her boot at the closed door for apartment 3A. She expected screams of panic and dismay from the family living within, but instead silence greeted her. No one was home.

Good. Makes things easier.

"I take it that was a door?" Becka surmised from what she heard over the comms channel. "You realize that smashing up other people's property cuts into our profit margins."

Zarra spent a moment gauging her surroundings. Moving again, she ran down the hallway heading toward the lounge and its large window. In most old action movies, the hero would place their arms protectively in front of their face and dive through the transparent material, emerging miraculously unscathed on the other side.

Zarra knew better.

This wasn't a movie – that cheap plate glass would slice her neatly to ribbons if she tried it.

Her eyes darted around the room and settled on a square, thick-bottomed glass vase on the coffee table, three quarters full of water and holding a bouquet of colorful flowers of a type Zarra didn't recognize. She wasn't a flowers kind of girl.

Whoever lives here, I'm real sorry!

"Pencil us down to replace a vase. And a window, too."

As she passed the coffee table, she snatched it up, and whipped it toward the window ahead of her. As planned, the heavy vase with the extra weight of the water shattered the glass on impact, raining deadly shards outward onto the pavement beyond.

She lifted her lead leg like a hurdler, clearing the sill, her trailing leg following suit. No fancy hitting the ground and rolling back up to a sprint like in the movies here – she knew better than to roll around in broken glass.

Zarra grimaced as her left shoulder blade caught a shard still lodged in the frame on her way past, slicing deftly through the leather of her combat suit and scoring her flesh. She ignored the pain and evaluated the injury calmly.

Minor flesh wound; may need stitches later, but I've had worse.

The shortcut paid off handsomely.

There you are! You big, ugly bastard!

The look on his face as she appeared from the shattered window was priceless. He had shifted back to Human form and was heading directly toward her but caught himself and skidded to a halt in his bare feet. She tightened her grasp on the grips of her weapons.

Here it comes.

It always came down to the final stand...and they always decided to fight.

"Got it, Zee," Becka said. "Possible type match on your runner. Harimau Jadian, if I'm pronouncing that right. Malaysian or Indonesian in origin. It's a shifter, all right. Big jungle cat...often a tiger."

She yanked her firearms free of their holsters, training them on the fugitive shapeshifter in an attempt to make her intentions crystal clear.

Don't mess with me.

From the look on his face, she didn't think that he got the message.

"He's a long way from home," Zarra mumbled.

"Warrant says alive, Zee."

"I don't think he plans to come peacefully, Becka. I may have to spill a little blood here."

"Just reminding you," her partner replied. "Says here that they're not usually hostile – only when driven by hunger or revenge. Try talking to it?"

Talk to it? That was her advice? Yeah, because that went over so well in the bar earlier.

Rising from her crouch, she drew a deep breath and relaxed her stance. The aim of her weapons remained an unspoken and overt warning. All his attention was now directly on her – a silent evaluation. She had an intuition for when a situation was about to slide sideways and paying heed to it had kept Zarra alive this long. She gripped her guns just a smidgen tighter.

He was being...twitchy.

She hated it when they were twitchy.

"Becka...if this situation slides, do we got any idea what will take this guy down?"

No answer was forthcoming. She looked at her opponent who was flexing his hands and closing them into cinderblock-sized fists.

Nothin' ventured, nothin' gained.

She took a deep breath.

"My name is Zarra Anderson. I'm a licensed Freelance Peacekeeping Agent workin' for the Federated States of Europa. You've been cited on an FSE Track and Retain Order as a person of interest in regard to some attacks reported in the area. Believe me, it's in your best interest to come quietly so we can conclude this without any bloodshed. So, I'm orderin' you...to stand down."

His face remained implacable. Either he didn't comprehend her, or he didn't care.

"Kenapa awak memburu kita? Kami tidak melakukan apa-apa kepada anda. Kenapa awak tak tinggalkan kami?"

He growled at her in a language she didn't understand, while walking menacingly toward her. An intimidating specimen, seven-foot plus of nakedness, wide and lean with muscles to spare. His hands remained balled into fists. Intuition confirmed.

"Becka?" she said uneasily, backing up slowly.

"No data on take-down criteria yet, Zee. Try the silvertips. Works on Werewolves...maybe it'll work on him, too."

The Webley & Scott F21 Freelancer was the firearm of choice for people in her profession. It could be loaded with a primary magazine of twenty untipped rounds, and a supplementary cartridge of twenty custom tips. A selection mechanism on the grip could be programmed to change the type of load attached to the rounds before firing. When it became clear he was a shifter, she had already thumbed the setting to give her the Werewolf-incapacitating silver-tipped rounds.

"No shit," she hissed back. "Thanks for your help. Really. Any idea what he said?"

"Nope. Don't even know what language that was."

"Jesus, Becka!" Zarra grumbled as she took another step back from the advancing behemoth. "Tell me again why I keep your useless ass around."

"My sunny disposition?" came the glib reply. "Chill ya boots, boss. I recorded it to run through linguistics later."

He was starting to shift back to his animal form, and now that she had a clear view, she could quite clearly see that Becka had been correct.

A goddamn tiger.

"Back it up, big fella!" Zarra shouted, but the creature paid no heed. "That's your last warning!"

He launched himself at her with unmistakably vicious intent – a blur of orange and black, fangs bared and claws un-sheathed. Every inch the cornered predator looking to fight its way out with deadly resolve.

Zarra dipped to the side and rolled effortlessly off her shoulder to evade him. She heard the scrabble of claws on the smooth paving slabs as her foe tried to turn, but the footing wasn't working in his favor. Her rubber-soled boots, on the other hand, provided the grip she needed to easily pivot.

Her left arm followed a smooth trajectory, and as her sidearm came to bear, she squeezed the trigger calmly. Her shoulder braced for the familiar recoil as the single shot was fired and the shell casing ejected.

She rarely missed.

The silver-tipped projectile struck fur at the creature's shoulder blade. Zarra waited on the reaction. Silver, while not lethal to a Werewolf, would cause an allergic reaction that was extremely painful and almost instantaneous. Yet, other than the crimson smear spreading slowly across his auburn fur, her prey showed no signs of being affected in the slightest by the flesh wound.

Zarra squeezed the trigger again and watched the second silver-tipped round hit her target, this time striking the other shoulder, producing the same bloody result. By now he had completed his turn.

"Dammit..." she muttered to herself and thumbed the grip back to the more numerous standard rounds. No point in wasting the silver-tips if they had no effect.

"That's a no-go on the silver-tips, Becka. Ideas?" There was an even greater sense of urgency in her voice now.

"Just not the hi-ex rounds, Zee. Alive, remember?"

"Yeah, yeah. No promises," she retorted, before muttering to herself, "Might come down to you or me, big fella."

Zarra had tangled with many a beast over the years, but she had to confess that this was the first time she'd picked a fight with a tiger. He was more measured in his approach on this occasion as he prowled toward her. She watched the muscles ripple down his back. Cornered and wounded with nothing to lose.

This was dangerous territory.

Zarra backed up, slowly distancing herself from her prey-now-turned-predator. She brought the second gun in her right hand to bear, too, hoping the threat of dual pistols would be enough to get the creature to back down. He continued to advance, apparently unimpressed. She continued her slow retreat.

Well, bang goes that theory.

Zarra squeezed the triggers of both guns simultaneously unleashing a round from each. The two bullets kicked up dust from the street just ahead and to either side of her opponent. He hesitated for a moment before continuing forwards, albeit with a hint more reservation.

This ain't gonna end well.

She briefly considered letting loose a volley of shots into his wide, flat skull, a result that would absolutely stop him in his tracks but would also diminish his value. The warrants paid out the most for targets brought back alive. The life of a mercenary wasn't a cheap one, and she couldn't afford to let money simply slip through her fingers when she had so many expenses to pay for, including the repairs to apartment 3A.

The FSE prided themselves on their moral stance of life preservation and, hence, the bounty for a live capture was a little above market price while the termination bounty was a long way below.

It's okay for them, she thought bitterly, *sittin' in their ivory wallpapered offices. But out here when you're faced with the teeth and the claws...chasin' the money is likely to get you killed.*

"Becka?" she grunted. "Any word on the warrant about icing?"

There was a brief pause on the line before Zarra heard the reply.

"Usual Federation bullshit. Alive by preference, minimal fee for a termination. Nothing in here about icing. You want to risk it?"

Zarra didn't respond. Her attention was now fully focused on defending herself as her target pounced. She backpedaled quickly, dropping the Freelancer from her left hand while her right arm jammed her other sidearm between the drooling teeth of the jaw reaching for her head. Falling backward, she heard the tearing of leather and felt the white-hot touch of claws sinking into her right shoulder. She grimaced as the blood began to ooze from deep gashes.

Curling into a ball, she braced her legs against the torso of the giant feline, pushing, trying to hold it at bay long enough for her left hand to reach for the pouch on her belt. The distraction of attempting to avoid being clawed to death had her normally nimble fingers fumbling at the fastener.

He was so strong! Her muscles screamed as her legs compressed. Her arm folded inexorably toward her own face while the powerful jaws crushed down on her gun. She cursed under her breath as the case of the weapon audibly cracked. Expensive repairs were going to be needed. The Harimau Jadian was so close she could feel his foul breath on her face as his saliva dripped onto her cheek. Zarra grimaced in disgust, but at last her left hand found what she was searching for.

"Fucker!!" she growled at the creature.

Not the pithy one-liner she'd been hoping for, but then real life wasn't a movie or comic book. Sometimes all your brain can find in times of stress is an expletive. Her hand whipped up and smashed the beast on the head...hard. She heard the breaking of glass and the sudden look of shock on his feline features as a subtle, ice-blue frost effect spread rapidly across his fur. Eyes grew wide, the deadly jaw slackened, and his body immediately became rigid. Dramatically frozen in place, his blade-sharp claws mere millimeters away from Zarra's face.

She hadn't realized she had been holding her breath until the sigh of relief whispered past her lips.

"Zee?" Becka hissed urgently into her ear. "You okay?"

Her head dropped back to the ground and she closed her eyes, summoning all her strength and shoving hard against the dead weight of the creature atop her with a grunt. The body rolled off to her side and lay still.

"Zarra!" Becka went up another notch on the urgency scale.

She lay on the ground for a second, composing herself while easing her damaged Freelancer back into its holster.

"Yeah, Bec... Yeah, I'm good," she said finally.

She reached out with her left hand, her wounded shoulder blade complaining mightily, and retrieved her other firearm. Weapons secure, she did a mental check of her condition. Nothing immediately life threatening. The flesh wound inflicted from jumping through the window seemed to have stopped bleeding, but the fresh claw wounds on her right shoulder were another matter entirely. That injury would require stitches.

"Gonna need a little of your needlework, but otherwise I'm dandy." A thought crossed her mind. "There any record of these things being venomous? This cut is pretty deep..."

"Two seconds..." Zarra heard the sound of Becka's fingers tapping on a screen over the open channel. "Nothing in the records. Claws, teeth, brute force. That's all we got on them. You should be fine. I'm dusting off to head your way."

"There's room on the street here. Bring *Diana* around and help me load him up. Ready the class-one containment. He's a big, strong bastard, so I'm not sure how long he'll stay iced for."

"On it," Becka confirmed. "Inbound to your location - ETA three minutes."

Zarra could already hear the engines of her dropship thrumming in the distance, getting subtly louder as it approached.

Rolling onto her side with a groan, she used her good arm to push herself to a sitting position. She pressed hard on her right shoulder with her left hand, trying to keep the wound as closed as possible. The warmth of her own blood oozed through the torn leather, slick against her fingers. She wasn't unduly concerned; this wasn't the first time she'd been wounded and certainly wouldn't be the last. That said, as the adrenaline high of the chase started to wane, the pain was becoming more acute and she was profoundly aware of the pounding of her own heart. She clenched and unclenched her fist repeatedly, trying to shunt aside the pain.

Closing her eyes, she imagined the feel of a stream of torrid water on her skin, soothing away the aches and pains of today's pursuit. She just wanted to load up their bounty, drop him off to the Federation base in Fort Nassau, get their money, and then grab a hot shower.

The dust swirled in the down draft of *Diana*'s engines as it hovered in closer, its running lights blinking rhythmically. The artificial wind started to whip up around her, ruffling her short ebony hair as Becka expertly guided their aircraft into a position to land in the street only a few meters away with the loading ramp pointed in the direction of Zarra and her prisoner.

Time to get paid, she thought, and allowed herself a smile.

| **3** |

KEEPING THE PEACE

– Jaymes Knightley –
– Monday – Nexus City, Iceland –

"Did she answer?"

"Voicemail. I just wanted to wish her a happy birthday, and good luck," Jaymes said sadly. "I'll try again later."

He returned to the seemingly eternal struggle to arrange the sash across his ceremonial robes, grumbling under his breath. He didn't mind wearing a suit, even a tuxedo should the occasion warrant it, but the ceremonial robes and sash were, in his view, taking it too far. Try as he might, he couldn't get the ensemble to look right. Fortunately, Jaymes Knightley had a wife with a talent for making him look respectable. Serlia shooed his hands away and took over the fettling of his accoutrements. Within seconds, the sash was draped correctly.

"You look wonderful, my love." Her melodic tone did little to assuage his annoyance.

"Ten years," he muttered, ignoring her compliment, "and every year we go through the same bloody rigmarole. You know, sometimes I loathe this job."

"Oh, hush, Jaymes. The Federated States of Europa could not ask for a better ambassador." His wife laughed lightly.

"They already have a great ambassador in *you*, Serlia. I sometimes think I'm just along for the ride."

"We're partners. In this together," Serlia reassured him.

"Now, if you've finished trying on your robes, you need to change, darling. We're meeting Allyson soon."

He glanced sideways at his wife, her smile the same brilliant white grin that had beguiled him almost thirty years ago. She still took his breath away. Still perfect after all this time, even though he no longer was. He looked back at his reflection in the mirror.

Jaymes had been twenty-five when they met; tall, slim, and fit due to the rowing hobby he'd started in his university days. The hair that had once been jet-black and perhaps a little too long, was now shorter and dominated by grey. Still thick, though...age hadn't thinned him out. He idly rubbed his stomach, which hadn't thinned either. He wasn't in bad shape for his age but had to admit that too many sit-down meetings and rich diplomatic dinners made those ambassadorial robes a little snugger than the last time he'd worn them. Still, the Summit wasn't for a few weeks. There was still time to lose a few pounds.

Who am I fooling? I'll just get the tailor to adjust them. Again.

"Why they insist I wear this ridiculous garb is beyond me," he continued to complain.

"You know why," Serlia sighed. "Sebastian StormHall will be the lead negotiator for New Victus, and he's from a very old House that values tradition..."

"So he says..." Jaymes muttered interrupting her.

"...so, this is ceremonial for them," his wife continued soothingly and then smiled, her green eyes glinting with a hint of loving mischief. "Besides, I think you look dashingly handsome; dare I say, quite sexy in your dress robes."

He waved his hand at her dismissively and snorted.

Yet it struck him how lucky he was to share these years with her. He had accepted long ago that time would eventually separate them. As he got older; she would be a fixed point. While Fae did age, they gained their years at a crawl in comparison to Humans. Serlia's lifespan would be measured in centuries...Jaymes in mere decades. Her complexion would always be perfect, her smile always white, her skin wouldn't weather, her body would never sag. While he was in his mid-fifties, she would never look a day over forty, and he knew looking even that old was done as a courtesy for him.

The traditional image of Fae was tiny beings given to flitting around on magical wings. Yet, if you inspected the myths and legends closely, there were a hundred different descriptions for them. And there was a good reason for this. Fae were shapeshifters. Physical appearance to them was a choice, not a genetic quirk. Height, weight, skin tone, eye color...everything about them was an option.

Serlia had been careful not to flaunt her abilities with him, but he knew the extent of her powers. She could be anything from a six-inch-high winged nymph flitting through the trees of the forest, to the six-foot beauty with raven hair, emerald eyes, and porcelain skin that greeted him every morning and kissed him goodnight every evening.

Changelings. The world seemed full of them these days. The Fae and the various breeds of Werewolf and Vampire, to name but a few.

"New Victus. Stupid name for a country. And ceremony and tradition, my arse!" he complained under his breath, forgetting how acute his wife's hearing was.

"Jaymes!" she admonished.

"Well, I'm sorry Serlia, but it's true. Sebastian StormHall has never shown any interest in these Summits before. When was the last time he actually came to one? Three years ago? Four? 'Ceremony' and 'protocol' is just his subtle way of exerting the petty influence of a petty man. Well, just this once I'd like to tell him where to stick his 'ceremonial dress robes'."

He muttered the words 'ceremonial dress robes' with not a little contempt while making air quotes with his fingers on both hands as he gave up adjusting his lapel. Despite his wife's best efforts, he continued his rant.

"What's more, if he really wants to play the 'old family' card then we should tell him how far back *you* go. That would show him."

"I'm not using my age, or my race, as a tool to gain political positioning over the Grand Chancellor. Or anyone else for that matter. I'm representing the FSE. Remember, darling, the Fae don't have a seat at the World Council and we try not to interfere in world affairs"

"Where's the fun in that...?" he muttered under his breath.

"Excuse me?" Serlia asked, even though he knew that she heard him.

"Yes," he conceded with a huff. "I know you're right. As usual."

The smile she shot him was radiant and lifted his mood. Just a little.

"That's because, as you've just noted, I'm considerably older and wiser than you, my dear. Which is why I know this mood you're in has more to do with Gayle than it does the impending Summit."

"Maybe one day you'll do me the honor of being wrong," he laughed. "Just once."

"I wouldn't hold your breath, my love. It hasn't happened yet. Two hundred and seventy-four years and counting."

As he listened to her musical laughter, he found the corners of his own mouth curling irresistibly upward. He knew that if she wanted to, she could use her Fae pheromones to enhance his mood. It was a skill all Fae had. A way of chemically guiding the disposition of another subject in varying ways, making it an extremely useful ability, especially for a diplomat. Thirty years ago, for example, the Fae had used it to help influence the end of the War.

And it was the reason why so many of the world's factions still distrusted the Fae. They maintained that this type of power was open to abuse...

Jaymes knew, however, the Fae very rarely used this ability outside of manipulation that was mutually consensual. This was what made the Fae such interesting, and sought after, sexual partners. Serlia had sworn an oath long ago that she would never influence him deliberately, lovemaking aside. She had also taught him how to easily recognize any form of intentional exploitation. Even so, at times like this, he wondered if she did it to him unconsciously, simply because of the love they shared. He was fairly sure, however, that for him, it was simply a reaction to her own happiness, almost Pavlovian in its nature.

Jaymes shuffled over to the bed and started to remove his robes. The smile was fleeting, already fading as his thoughts turned back to the daughter who had missed, or ignored, his phone call. She would be angry when she found out what he had done, and he was unsure as to how she would react. Ordinarily, their father-daughter bond would have seen them have words, but ultimately be okay. But since the Malta mission, she was angry, sullen, withdrawn...he didn't know how to reach her. All he wanted to do was help. Surely, she would see that...

"Gayle will be okay," Serlia said gently. "You'll see. Just be prepared to give her some time."

This was one occasion when he fervently hoped that his wife was right.

| 4 |

NEW VICTUS

– Lyssa Balthazaar –
– Monday – New York, New Victus –

They don't make music like this anymore.

Lyssa drummed her fingers against the leather steering wheel to the beat of 'Back in Black' by AC/DC. Her mood twisted to a darker, more melancholic place as she secured a rebellious strand of her long black hair behind her ear. Classic hard rock usually cheered her up, but today it just drew her thoughts back to how the world had stagnated since the War.

They don't really make music at all anymore.

The sunlight glinted off the metallic red of the Charger's hood as she rumbled down Broadway, her gleaming Dodge striking a sharp juxtaposition to the countless abandoned wrecks that littered the roadside.

Since the collapse of the motor industry, new cars had become an expensive luxury, custom built by small, private workshops. Thank the gods her position of relative privilege gave her access to some of the best mechanics in the state.

With over half a million miles on the clock, it was a minor miracle her car was still running at all. Spares were becoming rarer with every passing day as scavengers found all the best parts and rust took the rest.

The trip from her home in Albany to that of her bloodline in Midtown Manhattan was always a chore, but at least the city was peaceful these days. While it would get busier after sunset, gone was the white-knuckle experience of having to navigate a swarm of honking yellow cabs. Still, she missed the hustle and bustle of the old Big Apple. Lyssa mourned the beating heart of humanity that had once made the city feel so vital.

The signs of societal entropy were everywhere you looked. How do you take care of a city built for millions with a population now a fraction of that? Who maintains the streets? Removes the garbage or repairs broken utilities? Buildings stood derelict as weeds encroached on the roads.

The deep growl of her engine reverberated off Lincoln Center as she neared Columbus Circle, ready to loop counterclockwise and join Eighth Avenue. With pride, she noticed a distinct difference in the upkeep of the area. Her family was motivated to maintain their neighborhood to a high standard, and it heartened her to see that they were proactively pushing out farther. The greenery was immaculately pruned and the asphalt smooth as Hearst Tower came into view.

Lyssa had a soft spot for this building, which was the reason behind why she had chosen it to be her family home. A distinctive diagrid-patterned tower of steel and glass perched atop a six-story base built from stone eighty years prior. It perfectly blended the traditional with the contemporary, symbolizing the mantra of House Balthazaar – look to the future, respect the past. Storm would have changed the tower's name, but then he didn't *truly* understand the concept of tradition.

She brought the car to a gentle halt by the arched stone entrance and shut off the quietly burbling engine. Slumping back, she spent a moment gazing at the tower's stylish design through the tinted sunroof. Lyssa had worked here as a journalist before the War, when Hearst Communications had been a multinational, multimedia conglomerate. *The* place for world news. Now her people aggregated news and information, gossip and rumor, from all over the world, operating as an intelligence hub for New Victus. It kept House Balthazaar relevant.

More importantly, it kept Lyssa's finger on the pulse of everything that was going on globally. There was a Latin aphorism, 'scientia potentia est' – 'knowledge is power.' And while that wasn't entirely true, it never hurt to be the best-informed person in the room. Especially when you were attempting the kind of long-term subterfuge Lyssa was plotting.

The flag of New Victus rippled in the wind, hanging where the Stars and Stripes had once fluttered proudly. The blue sky was vacant of clouds, giving the dazzling sun nowhere to hide and forcing Lyssa to slip on her dark glasses as she reached for the door handle. Mercifully, the dash from car to the shade of the lobby was a short one.

A flurry of friendly acknowledgements greeted her as she entered. She idly replied in kind, but her attention was elsewhere, drawn to the Icefall, the water sculpture framing the escalators that led to the upper floors. The Tower's atrium was light and airy, a stark dichotomy to the sublevels deep below where Balthazaar lay sleeping in his darkened chambers.

"Good trip?" a familiar voice enquired.

"Same as usual," Lyssa answered, forgoing the usual banter and moving straight to business. "Did you find her?"

Mercy shook her head and her cascade of auburn hair moved in hypnotic waves. Her ice blue eyes, and the tight draw of her elegant cheekbones telegraphed the disappointing news even before she parted her lips.

"I'm sorry, Lys. We lost her trail at the border and didn't dare pursue into Pack territory."

Lyssa felt like expressing herself with an outburst of profanity, but instead simply nodded and bowed her head. She took a deep breath, gathering herself before entering the elevator, Mercy slipping in behind her. The floor buttons biometrically scanned her fingertips as she entered the code that would send their car to the private sub-levels.

"It looks like I need to make another trip north then." Lyssa sighed and massaged the bridge of her nose.

"I'm sorry," Mercy said. "Considering your sister's...affliction, I thought it best not to raise attention if we were caught following her there. I can order the tracking party to cross the border if you want. They'd be discreet."

Lyssa shook her head slowly.

"No. You did the right thing. As much as I hate to admit it...we're going to need his help. But that's the least of my problems. I've been summoned by Storm. He's on his way."

"He arrived twenty minutes ago. He's in the boardroom waiting for you."

"Shit." This time Lyssa did resort to cursing as the situation seemed to warrant it. "If he's found out what's happened..."

"He doesn't know," Mercy reassured her. "How could he? We've been careful to keep it quiet and, as the primary intelligence hub for New Victus, if we haven't heard a squeak about it then I guarantee no one else has."

Lyssa knew she was right.

"I'm also certain StormHall he has no clue about your...'extracurricular' activity up north,'" Mercy added to put Lyssa's mind at further ease.

"Thank the gods. But how long will that last?" Lyssa mused.

"You tell me. You're the one sleeping with his nemesis," Mercy shot back with an undercurrent of humor.

"I meant Vanessa," Lyssa said with an upward tilt of her eyebrow. "She's not the most...discreet of people."

"If she makes any noise, we'll hear it first," Mercy said firmly.

"We're so close, all our hard work..." Lyssa said quietly. "Too many secrets, Mercy. It makes me uncomfortable keeping them all."

"Worst case scenario," Mercy shrugged, "in the event she is hunted down and captured by a follower of Storm, she knows nothing about our other plans. She can't tell them what she doesn't know."

"But if he decides to reveal that my sister is a Su..."

"Lyssa, it doesn't matter what she is," Mercy interrupted firmly with a wave of her hand. "We have faith in you. We all have faith in you. StormHall has controlled our future for too long, and none of us will let anything jeopardize your plans. We trust you. Now you trust us."

Lyssa looked at her niece who had been her steadfast ally for more years than she could remember. She trusted Mercy implicitly and believed wholeheartedly in the depth of the woman's resolve.

"His time," Mercy said gently, "it has to end. This all...has to end."

Lyssa nodded.

"You're right. Of course, you're right." Lyssa bit her lip for a moment and started pulling together a plan of action. "Okay, please get in touch with our contact in the north and tell him that I need to meet. Today. Then get my flyer ready for departure. In the meantime, I'll go and see what Storm wants."

"You still refuse to call him StormHall."

"I refuse to acknowledge the union that created this mess."

"Well, in anticipation that this would be your course of action, I took the liberty of organizing things in advance. Your flyer is already on the roof ready to go."

"Sometimes I think you know me too well." Lyssa smiled with amusement.

An amusement mirrored by the glint in her niece's eyes.

"It's not hard," Mercy said with a light chuckle in her voice. "You go see 'his majesty' while I firm up your travel arrangements."

The elevator came to a gentle stop and the door opened onto a dimly lit corridor leading to an imposing arched door of solid ebony, etched with the ancient language of their people. She paused before heading toward it.

"One more thing," Lyssa said. "Project Lazarus?"

"Nyk's on it with her usual efficacy, so it's right on schedule. All we need is a test subject." Mercy pursed her lips. "You should come down to the labs after your meeting, see the progress for yourself. You can't leave until after dark, anyway, and it would be wise to give it some time after StormHall's departure."

"How close are we?" Lyssa asked.

"Really close," Mercy smiled. "You'll be pleased. Now go see your father."

With that she sashayed gracefully down the right-hand

corridor. Lyssa watched her leave while summoning up the courage to face her father. She glanced down at her outfit. She was dressed for business today – a black pencil suit skirt and sensible heels, which were a far cry from her usual comfort.

As much as she hated him, she had to at least acknowledge the decorum of meeting the leader of their nation, though she told herself that she was dressing up to visit her father. It was a self-delusion that made her feel a little better.

Moments later, she stood in her father's sleep chamber. She looked down at the resting place of her sire and placed her hand gently upon the polished black surface with its intricate pattern of carved writing. Her fingertips traced the letters slowly. It told the story of their beginnings...of the first twelve of their kind. The Progenitors.

The 'Children of the River.'

Her father was one of only four who still survived.

House Balthazaar was one of the oldest and most venerated families in New Victus. It was a bloodline that was pure and proud.

Pure bred didn't mean rejecting half-breeds. Mercy was a case in point, conceived and born into the family naturally from the union of a Vampyrii mother and a Human father. What it meant was that the House did not use the 'bite' to expand their numbers.

Legend spoke of Vampires as creatures of the night, stalking their prey and drinking them dry of blood, or turning their victims into monsters just like them. The truth, as always, was so much more complex and far less 'Hollywood.'

Vampyrii had no taste for blood and the bite itself was a sacred responsibility that the older Houses treated with religious reverence. The power to take or fundamentally change a person's life was not one to be taken lightly.

Alas, during The Rising, many younger Vampyrii had done just that – abused their privilege to remorselessly kill, or to half-turn, innocent Humans into the mindless slaves of their Vampyrii sires.

Trampyrii.

Three decades of suppressed anger surged within her. It

was a constant presence, simply ebbing and flowing depending on her mood. Today her mood was dark. Trampyrii were Humans doomed to live half-lives. Lyssa pitied them but hated what they represented.

"Please understand, Father. What I'm doing is for the greater good of our kind," she whispered to him in the silence of the room. "I promise I won't let you down. Not again."

Not for the first time, she wished she had her sister's telepathic gifts. If only she could talk to him...

Her fingers lingered briefly as she steeled her resolve for the meeting to come, summoning inner strength from her proximity to her father. Every finely tuned instinct she possessed was screaming at her about the potential danger Sebastian Storm's visit represented. He never travelled from his home unless he had a need to, which begged the question: why was he here?

Though she tried to push it aside, the sense of threat loitered, stalking her senses. A danger so tangible she could almost smell it.

| 5 |

NEXUS

– Allyson Knightley –
– Monday – Nexus City, Iceland –

Allyson chewed on a fingernail as she stared absently out of the window at the breathtaking view she was still getting used to.

Will I ever truly think of this place as home?

Iceland was where the last of the fighting had occurred during the final days of the War. A three-way clash between Human, Vampyrii, and Werewolf factions for control of a strategic steppingstone between North America and Europe. It ended with each faction holding a third of the country, slicing it into pieces like a pie.

Where all three of those sectors met was Nexus City.

It had been constructed upon the site of Goðafoss Park located in the Bárðardalur district of Iceland. Situated in Northeastern Region, it sat at the point where the Skjálfandafljót river split the terrain into three. The resulting tiny metropolis was a striking juxtaposition of modern architecture set against an Icelandic landscape that was vastly different to the English countryside to which Allyson was accustomed. A beguiling mix of deep green and gunmetal mountains, all set against a vibrant ice blue sky.

Yet, as magnificent as the terrain was here, it was nothing compared to the Goðafoss itself. Where the river cascaded into a turquoise blue basin surrounded by the black grey cliffs of rock covered in lush green, it formed the stunning natural feature that was known as the '*Waterfall of the Gods.*' Nexus had been built around the basin with the FSE territory on the eastern banks, Pack Nation to the North, and New Victus to the West. A trio of elegant bridges spanned the river in each direction forming a loose triangle between each faction.

As the morning sunshine filtered through the prism of rising mist and spray created by the tumbling water, it produced a vivid rainbow arcing upward and over the Pack Nation sector of the city. She sighed, closing her eyes for a brief moment and internalizing the view.

Its display of natural power had a calming, almost hypnotic effect on Allyson. No surprise there, really; it regularly stunned visitors with its splendor, but on days like today, it was downright breathtaking.

Yes, Nexus might be a very different place from the England she was used to. And it might not be home for her just yet, maybe never would be, but sometimes it truly wasn't a bad place to live.

So distracted was she by the stunning view, that she didn't notice the approach of her deputy.

"Chief Knightley?" Francesca Romano enquired in her usual stern tone.

"Mmm..." Allyson dragged herself back from her reverie. "What can I do for you, Fran?"

Fran's immaculate ebony locks were pulled back in a severe ponytail, making her face look older than she was. Ally stifled a yawn and unconsciously reached up to run a hand through her own unkempt hair, still damp from her hasty morning shower. Sleep had been hard to come by lately due to the stress of the upcoming Summit and, as a result, her appearance had somewhat suffered.

"Updated threat report," Fran said succinctly, handing her a data tablet.

Ally glanced at the items displayed on it.

"Getting to be a *long* list. Anything new since yesterday I should be aware of?" she asked wearily.

"At the top," Fran said pointing to the tablet.

Allyson looked back to the list. "Bomb threat? Note or phone?"

"Called in on the hotline. Female voice." Fran shrugged. "Anonymous, as usual. Not much detail. More of a warning really."

"Traced?" Ally felt the roll of her deputy's eyes.

"Of course. Public comm-station. And, yes, I checked the cameras, too," Fran said. "Likely another crank call. We get dozens of them every Summit. Usually nothing."

"Usually..." Allyson stared at the list thoughtfully.

Though their working relationship had thus far been brief, Allyson had quickly learned to trust her deputy's instincts in most things. If Fran wasn't unduly concerned, then *maybe* she shouldn't be either. But something felt...off.

"I don't know, Fran," Allyson muttered. "You get a recording?"

Fran's dark ponytail jiggled as she nodded.

"Okay. Send a copy to me to listen to, and a copy to forensics. See if they can find any clues as to our mystery woman." Ally exhaled heavily. "I'll take a look at it later after my meeting."

Fran nodded, but her eyes were looking past Allyson to the approach of someone behind her.

"Ambassadors," she acknowledged with a warm smile.

It was Allyson's mother who answered first. Her voice was silken, with a lyrical quality.

"Good morning, Francesca," Serlia said warmly.

"Hello, Fran," Jaymes followed up with his lilting baritone. "Everything well with you?"

"Business as usual, Ambassador." Fran's tone was noticeably friendlier.

Allyson tried not to take it personally. After all, her parents had served as Federated States of Europa ambassadors for over a decade, during which time they had worked closely with her deputy. Fran's disapproval was seemingly reserved solely for Allyson, a fact that she suspected was due to Fran being passed over for the job of Security Chief in favor of an outsider.

It had been merely a week since she had taken up the post, and while she wasn't regretting the career shift, she was getting a hard appreciation for just how complicated this job was. Hence the continually escalating stress headache. Planning security for a concert or sporting event in London had been a piece of cake compared to the complications she was discovering here in Nexus. World politics had never been her forte.

She doubted she would have applied for the role at all if it hadn't been for her uncle's assurances that it would be great for her career. He had been very persuasive, never doubting for a moment that she could do it. She had started to believe him – maybe she *could* do the job. When the call had come, informing her of her successful applications, she had felt happy for the first time in months. It seemed like the perfect job for her.

Then, reality had set in.

There had been more than a few moments during the last few days when she wondered exactly why she had succeeded in getting the position here instead of Fran, who had many years of experience living here in the city.

The meeting she had arranged with her parents this morning was an attempt to quickly bring her up to speed with the ins and outs of Nexus politics.

"Fran was just delivering the latest threat report," Ally said.

"Problem?" Serlia enquired.

"No. No problem." Ally shook her head. "A bomb threat..."

"Warning," Fran interjected.

"Ah, I see," Jaymes nodded. "Wouldn't be the first. Should we be concerned?"

"We're looking into it..." Ally started to say but was interrupted.

"I don't think so, Ambassador," Fran reassured him. "We may have seen dozens of these over the years, but we *always* take them seriously. We're looking into it. And with that in mind, I'll leave you to it."

Fran nodded and walked briskly away, leaving mother, father, and daughter alone on the promenade. Serlia looked serene, as usual, though tempered with a hint of concern over her daughter's fatigue – a topic that had been raised over breakfast that morning. Jaymes simply beamed proudly, still reveling in Allyson's new promotion and supremely certain his daughter could do the job. Allyson increasingly wished she shared his confidence.

She took a deep breath and brushed her hand back through her hair. It felt tangled and greasy. Washing it properly was *long* overdue. The quick morning showers aimed at waking her up were just not cutting it. Her natural blue was starting to reveal itself through the black dye job that desperately needed touching up. She mentally put a hair appointment on her mounting personal to-do list as she gestured toward the large wooden double doors behind them. The World Council Chamber awaited them.

"After you," she said wearily.

| 6 |

FIRST CLASS

– Michael Reynolds –
– Monday – London, England –

He prowled slowly back and forth, his rugged body a study in compact motion. There was always another mission, another job, and this one was no different from all the others. One more foray into unknown territory, forced to rely on his wits, intelligence, and experience. The poise of a veteran, every action concise and controlled; his current weapon of choice gripped tightly in his fingers. A surge of adrenaline created a ripple of butterflies that churned his stomach as the tiniest bead of sweat rolled down his forehead.

Embrace the fear...use it to your advantage.

He carefully surveyed the environment, his keen mind calculating the options. The biggest threats, the easiest targets, the potential escape routes. He slowly lifted his hand.

It was time.

"I'm Captain Michael Reynolds. Welcome to your first day at the HFA Defense Academy."

He looked around at the fresh-faced girls and boys that he was to train to be the next generation of Hunters. They all looked so young, barely in their teens. And nervous. They weren't the only ones experiencing something new today. Veteran soldier; rookie teacher.

"I'll be your Commandin' Officer during your time here.

Don't mistake me for a parent. Y'all are HFA Academy recruits, here to fight. My sole job is to get you ready for that fight."

His thumb prodded the stylus in his hand and gestured at the giant screen at the head of the class which started displaying a mass of slowly scrolling text, interspersed by a few photos.

"My military service record is, for the most part, an open book. You want to read it, go right ahead. The abridged version is that I joined the North American Alliance Army at seventeen and have been a soldier for almost twenty years. I've been everything from an infantry grunt to an NAA Navy SEAL and have fought on frontlines all over the world."

Every eye in the room was on him, enraptured. Michael Reynolds wasn't afraid of much in this world, but these kids and their abilities, untrained and with no moral compass...that truly terrified him.

Each of them carried the potential to be a weapon greater than almost any form of ordnance that he himself had ever wielded. They were raw power that needed to be molded before they became adults and inherited all the flaws that came with age. It was his job to instill into them a sense of duty, of honor, while they were still young.

"During classes you will address me as Captain Reynolds. On trainin' operations, I go by the call sign 'Rogue'. Each of you will get a call sign of your own in due course.

"Every mornin' you will join me, or whichever tutor is assigned to you that day, promptly in this classroom at oh eight hundred hours, ready for roll-call at oh eight thirty. Do not be late. It takes discipline to be a soldier, and discipline starts in the small things. If you can't maintain the discipline to be on time for your classes, don't expect me to trust y'all with the more serious aspects of your trainin'.

"I have no problem washin' you out of this unit if I don't think you've got what it takes. Any abilities you may have do *not* earn you a free pass with me."

The recruits breathlessly hung on his every word.

"You will *not* use your abilities with me. Teachin' you how to use those is not my job. In my classes, you will be learnin' to rely on your intelligence, your wits, and your ingenuity. There will be no short cuts. In my classes I will teach you how to be a soldier."

He paused and took a breath. With the formalities over, it was time to move on to the fun stuff.

"Y'all have your class schedules now. While you missed out on the first physical education class this morning, due to your induction, we *will* be starting this afternoon with your first Enemy Recognition and Intelligence class." On his cue, a word popped up on the video screen. "What can any of you tell me about Therianthropes?"

None of the kids volunteered an answer. He hadn't expected them to. With a push of a button, a holographic image manifested above his desk. An animation of a man transforming into a wolf and back again.

"Big word, I know. But how 'bout now?" he prompted.

Realization dawned abruptly on the young faces, but still none seemed brave enough to raise a hand and give an answer. He brandished the stylus in the air like a wand and the definition appeared beneath the word on the screen.

"The term 'therianthropy' is derived from two Greek words. 'Theríon,' meanin' 'beast,' specifically a mammal; and 'anthrōpos,' meanin' 'Human.' There are many types of Therianthrope. In Africa, there's a race called the Bultungin who can change into large hyenas. The Harimau Jadian, from Malaysia and Indonesia, transform into tigers.

"Before you ask, your kitty-cat at home ain't a Therianthrope in disguise. Unlike Fae, Therianthropes don't alter their body mass significantly durin' transformation. So, in addition to wolves, we're talkin' about lions, tigers, and bears...that kinda thing. Today, though, we are gonna start with the most basic, and most prevalent – those that inhabit what was formerly Canada, now known as Pack Nation.

"The Werewolf.

"Y'all have skills and abilities, and you'll be taught how to use them in good time. But...the most important thing you'll learn within these four walls will be to know your opponent. Pop culture has filled your heads with contradictory stories of

Werewolves, but in this class, you'll get the facts. Nothin' more...nothin' less.

"I'll teach you every strength, every weakness, every tiny detail, and every dirty little secret. I need y'all to take it in, learn it, and remember it. Because I promise you, what you learn in here will save your life a thousand times over. What you don't learn...will get you killed."

He looked at the young faces, now ashen.

Michael didn't want to scare them — that had never been his intent. He knew, though, that he had to expose these kids, barely in their teens, to how unforgiving life on the front lines could be. Anything else would be a disservice to them. Yet watching the gravity of their role finally start to sink in sobered him. They were asking children to grapple with the concepts of life and death in a way that had likely never crossed their adolescent minds before.

He knew better than most the price you pay when you give your life to the defense of others. To walk away from every battle, with everyone unscathed, was a rarity. Every mission would bestow on them its own brand, scars both physical and emotional.

The only immutable truth in their line of work was death. It would be all around them, all the time. They would be responsible for death, and death would also come for them and their friends. All you could do was accept it without fear and strive to postpone your appointment with it.

Easier said than done.

| 7 |

THE ASSIGNMENT

– Gayle Knightley –
– Monday – London, England –

The chair in which Gayle was sitting was disconcertingly snug. As she waited for her uncle to settle himself into the chair across his desk from her, she glanced around the room. It was exactly how she remembered it. With the plush carpet and the majestic fireplace, it felt more like a lounge than an office. The room was a love letter to the sensual nature of the Fae. Something seemingly coded directly into their DNA.

To be around a Fae generally meant being drawn into their world of beauty, from their perfect features and physiques, to their embracement of opulent luxury. It wasn't an exercise in status, simply an affinity for nature and its materials. The softest woolen furnishings, the finest art, and the most exquisitely carved woods made most Fae homes places of abundant comfort.

And then...there were the pheromones

The subconscious ones.

Fae exude pheromones as a natural by-product of their physiology. Unfortunately, these chemicals were known to cause a very mild aphrodisiac effect in Humans. It was this innocent consequence that usually caused Gayle's 'comfort' issue when she met with her uncle.

Like all Hybrids, she was heavily resistant to the conscious pacifying ability of the Fae. Regrettably, the combination of her Human and Fae DNA seemed to make her particularly vulnerable to the aforementioned passive effect. She wasn't entirely sure why. Maybe it was because she could consciously manipulate a somewhat watered-down version of the same ability, but whenever Gayle was near a Fae, especially a masculine one, her own sexuality unintentionally went into overdrive.

Embarrassingly, being related to the Fae in question did not provide immunity to the effect. Her ride through puberty had been a bitch! Her mother tried to help, removing her from school to be home studied, and trying to keep her away from other Fae, but Uncle Norbel was family. It categorically wasn't his fault at all, but his visits, while limited, became somewhat...uncomfortable for Gayle.

And it was a situation that got worse when she arrived at the Academy, where *all* the teachers had been Fae and all the students had been Hybrids like herself. She, along with her fellow classmates, were forced to experiment with various coping strategies. Alcohol had been an early candidate, but Gayle had quickly discovered that being horny *and* having her inhibitions removed was a recipe for disaster. It took her a while to learn that you either went along for the ride, or you tried to bury it under another emotion.

Today she was experiencing a seething anger that seemed to have defused any sexual urges before they even attempted to surface within her.

"How is the knee?" Norbel asked as he slipped gracefully into his own padded leather chair.

"Fine," she answered tersely. "I'm ready for active duty."

She was in no mood for further civilities. All she wanted was to leave the Academy as soon as possible with an assignment to somewhere where she could punch something. Where she could fight something real, rather than her demons.

"I had assumed that you would prefer to stay away from the front lines for a while," Norbel gently probed. "After Valletta—"

"It's been more than long enough," she interrupted. "In my

opinion."

There was a pregnant pause before Norbel finally gave Gayle the news she had been dreading.

"It is an opinion we do not share," he said in a flat measured tone. "We think that you would benefit from an extended rehabilitation time. Teaching, here at the Academy."

"You've got to be fucking kidding me!" she hissed and shook her head slowly.

Adrenaline flooded her system as she prepared herself for the verbal conflict to come. Her hands balled into fists and she tried to subdue her angry trembling.

"I assure you, Captain, that this is a serious consideration."

"General," she tried her best to reciprocate his calm, "we both know there are no classes to teach here at the Academy. The program was suspended after my team graduated. Unless, of course, the rumors are true, and you *are* trying to replace my team already?"

It was a rhetorical question at best. Before Norbel even answered, Gayle knew that Torbar had been right.

Fuck!

"Gayle, the loss of your team saw it necessary to restart the Hybrid program. The 136th alone is not enough. Captain Torbar's squad cannot cope with the demand the FSE puts on our resources. We need two units, that much has always been true."

"Then you go right ahead and train them up. But in the meantime, put me back on active duty and I'll pick up the slack as a solo operative. I'm more useful in the field..."

Norbel looked at her, his eyebrow jerked upwards as he interrupted her.

"The new cadets are *already* enrolled and about to start their training. We think that with your current invalid status—"

"Invalid!"

"—your temporarily suspended field status, and your wealth of experience, you would be best utilized at the Academy as a teacher and mentor."

Gayle took a deep breath before growling her angry reply

through gritted teeth. "I repeat, with all due respect...you have *got* to be fucking kidding me."

"Gayle, please," Norbel implored. "Less of the profanity. I may be your uncle, but I am also your superior officer. There is still a chain of command in effect here and I would ask you to respect it."

She tried to decide what was worse. Feeling that she was being side-lined? Or that Torbar had been right? A fact he would likely be insufferably smug about the next time they crossed paths.

"My apologies, *General*," she said with a calmness she didn't feel. "But I honestly fail to see what possible benefit I could be to you here at the Academy. You've just remarked on my attitude, so you know I'm not really kid-friendly. Surely my skillset would be better deployed in the field somewhere? And who is '*we*'? I thought this was your decision."

A daughter of two diplomats, Gayle understood the subtleties of language. Her uncle's use of the plural pronoun was like waving a red flag in her face. If this *was* a joint decision then she wanted to know who was party to it, though she already had her suspicions. Norbel, to his credit, met her glare directly, slowly steepling his fingers as he leaned against the desktop.

"I have seen the surgeon's medical reports. I have also seen the reports provided by your physiotherapist. The knee is—"

She knew where this was heading.

"—is fine," she interrupted.

"—is not healed sufficiently. We cannot in good conscience put you back on active duty. You and I both know you would struggle with the physical."

"Let me try. Watch me ace it."

"Of that I have no doubt," he admitted. "Just as I have no doubt you would aggravate the injury further in the process. I have witnessed firsthand your tenacity and your...stubbornness over the years. Sometimes, however, you need protecting from yourself. A full recovery will take time. Time you refuse to give to yourself."

"So, this is your way of forcing me to take care of myself. Treating me like a child?"

"Treating you like a valuable asset. You'll be put back into the field when we are confident that you are physically and mentally capable," he retorted angrily.

"Mentally capable?"

"Dr. Griffin informs me that you have been skipping your weekly therapy sessions," he said simply. "What you have been through takes an inevitable toll."

"I don't need therapy. Besides, no one ever specified that it's mandatory." She shrugged and slumped back in her chair.

"From this point forward, it is. While the physical aspects of your injury are healing as expected, your mental state is another matter. We cannot clear you for active duty until we have the sign off from both your physiotherapist and your psychiatrist."

"*Who*...is 'we'?"

This time she wouldn't allow Norbel to dodge the question with vague statements and as she fixed him with a determined stare, he looked uncomfortable for the first time since the meeting had begun. The final piece of the puzzle dropped into place. Before her uncle could say another word, she had already deduced the answer for herself.

She could tell by his discomfort that the 'we' he kept referring to was someone personal rather than simply the military chain of command. Gayle was positive that her sisters would not be a party to this. No matter how concerned they may be about her, neither Ally nor Carrie would be whispering conspiratorially into their uncle's ear. Which left only one other alternative...

She repeated what was fast becoming her phrase of the day.

"You've *got* to be fucking kidding me!?" whispered almost in disbelief this time. "My *parents*?"

"Your father made it clear that he was worried about your current state of mind. He mentioned in his communications with me that you seemed excessively angry..."

"I'm always angry. *You* know that. It's the way I am," she interjected angrily, proving his point.

Norbel sighed wearily, realizing that he was about to engage in the very argument that he'd been looking to avoid.

"I understand the events of Valletta are something that—"

Gayle shot out of her seat. There was venom in her voice when she spoke.

"I wish to *fuck* people would stop talking about Valletta. Using it as excuse or, worse than that, a reason for every tiny bit of..." her voice held a tremor as she paused momentarily. "Whatever the fuck they are accusing me of! Look, it happened. They're dead. These things happen all the time in war. We deal with it. We move on. I've dealt with it. It's done."

"Your father does not think so. I do not think so. More importantly, your psychological evaluation came back...and your therapist concurs."

"Well, the *therapist* can go fuck himself, as can my father. And, excuse my language, *sir*," the last word spat with disdain, "so can you."

General Norbel stood, drawing himself to his full height.

"I'm warning you for the last time, Gayle. I've tolerated your insubordination until now, but you're stepping a long way over the line."

Gayle gritted her teeth and straightened up. Her eyes remained locked with his, but she suppressed the angry, expletive-laden retort that her brain instinctively prepared. She refused to back down.

"General. I respectfully disagree with your assessment and your decision. I hereby tender my verbal—"

"Don't finish that sentence," Norbel cut her off, holding up his hand. "You want to quit now and do what? Become a mercenary? Go freelance and hunt in the outer territories? You could, if that's what you truly want. But we both know it is not. Consider, also, these cadets. Where do you think your skills and expertise are more valuable right now?"

"I'm sure you already have good teachers here," she retorted.

"We did. However, as you stated earlier, the program was warehoused after your graduation, and the faculty disbanded." His voice remained calm. "If you were even close to field-ready, believe me, you would be back in the fight. But you are not, and we both know it. Only you are too stubborn to admit it."

His expression changed from one of anger to one of regret.

"We have a golden opportunity to correct past mistakes. We did not understand what you were going through as teenage hybrids. These children are younger than you were when we trained you, and we can influence them positively as they mature. You can relate to their experiences in a way that, ten years ago, I could not.

"I need you here, Gayle. To give these students the benefit of your experience."

Fuck.

Angry as she may be, she could see the wisdom in his words. Her Hunters had all been between fifteen and seventeen when they were enrolled into the program. A seething mess of hormones mixed with their inherited Fae ability to influence people with their pheromones led to a mess for which none of their tutors had been prepared. There was a direct correlation from those early years to the downfall of her team nine months ago.

In hindsight, she could see it clearly – the point where the looming disaster had become an inevitability.

Gayle could recognize the logic. Enroll the kids younger and be prepared to usher them through the maelstrom of balancing puberty with powers. He was also correct that she was the perfect person to help steer them in the right direction, guiding them to avoid the mistakes she herself had made.

That her team had made.

"Fine," she begrudgingly accepted. "Have it your way. I'll teach your kids until I'm fit for active duty."

Norbel didn't gloat in his victory. That wasn't his style.

"We do have one other faculty member – Captain Michael Reynolds. He has been working with me on the project for several weeks now and is well-versed on what we are looking to achieve. You and he will be partners on this moving forward, and I want you to work closely together.

"A copy of his service record has been emailed to you along

with the class schedule. While both of you will share the responsibility for most classes, you will be mainly responsible for teaching them how to effectively harness their abilities. Captain Reynolds' focus with them will be physical education, bearing in mind your injury. To be clear, you are not working with these recruits unilaterally. You *will* liaise with each other and work together."

"Yes, sir," she surrendered.

His voice softened. "Gayle, there are some...special recruits in this class. Unique children as you once were. Please, do not let your emotions – your anger – influence how you treat them. We owe them our best. Teach them better than I taught you."

Gayle nodded. It would be churlish of her to make these kids suffer just because she couldn't put her grown-up pants on.

"Reynolds and I will work together."

"Thank you," Norbel smiled. "The cadets arrived last week and have been settling in. Captain Reynolds has started classes this afternoon, so I suggest you go and introduce yourself to them."

Gayle simply nodded.

"I would like you to start your classes with them a week from now. You should take the rest of this week to get up to speed."

"No problem, sir." She tried, but failed miserably, to hide the sarcasm in her tone. "Will that be all?"

At this point, she just wanted to get out of this office as soon as humanly possible. Her uncle got the hint and nodded.

"Dismissed, Captain."

She left without a further word. The moment she was out of earshot, she pulled her phone from her pocket and thumbed one of the quick-dial numbers.

"Dad, it's Gayle. Call me back. You know why. I'm at the Academy."

She ended the call angrily without her usual display of daughterly affection.

She hated feeling like this. Gayle's relationship with her father had always been very close. In comparison with her sisters, she recognized that she was regarded as the black sheep of the family. Gayle knew her mother sometimes despaired for her eldest daughter's attitude toward life and her embracement of the soldier's lifestyle. Her father, though he had wanted her to follow him into diplomacy, had always understood and supported her.

Gayle scrolled to Allyson's number; her sister was usually her sounding board in moments like this. She briefly hovered her thumb over the call button before deciding against it, exhaling heavily.

Let's go meet my new partner, then, she thought bitterly, already determined not to like him.

She orientated herself and stalked off with a purposeful stride. The fury still churning unabated in the pit of her stomach.

| 8 |

PROXY

– Lyssa Balthazaar –
– Monday – New York, New Victus –

Lyssa suspected Mercy made Storm wait in the boardroom simply because she knew he would loathe it. The glass walls and dark glass table with its comfortable modern chairs ran counter to his personal tastes. The man was deeply mired in the past, in both his thinking and his attitudes. It wouldn't have surprised her if he'd turned up today in a horse drawn carriage.

As she approached, she recognized the pair of burly identi-kit security guards who formed his usual entourage and breezed past them.

Sebastian StormHall sat at the head of the conference table, a strange contradiction of a man. For a person of his power and reputation, you would be forgiven for assuming he would present an intimidating physical presence. Yet he was anything but. Average height, a little overweight, with spindly arms that looked too long for his body while his legs looked a little too short. His whole physical demeanor was...awkward.

His face was almost gaunt with angular cheek bones and pencil thin lips. His pale sand-colored eyes looked a little too close together aside his narrow nose. A look that made him appear shifty rather than interesting. His hair was a dull brown bordering on black and was cut in a style that was at least fifty

54

years out of date.

Yet, Lyssa could not deny...there *was* something about him.

A brand of malevolent charisma, for want of a better word. He found manipulation to be the easy path to power and you needed a strong will to be in Sebastian's presence and not be bent to his whim. Fortunately, Lyssa was every bit as strong a personality as the man before her. *Un*fortunately, he was the one in the elected position of power.

For now.

"Colorado to New York City. Long way to come. To what do I owe the pleasure, Grand Chancellor?" Her question was laced with barely disguised contempt.

She had no intention of dragging this meeting out any longer than was necessary. A sentiment Storm evidently did not share.

"A long overdue visit," he launched into the customary political small talk. "I thought it was about time I came to pay my respects to your father."

"My father is still in hibernation," Lyssa replied dryly. "I'll relay your respects when he rises in another fifty years or so."

"I'd be honored to visit his chamber..." Sebastian said in a low, leading tone.

"So would a great many people, but the chamber will remain locked down until his time to awaken." She had no intention of taking him to their most sacred place. "I'm sure you understand how seriously we take his security."

"Surely you don't think I, the Grand Chancellor of New Victus, present a threat to Lord Balthazaar?"

A more modest man would have gone with 'President' or maybe just 'Chancellor,' but Storm wasn't one to accept a title that sounded anything less than grandiose. She was a little surprised he hadn't just decreed that he should be called the 'Emperor.' Or 'Illustrious Emperor.' Or 'Grand Illustrious Emperor Sebastian StormHall of New Victus, The First of His Name.'

Either way, his official title pissed her off to no end.

"We live in a world populated by shape-changers. You arrive here on short notice, waltz past my security without official checks... How do I know you even *are* the Grand Chancellor?"

He lounged slightly in his chair, casually interlinked his fingers across his stomach, and smiled.

"You're implying I'm...what?" he said with a tone of amusement. "A Fae in disguise looking to assassinate your father?"

"It's not about your threat level, Sebastian," Lyssa shrugged, refusing to take the bait. "It's about tradition."

Her last word was the dagger. The simple fact was that the only thing that held more influence in their society than those elected to the Council of Blood were the Progenitors. In a culture where tradition was sacrosanct, House StormHall held no currency, and StormHall knew it. Lyssa knew he didn't *actually* want to see Balthazaar – he simply wanted to see if he could make Lyssa yield to his wishes.

It was a power-play, and she had reached her limit of tolerance for this verbal sparring.

"Maybe you could do us both a favor and get to the real reason for your visit," Lyssa said, diverting the conversation back to the pertinent topic.

He met her stare, both refusing to back down. To do so would show weakness. She was expecting the inevitable biting retort, but instead he merely smiled. It was a gesture meant to look friendly.

"You...will be representing New Victus at the Nexus Summit this year."

Even stunned as she was, Lyssa was savvy enough to bite her tongue and swallow down the initial urge to tell him to go fuck himself.

Instead, she tempered her response, buying herself time to think this through. It was clear that Storm wanted something more from her than simply fronting New Victus at the Nexus Summit. It was why he was here in person. That gave her leverage.

"You're dropping out of representing New Victus at the Summit," she stated, trying not to roll her eyes. "Again."

"As much as I recognize the importance of the Summit and

savor the responsibility of representing our kind in Nexus..." Such smoothly told lies that Lyssa almost laughed out loud. "...for what I am proposing this year, I think you will be the better choice to attend. It is important that what we offer is taken seriously."

Damn him.

Against her better judgement, she found her curiosity was piqued.

Despite his flowery words, she knew that Storm thought the Summit a useless waste of time. The original Summit had been an attempt to reign in the hostilities that were tearing the world asunder. As a result, much of the world was now in a holding pattern of truces and paper-thin peace treaties. In recent years, New Victus had always made the same demands that were never met. Vetoed by the other World Council nations who voted against such demands, because to cede to them would skew the delicate balance of power firmly in favor of New Victus, which was something that the rest of the world could not allow.

To be honest, Lyssa agreed with them.

This was why sending her as their representative seemed more than a little...unconventional.

"To be frank, Sebastian, you know my political stance and it has always opposed yours. Surely sending me as your delegate would be simply seen as more evidence of your indifference toward the Summit."

"Perhaps at first. But I'm about to make a proposal that is, dare I say, historic. The nature of it... Well, coming from me, I fear it would be viewed with suspicion. Coming from Lyssa Balthazaar, though? You head a House that is old, revered, and widely respected and are well known as someone who opposes many of my policies. If you are delivering our offer, then I suspect it will be taken far more seriously."

He paused and looked down for a moment, seemingly introspectively, at his own reflection in the gleaming black glass.

"Lyssa," he finally said. "I understand how I am regarded by the other nations. They do not trust New Victus while I sit on the throne."

Interesting choice of words.

"I can also understand how what we have historically asked for has been perceived. As concessions intended to tilt the balance of power in our favor. I can assure you, Lyssa, that our requests for trade were simply to strengthen our economy, *not* to increase our powerbase."

Bullshit.

Lyssa had a seat on the Council, and she knew full well that Storm and his followers were desperately eager to link up with their cousins in Africa. They were fighting a war on too many fronts and the vampire breeds that had infested Africa would make excellent foot soldiers in their fight with Pack Nation and the North American Alliance.

"To be perfectly honest," he continued as if reading her mind, "New Victus is too large and our population is too small. On the San Andreas line, we are in conflict with the NAA *and* the FSE. To the north, we are holding an uneasy ceasefire with Pack Nation, and to the south we have a less than stable relationship with The Cartel. It is an untenable situation.

"The NAA is mobilizing. Their 6th Fleet has been spotted gathering its strength in the Gulf of Mexico, possibly with the intention of invading Texas. At some point they will push inland again from the west. It's only a matter of time. While to the north, one small incident could easily incite the dogs back to war."

He paused before continuing, looking her in the eye as if making a point. The look gave Lyssa a moment of concern, but her poker face did not crack.

"Meanwhile, The Cartel is controlled by DeMarco Santana and his group. While we have a trade agreement in place that keeps things...peaceful, you and I both know that The Cartel elects its leader on a Darwinian basis. DeMarco could be gone tomorrow and who knows what the political stance of their new leader may be?

"New Victus simply does not have the manpower to be able to sustain a workable economy while waging a war on multiple fronts. It is, therefore, time to pursue peace. Our offer at the Nexus Summit will be our first step."

She raised her eyebrows in astonishment.

Now that, Lyssa thought, *is the first intelligent thing that you've said since you walked in here.*

She pulled out one of the chairs at the conference room table and sat down opposite where Sebastian had positioned himself.

"Go on...I'll bite. What are you offering?"

He paused for a moment and took a breath; she couldn't be sure if he was actually nervous or just faking it for show. The latter seemed much more likely. Storm wasn't the kind of man who typically demonstrated nerves. Eventually he leaned forward conspiratorially.

"I want you to announce at the Summit...our intention to relinquish control of the Western states as far inland as Texas...back to the NAA. We will surrender North Dakota, South Dakota, Nebraska, Kansas, Oklahoma, Texas, and all the states between those and the San Andreas front."

Lyssa sat back stunned. "That includes Colorado."

"A small price to pay for peace," he said with not a flicker of sentiment. "Besides, I'm thinking of moving to Manhattan."

"I'm not sure we have space here for the construction of a castle as grand as yours."

"I've always been partial to Central Park." He was attempting a joke, but it came across more like a subtle threat. "Essentially, we're willing to split New Victus down the middle. The eastern states will remain in our hands and we will relocate our population accordingly. The west will go back to the NAA to do with as they please. In return, we want a peace treaty in place that will establish a 'No-Man's Land' between us and them. Furthermore, we would like to instigate a trade deal with them to stimulate both our economies."

Lyssa mulled over Storm's statement for a moment or two. While the idea of a trade deal with the NAA might be a step too far for now, she couldn't deny the fact that this was perhaps the most sensible plan of action for their future that he had ever put forward. One remarkably similar to that which she had been pushing in Council meetings for years now.

Which is why she doubted it was genuine.

Storm's whole path to power was built on the manifesto of Vampire superiority. Vampires were stronger, faster, tougher, and lived longer than Humans. He maintained the point of view that it was only intervention of the Fae that prevented them from ruling the world. Handing large pieces of territory back to the Humans would be an abhorrent idea to him. More than that, she knew that The Collective were cut from the same racist cloth that Storm himself was.

If this offer *was* genuine, then how could he have possibly sold it to them?

"You're wondering how I got this plan past The Collective," he said, as if on cue. "It wasn't easy. You and I both understand that New Victus does not have the numbers to populate a country this size. We bit off more than we could chew. We have barely ten million citizens living in a country that used to hold thirty times that. Many of the states I'm proposing we hand over are...sparsely populated at best. And I'm generously counting Trampyrii in those numbers."

Lyssa was far too jaded to be taken in by this false sincerity. She had to admit that what he was saying was true, though. Vampyrii were not happy in the hot and sunny States, and the more temperate East Coast States were far more conducive to their physical limitations. The population tended to congregate in the major cities on that side of the country. Even so, they were hardly the bustling metropolises of yesteryear. New York City was a perfect case in point.

"Our army is stretched too thin," he continued. "If the NAA invaded along the coast of Texas, we would be unable to muster the required forces to repel them. During the War, we had the element of surprise and the advantage of being able to recruit by way of turning our enemies.

"Now, without a Human population to turn or enslave, that is no longer an option. Additionally, the forces we face are now familiar with us as an enemy. They are armed with knowledge and weapons capable of defeating us, hence our margin of superiority is reduced. They won't even risk placing Humans on the front line when they can pave the way with drones and fight us from range using their control of the GPS network.

"While we inherited much of the US military land forces and a portion of their Air Force, we haven't had the technical expertise to advance that technology. We're fighting a modern war with antiquated tools."

He paused for a moment to take a breath in the middle of his monologue. Lyssa didn't interrupt. She strategically maintained her silence until he eventually continued.

"Our Air Force, for example. Almost three thousand aircraft with limited numbers of our most advanced fighter jet, the F-22. While the bulk of their Naval Air Force is also comprised of F22s, intelligence indicates the USS *Nimitz* and the USS *Abraham Lincoln*, who are currently stationed in the Gulf, are about to each receive a complement of ten De-Havilland Hornets. An aircraft far superior to anything we can put in the sky."

All true. Lyssa's people had uncovered that snippet of intelligence themselves.

"Those twenty Hornets won't break the stalemate for them, but how long before they have fifty? Or one hundred? These are the *facts*...and even the most stubborn member of The Collective could not argue against them.

"Pulling our territory back to those proposed lines and forming a truce with the NAA will enable us to more comfortably protect our territory by shortening our border with Pack Nation to only the geography around the Great Lakes. Plus, it will rid us of the Cartel problem altogether."

"I've been an advocate for annexing the western states back to the NAA for years," Lyssa finally broke her silence. "But why the change of mind? Why now?"

"The world is more at peace now than it has been in years. Peace has allowed our enemies time to consolidate their positions. We've had nine years of Nexus Summits, how many more before they put their differences aside and bring their forces to bear as a united front? Another war is coming, Lyssa, and it's a war that we cannot win. This is purely a matter of safeguarding our future."

He was preaching to the converted. Lyssa knew that war was a folly they could not afford. Still, he hadn't answered her question.

"Regardless, this doesn't explain how you sold it to The Collective."

"Money." StormHall sat back in his chair as Lyssa leaned forward.

"You bribed them?" she asked.

"In a way. We give half of New Victus back to the NAA," he said by way of explanation. "That's almost two million square miles. By rough estimate, there are no more than ten million former US citizens left in exile and many of them are happily resettled in other countries by now. Once they have their land, they'll be in the same position we are. Too much space, too few people.

"It'll be decades before they're able to muster up any kind of population that would allow them to threaten our hold in the Eastern States. They're currently relying on the charity of other nations, but when they resettle the Western region, they'll need to establish their cities, economy, and manufacturing base... It all takes time and people. This is the easiest way to remove a threat off the board."

"What does this have to do with money?" Lyssa pushed.

"Because, my dear, in order to re-establish their economy, they will need trade partners."

"You expect the NAA to establish trade relations with the people that took their country off them?" Lyssa almost snorted derisively.

"Will they have a choice?" Storm countered. "New Victus will be their closest possible avenue for import and export. They will flourish and benefit. And so will we. The members of The Collective are all businessmen and the promise of profit is a powerful motivator. Even so, it has taken me months to gather the support I needed to get this approved. I know precisely what I am and where my strengths lie. I'm not a warrior, Lyssa. I'm a politician and a realist.

"Yes, I instigated the War. I used my position and my power...and I don't regret that decision. We, as a race, have gone from a hunted and persecuted people, to a nation with our own territory and a seat at the table of world power."

"All true," Lyssa shot back. "But at what cost, Sebastian?

How many billions of people had to die for you to realize your vision of the world?"

"Humans," he shrugged.

"Humans are still people. Their lives matter, and I – and many like me – have an issue with your casual disregard of that fact. Many of us worked hard to integrate ourselves into Human life, to live alongside them. Pop culture had already painted a less than flattering picture of us as a race, but your actions cemented that image. We were already feared. Now we are mistrusted. More than that...we are hated. We are contained in a trap of our own making.

"You just said it yourself... Pack Nation stands to the north and the NAA control the West Coast states. The Cartel hold Mexico and most of Central America in their influence and the FSE naval forces dominate the waters of the Atlantic. You talk about us finally having a place in the world, but other than the tiny sliver of a flight path that allows us to travel to Nexus City and our small section of Iceland, we're utterly isolated.

"Borders are closed to us. Everywhere.

"You may have gained us a place at the table, but we'll never be invited guests."

She saw Storm visibly bristle at her assertion that Humans were of equal importance. For all his bluster and his supposed intention to play nice, he couldn't hide the fact that beneath it all he was still as prejudiced and racist as he had ever been. To his credit, he swallowed his retort and smiled.

"Then, Lyssa, my dear, maybe *this* is the first step to us being given that invitation. To change that perception. So...will you deliver my proposal to the Nexus Summit?"

Her mind whirled trying to figure out his endgame. There was no valid reason to refuse him. He was the elected leader of their country and he was putting forward a proposal that was something for which Lyssa herself had been a leading proponent. This was Storm giving her everything she had been asking for on a platter.

So, why did it feel like a trap?

| 9 |

THE ROUND TABLE

– Allyson Knightley –
– Monday – Nexus City, Iceland –

Designed and constructed by the Fae, the World Council Chamber followed their unique aesthetic, combining natural and man-made materials in achingly beautiful ways. The diplomatic chamber was a modest amphitheater of steel, stone, and wood. Its high-domed roof of wooden arches curved gracefully to an apex, framing clear crystal windows that kept the room diffused in natural sunlight.

The room's centerpiece was a huge AuthaGraphic map of their world sitting in a shallow-dished area, around which fourteen sturdy mahogany tables were arranged. It was a colorful work of three-dimensional holographic beauty detailing the peaks and valleys, deserts, jungles, and ice plains of their planet. The cities twinkled and gleamed, while the blue-green oceans and seas ebbed and flowed in animated real-time. Exquisite as it might be, the map did have an important function. It accurately displayed the fluid borders of the world's factions, around which there was often much heated debate.

But then, debate *was* the very philosophy behind why this room existed.

"So, do we know who's actually coming to this shindig?" Allyson said, looking around the chamber.

"It's not a shindig," Serlia admonished gently. "It's a Summit."

"Although," Jaymes said as he scratched his neatly trimmed beard, "the evening gala could be called a shindig, I suppose. You will be coming to that, yes?"

"Mmmhmm," Ally idly nodded as she tapped the nail of her forefinger against one of her teeth, only half listening to her parents.

"Excellent!" Jaymes exclaimed. "Your mother and I want to be able to show off our daughter to the assembled delegates."

That last bit caught her attention.

"Dad! No. I'll be there, but I'll be working security for the event. Not socializing."

"Fran can handle it," her mother answered. "I'm sure you can take *one* night off. As your parents and Federation Ambassadors, we would like our daughters around us at the gala."

"It's a special occasion," Jaymes nodded. "The 10th anniversary of the Nexus Summit."

"Then why isn't Carrie coming? Or Gayle?" Allyson shot back.

"Carrie *is* coming," Jaymes confirmed with a hint of joy in his voice which quickly disappeared.

"But not Gayle?" Ally shot him a sideways look.

"No, I...I don't think so." There was a sadness in his tone. "Well, we'll see."

Something was evidently awry between her father and her older sister. She decided not to push the issue. Not right now, anyway. She was due a conversation with Gayle later that day, so would endeavor to prize whatever the issue was out of her. If her father wanted to talk about what was bugging him, he would. Still, it was hard to imagine anything driving a wedge between Gayle and her father, so whatever was happening, it must be serious.

Allyson had grown up the stereotypical middle child, never truly bonding with either of her parents closely. Gayle, the eldest, was strong-willed and charismatic – traits she inherited from Jaymes. The two would talk for hours, and Ally knew that her father secretly wanted Gayle to follow in his footsteps as a diplomat.

Conversely, Carrie-Anne was more reserved and introspective. A bookworm, something their mother had encouraged in her. Serlia fed her youngest daughter's insatiable appetite for knowledge by bringing her books from all over the world. She was thrilled when Carrie pursued a career as a journalist.

Allyson, meanwhile, always struggled to find an identity apart from her sisters. Her parents had never been anything but loving and supportive, but as an adult she recognized how difficult it must have been for them to deal with the 'troublesome' middle child.

"Maybe you could even dress up nice. Bring along Dannielle, make a night of it." Her father was still chattering about the gala.

"Oh, Jaymes," Serlia said quietly. "Allyson broke up with Dannielle months ago."

"Really?" he sounded disappointed. "You seemed so happy together."

"We were," Ally shrugged. "For a while."

"I'm sorry, Ally." His note of concern made her smile.

"Don't worry...I'm not heartbroken. There are plenty more fish, as they say."

"Very true," he nodded. "Maybe you'll even meet someone at the gala..."

"Jaymes!" her mother admonished.

"Fine! You win. I'll be there," Ally laughed. "I'll even dress up nice."

"Thank you," her father sounded genuinely pleased.

"Now, let's get back to business, shall we?" She gestured around the room. "Who precisely is coming to this shind—to the Summit?"

"Well..." Jaymes thought for a moment. "Ambassador Sabadini from Pack Nation, of course. You've met him before. He pretty much resides here in Nexus these days. Grand Chancellor StormHall sent word this afternoon that he's sending a representative in his place. Again. Lyssa Balthazaar..."

"Problem?" Ally asked as her father trailed off, deep in thought.

"Hmmm," her father blinked. "No, no...I don't think so. It's just... If I recall correctly, the House of Balthazaar opposed the election of StormHall, inciting the other Progenitor Houses to follow suit. She seems an...odd choice for his replacement."

"I'll check up on that," Ally noted mentally. "Any idea why?"

"Not a clue," Jaymes mused. "But I do know StormHall, and nothing he does is without some form of self-interest."

"Duly noted."

"I've played this game long enough to know when the wind is changing. This alteration of plans by StormHall..." Jaymes paused.

"Alteration?" Ally asked. "I heard that StormHall never comes anyway. What makes this year any different?"

"Because he has announced it early, rather than just not showing up and giving us platitudes and excuses. This is out of character for him and my gut tells me it means something unpleasant. Something we need to make sure we prepare for."

"Great," Allyson snorted through her nose. "My first Summit in charge of security and New Victus are up to no good already."

Her mother smiled and tutted. "Not New Victus, Allyson. StormHall. First rule of diplomacy – don't confuse a people with an individual. Now, then..."

Serlia gestured to the oversized wooden chairs at the table just clockwise from where they stood.

"Ambassadors Alzim and Yetu will be here. They *always* attend."

"What are they like?" Allyson asked with interest.

"The NordScanians?" Jaymes said.

Ally nodded. While her sisters were well travelled, Ally's career choices had given her a far more insular life until now. NordScania was a nation populated by three races living in harmony together. While the Humans needed no explanation, the Ice Giants and Trolls were unfamiliar to her. She had to admit, she was kind of looking forward to meeting them.

Jaymes considered for a moment before responding. "Your mother deals with them more frequently than I do. I'll let her answer that question."

Serlia contemplated her reply and then smiled. "Assuming you're talking about the non-Human races... The Trolls are ancient, not at all what myth and legend paint them to be. They love to talk. Ambassador Yetu is soft spoken, charming, kind, and funny. He's also judged to be quite handsome in his culture."

"And the Giants?" Allyson prompted.

"Beautiful," Jaymes said simply in response. "Literally living ice..."

She believed her father in his assessment. She had seen photographs of the huge crystalline creatures and was eager to meet them in the flesh, so to speak.

"Really quite exquisite to look at," Serlia agreed. "Peaceful, secluded. They're listeners, but when they do talk, what they say is always considered and wise. Their voices are very...singsong. Lyrical. Hauntingly beautiful."

"And *very* tall," Jaymes continued. "Ambassador Alzim is almost twice the height of Yetu and by all accounts he's on the short side for an Ice Giant. I think he got the job here because he does at least fit into the room. Back in Norway, the largest Giants are at least twenty feet tall, I hear."

"How did they stay hidden for so long?" Ally asked.

"They didn't," her mother took up the answer. "The Scandinavian Governments knew about their existence but kept it secret. They're mountain dwellers, mostly living underground. Despite their size, they're superb at being discreet. I enjoy dealing with them very much."

"They are a straightforward people – in a complicated world," Jaymes finished.

Sadness tinged his voice. Ally often forgot that her father remembered a time before the age of gods and monsters.

"Do you miss it?" she asked softly. "The before."

He took a moment to collect his thoughts on the matter before looking at her with a twinkle in his eye.

"It was, in some respects, a simpler time. But also one very much complicated by politics."

"More complex than all this?" Ally gestured around the

room.

Her father chuckled lightly. "Oh, heavens, yes. Many more countries, all with their own interests. Terrorism and petty wars over religion and territory. Governments came and went, changing policies and unpicking each other's work. There were constant struggles with things we take for granted today. Climate change, gender equality...as a gay woman, you'd have found the world back then a very different – more difficult – place. We'd seemingly swing from walking a path of cultural enlightenment to regressing to the Dark Ages every few years.

"Yet, for all the horror the world saw almost thirty years ago, for all the death and destruction...we came out of it all in an oddly better place."

"Really?" Ally felt a little taken aback at her father's admission.

"Humanity is more united now." He looked at Serlia and smiled. "The Fae united us as faction states rather than individual countries. While politics will always be politics, the ground we stand on doesn't tend to shift as much these days."

For her father, the term 'united' in reference to the Fae had a more personal emphasis. After all, he married a Fae with whom he had three daughters.

"I've never been a great believer in the Gaia philosophy, but it does seem like the planet is healing itself," he continued thoughtfully. "The regrettable culling of humanity is allowing mother nature to repair the damage that we did. Scientists say that the environment has never been healthier, the ozone layer is well on its way to recovery, and..."

Ally grinned in amusement. Her father the diplomat, she knew well. Her father the philosopher was something new. He suddenly noticed her expression.

"I'm so sorry. I was rambling, wasn't I?"

Allyson shrugged. "No, it's nice..."

"Anyway," he continued, "without The Rising, I wouldn't have my wonderful wife and my beautiful daughters. I have to admit, your mother and I had reservations when you said you wanted to join the Police Force, *and* when you told us you were applying for the job here."

"Thanks," Ally frowned at her father.

"I'm simply admitting we were wrong to be apprehensive," Jaymes said. "Look at what you've accomplished, Ally. Twenty-six and Head of Nexus Security. We're so proud of you."

Ally blushed. Compliments never sat well on her shoulders.

"We should get back to discussing the Summit arrangements," Serlia interrupted coming to her daughter's rescue.

Jaymes smiled knowingly and gestured to the smaller chairs at the NordScania table. "Of course, there are also Humans amongst the NordScania ambassadorial party. We could learn a lot from how they co-exist. A model for the world going forward...if only we could all be so enlightened."

Ally pointed across to the other side of the chamber to a table lacking the accoutrements of the other areas – just a single banner hanging forlornly.

"Tell me about China."

"Zǔguó. Though many still call it China for sake of ease, and as they aren't here to disagree..." he shrugged. "Translates as simply '*Motherland,*' if I recall correctly, though that may be a tad inaccurate. Mysterious nation – we know little about them these days."

"They've been at war with the Japanese Empire for decades now," her mother continued. "Though a truce appears to have been called lately according to the FSE fleet working out of Australasia."

"Curiously, their national flag changed about twenty-five years ago." Jaymes stroked his beard thoughtfully. "Though that's never been officially confirmed. A reconnaissance drone snapped one of their warships in the South China Sea flying that banner."

He pointed to the crimson flag and it's contrasting golden stars.

"The same traditional large star, symbolizing Communism," he continued, "now has *five* smaller stars surrounding it rather than the original four. They used to represent the social classes of the Chinese people, so we assume that adding another implies a new class..."

As her father trailed off thoughtfully, Ally looked at the spartan array of furniture arranged neatly under the striking red banner.

"So," she said, "what you're saying is...don't spend too much time worrying about them as a security risk?"

"If I were you," Serlia laughed lightly, "I'd spend more time worrying about the ones who are actually going to be here. But, while we're on the subject of potential no-shows..."

She pointed towards the area that had the large golden flag with the red circle on it.

"The Japanese Empire," Jaymes nodded sagely. "They were a founding member of the World Council when we first broke ground on Nexus City, twenty years ago. As was China. Neither have been back here since."

"Any idea why?" Allyson asked, genuinely curious.

"They disagreed with the contents of the Nexus Treaty," Jaymes shrugged. "They wouldn't sign it. It was quite an acrimonious affair, and both swore never to come back to the World Council while..."

His voice trailed off, leaving his explanation incomplete.

"While what?" Allyson pushed.

It was her mother who answered. "While the Fae have a say in world politics," Serlia said quietly but elaborated no further.

"Suffice it to say, the Fae tried to alleviate the issue by refusing a place at the World Council," Jaymes quickly interjected. "Yet, even though the Fae no longer...interfere, neither Zǔguó nor Japan have come back to the table. Rumor has it they will be here this year, though. It would be exciting to have some new faces."

As the briefing went on, she found that working with her parents was fast becoming an enjoyable bonding experience for both sides. Even if they or her uncle *had* pulled strings to get her this job, she was grateful for the opportunity to prove herself. A determination surged within her; the Summit *would* be a success.

Even if she had to wear a pretty dress and make nice at the gala dinner.

| 10 |

FIRST IMPRESSIONS

– Michael Reynolds –
– Monday – London, England –

Teachin' ain't so hard.

Granted, thus far he had only experienced roughly forty minutes of the profession, but Michael felt like he had really started to get into a rhythm. The cadets seemed to be engaged and taking in all he had to say, and he found that a flickering ember of enjoyment displaced the butterflies of earlier.

All that was about to change.

An abrupt knock on the classroom door rudely interrupted his flow, seizing the attention of everyone in the room. A face appeared in the tiny window in the door, and without even seeing the signature pink hair, he recognized Gayle Knightley from her file. She looked subtly different, though. In her pictures, her eyebrows had been softer, less arched and angry. Her lips less pursed and hard.

He beckoned for her to enter.

She pushed the door open and strode in, the cadets gazing at her, awestruck. Here she was, the physical form of a battlefield goddess walking amongst them. Michael, of course, knew better. He had read all the files to which they weren't privy.

"Captain Knightley." He offered a smile. "Glad you could join us."

She spared him barely a glance, her eyes already scanning

the students one by one, evaluating them. He had to admit, reviewing her file and combat logs had not prepared him for her presence. Power and confidence emanated from her in palpable waves.

And anger.

Resentment.

"Commander Norbel said I should come down here and introduce myself." Her voice had a hard edge. "I'm Captain Gayle Knightley. I'll be working with Captain Reynolds here to teach you all the shit you'll need to know before you're ready for active duty. I'll be getting up to speed this week, so our first class together will be next Monday."

She swiveled her head in his direction slowly, her eyes meeting his with a hard stare of judgement. There was a fire of bitterness burning in those jade eyes. If he had to hazard a guess, she was likely pissed about being given this assignment.

"Till then, they're all yours, Captain."

Her parting words.

She spun on her heel and exited via the door through which she had entered mere moments ago. Her brevity left the cadets stunned and triggered an irritation in Michael. The urge to pursue her out into the corridor was strong, but there was still a class to teach. He summoned a calmness and picked up his tablet from the desk.

"So...back to Werewolves," he said loudly to draw his class back into the moment. "Throw out some things y'all reckon you know about them. We'll play a lil' game of true or false."

A flurry of hands shot up amongst the students. Werewolves were common creatures in myth and legend, and everyone knew something about them.

"Miss Hudgins." He picked the young red headed girl who was sitting on the back row of the class.

Michael knew all twelve of the students by name. He had studied their dossiers when he accepted the position.

"Werewolves only change on a full moon," Rosario said confidently, her accent betraying her Canadian parentage.

"The top fact on any Werewolf list, but false. Werewolves

can change anytime the mood moves them."

He tapped his stylus against the tablet and the first item on his pre-prepared list popped up onto the video screen. There were still hands in the air.

"Mr. Jager?" he called upon the dark-haired Icelandic boy.

"Silver bullets kill them," Tomas Jager said seriously.

Michael smiled and nodded. "As much as anybody will be killed by a silver bullet, yes." The response elicited giggles around the classroom. "But seriously, there's a grain of truth to that. Werewolves are allergic to silver, but it won't kill them immediately. Think of it more like a hypersensitivity. Like to bee stings or peanuts.

"Any more?"

Emboldened, the rest of the class started to offer other bits of Werewolf folklore they had picked up through pop culture or hearsay. With the ice now broken, answers began to come thick and fast.

| 11 |

LONE WOLF

– Alex Newman –
– Monday – Mont Tremblant, Pack Nation –

The breeze rippled his thick midnight fur as he sampled the rich cross-section of scents it carried to his sensitive nostrils. He panted uncomfortably; it was an unseasonably torrid night in the forest. Quiet, too. The presence of an apex predator amongst them muted the voice of most wildlife. Why draw the hunter's attention when it was far more prudent to quietly wait for it to pass? Their fear was misplaced – none of them were prey tonight.

He sniffed the wind again, this time finding the scent he was seeking. It was very faint, yet distinct amongst the more mundane aromas of the forest, like a diamond sparkling in a sea of glass. He padded a few degrees clockwise to catch a subtly different part of the gentle wind.

Better. Stronger now.

Alex edged forward and cocked his head curiously. His quarry's scent was still there but was somehow...different. Now that the wind worked in his favor, he could distinguish a new aromatic edge. Instantly recognizable, where it hadn't been before. The distinctive fragrance of intimacy. Sex and its predictable side effect. Two people; one intermingled scent. Male and female. He concentrated, trying to separate them.

A buried memory teased him as he isolated the female, but

nose and brain weren't quite in sync just yet. The answer remained tantalizingly out of reach. Regardless, the couple had split to follow different paths. The male continued on the same heading as before, but she was now circling to the east. Not too far away, though. Were they flanking something maybe?

Hunting something?

Or someone.

The target he was tracking was dangerous on its own. This new discovery ratcheted the threat level up another notch. Alex pushed aside the characteristic aroma of his target and refocused as he continued his wary advance. As his nose broke the tree line into a small moonlit glade, he stiffened and immediately stopped. The third scent was delivered to him on the breeze. Unique and unmistakable. The metallic aroma of Human blood.

No...

Not *just* Human blood. Something unfamiliar to him. Sweet honey with a hint of citrus. A subtle, pleasant odor mixed amongst a heady perfume of adrenaline and nervous sweat.

Alex backed up slowly, returning to the shelter of the forest. It was clear his quarry had tracked the sweet-smelling Human to this clearing. Had this been a trap? Was it *still* a trap?

A tiny gust swept gently across the glade teasing the leaves into a gentle, whirling dance and gifting him with a wealth of new scents. He listened carefully, scanning upwind where the direction of the breeze worked against his nose. Ears standing tall and twitching, he panned his head around deliberately, eyes darting from tree to tree evaluating them for danger.

Impatience got the better of him. He prowled forward once more, leaving the relative safety of the forest. Creeping low to the ground, his body a coiled spring. The unmistakable aroma of blood led him to a bramble near the center of the clearing, its thorny betrayal evident by the dry claret painting its sharp thorns. He sampled the perfume of the dark stain seeking to decipher its identifying markers.

Female. Early adult in her late teens, maybe early twenties. Human?

It was oddly hard to tell. There were the definite Human markers, but something was just slightly off. A sweetness, of sorts. He couldn't place the scent, so he filed it away in his brain for later.

Assuming she was Human, her profile in conjunction with their current location prompted a worrying thought. Could it be *her*? He needed to call this in and let Damian know. Let him check.

His attention flitted back to the identity of the other odor. The answer hovered on the periphery of his mind but remained resolutely elusive. It was something familiar, a variation on something he had smelled a million times before.

Fuck, what is it?

His brain examined his memories searching for the match to this particular sequence of scent molecules. Female. Similar to Vampyrii but subtly different. The memory unlocked at last, revealing the true extent of the danger he faced.

Oh, no!

He closed his eyes, willing forth the transformation. The flood of endorphins surged through his body numbing him to the agony of his impending transfiguration. From the painful splintering and mending of his bones, to the stretching of his skin over his new form. The transition from Wolf to Man was completed in a handful of heartbeats.

He stood exposed in the moonlight, a pleasant buzz dulling his brain momentarily, a side effect of the natural painkillers pumping around his bloodstream. Technology had provided them with body hugging-outfits and smart equipment that could meld to whatever form their wearer took. He tolerated the backpack and its malleable straps but, like many of his kind, he eschewed the clothing as being too restrictive.

The pack was quickly shrugged off and placed on the ground where he squatted to access its contents. He extracted a rugged looking phone from one of its pockets.

"Basecamp. This is Lonewolf."

A female voice, crisp and clear replied. "This is Basecamp, Lonewolf."

"Confirm transmission is secure," he said in a low voice.

"Confirm secure," came the immediate reply.

"I need to talk to Alpha."

"Is there a problem, Lonewolf?"

"I need to talk to Alpha," he repeated his request more forcefully.

There was a pause on the other end of the line before the voice came back. "Lonewolf, cut transmission. Alpha will contact you directly."

"Affirmative, Basecamp. Lonewolf out." Alex cut the transmission.

It didn't take long. A few minutes later the phone vibrated in the palm of his hand. A new voice, that of Damian Dane, came quietly through the tiny speaker.

"Alpha. Transmission is secure."

"Target is no longer alone. Female. Code 11," Alex growled in a low tone.

A pause.

"You're *sure*?"

"Positive," Alex confirmed.

A pause as the voice at the other end processed the information.

"Do you need back up?" Alpha finally asked with a hint of concern.

"Affirmative," he stated simply.

"I'll have them standing by," an undercurrent of concern in the voice.

"Not our troops," Alex interjected. "The targets are heading toward New Victus. If they reach the border..."

"MercNet?" Alpha understood the situation.

"Yes," Alex confirmed.

"I'll raise a contract—" Alpha started but Alex interrupted.

"You *know* who to call," he said quietly. "We'll need her on this one."

Silence. Alex knew what he was asking for and the ramifications for both of them.

"You're sure?" Alpha eventually responded.

"I'm sure." No hesitation from Alex.

"You're absolutely positive it's a Code 11? Been a long time since we saw one."

"Three years," Alex confirmed. "Took me a while to put the pieces together. She has the experience with this…not many do."

"You'll be able to work together?"

"We'll be fine," Alex said assertively. "There's more…"

"More?"

The reason I needed to talk to you.

Alex took a deep breath. He truly hoped he was wrong about this.

"They're hunting. Human female, late teens or early twenties." Alex glanced at the blood on the ground again. "She's wounded, which will make it easier to track her than them. They may already have her. I thought you should know…considering where I am."

A pause before the measured response. "Is it her?"

"I don't know," Alex said truthfully. "The trail *was* heading towards Lac Reynard until I found this more recent scent. It looks like they crossed their own track, so he could have been there already. You want me to head down and take a look?"

The pause was so long it made him think that maybe the connection had been lost. Finally, the voice came back again.

"No. Stay on them. I'll check the commune from my end and sort out your backup. In the meantime…just be careful."

"Always am. Lonewolf out." Alex cut the transmission.

Stowing the phone, he shifted back to his lupine form.

All the better to track you, my dear, he thought and set off in the direction the scent of blood led him.

| 12 |

REGRETS

– Gayle Knightley –
– Tuesday – London, England –

"Urrggghhhh."

It was, perhaps, an understatement of how Gayle felt as she cracked her eyelids open, allowing the early morning sun to painfully seep through.

She wished she could blame excessive drinking on her delicate condition, but no alcohol had been imbibed on her late-night phone call to her sister. Not by her anyway. Allyson, on the other hand, had likely knocked back at least a few glasses of wine while she helped Gayle get through her angry discourse. Allyson had always been good at talking her down.

She looked at the clock on the bedside table. It displayed an utterly unreasonable seven a.m. Three hours sleep. No wonder her brain felt like her thoughts were trudging through treacle. What had she been thinking setting her alarm so early?

"Fuck," she whispered under her breath as the memory surfaced.

She stared at the ceiling and gave a sigh that morphed into a huge yawn. The truth was that after all the anger had subsided – or had been placated by her sister's reasoning – she felt pretty shitty about how she had treated Captain Reynolds and the cadets. As angry as she had been, there was really no need to be such a bitch. So, a plan was hatched for her to rise early in the morning and head to the Academy to make amends with her new faculty partner.

Rubbing at the corners of her eyes, she fumbled for her phone and squinted at the screen that seemed to be set far too bright. Two notifications awaited her. A *'good luck'* message from Ally, and a missed call notification from her father. She debated calling him but felt a twinge of anger flicker anew within her. Best leave that until she could be calmer about it.

Forcing herself to sit up, she glared at the clothes laid out on the back of the chair next to her dressing table. Black jeans, a red sweater, and a pair of black suede boots with modest heels.

Too casual maybe?

Her gaze flicked to the other outfit, hanging from the wardrobe. It's red-and-white color scheme a stark contrast to the dark wood of her furniture. State-of-the-art military technology wrapped up in a bespoke synthetic catsuit that fit her like a glove. Her 'CombatSkin' was probably the most comfortable thing she had ever worn, but the outfit that had come to define her life in the 137th was now a painful reminder of her loss. She knew that at some point she would have to slip it on once more, but today was not that day.

She hadn't worn it since Valletta.

Her eyes flicked back again to the clothes on the chair. It wasn't military, but it was smart enough to not be disrespectful. While she accepted the fact that she was going to be teaching at the Academy, she wasn't ready to go the whole hog. Not just yet. Her acceptance was a work in progress.

The phone in her hand vibrated abruptly, startling her.

"Y'ello," she said sleepily.

"Happy birthday!" Allyson's voice came through the speaker louder than Gayle felt comfortable with. She winced.

"How can you be so...loud?" she croaked. "And my birthday was yesterday...you missed it."

"Really? September 25th, right?" Ally said, sounding a little confused.

"Yeah, but today's the 26th..."

"You sure?" her sister asked with a puzzled tone, "If that's true, then why didn't you mention it when we spoke last night?"

"I know my own birthday, Ally," Gayle yawned. "And I wasn't in the mood to celebrate it. It's actually a concern that a woman in your position doesn't seem to know what date it is..."

"You have no idea how busy it is here, Sis," Ally sighed. "The days are blurring one into the next as the Summit approaches. Sorry. I'll make it up to you when I'm there, I promise. Anyway, my other reason for the early morning wake up call, was to make sure you're up..."

"Barely."

"And that you remember what we *did* talk about last night?" Allyson asked animatedly.

"Yeah." Gayle took a deep breath. "I'm accepting my situation. I'm gonna go in and apologize to Reynolds. And blah blah blah."

"Don't forget the blah blah blah," Ally laughed. "That's the important bit."

"Duly noted," Gayle yawned, scratching her head. "So, I'm sorry I didn't ask last night, but how was *your* first week on the job?"

"Ugh," was Allyson's grunted response. "I'm not sure how I let Uncle talk me into this. Starting to feel like I'm in *way* over my head."

"That's bollocks, Ally, and you know it"

"Do I?" Ally sounded doubtful.

"Unc' wouldn't have recommended you for the post if he didn't believe in you."

Gayle knew what her sister was going to say even before her voice echoed down the phoneline.

"Maybe you should trust him with your 'situation' then?"

She sighed, knowing deep down that her sister was right. She was genuinely appreciative of Allyson's support. Both her siblings had been a constant presence in her life since the incident, and she felt a pang of regret at how she had treated them prior to that life-changing day. She had been horribly neglectful of both Ally and Carrie, but when it mattered, they had been there for her. No questions asked.

"I said, I am accepting the situation," Gayle sighed in response. "But that still doesn't mean I have to be happy about it."

"Seriously, I think this will be good for you," Allyson said sincerely. "Give it a chance, okay?

"Thanks, Ally," Gayle said softly.

"What for?"

"For talking me down off the proverbial ledge...again."

"That's what I'm here for," Ally said. "And now, thanks to you, I shall be heading to work this morning brimming with confidence!"

"Is that sarcasm I detect in your tone, Ally?"

Gayle heard Allyson laughing as she said it, a sound that brought a tweak to her own lips.

"Love is a two-way street, Sis," Allyson continued. "Good luck today. And call Dad. *Don't* let it fester. Got to run, early morning briefing. Talk later. Love ya. Bye."

The line went dead, and Gayle stared at the phone for a moment. She wouldn't let it 'fester,' but now was not the right time. She turned the screen off and got up from the bed.

Time to try and make a better second impression.

| 13 |

OLD WOUNDS

– Damian Dane –
– Tuesday – Domaine Saint-Bernard, Pack Nation –

I have a very bad feeling about this...
All Damian could think about was Schrödinger's cat, and it was making him sick to his stomach. He felt overwhelmed with a sense of nervous foreboding. Lonewolf was either right, or he was wrong. Until he landed at Domaine Saint-Bernard, both results were in play. It was the uncertainty that was the cause of his suffering. If right, then Damian's impromptu visit would be the least of their problems.

If Lonewolf was wrong...

Either way, this would not be a pleasant visit.

Damian resisted the impulse to reminisce, trying to concentrate on the matter at hand. For his own sanity, he had avoided coming here for over twenty years. He hadn't been sure if he would remember the way, but his hands moved on the controls of his flyer with unerring precision. Even when the mind forgets, the heart never does.

Eloise was the last person he had truly loved.

It hadn't been his first clandestine affair, and it wouldn't be the last, but she had been the one. His secret love and the reason everything changed.

The spark that lit the fuse. The fuse that ignited the War.

The War that brought the secrets of their kind out of the shadows and into the light of day.

How many Humans had died because of him? How many of his kin had been hunted down and slain, like his own mother?

With her death, his role in this new world was irrevocably altered. Responsibility forced upon him a hard choice.

His heart or his duty?

Uneasy lies the head that wears a crown.

It was no choice – simply the illusion of such.

Years passed, yet her golden hair had not changed. She had come to him for help, tears filling those sparkling blue eyes he still dreamed about. She wanted to return here, to the place where they first met. Where they walked and ran, laughed and loved.

To this place of safety.

Safety for her.

For her husband...and for her unborn child.

True love is like a tattoo, indelibly inked across your heart for all eternity. He tried to put her behind him, enjoying the company of many women. He had grown fond of a handful, even fallen in love with a few. None could break the spell Eloise had cast upon him. The day she begged him for his help was the day he learned that a heart can be broken more than once.

Eloise always had an eye for the idyllic and it didn't surprise him that she had chosen Domaine Saint-Bernard. The calm waters of Lac Reynaud and the rich green of the forest created a tranquil backdrop to life here. The mountain-top provided stunning vistas and at night a thousand fireflies danced along the riverbanks.

For twenty years he had protected her. Kept her safe.

He landed near the lake, his jets kicking up twisters of dust and debris, and tires bouncing rigidly on the hard-packed dirt. The canopy was open, and he was already hopping out before the engines finished whining through their shutdown routine.

Damian paused for a moment to pass his sword over his shoulder and into the electromagnetic sheath incorporated into the back of his combat harness. As the clamps of the sheath closed around the blade, he prayed that he wouldn't have to use it.

As the glinting rays of sunrise bounced golden from the mirror of the placid waters, he hastened towards the buildings that formed the commune in front of him. The location had been a superb choice, more than suitable for Eloise's requirements. Once a relaxation retreat, over the years other refugees from the War made their way to the safe haven it represented and established a small hidden community. He headed for the largest building, the Grand Saint-Bernard pavilion. At last count, there were thirty-two people here – men, women and children.

Families.

No.

His stomach flipped as his nose confirmed his worst fear. The distinctive bouquet of spilled blood.

| 14 |

TEMPTATION

– Zarra Anderson –
– Tuesday – Nassau, Bahamas –

Her namesake was *Diana,* the Roman Goddess of the hunt. *Diana* had stubby, repulsor-lift wings, an aggressive drop snout, and a long double-tail straddling her loading ramp. The de Havilland DH 426 Dragonfly III was an example of early attempts to achieve hybridization of Human design and Fae technology. Becka had once, rudely, called her fat-bottomed and ugly. She wasn't totally wrong in that assessment, but to Zarra she was a misunderstood beauty.

She'd bought the second-hand dropship three years ago and had spent a significant amount of money modifying her. In her prime, she was operated by a flight crew of four and had ample room for a dozen fully equipped soldiers and six tons of military cargo. The bulk of Zarra's refit saw the ship extensively rewired so it could be piloted solo, while the cargo compartment was converted to holding cells for her captured bounties. All necessary additions for her profession.

Her favorite part of the conversion, though, was the small but comfortable living quarters that replaced the troop compartment. One for her and one for her Becka. *Diana* was more than just a dropship – she was Zarra's home.

She grimaced in pain as she sat down gingerly on her bunk, falling back onto the mattress. Her old army buddies might scoff, but a soft bed was the one luxury she had happily afforded herself. And right now, the freshly stitched shoulder along with an aching and bruised body thanked her for her foresight. She glanced at the supple, worn leather of her combat suit draped over the back of the chair and sighed. Repairs were needed.

Again.

Zarra yawned. Before heading out on this excursion to the Bahamas, she purchased six new combat suits, all of which were now either damaged or ruined entirely. A needle and thread had saved her a small fortune, but there was a limit to just how much you can repair. As a freelancer, she was responsible for her own fiscal bottom line and this kind of damage hungrily ate into her profit margin. Maybe it was time to get one of those fancy new CombatSkins. They weren't cheap but would probably be more cost effective in the long run.

She idly picked up the datapad that was lying on the bunk and accessed her current financial balance. The numbers brought a weary smile.

They had undertaken seventy-nine hunts over a brutal six months. Their reward for all their hard work was a total bounty collected of almost three-quarters of a million credits. Minus expenses, the percentage MercNet took, and operating costs for *Diana,* it left around four hundred grand to be split between Becka and herself. They could easily take some time off; head back to Europa to spend some of that well-earned cash. Maybe a CombatSkin *was* in the cards after all.

She heard the familiar footsteps of Becka's approach on the metal deck plates. The young woman knocked on the bulkhead and promptly stuck her head through the door without waiting for permission. Her unruly brown-blonde hair was tied haphazardly atop her head, just a few strands loosely framing her youthful face.

Zarra knew that Becka had some military training. There were certain elements of her skillset that transcended her obvious youth. She could pilot the hell out of a dropship, for example. However, Becka didn't do well with authority and, while Zarra never pushed for details, she had clearly washed out of whatever program in which she had been. She was on the proverbial scrapheap at just twenty-four when Zarra found her and made her an offer she couldn't refuse. The exciting life of a mercenary. The thrill of the hunt, but without any of the starch of military life.

"So," Becka smiled, plunging her hands into the deep pockets of her overalls and leaning against the doorframe. "How was Havana for you?"

"Painful," Zarra confessed.

"Yeah, didn't sound like you slept much last night. Our catch is on ice in cargo two. Containment level one, as requested."

"They've still not picked him up?"

"Bureaucrats dragging their feet as usual," Becka said. "But Fort Nassau are sending a team to unload him as we speak. So, I'm going to need your signature to process our claim through MercNet for payment. How's the shoulder?"

The young woman also had a gift for organization and blitzing through red tape, a skill that Zarra herself lacked. She yawned and absent-mindedly scrawled her initials on the tablet with the stylus Becka handed her.

"It's fine. Thanks for the great job with the stitches. Again." Zarra handed the tablet back to her partner.

"I know you can do it yourself, but with me around you don't have to." Becka shrugged. "I'm at your service, whatever your needs. Within reason."

Said seriously, but with an undercurrent of innuendo. Becka furrowed her brow for a second before handing the tablet straight back. Zarra glanced at the signature box and cursed mentally.

"Sorry," she muttered as she redid her signature.

"Been a long couple of weeks," Becka chuckled.

"Been a long six months!" Zarra yawned and closed her eyes.

"Still, it's been a while since you've made *that* mistake. That's almost the last job on the docket, so you should get some rest while I liaise with the Fort Nassau people."

"That's the plan."

Her young partner loitered in the doorway and Zarra cracked her tired eyes. Becka had a look on her face like she wanted to say something but wasn't quite sure how to broach the subject. As her mental faculties caught up, she realized what Becka had just said.

"No," Zarra shook her head.

That's almost the last job.

"Hell, no," more firmly this time. "That *was* our last job."

"Well, boss, there's a job flagged on MercNet..."

Granted, it was part of Becka's role to find them jobs on the Warrant Service – MercNet was the unofficial name for it – but they had both decided days ago that this hunt would be the last for a while.

"Becs..." Zarra sighed, "we agreed to have some downtime after this last hunt. I seriously need some R 'n R. You literally just said it yourself."

"Yeah, I realize that, but..." Becka pursed his lips briefly.

Zarra could see the cogs in her brain turning as Becka debated her next move. Zarra, for her part, just preferred she stop beating around the bush.

"Just spit it out."

The young woman launched into her pitch.

"Now, I know you said we never ever, *ever* take jobs up north..."

"Dammit, Becka, you know better than this. We don't go huntin' in Pack Nation for a very good reason. It's just not worth it—"

"Two. Million. Credits," Becka interrupted.

Okay, now I get it.

"Two million," Zarra said slowly.

"Two million. It was a half million, but took a jump, a big jump, about an hour ago."

"That's... That's a whole lotta money."

"I know, right?" her partner grinned mischievously.

Zarra slumped back onto the bed, her brow furrowed in thought. Much to her chagrin, Becka *had* piqued her curiosity. At least enough to be interested in the details of the job.

"What's the mission? Take down New Victus on our lonesome?"

"No idea. Details on application. But...it's got gold status, so the money is guaranteed. What's more, it's non-competition flagged."

"Not open competition or assigned?" Zarra was genuinely puzzled.

"Nope. Invite only. Which is how it came to my attention."

"We got an invitation? Who's the contractor?"

"Well..." Becka hesitated, her grin fading. It didn't take a genius to figure out the news was bad.

Zarra cocked an eyebrow at her.

"Damian Dane," Becka eventually muttered, almost under her breath.

"No."

"No?"

Zarra shook her head vehemently to underscore her answer. There was no way she was going to Pack Nation at the best of times. Especially if the contractor was Damian Dane. Not even for two million credits.

Two million.

It was a number that gave her pause for thought.

"Maybe." Zarra hated herself for contemplating it.

"Thing is," Becka said slowly rolling her eyes innocently, "we're the only invited party, and the job was flagged directly to our inbox...from Dane himself."

"Fuck off!"

"The Wolf King himself," Becka confirmed.

"There is no way on this planet that Damian Dane is sendin' me emails requestin' my presence on a job." Zarra laughed at the absurdity. "No way at all."

"You think I'd bring this to you without confirmation? I know you guys have history. Well, I checked. It's *definitely* from him."

Becka loitered in the doorway and said nothing more as Zarra processed her thoughts, silently arguing the case with herself. Zarra knew this tactic well – Becka had used it before. Annoyingly, often with a high success rate. Not this time, though. This time Zarra was determined not to buckle.

The problem was, however, her rational mind was fighting a rearguard action against her increasingly insatiable curiosity.

She couldn't help but wonder... Why would Damian Dane personally send her this invitation considering their rocky history? What would prompt him to try and bridge the gap between them?

Two million credits.

Something very bad must have happened.

Maybe it was worth at least replying to the email.

Becka grinned in her triumph.

| 15 |

SECOND IMPRESSIONS

– Michael Reynolds –
– Tuesday – London, England –

"Nice." Gayle Knightley stood in the doorway grinning. "Who do I need to fuck to get an office like this?"

Michael glanced up from his paper-strewn desk and gave her a look that suggested he wasn't impressed by her opening gambit. She slouched against the doorframe and jerked her thumb over her shoulder at the door directly opposite.

"Mine's across the way," she continued, undeterred by his silence. "We're neighbors."

His eyes flicked briefly toward the door and the name etched into the brass plate attached to it.

Captain Knightley.

Her demeanor was a far cry from the display of the previous day. There was no anger today. Instead there was…something else. Something calming. He took a deep breath.

At least she's trying, he mused and resolved to reciprocate the gesture.

"I got here two months ago to head up this project, hence I got first pick," he stated. "Hence, the nice office."

She took his reply as an invitation to enter and make herself comfortable, sashaying into the room like she owned it. Settling down into one of the chairs across the desk from him, she slouched slightly sideways as she crossed her legs and scanned the room with feigned interest before finally looking directly at him.

"Y'know...for all my wit and charm," she said, "I'm getting the *distinct* impression you don't like me very much."

She wasn't wrong.

When Norbel proposed her participation, Michael had his doubts. Doubts she justified in her earlier fleeting introduction. A large part of him really wanted to give her a piece of his mind, but he bit his tongue. Instead, he calmly leaned forward and folded his arms, remembering something Alex had once said to him.

You're too quick to judge people, brother. Give them a chance to show you who they really are before you write them off.

"To be honest," he said slowly, "your first impression left a lot to be desired. Not sure the cadets took it that well, either."

"I'm not here to be their best friend. I'm here to do a job." She shrugged. "And that job starts next week. In my defense, yesterday...was not a good day for me."

"I'm not rightly sure that's a valid excuse, ma'am," Michael commented.

Gayle just bit her lip and studied him for a moment. He got the impression that this meeting was not going entirely the way she had planned it. She got up and began idly walking around the room, inspecting the few personal effects he had, seemingly considering her new course of action.

"So, is there anything I can do for you?" he prompted.

"I was thinking. Norbel says we have to work together, so maybe we could get dinner or something later. Maybe get to know each other a little better." She perched one hip on the edge of his desk and turned her attention directly to him.

Michael reclined in his chair and eyed her warily.

"You're serious?" he said.

"Why not?" she responded with a sly smile.

"Look, Captain Knightley..."

"Call me Gayle. Or 'Knightingale' if you prefer," she purred.

He rubbed at his temple where the nub of a headache was taking root. It was difficult to reconcile the seductress perched on his desk with the angry bitch he had met yesterday.

"Call signs should only be used on operations when..." he started.

"I know the regulations," she retorted. "But I don't know you well enough to call you Michael, Mike, Mikey, Tex, or whatever your friends call you. And I fucking hate the military etiquette bullshit of calling you Captain Reynolds. In the 137th, we would simply use our call signs, so I'm suggesting we compromise. Yours is 'Rogue,' isn't it?"

He said nothing, realizing that this was a battle he wasn't likely to win. She was going to call him whatever she wanted to. He saw it for what it was – a subtle way of exerting her influence over a situation she didn't like.

I'll give you this one.

He was sure that this wouldn't be the last battle of wits they were going to have in their co-stewardship of these students.

"'Knightingale' it is then," he finally capitulated.

"It gets shortened to 'Knight' a lot, so feel free to use that if you prefer." She beamed at him in her tiny victory.

"But don't ever call me Tex," he added.

"That's where you're from, right?" she asked, "The accent?"

"I left Texas when I was seven."

"See!" Gayle grinned triumphantly. "This is why we should get to know each other, so I can learn important information like that. So...dinner?"

She shimmied back on the desk going from a hip perch to a full sit, seductively crossing one of her long, slender legs over the other.

"We could get to know each other *much* better..." she purred.

He shook his head slightly and pushed back against the rising biological urge. Realization dawned. Pheromones.

He had been warned.

"I don't think that's a good idea," he said slowly.

"Come on!" she pleaded softly. "Let me make up for my earlier behavior."

"Look," he said firmly, "if you wanna go over the curriculum, or have ideas on what you want these kids to learn, then pull up a chair and get comfy. I want us to have an effective working relationship movin' forward so that these kids learn to be the best—"

"—the best that they can be," Gayle muttered sarcastically.

"Considering Valletta, isn't that somethin' you'd have a vested interest in?" Michael continued unperturbed

He struck a nerve.

There was the woman from the classroom again. The pressure in his head suddenly lifted as the flirtatious smile faded and her lips drew a tighter line. Her vivid green eyes hardened, and Michael could feel her mood shift dramatically. It was like a switch had been thrown, and now the same waves of anger he felt yesterday buffeted him again. More evidence that she had indeed been chemically manipulating his mood. A flicker of something passed across her flawless features.

After a few awkward moments of silence, she quietly responded to his question.

"Don't *ever* ask me that again."

He felt like he should apologize, but instead he let the silence between them linger until she slid off the desk and stood up. She plucked an elastic hair-tie off her wrist and, in one smooth, practiced motion, she used it to tie her long pink hair into a loose ponytail.

As she moved the strands from around her face, she exposed her left ear for the briefest of moments. What he thought had been flawless, unblemished skin, actually wasn't. Roughly four inches in length, a pale scar ran gracefully from her ear down to her throat. A moment later, it was hidden again as she draped the ponytail deliberately over her shoulder to obscure it. Returning to the chair opposite, she sat down, now all business.

"Let's talk curriculum then," she said sternly. "What do you want me to teach these little fuckers?"

| 16 |

OLD FLAMES

– Zarra Anderson –
– Tuesday – Nassau, Bahamas –

Her foot jiggled nervously beneath the desk as her computer purred at her. She took a deep breath, mentally preparing herself to talk to the man that, for the sake of her own sanity, she had said goodbye to.

Damian Dane.

His response to her email, sent against her better judgement, had been almost immediate. She had opened it nervously and found that a broken heart and three years of distance had bought her a simple five-word response:

> *Please. I need your help.*

She sighed. In truth, it was probably about time that the two of them talked. Old wounds would surely have healed by now.

Wouldn't they?

She took a deep breath, and answered the call, trying to appear casual as it connected, and *his* face filled her monitor. She swallowed hard at the sight of his ruggedly handsome features; he hadn't changed one bit. Her memory started to pick at the scabs of those old wounds.

"Damian."

"Lexy," he said with a disarming smile. "How have you been?"

A small measure of relief surged through her. Maybe this wasn't going to be quite as awkward as she had envisaged.

"It's Zarra these days," she corrected him, trying to keep her tone casual. "I'm good. Been busy...you know how it is. How's things being the King of Pack Nation?"

Despite their estrangement, she knew him well enough to see the subtle clues. There was a real pain in those grey eyes. His answer, though, was light, his voice laced with a forced levity.

"Same old shit. Can't get the Packs to agree on anything, as usual, and StormHall is still making his presence felt."

"I'm sure you'll figure it out," Zarra replied.

With that, the pleasantries ran dry and the conversation stalled. Damian was clearly distracted, so she moved to break the ice on the subject of the job.

"So..." she said. "Two million credits..."

"Due to recent developments, it's likely to be a long and...difficult job." He paused for a moment. "I can pay more if two million isn't enough."

Interesting.

"All that cash to try and entice *me*?" she asked.

On the video image, Damian hesitated before replying. "It's...complicated."

"Always is," Zarra muttered. "Damian, you're the one that put the job out on MercNet. You're the one who invited me personally. You really didn't expect to have to tell me what this is all about?"

Damian looked down, averting his gaze momentarily from the camera. Finally, he resolved whatever internal struggle he was having and looked her directly in the eye.

"It's Eloise."

"Oh, hell no! Are you fucking with me? You do know there's a reason that we haven't spoken for three years and that...woman...is at the root of it."

Anger surged within her. She had been wrong. It wasn't possible to let bygones be bygones and rationally deal with her ex. Another verbal barb was on the tip of her tongue when Damian interjected with two simple words.

"She's dead."

Zarra bit her tongue. The anger simmered, but she knew what that woman had meant to Damian.

"I'm...sorry for your loss," she said quietly.

"She was murdered."

"Vampyrii?" Zarra asked.

"No," Damian shook his head. "One of our own."

"Werewolf? You're sure?"

He nodded soberly. "I..." he hesitated, emotion raw in his voice. "I have seen... I went to Domaine Saint-Bernard and..."

"Damian, stop," she said softly. "I'll need to see it myself anyhow."

He nodded; a look of gratitude flashed across his face at her empathic interruption.

"It's..." he paused, searching for words. "It's hard to witness."

Silence hung between them for a moment before she eventually broke it.

"So, this is a revenge mission? Hunt-Kill contract?"

"No," he replied softly. "It's a rescue mission."

"You said she was dead..." Zarra furrowed her brow.

"Her daughter isn't."

"Kareena?" Suddenly Zarra understood. "You're sure?"

He nodded. "She's missing. We think she was taken."

"Shit."

She pushed away from the screen and leaned back in her chair, rubbing her forehead, deep in thought. She needed a moment to process the details of what Damian was telling her.

"Why me?" she said eventually.

"Alex asked for you specifically."

"Lonewolf?"

Damian nodded again. "He's tracking those we think are responsible for her abduction. I told him I'd see what I could do. I'm glad you made contact."

"I haven't said yes yet," she reminded him.

"I want the best on this, and that's you." Damian paused as a haunted look flickered across his rugged features. "I went to

Domaine Saint-Bernard. I saw the carnage...the way he butchered his victims. He's dangerous enough alone, but now Alex is reporting that he's tracking two targets. It took him a while to recognize the second scent... He's reporting a Code Eleven."

"Code Eleven?" Now it made even more sense. "A succubus? You're absolutely sure?"

Damian's face never strayed from serious. This was no joke.

"Same scent profile as three years ago. That's why Alex asked for you."

"Dammit, Damian," Zarra sighed. "You've got all kinds of crack troops at your disposal to support Alex. You don't need me."

"You're a licensed FPA. and I've seen your MercNet record..."

"That's not what I mean, and you know it," Zarra interrupted. "To track through the forests of Montreal will be next to impossible without—"

"I know." He moved forward on the camera, his eyes hardening. "I know the vow you made three years ago. I'm not asking you to break it. I'm asking you to do something only you can do – to help Alex track these targets. He's good, but he's not you. He's not as patient and not as cool under pressure as you are."

Compliments were *not* going to push her into doing this job.

"You have squads y'all can send. I can brief them," Zarra offered.

"If this were just about putting down a rogue wolf and his bitch, I'd have sent the troops in by now. But I want Kareena brought back safely. I don't want her caught in any crossfire. Additionally, they're heading toward New Victus territory. I can't send my soldiers in there."

"But Alex will cross over?"

"He knows the risks. We can get away with a lone wolf, no pun intended, wandering into New Victus without sparking a war."

"You realize, I'll be with him?" Zarra laughed sarcastically. "*If* I take this job."

"*When* you take this job," Damian said firmly. "Zarra, I need you to put aside any problems you have with me because there's an eighteen-year-old girl who is lost and alone. Kareena needs rescuing. That's the job."

"What if we catch up with your Wolf and succubus?"

"You terminate them. I'll pay extra if you do, because they need taking off the board, but that's not the primary mission. The two million, that's for bringing Kareena back safely. And I *know* she'll have a better chance if you're partnering up with Alex."

Bad choice of words. She winced and saw the flicker of recognition from Damian of his unintended faux pas. He opened his mouth and started to offer an apology.

"I'm sorry. I—"

She cut him off. "Two mil' for the rescue. Five hundred-K each for your Code 11 and her friend. We'll dust off within the hour and be with you tomorrow morning."

"Can you go directly to Alex's co-ordinates if I relay them to you?"

"Send 'em over, but I want to swing over to Domaine Saint-Bernard before I meet up with him. I want to see the scene for myself."

"As you wish. I'll forward over the pictures I took so you can prepare yourself. I have a team on standby to retrieve the dead and cleanse the site, but except for my visit, it'll be untouched when you get there."

"Noted," she said flatly. "I'll let you know when I'm done."

"Thanks. And Lexy...be careful. Please."

"Always am," she said with a shrug that was supposed to be casual but came off looking awkward.

"Thank you."

"Relay the co-ordinates and the images. I'll be in touch."

"It was good to see you." There was genuine sincerity in his voice.

Don't say it, don't fuckin' say it!

"It was good to see you, too, Damian."

Goddammit!

She cut the connection before saying anything else that she

really shouldn't verbalize. Broken hearts never truly healed; the scars always lingered. Her fingers drifted to her neck, touching it tenderly. She had tried to move on since that day three years ago.

She wondered if he felt the same way.

| 17 |

REBORN

– Kareena St. Claire –
– Wednesday – Mont Tremblant, Pack Nation –

There was no comfort to be found in her restraints, nor was there any escape. Initially, the nature of her bondage had given her hope. Her hands were small; surely she could work the ropes loose and slip free? But the abrasive fibers that held her snugly only promised prolonged captivity.

She shivered.

Darkness had been her sole companion for days now. Kareena's eyes blinked uselessly behind the rough sackcloth bag that had been pulled over her head and cinched around her neck. Her long eyelashes brushed the coarse material that pressed against her perspiration-soaked face. Without daylight as a reference, time had lost its meaning. She just knew that she had long past the limits of her ability to stand in this spread-eagled position. Yet the ropes gave her no choice.

Her shoulders burned terribly, as did her calves and thighs. Simply hanging by her wrists didn't help. Soon she started to lose feeling in her hands and was forced to stand again.

Why is this happening to me?

Dank air whistled gently through the weave of the makeshift hood as she pulled weakly on the ropes and moaned gently. Even her voice had been taken from her. They had torn the hem off her skirt, wadding it up and forcing it into her mouth where the tight sackcloth prevented her from expelling it. Her jaw ached unbearably, while an unremitting stream of drool oozed slowly past her lips to soak into the material of her ruined shirt.

The stress of her current predicament, and her terror over what might happen next, made breathing calmly a challenge. Her chest rose and fell rapidly with short ragged gasps.

Would they assault her? Physically? Sexually?

Would they kill her?

Sacrifice her?

She heard them use the word 'ritual.'

They had also used other words of which she didn't understand the context.

Feeding.

Rebirth.

These words had been preying on her mind since the meticulous *preparation* had begun. Was she being groomed for some sadistic ceremony?

Soft, feminine hands had gently massaged an oil into her skin at regular intervals. Daily, maybe? It was hard to tell. Despite allowing her the continued modesty of clothing, the hands spared no inch of her flesh. Their touch was humiliatingly loving and intimate. Whatever this emollient was, it acted like an intense aphrodisiac She felt a heat spread through her that she couldn't resist. Tormenting her for what seemed like hours.

Yet, there was nothing overtly sexual about her treatment. The hands caressed, but never strived to stimulate or arouse. They were simply...diligent. Not that it mattered. This was a physical contact to which her virgin body was certainly not accustomed. As she was touched, she found herself moaning softly. Kareena felt like a stranger in her own body.

Her stomach growled.

Food and water weren't offered often, and she had learned to accept anything she was given without hesitation. She wouldn't make that mistake again. She recalled the first time they had carefully lifted her hood, removing the gag but leaving her eyes shrouded. The cool touch of the cup against her lips. She thought she heard someone say, "*Drink.*" The water tasted so sweet.

"*Eat.*"

Had those words just popped into her head?

She had eagerly opened her mouth to accept food, but what they spooned onto her tongue made her splutter and retch. She spat it out, sobbing, resolving angrily to hold out until they gave her *real* food. Time passed and her stomach grew emptier. Her head grew dizzy and light. Her resolve shattered. When sustenance was next presented, she took it without hesitation. Wolfing down the food and taking great gulps of water while babbling her gratitude. The food was oddly sweeter than she remembered, the water more bitter. She recalled wondering whether it might have been drugged.

Now she was certain of it.

Whatever it was, she now felt more alert. More *alive.* She was intensely aware of her body, which compounded the effects of the oil tenfold. She felt like she was changing somehow, fundamentally at her core.

A subtle displacement of air raised goosebumps across Kareena's sensitive skin, and she whimpered quietly. Without sight and with her senses so heightened, the signs were undeniable.

They were here.

"*Her true nature finally surfaces.*"

The voice was feminine and seductive. Ethereal almost. She turned her head frantically, searching for it. Was it in her mind? It whispered things to her, things that made her blush. Always fanning the fire that was building deep within her.

True nature? What did that mean?

Hot breath raised the hairs on the nape of Kareena's neck and she whimpered faintly. Something soft brushed her shoulder. Fur maybe? She shivered. Her sensitivity was off the charts and this time she *knew* it wasn't the cold that made her tremble and shudder.

"I told you what she was," a deep masculine voice growled behind her. "I could smell it on her."

"Poor child. She has no idea." The female voice had a sing-song, seductive quality. *"It will certainly make things interesting. What will we birth today?"*

"Is she ready?" he said.

Their voices moved constantly. Circling her. Like predators stalking their prey. They were acting differently, and it scared her.

She shook her head frantically as she felt the waistband of her skirt being sliced through. It fell to the floor. Her blouse followed as the material was meticulously cut from her body. Suddenly she felt more vulnerable and exposed than she ever had before.

Have to get free, she thought. *Have to escape!*

Yet her flesh was also yearning for a different kind of release. Kareena couldn't help squirming slowly, whimpering in despair. Who was she? All the willpower in the world was unable to prevent the slow writhing of her body.

"Close. She is scared, humiliated and ashamed. She doesn't want to feel what she's feeling. She fights it."

How can this strange woman know my thoughts? My feelings?

"I know, child," the seductive voice whispered, *"because I'm the one putting them there. Your mind is my playground."*

A laugh with a hint of sadistic pleasure echoed in her head.

"Let her fight," the male rumbled dispassionately. "We both know better than most that *nobody* can fight their true nature."

Kareena twisted desperately in her bonds as the voices spiraled. She tried to move away, but there was nowhere to go, held as she was by undeniable ropes. Still, she pressed anyway, awkwardly teetering on the tiptoes of her widely spread feet.

Velvety fur pressed against her exposed back; rough claws caressed her flanks. Something sharp grazed the soft skin of her neck, sharp, like tiny daggers. They dimpled her skin but did not pierce it. Kareena choked back a sob of fear as she felt the hot breath of her tormentor and realized what they were.

The teeth of the Wolf.

"She tastes...delicious!" The melodic female voice sounded slurred. *"An ambrosia..."*

Kareena suddenly felt the press of supple naked skin, the unmistakable contours of a woman's breasts against her own. Gentle hands stroking her hips, her flat stomach, and then wandering teasingly between her thighs with the threat of something more intimate.

"I have never tasted her like before," he growled.

Please, Kareena found herself pleading in her head. *Please, just do it.*

Words she would never say out loud.

"*Are you sure little one?*" the seductress enquired. "*You wish to be reborn tonight?*"

Kareena was past caring where they were driving her. She was on a journey and simply – desperately – wanted to reach the destination.

Reborn...yes. Yes. A thousand times, yes.

She surprised herself with her urgency.

"*She is ready, my love,*" The voice was like a feather down her spine and the promise it brought made Kareena shudder.

Equal parts fear and lust rose within her, both approaching a crescendo. Kareena braced herself as best as she could, expecting her virginity to be roughly taken against her will. Claws gripped her tightly as the creature behind her drew her close to him. She screamed as loudly as she could into the gag when her mind finally lost the battle with her body. As the primal lust overwhelmed her, she stood shaking...awaiting her fate.

A fate that didn't come in the way she expected it.

The claws scratched at her back, leisurely tearing at the skin. Her screams grew even louder as her senses exploded with exquisite agony. She felt blood pulse from the wounds. She arched throwing herself at her bindings and pulling with all her might as she strived to free herself from the sensations overwhelming her. But the woven fibers were tight. Unbreakable.

Yet, despite the pain behind her, delicate lips and fingers danced across her breasts, her stomach and thighs. Briefly touching her intimately, lovingly, but never lingering. Kareena babbled deliriously, unable to resist. The peak of her long climb beckoned. A confused mix of gentle pleasure and sweet agony simply served to stoke the furnace within her. Driving her inexorably toward something...final.

Her last act of defiance was to pray to a God in whom she didn't believe to save her from these monsters.

"Beg and plead all you wish, little one. There is no God to help you. It is just you and us, and our numbers grow...for tonight we birth a child."

Kareena felt the soft breasts pressed against her own. Felt her own leg being straddled by a pair of silken thighs, slick against her skin. A pressure, grinding sensuously and rhythmically against her. Fingertips and soft lips moving from her breasts, to her stomach, to her thighs...teasing her.

It was all too much, and as her body finally betrayed her, Kareena heard the terrified screams that gurgled in her throat turn to something more guttural as she spasmed and convulsed, giving herself over to orgasmic ecstasy. As ashamed as she was to admit it, she *craved* it. Overwhelming sensation blinded her rational thought. All Kareena could do now, as her head was yanked back by the hood to expose her throat, was *feel*. But the blissful detachment didn't last long.

As she was peaking, she felt the sharp teeth pierce the perfect flesh of her shoulder. Agony lanced through her again, in perfect synchronicity to the pleasure. But this time those contradictory feelings were joined by something far more primeval. Something powerful. Kareena struggled to understand what was happening, her mind spinning.

"It begins with the teeth of the wolf," the seductive voice in her head said gleefully, *"and is complete with the maternal kiss of my own."*

Even while her addled brain tried to put meaning to the words, fangs pierced her thigh. She cried out as she felt herself slipping away, her body wracked in uncontrollable waves of transcendent pleasure. Waves that finally crested when something deep within her irrevocably changed. Whoever she had been in her previous life, that person was suddenly now gone.

Now she was something else. Something more. Something stronger.

She felt the hood being loosened and lifted just above her mouth; the gag finally removed.

"Please..." she begged.

Her brain was a tangle of confusion. Instinctively, she had a compulsive need, but for what she did not know. Her captors understood and gave her what she craved.

"*Feed.*"

She felt a presence, a pressure on her lips. Without thinking, she opened her mouth and bit down hard.

Self-defense, she lied to herself, *my only weapon.*

She heard the moan of pleasure from her seductress as Kareena's teeth pierced her flesh with ease.

How did I do that?

She felt something trickle into her mouth, a coppery taste.

Blood.

Not her own.

Disgusted, she shook her head, trying to pull back, but his grip was strong. Her scream turned to a gurgle as the thick liquid ran down her throat, choking her until she swallowed.

Kareena's rebirth hit her like a battering ram. Her body spasmed *hard*. The ropes that held her wrists and ankles snapped like delicate silk. She stumbled forward on unsteady legs, tearing at the hood with nails that felt hard as diamond and sharp as razors. They made short work of the tough canvas and, as she fell to the floor, she blinked in the dim light. She stared at her hands, now barely recognizable claws. Her body felt alive, her senses heightened to an astonishing level.

Her injuries...

The wounds to her back, the bites on her shoulder, her thigh... All healed. Had they existed at all? Only the smear of her own blood on her smooth skin bore witness to their passing. Across the room, her assailants smiled at her like proud parents.

Beauty and beast. She was naked and beautiful, her eyes pale, her canines pronounced. The beast was like something from a nightmare fairy-tale. Man and Wolf combined as one.

What have they done to me?

"*You are of us now.*"

The reply was in her mind, not spoken out loud.

"*One of us, but more than us. Vampyrii and Werewolf and more in one body. Welcome, daughter.*

We love you."

| 18 |

THE WOLF KING

– Damian Dane –
– Thursday – Montreal, Pack Nation –

"I was told that I'd find you brooding in here." The voice was gently chiding.

"Welcome back," he said flatly.

"Thank you, Your Majesty," she replied.

"Don't." He wasn't in the mood. "You know I don't like it."

"Maybe that's why I do it."

Her tone was flirtatious, but her ice-blue eyes told a different story. He could smell it on her, too – the anxiety. Lyssa Balthazaar was not someone prone to showing extreme emotion, but something had her concerned enough to come to him outside of their usual arrangement and at great personal risk.

"Every time I see this room, I understand why pop culture thinks we're *unrelentingly* dour. Sometimes I wonder if our ancestors knew what color was."

Despite the softness of her tone, her voice reverberated around the room. An acoustic feature of the Great Hall that Damian suspected intentional. When the King sat on the Moon-Throne, every voice could reach his ear. Not that the Great Hall was used much in the modern era. These days, its exclusive purpose was for greeting foreign dignitaries and holding banquets.

Lyssa sat cross-legged next to him on the wooden floor and

joined him in staring at the mural on the wall opposite.

"I sit corrected. That's quite beautiful."

A deep indigo sky with bright white stars over a lush green forest surrounded the azure waters of a lake. The Laurentian Mountains sat in the background; the same vista he saw every morning from the window of his bedroom. The full moon had center placing, rendered to look much larger than it did in real life.

"'*The Children of the Stolen Sun*'..." Lyssa continued, reading the script beneath the artwork. "It depicts a story, I assume. A myth? Legend, maybe?"

"A lie," he said sullenly.

"Indulge me." Lyssa smiled.

Even in his darkest mood, he found her presence comforting. Both because of who she was, and because of what she represented. He sighed and pointed to the mural.

"It tells the tale of the Sun and the Moon, lovers who shared the sky in equal measure," he said. "One day they quarreled, as lovers often do, in a cloudless sky, over an arrowhead mountain. The victorious Moon smothered the Sun and, as his darkness stole her light, her children rose from the lake. Neither beast nor man."

He gestured to the twelve naked figures with Human bodies and monstrous lupine heads.

"As they emerged from the waters, they howled for their mother, the stolen Sun. They howled so loud that the Moon fled. The children bathed in the light of their mother once more, restoring them to their Human form. It is supposedly the legend of how Werewolves came to be."

"That's no quirkier than some Vampyrii legends, to be honest." Lyssa shrugged.

"I suppose not."

"But you said it was a lie?"

"The more you stare at it, the more of a lie it becomes. Where to even start..." Dane said dourly and pointed to the painted stars. "That's the constellation of Lupus, the Wolf. Which, as any competent astronomer will tell you, is only visible in the Southern Hemisphere. Also, the original twelve are pictured as Caucasian men, which is bullshit. It is known that half of them had been female and the group had been a mixture of ethnicities. Case in point..."

He gestured to himself and his rich umber skin tone as if to prove his statement.

"I'm pure blood through and through. My family name is descended from Dane herself, who was one of the original twelve. We know for a *fact* that she was from somewhere in Africa. Not Canada, as this painting shows."

"We have the same issue in Vampyrii legend. Old societal prejudices coloring our history."

Damian nodded before gesturing to draw Lyssa's attention back toward the wall-art once more.

"Then, of course, there's the Sun and Moon stuff."

The mural presented a moon encircled by the diamond-ring effect of the sun's transition out of the lunar shadow. He had seen the phenomenon enough in his lifetime to recognize what the painting represented.

"A solar eclipse." Lyssa nodded.

"Which takes a little of the poetry out of the legend," Damian said with a sigh.

"They're still beautiful things to watch."

Her voice was soft, almost a whisper. Damian glanced sideways at her with a smile. Even disheveled and anxious, she was staggeringly pretty. He reached across and gently brushed the loose strands of her white streak back behind her ear.

"Yes," he said quietly. "Yes, they are."

She didn't turn her gaze away from the mural, seeming not to notice his tenderness. There was something else on her mind. A distraction.

"Do you know much about where the rest of your people originated?"

"Outside of my own family line?" Damian shrugged. "Not really. Just fables, myths, and legends. Written on parchments or painted on walls."

It struck him that, in all their meetings and the time they spent together, they had never discussed the origins of their respective races.

"What about the stories of the Night War?" Lyssa asked. "Do you believe them?"

"I don't know," Damian admitted. "My mother used to tell tales of crystal men taller than trees, of Gods who could scorch the land and sky, of winged beasts of fire and ice... Always sounded crazy. But...I'm more inclined to believe it since The Rising."

"Me too," Lyssa agreed, but said nothing more.

He glanced down at *Fangsbane*, the ancestral sword that lay across his lap. The blade was heavy with legacy. If only it could talk, it would likely reveal the truth regarding their history. It had been wielded by his ancestors thousands of years ago, used to establish a lasting age of peace. It weighed on his conscience that his own rule had started with the collapse of that era, a burden heavier than a thousand blades.

"I wasn't expecting you for two more weeks." A subtle verbal nudge.

"Something came up. It's about my sister..."

"Vanessa or Nykola?" he asked.

Lyssa raised a surprised eyebrow, seemingly impressed that he remembered the names of her family members.

"Vanessa," she said. "She's...loose. For want of a better word."

"Loose?"

Lyssa nodded hesitantly.

"You're going to need to give me a little more than that. Like, why it is any concern to me that your sister is...loose."

"Because I may not have been entirely honest about my sister's...condition," Lyssa replied cryptically.

"You said she suffered from some form of autism..." Damian tried to recall the details.

"No...I said she had 'special needs,'" Lyssa confessed nervously. "In Vampyrii families, her condition is *exceedingly* rare – maybe one in ten thousand is born with it. She's a..."

His brain started to assemble the pieces of the puzzle.

"She's a succubus." he interrupted abruptly. "And she's here in Pack Nation, isn't she? That's what you're here to tell me."

Using *Fangsbane* as an aid, he pushed himself to his feet. Though middle-aged for a Werewolf, his body had seen many battles and had taken many injuries. With the cold of autumn setting in, his formerly broken foot had started to ache painfully.

"I feel like I'm missing something..." Lyssa said quizzically. "How did you know?"

"About Vanessa?"

Lyssa nodded, likewise rising from the floor. "Of course, Vanessa!"

He sheathed the long blade, striding out of the Great Hall. Lyssa followed.

"So, are you going to tell me or keep me in suspense?" she said impatiently.

"Because I've just had to make a difficult call to an old acquaintance about possibly pursuing and killing her."

"Killing her?" Lyssa exclaimed.

"You should have told me. You always referred to your sister as ill. You never told me *what* she is."

"Because it's nobody's business but ours and *we* don't have that kind of relationship."

That last comment stung him more than he had thought it would.

"Lyssa..." Damian shook his head and sighed. "The situation is *so* much worse than you can imagine..."

| 19 |

SCENE OF THE CRIME

– Zarra Anderson –
– Thursday – Domaine Saint-Bernard, Pack Nation –

Sometimes finding your target was as simple as A, B, C.
Quarry 'A' likes to drink in Bar 'B' with Contact 'C.'
Easy.
Other times you needed to use the whole alphabet to find the person you were looking for. Occasionally, you needed both letters and numbers and an extensive system of cross referencing.

Zarra was experienced enough to know that, in this job, the quickest way to an early grave was to stumble into a situation unprepared. Too many of her peers, her friends, had died horrible deaths because they were ill-equipped to handle the peril in which they had put themselves. What made Zarra excellent at her profession was her attention to the minutiae of the hunt. Planning was key. It was a philosophy that had been drilled into her in the NAA Marine corps.

Seeing Domaine Saint-Bernard for herself would reveal information about the monster she would be tracking that she couldn't get from Dane's scant testimony and a few hi-definition photographs. She wanted to *feel* the crime scene. Experience it. She needed to get into the mind of the killer to understand how to hunt him. She was under no illusion – she knew what she was about to see would be mentally scarring. But it was important. It was part of the preparation.

Becka banked *Diana* around the mountain, swinging low over Lac Reynaud and sending up spray from the placid waters. Zarra activated the comm-piece in her ear with a gentle tap of her fingertip.

"Hover by the lake. I'll drop and scout while you get some altitude. Keep your eyes peeled, Becka – I don't want any surprises."

"No problem, Zee," came Becka's voice in her ear. "Be careful."

Zarra checked her weapons as she walked through the cargo bay, thumbing the biometric safeties off both holstered Freelancers. Dane's email said the site was clear, but Zarra didn't take unnecessary chances. The green LEDs on each grip turned red.

As *Diana* pivoted slowly, Zarra lowered the loading ramp. The cargo bay depressurized, and she peered down at the tiny settlement below. The telltale swirls in the dust and grass left by Dane's own flyer were swiftly obliterated as Becka fired *Diana*'s repulsors, bringing the dropship to a hover about ten feet from the ground.

Zarra walked down the ramp and stepped off the end with practiced ease, dropping gracefully toward the ground. A flex of her knees easily absorbed the impact. Straightening up, she unsnapped the retaining straps on her holsters and placed her hands reassuringly on the grips of her Freelancers as she strode slowly toward the lodge.

There was an old adage: 'Fools rush in where angels fear to tread.' Zarra was no angel, and she wasn't afraid of what she would find. Damian's photographs had braced her for the gruesome reality, but even prepared as she was, she had no desire to rush toward it.

Downwind from the buildings, the gentle breeze carried the sweet scents of the forest, yet also the stench of something just as familiar and far more unwelcome. Death. Its unmistakable aroma stung her nostrils. The hairs bristled on the nape of her neck.

She paused in the roadway between the buildings – Le Pavillon de Chasse to her right, and a little further ahead and to her left, the Grand Saint-Bernard. If something *were* still lurking, she could not sense it. She crouched warily to inspect the flurry of footprints in the dirt, crisscrossing between the buildings. Two sets drew her attention.

The first, delicate and barefoot, headed northwest toward the lake. Kareena maybe? The second, oversized and inhuman, sharp claws leaving distinctive furrows, had begun to follow before turning to sprint toward the Grand. Her target, Zarra presumed.

She followed his tracks. The building's door opened easily with a hint of a creak. The windows were not boarded, the entry not barricaded. It had been a hurried retreat to a place where the people naively thought they would be safe. A large sideboard lay broken on the floor, as if they had been trying to fortify the entrance. Too little, too late. They had locked the door, but it was the frame that had given way. The strike plate torn from the splintered wood by the force of his impact. The heavy sideboard toppled easily, providing little resistance.

Her target was strong. Fast.

Even primed, the rest of the lobby was an overwhelming and brutal assault on Zarra's senses. The stench made her stomach heave and the persistent buzzing of blowflies provided a constant soundtrack to her distress. Her brain worked to process the information; the fully hatched flies told her that the people here had been slain many days ago. Left to rot for over a week.

She closed her eyes, lifting the back of her hand to her mouth. Swallowing down the rising bile that burned the back of her throat, Zarra took a deep breath and forced herself to view the scene again. She tapped open a channel to *Diana*.

"You okay, Zee?" Becka sounded worried.

She cleared her dry throat; words were hard to find.

"Yeah," she said quietly. "I'm peachy. It's just...it's worse than I imagined."

"That bad?"

"The pictures don't do it justice. Be thankful you're not

standin' here after the lunch you had earlier." Zarra wasn't joking.

"Talk me through it," Becka said calmly. "Tell me what you see."

Her composed gravity belied her youth – Becka knew *exactly* what to say and how to say it. This wasn't a time for flippant humor. Her voice instead soothed and steadied.

Process the scene, Zarra thought to herself. *Be the hunter…*

Carefully, she cast her eyes around the lobby, trying hard to be clinical about such a horrific chain of events.

"Twelve victims. Five adult females, four adult males, three…children." She swallowed. "Two girls and a boy."

"How did he kill them?" Becka prompted quietly, professionally.

This exercise was about more than just *witnessing* the horror, it was about *understanding* it. Getting into the mind of their target.

"Evisceration in most cases. Brutal…" Zarra said in a whisper. "The adults were tortured. Casually…but quickly. Each was suspended by the ankles as he bled them out. They wouldn't have lasted long. The slashes are precise…surgical almost. Not a frenzied assault; he took pleasure in this…but he didn't draw it out…"

She heard her own voice trailing off, echoing in her head. Her mind circled the words… Casually. Quickly.

What did that mean?

"The children?" Becka interrupted her thoughts.

"Same precision, but…" She paused. "no torture…"

The drying blood grabbed at the soles of her boots as she walked slowly around the lobby. Each footfall crunching softly as she crushed the blowfly maggots still searching for their next rotten feast. Zarra crouched to look closely at a young girl of maybe ten or eleven. Her tiny body was a grisly canvas of slashes similar to those inflicted on the adults, but with one intriguing difference.

"Zee?" Becka prompted.

"The kids were killed quickly. He slashed the carotid artery;

they'd-a been dead in seconds. The other injuries were in-flicted postmortem... He closed their eyes, Becka."

"Surprising amount of compassion for the children," Becka commented. "For a brutal and sadistic killer, that is."

"Yeah," Zarra said distantly, "that's what I was thinkin.'"

"You think he's a father?"

"Maybe," she contemplated. "But I reckon he cut up the children to torture the adults."

"You're sure? Maybe he was torturing them for infor-mation."

"No." Zarra thought back to the other set of footprints, barefoot and delicate. "He had already found what he was lookin' for. He'd already split Kareena from the group. He gave her a head start... She ran toward the lake while he tidied up loose ends here."

She stood and looked around the room as she spoke.

"He flayed flesh, carving each victim to the bone. He en-joyed the screams, the feel of their blood on his hands – but he didn't prolong it. He went through them one by one in a few hours. This place is remote...nobody would have been any the wiser for a very long time. He *could* have strung his pleasure out for days, weeks maybe. If Alex hadn't called this in with his suspicions, it could have been months before anyone thought to check on them."

Casually. Quickly. The two conflicting words suddenly made sense.

"He was on a schedule," Zarra whispered.

"A schedule for what?"

"That," Zarra admitted, "I don't know."

"So, what now?"

Standing, Zarra turned her back to the horror. She desper-ately wanted to cut the victims down and give them the re-spect they deserved, but she knew she, too, was on a schedule. Besides, Damian was bringing a crew to do that job himself. A job she knew he took extremely seriously.

"I'm headin' upstairs to check for..." she paused, not want-ing to say *her* name, "...for other victims. Message Dane. Tell him it's all-clear for his clean-up crew and bring *Diana* around for pickup. I won't be long."

She closed the channel without waiting for a response. The rising engine noise in the distance acknowledged Becka's receipt of her instruction. She swallowed and started up the stairway, bracing herself for the final piece of the gruesome puzzle. Damian knew that she would want to see the scene intact, and she quietly recognized how hard it must have been for him to leave Eloise like that.

She wondered how he would ever get over this.

| 20 |

STRANGE BEDFELLOWS

– Lyssa Balthazaar –
– Thursday – Montreal, Pack Nation –

"Fuck…" Lyssa cursed breathlessly.

She rolled onto her back, basking in the afterglow as she descended back to normality.

Now that…is how you scratch an itch!

The unmistakable musk of their lovemaking lingered heavy in the air. She wondered how it must smell to his far more sensitive nose. As usual, with the post-orgasmic bliss came the accompanying wave of guilt.

"We really have to stop doing this," she whispered.

She felt the roll of Damian's eyes. "Every time…" he muttered quietly.

"What?"

This was their usual post-coital dance.

"The guilt."

"It's not guilt—" Lyssa started, but he interrupted her.

"I understand this is not Romeo and Juliet…"

"I'd hope not." Lyssa laughed. "That 'relationship' lasted just four days and ended in a double suicide!"

"You know what I mean, Lyssa. This is not star-crossed lovers – it's just sex. Simply a welcome distraction after a bad day… For both of us."

It was a lie; she knew this meant more than that to him. He

was right about the guilt, though.

She had told him about Vanessa. He had told her about Eloise St. Claire, her daughter Kareena, and the attack on Domaine Saint-Bernard. They had commiserated, empathized, and held each other as tears had come to them both. From there, it was a short hop to the comfort of the no-strings, forbidden intimacy they had enjoyed so many times before.

"But..." she began.

"Like you, Lyssa," he interrupted her again, "I simply enjoy the recreation of it. In our positions, having a paramour is...complicated. Difficult. I'm *not* a lovesick puppy..."

"No, *you're* the Wolf King!" Lyssa laughed.

"...and this is just sex."

Even though that was a half-truth at best, she understood the sentiment. As the head of House Balthazaar, she faced a different, albeit similar, issue. The people of Pack Nation were enlightened in a way that Vampyrii society wasn't. The Werewolf packs were generally ambivalent toward an individual's race, color, gender, or sexual orientation. Acceptance was the tenet upon which their society was built.

It was their touchstone. Their belief.

Lyssa had long wondered if that acceptance was programmed into their genetics. Or were young Werewolves simply raised in a more liberal culture than the one in which she had been raised? Vampyrii society did not embrace 'deviant behavior,' thus Lyssa had been forced to repress her bisexuality.

Her position as leader of a Progenitor House also added another level of complexity to the situation when traditional Vampyrii family dynamics were a consideration. Once you removed the women, Humans, half-bloods, and Vampyrii of lower social rank from the dating equation...living in New Victus severely limited her options romantically.

Whereas here in Pack Nation, she could be herself.

She loved Damian, but not in that way. Not that she had objections to a male partner. Or Human or half-blood for that matter. His being a Werewolf no more bothered her than the color of his skin. But truly her preference was skewed toward somebody a little more...feminine. Kind of like how some people prefer blondes to brunettes.

Damian, however, *was* a romantic and so she had tried to be open and honest with him from the start. He knew how she felt. But while sex between them was simply a means to an end for her, for him it was a thread of hope that one day she *might* change her mind. Hence her guilt when it was all over, and she still felt the same as she always had.

"I actually just came here on business," she said.

"You just '*came here on business*' a lot..." he chuckled.

Lyssa's lips crinkled in a wry smile at the crude double entendre. She tilted her head sideways to look at him, while his eyes hungrily traced the curves of her naked body. A hint that he wasn't quite done yet. She glanced down, confirming her suspicion. Lyssa, though, was satisfied.

"Down, boy," she said lightly with a gentle smile.

"Really?" Damian laughed. "I'm your pet dog now?"

"Of course not," she giggled girlishly. "As we just agreed, you're the King, the Alpha Wolf. Leader of the Pack. Your Majesty, Your Highness..."

"I agreed to nothing!" he laughed at her. "I leave that kind of pomposity to the likes of your glorious leader."

"Only in sarcasm would you put the words 'Sebastian Storm' and 'glorious' together in the same sentence," she laughed.

They lay in silence for a while, both lost in their own thoughts. Outside the window, Lyssa could see the full moon high in the night sky, its light bathing their naked bodies. She idly recalled what the myths and legends said such a beautiful night would do to her lover.

"Are you okay?" she asked with quiet empathy.

His earlier introspection in the Great Hall had been a direct result of his trip to Domaine Saint-Bernard. Lyssa knew the trip had been extremely difficult for him. There was a limit to how much he would open up about it and sex had been a distraction tactic on his part. Lyssa willingly went along for the ride, proverbially and literally. Delaying a conversation, though, did not mean that she was going to simply forget about it.

"I'm serious, Damian." She placed her hand over his comfortingly. "If you need to talk…"

He sat quietly in the rumpled sheets; their intimacy of a few minutes previous now seeming an eternity ago.

"Thank you, but I'm fine," Damian eventually said.

Damian reclined back onto the bed, trying to appear casual as he linked his hands behind his head. But his tense body language told a different story. Lyssa sighed; she had hoped the distraction would last longer. Especially as she was about to drop another bombshell on him.

She took a deep breath.

"Actually…" she muttered, "talking about Storm reminds me… There's something else I need to talk to you about."

Damian raised an eyebrow but said nothing.

"He wants me to front New Victus at the Nexus Summit," she said. "He has a proposal he wants me to table."

"What sort of proposal?" he asked.

"If I tell you," she said hesitantly, "you *cannot* tell another soul. Nobody. Not Sabadini or any of your other Nexus staff. This is between us."

"Of course." Damian shrugged as if his discretion was a given.

"I mean it. If even a sniff of this gets back to Storm…" she let the statement hang.

"I know the consequences, Lyssa. Not a word. On my honor."

Satisfied, Lyssa launched into the pertinent aspects of the proposition just as it had been detailed to her. The emotions danced across Damian's strong features as he listened in silence. From shocked disbelief, to deep suspicion. He lay on the bed quietly for a moment before responding.

"So, he's sending you to submit this proposal on his behalf because…" he paused. "I assume he considers you a better face?"

"Something wrong with my face?" Lyssa couldn't resist the set up.

"No complaints here," Damian smiled.

"You're correct, though," Lyssa said seriously. "I've been an outspoken opponent to his regime. I won't be seen as one of his lackeys."

"You're not buying that?" Damian sensed her hesitation.

She shook her head. "There's something more in this for him. Something I am not seeing."

"Does it really matter?" Damian said unconvincingly. "*If* that proposal is tabled and *if* I agree to it, and *if* the FSE and the other nations sanction it...we stand to make huge gains."

She nodded. That was *exactly* what worried her.

"If the benefit to us is that big..." she said, "then the pertinent question becomes...how big is the payoff for Storm?"

| 21 |

APOLOGIES

– Michael Reynolds –
– Thursday – London, England –

Gayle threw open the door to Michael's office and blew into his room like a pink-haired hurricane before slumping heavily into the seat across from the desk. Her face was plastered with a grin.

"I've got call signs for the kids..."

"Cadets," Michael corrected.

Gayle ignored him. "Want me to run them past you?"

He glanced up from his paperwork-strewn desk. "It's only been three days!"

Gayle nodded. "Yes, I know... But I want call signs to be second nature as soon as possible."

"Your call," he capitulated gracefully.

"What're those?" she said, changing the subject.

Clearly, she had no intention of leaving anytime soon, but her body language was conflicted. She crossed her legs trying to look casual in the plush leather chair; yet she drummed her fingertips on the cushioned arm while bouncing her foot impatiently.

"Class assignments. I need to grade them before morning."

Gayle either didn't pick up on the heavy hint or, more likely, simply ignored it.

"On paper?" She raised an eyebrow. "We do have these

things called computers these days."

Michael returned the gesture. "I prefer to grade with pen on paper."

"Old school." She pursed her lips and nodded. "I can respect that. What's the subject?"

"Battle of the Bay."

"The San Francisco Evacuation? For their first class? You do know we lost that battle, right?"

"Matter of opinion." Michael shrugged. "Without that battle, many more Americans would have died that day."

"Maybe, but it was still the last time you guys set foot on mainland United States for almost two decades."

"I know," he said quietly.

This time Gayle didn't ignore the subtle hint in his voice. She nodded; subject closed.

"Actually," she moved to shift the topic, "I have a couple of other things to discuss with you. I've done something...something which I probably should have asked you about first... I was thinking about *Artemis*..."

"I'm familiar with it," he nodded. "It's currently bein' repaired and overhauled at Brize Norton. It'll be back here when it's ready for service."

"Repaired?"

"The *Minerva* needed some spare parts that were in short supply. I allowed them to take parts from the *Artemis*, as we weren't usin' it anytime soon," Michael explained.

"Ah. Well, she'll need a pilot. We're going to need to get these kids training in the field soon for combat, and that is going to include dropship etiquette, etcetera. I've put in a request to have Captain Fordham reinstated to duty."

"Fordith?"

A momentary flicker of shock flashed over Gayle's features at his casual mention of Captain Fordham's call sign. Then the penny dropped – of course he had read the dossiers regarding all former members of the 137th. His familiarization with the captain, however, was based on a little more than simply reading a name in a file.

"Yeah," Gayle said. "I also think she would be a great addition to fill some of these course timeslots with self-defense classes. She knows Karate and other...fighting skills. You okay with that?"

"I went to see her a coupla weeks ago for the same reason. She politely declined."

"Declined?" Gayle was genuinely surprised.

He nodded.

"Declined," she repeated quietly to herself.

"We spoke. She had her reasons." Michael shrugged. "I've been sorting through other candidates for the position but was waitin' to talk with you before a decision is made."

"Do you mind if we hang fire on that? I'd like to go talk to her myself."

"Go for it. I figured you'd probably want to do that anyway. It was, admittedly, the other reason I delayed."

"Am I that predictable?" Gayle looked at him with a wry smile, which he returned.

"No," he said. "But you strike me as a woman who has ways of gettin' what she wants and rarely takes no for an answer."

He expected her to lash out at what she would no doubt perceive as an insult. But, surprisingly, her only reaction was to blush profusely as she bit her lip and averted her eyes. She suddenly looked extremely uncomfortable. Sheepish even.

"I actually..." she started and then hesitated. "Okay, here's the thing... I realize that in trying to apologize for my first impression...I fucked up my second impression, too. So, I wanted to say sorry. Again. Not just for Monday, and being a complete bitch, but also for...well...the whole pheromone thing..."

Clearly, this was a difficult subject for her. She was struggling to express herself.

"When a hybrid like myself, when we...meet someone, my Fae side...it... I'm pretty used to getting my own way when it comes to the opposite sex, and that's...that's not an excuse."

Her eyes locked with his, and he was startled by their emerald depth and the emotions on display. There was a sadness within them, but also a need to be understood.

"I'm..." Words were not coming easily to her. "I'm trying

hard not to be that way anymore. I was angry. It was a moment of weakness. It was...unprofessional of me, and I'm *truly* sorry."

Michael simply smiled warmly at her as she finished. He didn't doubt her sincerity. It was all there on her face.

"Apology accepted."

The gesture immediately seemed to put her at ease. Relief flooded her features.

"Monday was a rough day," she said. "No excuse, as I said, but...you know how it is when you have a rough day. And Tuesday was just...unprofessional. Sorry."

"How about the next time you're havin' a rough day, you just come talk to me about it? We're in this together, after all." He laughed gently. "And, honestly, Norbel warned me about the pheromones in advance. Still, it was quite something to actually *experience* it."

Gayle blushed anew but reciprocated his smile.

"Honestly...you surprised me by resisting so easily."

"It wasn't so easy," he admitted.

What the hell are you confessing that for?

"You, Captain Michael Reynolds," she said lightly, "are far too gentlemanly."

The book on Gayle Knightley was a tale of duality. An abrasive maverick who frequently went off plan; yet the leader of a fiercely loyal team that got results. He had questioned the wisdom of employing her in a teaching role for which she seemed hugely unsuited. Wondered if this was purely a case of nepotism. Now, though, he was beginning to understand Norbel's reasons as he began to discover just how much more complex she really was.

Buried beneath the façade of anger and bad habits, there was *something* about her. Something effortlessly charismatic. Plus, she had skills and knowledge that would undoubtedly be a valuable asset to the program. She *knew* what these hybrid kids would go through better than he ever would. She had a genetic advantage in that respect.

"I can see why Norbel had us work together on this," Gayle said as if reading his mind. "I need a good influence to counter my bad one."

Her face turned serious; the smile faded.

"Look, Rogue, cards on the table," she said leaning forward. "I *am* very used to getting my own way. I need someone who isn't afraid to put me in my place from time to time. Especially now. Can you do that?"

He nodded. Twenty minutes ago, he was bordering on the opinion that it was impossible for them to work together. Yet here she was, taking ownership for her mistakes and asking for his help moving forward. She was more astute than he had given her credit for.

"I also want you to know," she continued, "that the pheromone thing won't happen again. Things between us will be *totally* professional, from this point on."

There was something unspoken in that statement. An inflection in her voice, the lack of profanity and the way she held his gaze. Like she was confessing something greater than the sum of the words that left her lips.

"Totally professional?" he said with a sly smile. "Yeah, sure..."

At first her face flickered with a hint of anger, then she realized that he was teasing. Defusing the tension of the situation. Her relief again subtly softened her features, and a genuinely happy smile twisted her lips. Michael was struck by how attractive it made her.

"I'll go talk to Lana tomorrow. See if I can change her mind."

"Good luck."

She pushed herself up out of the chair and started toward the door. Oddly, Michael found himself wanting to delay her leaving.

"You know...I reckon that's the first conversation we've had without you cursin'."

She stopped and looked back at him and, just for a moment, he thought she was going to curse at him. Just to spite him. He could see it dancing on the tip of her tongue.

Fuck you, Captain.

The words never emerged. Instead, it seemed like some

other shard of her personality won the battle, her need to prove that she wasn't always foul-mouthed. She laughed gently.

"You want me to?"

"Just bein' honest." He spread his hands in a gesture of innocence.

"Yeah, from the man who couldn't be honest enough to just tell me to fuck off because you're busy."

"And there it is..." he chuckled.

Her face warmed over as she realized her genuine slip. She shook her head and cursed again under her breath.

"Okay, so...I'll leave you to it. I'd be really interested in reading those papers when you're done. See how the kids are thinking about things."

"Really?" he said with a raised eyebrow.

She nodded, and as she headed for the door, Michael remembered the reason she had graced him with her presence in the first place.

"You were gonna go through the kids' call signs with me?"

She paused and looked back over her shoulder, rolling her eyes mischievously upward.

"The cadets," she corrected. "Nah. I just needed a reason to come talk to you. It's only been three days. I'll figure them out next week. Have a good night...Captain."

There had been the briefest of hesitations, and he felt like she had *almost* said his name. Almost made an effort to be warmer. Friendlier. At the last second, however, her vow to be professional had kicked in and she substituted his rank instead.

"You too, Gayle," he said with a smile.

As she exited, he shook his head, continuing to smile to himself for a moment. What would she do next to surprise him? Working with her would never be boring, he felt sure of *that*.

| 22 |

FAMILY MATTERS

– Lyssa Balthazaar –
– Friday – Vermont, New Victus –

Lyssa *loved* to fly.

In her dreams, the wind caressed her skin as she spent countless hours soaring through the clouds of a bright sunlit sky. It always ended with disappointment as her eyes opened and she realized that the fantasy would never become reality. Vampyrii had many unique abilities, but flight was not amongst them.

The closest Lyssa could get to experiencing that sensation was sitting behind the controls of her secret pride and joy. Personal flyers were not cheap, especially when acquired through the black market. The expense, however, was easy to justify as an investment in their future. The little de Havilland Butterfly was state-of-the-art and included Fae-derived technology, with both speed and stealth far in advance of any conventional aircraft in New Victus. Considering her illicit meetings across the border, both those attributes were essential.

Lyssa called her flyer *Tawaic'iya*.

She nudged the flight-stick, rolling the tiny flyer into a dive toward the calm waters of the aptly named Lake Placid, the sun glinting off its iridescent wings. She skimmed the surface of the water briefly, creating a spray that cast rainbows in her wake as she sped toward the shoreline. Lyssa throttled back, gently slowing her approach to the clandestine hangar on the western bank, hidden amongst the trees.

It wasn't an easy maneuver to pitch the aircraft down through the treetops and into the large camouflaged hangar doors, but Lyssa was an excellent pilot. As she gently brought *Tawaic'iya* to a safe landing, she spotted Mercy reclining casually against her little coupe, parked next to her own Charger. Lyssa had offered to source her niece a new car, something more in keeping with her station, but Mercy professed a nostalgic love for the little two-door Mazda.

"Welcome back," Mercy greeted her as she popped the canopy and started to climb out of the cockpit.

"Thanks."

"Productive trip?"

Lyssa nodded.

"He'll help us then?" Mercy prompted.

"He already has people on it. But it's become...complicated."

"Complicated?"

"Vanessa isn't alone." Lyssa sighed. "She has a companion. One of theirs...an incubus, they think."

"Theirs?"

"Wolf," Lyssa clarified.

"No kidding," Mercy said quietly. "Lyssa, your sister's condition is so rare...the odds of her, a Vampyrii succubus, breaking out of her protection and then finding a companion that is her Lycan counterpart..."

"Oh, it's no coincidence," Lyssa agreed firmly. "I need you to take a closer look into this."

"Already did. Something didn't feel right, so I had our security experts take a look at it. I told them it was a security exercise."

"They find anything?"

"Someone hacked our security system," Mercy said, "from the outside. Local, though. Inside Burlington."

Suspicion confirmed.

Vanessa *must* have known about the hack in order to co-ordinate her breakout. Which meant that Vanessa and her new companion had to have been in communication.

"They were talking," she muttered.

"I checked her emails and her chat programs. Nothing suspicious. But there are other ways...ways beyond my level of expertise. I can try to find a techie I trust, but the more people we involve, the greater the chance your sister's secret gets out."

"Risk it," Lyssa ordered. "We need to know."

"If StormHall finds out—"

"He already knows," Lyssa interrupted. "He's behind this. I feel it in my gut, Merce."

"Okay. If that's true..." Mercy asked, "then what's his plan? What's his endgame? Why publicly make *you* his proxy if he's working behind the scenes to bring you down?"

"It's worse than that. *How* did he find out? And does he know about Damian and my trips over the border?"

Mercy said nothing. She could no more answer these questions than Lyssa could. Was this simple paranoia? Or a masterful game Storm was playing with her?

Lyssa slumped back onto the hood of her Charger and sighed. Neither spoke for a minute or so, both deep in thought. It was Mercy who eventually broke the silence with another pertinent question.

"Why were Dane's guys already tracking the incubus?"

"It started with a particularly gruesome murder out near Sherbrooke. The perpetrator fled south, leaving a bloody trail of destruction and escaping by crossing the border into New Victus," Lyssa explained.

"And they didn't feel the need to inform us?"

"You know as well as I do, our nations don't have *that* kind of relationship," Lyssa shrugged.

"How long ago?"

"About six weeks," Lyssa recalled from her conversation with Damian. "He said it was quiet until five days ago when one of their border patrols didn't report in."

"Killed as the target crossed back into Pack territory, I assume?" Mercy surmised.

Lyssa nodded. "They've been tracking his scent, and

Vanessa's, ever since. Their nature and their location make it hard to get a team in to take them down. Damian hired a specialist off MercNet to deal with them..."

"Kill contract?"

"Yeah," Lyssa said quietly. "But I've asked if he can specify Vanessa be brought back alive, if at all possible."

Mercy quietly processed the information she had been given for a moment.

"So, I have two questions," she said eventually, looking Lyssa in the eye. "First, he's an incubus with an insatiable lust for blood...and the murder in Sherbrooke was the *first* Dane's people heard about him? Where was he before that?

"Second, he crosses the border and *then* goes quiet. From a murderous rampage to a period of five or six weeks of silence. Time that he looks to have spent seducing Vanessa. You're right, Lys...this is definitely no coincidence."

This was why Mercy was her second-in-command – her uncanny ability to home in on details Lyssa herself overlooked. The timeline *was* intriguing, and prompted more questions than answers, including one that had been niggling Lyssa since Damian mentioned her name.

"Kareena St. Claire..." Lyssa whispered.

"Who's Kareena St. Claire?" Mercy asked, with a hint of confusion.

"Exactly," Lyssa muttered cryptically.

| 23 |

REUNION

– Alex Newman –
– Friday – Mont Tremblant, Pack Nation –

He listened carefully.

Even with his Human ears, he could discern the low-pitched whine of repulsor-lift engines in the distance. Moments later, a tiny dark shape appeared above the treeline in the distance and quickly started to grow. As he watched the dropship approach and begin to slow, a small smile of anticipation wrinkled his lips.

The incline and the heavy tree cover gave scant opportunity to land, but then landing had never been part of the plan. The engines edged up in pitch as the aircraft started to hover, spinning gracefully on its axis until he could see the already deployed boarding ramp between the double struts of the tail. Standing on the end of the ramp was a familiar figure. His new partner.

Or old partner, depending on how you looked at it.

As the dropship held its position, she stepped confidently off the ramp. Gravity took her as she dropped the twenty or so feet to the ground, one leg extended and the other bent gracefully. Her arms were outstretched, as if she was using them to arrest her fall. She absorbed the landing with a perfectly timed flex of her legs.

Flawless.

Another leisurely rotation brought the cockpit back into view, a young woman clearly visible behind the plexiglass. She waved at them and Zarra reciprocated with a casual salute, upon which the engine note quickly rose to a howl and the dropship leapt forward. Within seconds, it disappeared out of sight across the treetops.

"Lexy. It's been a while," he opened warmly with a smile.

"Zarra," she corrected him coldly. "It's just Zarra these days,"

"I wasn't sure if you'd agree to come,"

"Almost didn't," she shrugged. "Turns out it ain't easy turnin' down three-million credits when you have a dropship to service and a partner to pay."

Even though he had expected it, her cold shoulder still stung. Alex started to wonder if he had been wrong. Perhaps they couldn't work together.

"Look, about Sawtooth...you know I..."

Her glare stopped him mid-sentence.

"I'm not here to take a mosey down memory lane. I'm here to track your targets and bring the girl back safely. If possible, I'll kill your rogue Wolf and, if necessary, the succubus, too. That's all. So...bring me up to speed. Crib note version."

Three years had passed and, evidently, she was *still* pissed. Not that he blamed her. That fateful day in Idaho had changed her life irrevocably.

He decided against trying to prod her into clearing the air between them. In her current mood, it would likely just irritate her and make a difficult situation worse. If she was acting chilly with him now, continued badgering would only make their working relationship frostier.

Maybe she would mellow a little as they spent more time together on the hunt.

Alex could only hope that would be the case.

"Okay, short story. We got a series of reports from local communities concerning a string of violent murders. Looked like the work of a rogue Wolf, so I was sent in to deal with it. He seemed to be targeting families living in isolated areas. His last two attacks resulted in missing persons. One male, one female, both just eighteen. No idea why they were taken, or where.

"I tracked him from Sherbrooke but lost him when he crossed the border into New Victus about five weeks ago. When one of our border patrols picked up his scent five days ago, they called me back in. Then yesterday I came across something that prompted some concern regarding the Domaine Saint-Bernard community and the fact that he was no longer working alone. Which is when I called Dane and asked for your help. He said you went to Saint-Bernard on your way here..."

"I did," Zarra nodded.

"Find out anything interesting?"

"Our boy is big, fast, strong as an ox," she reported succinctly. "He made short work of their locked door. He's smart, separating Kareena first and drivin' her toward your succubus. He's patient; a sadist, but not to the point of wastin' time. He tortured the victims for fun but didn't prolong the experience. Professional. Like he was on a clock. Maybe he simply had to catch up with his partner and the girl. Or maybe somethin' else entirely. Prefers his Wolf form, or possibly he's a mid-shifter. He's not a feeder as far as I can tell."

She slipped so easily into the slang that Alex wondered how many jobs Zarra had taken over the intervening years.

'Feeders' were rogue Werewolves who had developed a taste for Human flesh. Rare, but not unheard of. 'Mid-shifter' was a reference to the ability of some Therianthropes to maintain an intermediary transformation where they had attributes of both their Human and lupine forms. Usually a humanoid form with the head and claws of the beast; sometimes the tail, too. Alex had never mastered the art but knew that Dane could do it. The best he could do was to shift his vocal cords to allow Human speech while in his Wolf form, which wasn't unusual, and most Werewolves could do it.

"His claws are hella sharp, and he has zero compunctions about usin' them to torture his victims," Zarra continued. "Uses them like scalpels, surgically precise flaying of skin and flesh, often to the bone."

"Did he assault any of the victims sexually?"

Surprise flickered across Zarra's features, but he could see her thinking about it, reliving the scene of the grisly murders. She slowly shook her head.

"No..." she said with a hint of uncertainty. "I mean, it never crossed my mind, so I can't be absolutely sure, but nothin' stood out. The adults were all treated the same, but the kids...he killed them quick. He made it *look* like he'd tortured them, but he didn't. Why'd you ask about the sex?"

"I'm working on a theory..." he said hesitantly.

"Theory?"

"Dane confirmed the woman *is* a succubus. I thought that maybe the rogue Wolf was under her influence, but...I think maybe it's actually the other way around."

"That don't make no sense," Zarra said. "Succubi use pheromones to control male subjects; there's no long-term protection against that...unless..."

Her train of thought jumped neatly onto his tracks.

"...unless he himself is predisposed to the same condition," he finished for her. "I think he's an incubus."

"That'd be a hell of a coincidence," Zarra mused. "You realize how rare they are? To find succubi outside of New Victus is...I dunno, one in a million. And Vampyrii-based incubuses are as rare as rocking horse shit. A Werewolf incubus? If there has ever been a reported case, I ain't heard of it."

He had to admit, she was right. His theory did have significant holes in it. Yet every instinct he had was telling him it was right.

"You told Dane this theory of yours?" Zarra sounded skeptical.

Alex nodded. "There's more..." he said hesitantly. "It looks like they captured Kareena not long after that clearing. She cut herself..."

"Blood," Zarra understood where he was going.

"Made her easier to track, which worked for me, too. It was easier to follow the trail of her blood than their scent. It led me to a cave where I think she was held for a few days. Place reeked of...sex."

"They assaulted her?"

"I don't know..." Alex shook his head. "I don't think so. Something *did* happen there, though, and our *targets* certainly had a lot of sex... But Kareena..."

His voice trailed off as he struggled to put into words what he had found. Finally, he looked at her and continued.

"She'd been tied up, stripped...and there were a lot of weird scents in the cave. I dunno... I didn't stay long enough to check it out properly; my priority was to track them."

"Is it far from here?" Zarra pursed her lips. "I'd like to see it myself."

"Couple of days back maybe."

"And what kinda head start they got?"

"Three days, maybe four," Alex replied.

"Well, shit, I guess that answers that question," Zarra muttered. "We can't afford to lose any more time, or the trail will go colder than the fur on a polar bear's ass. You got any idea where they're goin'?"

Alex shook his head.

"Their heading is...erratic. It's Kareena's doing. She's really pushing the pace. At first, I thought it was fear, an escape. But there's also something different in her scent now...something I can't put my finger on. The other two position themselves upwind of her and travel under the cover of the forest, staying out of direct sunlight. And they keep separating. Vanessa always stays with the girl..."

"Vanessa?" Zarra raised an eyebrow. "You know the Code 11's name?"

"Yeah. The succubus, she's the sister of Lyssa Balthazaar."

"Jesus, fuck," Zarra cursed. "Are you kiddin' me?"

Alex shook his head

"I thought you knew. Dane urged us to try and bring her in alive. Said to tell you he'd pay extra for it."

Alex said nothing more – it wasn't his secret to tell. Not that Zarra needed any more clues.

"So, we can kill the incubus...but Lyssa Balthazaar's sister is off limits?" Her agile mind connected the dots with equal amounts of deduction and intuition. "He's screwing her, isn't he?" she concluded angrily. "Lyssa? He's fuckin' a Vampyrii. Never could keep his dick in his pants when it comes to women outside his own race."

Every growled word dripped with bitterness. He didn't blame her. He would follow Damian Dane through the fiery inferno of Hell and to the ends of the Earth, but he'd never give countenance to the way he had treated Zarra. There was nothing Alex could say that wouldn't make the atmosphere worse than it was, so he kept his mouth shut.

"So, shall we go get these fuckers then?" she said eventually, breaking the awkward silence.

Figuring that the last thing Zarra would want to be greeted by was his nakedness, he had slipped on his morph-suit. It fit like a sleeveless wetsuit, snugly hugging his torso and cut short on the arms and legs. As he started his transformation, the material adhered to his changing shape, snagging uncomfortably on his fur. He hated wearing the suit in his Wolf form.

The scent was simple to find again. He turned his canine head toward Zarra, grinning a large, toothy grin.

"This way," he growled. "Can you keep up?"

His heart warmed a little as she smiled back at him, a sly look in her eyes. It briefly reminded him of old times.

"Don't worry 'bout me." She flicked her eyes, a gesture urging him to get moving.

Alex padded down the rocks into the forest, Zarra at his heels.

| 24 |

HOMECOMING

– Gayle Knightley –
– Saturday – Cambridgeshire, England –

"I don't know, Gayle..." Lana shook her head slowly.

"Have you got something better to do?" Gayle had come too far to give up so easily.

"No," Lana admitted. "But to be honest, I *am* enjoying having nothing to do besides look after the farm."

Gayle had to admit, she had a point. Lana's farm was a pocket of tranquility hidden away amongst the Fens. Only the wind sedately rustling the trees and the gentle sounds of livestock did anything to disrupt the peace of this beautiful autumn evening. It was the perfect place to process the troubled thoughts in your head. She wondered why she hadn't visited since Valletta.

"After Malta," Lana said as if reading her mind, "I felt I needed to step away from the Service. I didn't want to fly for another squad. The 137th was... To be honest, I'm surprised to see *you* back in uniform. Metaphorically speaking."

Gayle took a long sip of homemade lemonade. The ice made the glass cold to the touch, encouraging condensation to gather across its surface.

"I didn't have much of a choice. I couldn't leave the Service while they were still paying for my treatment and rehab. Then Norbel ordered me to the Palace..."

"That's bull," Lana interrupted. "You could afford the rehab yourself, and you've never shied away from using a few choice words to get your own way."

"Like Valletta?"

Lana wouldn't be baited. Instead, she changed subject. "Shouldn't you be teaching today?"

"Not till Monday," Gayle shrugged.

"Then shouldn't you be prepping for your first day as a molder of young minds?"

"I felt it was more important to come and talk to you."

"To try and persuade me into coming back? Captain Reynolds already came and pitched a job at the Academy to me. I politely declined."

"I know. Michael told me."

"Michael?" Lana raised an eyebrow.

"Captain Reynolds," Gayle sighed. "Look, we need you, Lana. We need someone to fly *Artemis*."

"We?"

"Yes," Gayle nodded. "Michael and I."

"Last I heard, 'Michael' was already looking into other pilots to take the job. I even gave him some recommendations."

"I told him to press pause on that. I wanted to come talk to you myself."

"So, *who* needs me to come back?" Lana asked knowingly.

"Okay, I," Gayle admitted. "*I* need you."

She cringed, hearing the desperation in her own voice.

"I don't know..." Lana muttered. "There are *dozens* of qualified pilots. Maybe your new team needs a new pilot. A fresh start."

Gayle had known that Lana would not be easily persuaded, but all she was hearing were excuses. Not reasons.

"They *need* the best," Gayle stated firmly. "Lana, I don't know if I can do this alone. I walk around the Academy and all I see are memories. Good memories...and bad. Truthfully...it's the good ones that hurt the most. I see ghosts *everywhere* I look, reminding me of how I let everyone down."

"Gayle, you didn't let anyone down."

"It was *my* reckless decision..."

Lana raised her eyebrow. "What happened to the woman who faced down admirals and never doubted her team or her decisions? This second-guessing is new."

"I lost my team," Gayle said sadly.

"I know," Lana's tone softened. "But we took on a dangerous profession, and we all accepted the risks going in. We knew there was a strong likelihood our careers would end one way, but over ten years, *your* decisions kept us safe. The 136th had a far greater casualty rate than we did."

"Torbar never suffered a team-wipe," Gayle countered.

"True, but that doesn't change the fact that under your command, historically the 137th was the safer *and* more successful squad. You can't blame yourself for a single bad decision."

"Can't I?"

"Maybe," Lana shrugged. "But, putting all that aside, if that is how you feel...then why go back at all? Walk away. Get your FPA license; you'd do well with your skills."

Gayle chewed thoughtfully at an already thoroughly nibbled thumbnail. That was the question, wasn't it? Lana was right. She did have a reputation for being a strong-willed maverick, so why not go her own way now?

She *could* leave. Freelancing was certainly an option, but Norbel had manipulated her into staying by suggesting she had a responsibility to pass on her knowledge. Emotional blackmail. It had been a powerful fuel to the inferno of her fury. Yet, as the week passed, her mood had mellowed. Realization dawned. The anger that burned inside was aimed at herself.

She had allowed her uncle to manipulate her to stay because he understood the one thing that was only now becoming clear to Gayle – the Academy was her home. Lana, of course, knew that already. She had been guiding her toward this epiphany.

"Bollocks," Gayle sighed. "You *know* why I stayed. In a fucked up way...it's where I belong. I see these kids they want me to teach, and Michael... He's such a good role model..."

"For the kids? Or for you?"

"For the kids," Gayle said too quickly.

Her friend raised an eyebrow.

"Okay," Gayle sighed. "Maybe for me, too."

"So why do you need me?"

"Because I feel like I'm alone and…" Gayle hesitated. "It's hard to explain but I need something there that's familiar. Someone… You're all that's left of the 137th…"

"I'm not the only one left," Lana interjected.

"No…but we've been best friends since we were children." Gayle averted her tear-filled eyes. "You're the only one who will forgive me for what happened."

"You really think you need forgiveness?" Lana said softly with a hint of surprise.

Yes. Yes, I do.

A tear meandered down her cheek. She tasted its salt as her tongue caught it, while she tried to nonchalantly dry the track with a swipe of her finger. It had not gone unnoticed, but Lana said nothing, and Gayle shrugged.

Lana stared out across the fields deep in thought and Gayle *knew* she was deliberating her request. She had always been the calm voice of reason, never afraid to play Devil's advocate or call Gayle out on a bad decision. Maybe if she had been there on that day in Malta…

Maybe she could have talked me out of it.

"Fuck it," Lana finally broke the silence. "I'm in."

Lana's head remained still, but her eyes flicked sideways to look at Gayle, who knew what that sly look meant.

"What's the catch?" she asked, her voice laced with suspicion.

"No catch…" Lana said innocently. "What kind of a best friend would I be to impose conditions on something like this? I'll need somewhere to stay, though…"

"I got space," Gayle interjected. "You can stay with me."

"…and I want you to call her."

Gayle bit her lip and swallowed hard. "I don't think she wants to hear from me…"

"You're scared, I get that." Lana's voice was gentle. "But while you may be consumed with anger for yourself, I know for a fact that *she* isn't."

Gayle opened her mouth to respond, but Lana's expression told her that whatever fabrication she was about to peddle, her friend was not interested in buying it. The anger was ever present, simmering just below the surface. It took every ounce of Gayle's willpower to keep it suppressed.

Instead, with a deep breath, Gayle nodded her acceptance of her best friend's conditions.

| 25 |

NEW SENSATIONS

– Kareena St. Claire –
– Saturday – Mont Tremblant, Pack Nation –

She ran.

Exhilarated, invigorated. Urging her energized legs to move faster and faster, feeling the addictive pull of something she had *never* felt before.

Power.

She tore through the same forest that had stymied her escape, but now *she* had the upper hand. This time she wasn't running away from something. She wasn't the one who was afraid.

Now *she* was the hunter.

Something within her was fundamentally evolved. Her senses were alive in so many confusing yet thrilling ways. She ran with power and grace, tearing through the forest faster than she had ever run before. Tree branches whipped and stung her as she passed by, thorns grabbing at her possessively, but all they did was tickle her with the promise of a pain she no longer felt.

She broke through the tree line into a clearing and skidded to a halt.

Placing her hand on her chest, she felt her heart beating slow, steady. Which felt odd considering her excitement. Her mind struggled to process this new Kareena. What was she capable of? How long had it been? How far she had run? She closed her eyes, vividly remembering the thumping of her heart against her rib cage, feeling like it would explode. She remembered the overwhelming terror, her frantic thoughts of escape, and the horror when she realized there was none.

But now... She wasn't even out of breath.

Kareena looked at her body, and the unexplained changes it had undergone. She had always been slender, but now she looked athletic, too. Her legs were muscular and well defined. Her stomach was a washboard – no more puppy fat. She held her arms in front of her, observing distinct veins and muscles. How strong was she?

What had happened to her?

You are of us now.

Had they really spoken in her mind? Or had she imagined that?

She didn't understand the terrible things they had done to her. She struggled to process the feelings and sensations they had put her through. She had felt afraid, violated, then thrilled and excited and finally...

Reborn.

We love you, Kareena.

Was she still Kareena?

One of us, but more than us. Vampyrii and Werewolf and more in one body. Welcome, daughter.

Dropping to her knees, she cast her eyes to the bright blue sky, filling her lungs with fresh forest air. It tasted different – fertile with stimulating new flavors and textures that burned on her tongue and seared her nostrils with sensations she didn't comprehend. Her head began to spin. It was overwhelming. Screwing her eyes shut, she heaved, a recurring pattern of dry retching and strings of spittle. Her empty stomach had nothing to expel.

She tried to focus once more on the scent she had been hunting in order to settle her equilibrium. She didn't yet have the experience to know what it was, but it was swifter than she. A deer, maybe? It mattered not; it was ideal for her needs.

She could use it to hone her skills and block out the sensory overload that happened every time she stopped to smell the flowers.

No.

She had to conquer this, not be ruled by it.

Smell the flowers!

Kareena forced her eyes open and focused her gaze on a flower, tiny and blue, hiding amongst the untamed grass. She absorbed every intricate detail, perceiving it in a way she never had before. Its blue was brighter and more vivid than any color she had ever seen. And the smell...

She inhaled deeply – like spring and summer rolled into one. Like the feeling you get when the sunlight bathes your skin.

Her eyes eased gently closed again.

What have they done to me?

Chased her from her home. They called her their daughter.

They are not my parents!

Her mother had told her tales of the Wolves. Friends, a force of good to protect us from evil. The howls at night were just the wolves wishing her a goodnight. Pleasant dreams, little one, we'll watch over you as you sleep.

Lies.

She had met the Wolf; his howls were the gloating song of sadistic pleasure. A monster – no more, no less – looking for sport with innocent, defenseless people. The Wolf had *not* protected them.

It had *butchered* them.

Grief punched a gaping wound through her terror and a white-hot anger ignited within her. An acrid odor stung her nostrils. Her eyes flicked open and she stared at the tiny blue flower.

Its charred leaves wilting, as the delicate petals burned away.

| 26 |

POWER STRUGGLE

– Gayle Knightley –
– Monday – London, England –

"This *isn't* Hogwarts and none of you are Harry Potter. What you all have is not *magic*. It's *power*."

Gayle's heels beat a slow rhythm on the hardwood floor as she paced back and forth. The cadets remained silent in her presence. She wasn't sure if that was through respect or fear, but regardless, they hung on her every word.

Good, she thought. *They* should *be fucking listening.*

"You're all here because you're children of dual heritage. Fae father or Fae mother, it doesn't matter. Your DNA allows you access to something more, something special..."

She paused for effect and cast a look around the classroom, catching each cadet by the eye.

"...but don't even contemplate the thought that you *are* special. Because you're not."

She gestured toward the window and the city outside.

"Thirty years ago, the United Kingdom had a population of sixty-six million people. Between The Rising and The Purification, it is now less than a quarter of that. London itself used to be home to nine million...now it's less than one."

She walked slowly down the aisle between the desks toward the back of the room.

"That's just the UK. In America, the death toll was significantly higher. Africa, South America, the Middle East…the attacks were brutal, the cost of life high. Whole countries were wiped out in days. Russia went dark twenty-eight years ago and hasn't been heard from since.

"You want some more big numbers? The Human population of the world *right now* is somewhere around one billion people. Sounds like a lot? Well, before The Rising that number was almost seven and a half billion. Look at your classmates…"

The cadets all looked at each other in mutual confusion.

"Twelve of you in this class, so, by my math, at least ten of you would be dead now."

That last statement hit a little too close to home, and there was a catch in her throat as she finished it. Gayle reached the back of the classroom at an opportune moment; she wasn't facing them when she faltered.

"This is a dangerous job, but don't think you're special to do it. Special implies that you're better than everyone else, that you're more valuable than everyone else."

She stalked back to the head of the class and turned to face them, her look stern.

"Bollocks. That last one billion Humans, *they're* the special ones. When you consider that the War culled over six times that many people in a matter of months, you realize how fragile that number really is. Humanity *is* an endangered species, and *you* are the thin line between their survival and their extinction.

"Your parents and your grandparents thought Vampires and Werewolves were simply fodder for action movies and romance novels. Now we know they're real. We've seen them. We've touched them. We've killed them. And *that,* kids, is just the tip of the iceberg. This world has *never* been more dangerous."

She snapped her fingers, and a flame sprang forth from the tip of her index finger. It swayed hypnotically as it burned. She felt the power course through her, mesmerizing and addictive. Gayle tilted her head as she watched it, her face softening, her breathing becoming labored. She had forgotten how it felt. She hadn't done this in over nine months, yet still it came so easily to her.

"This..." she said breathily. "Some people heralded our embrace of this power as the moment we saved our world. Others think that we're sitting on a bomb...and we just lit the fuse. There will be times when you agree with the latter...and pray for the former."

She watched the flame dance from finger to finger as she turned her hand slowly. Gayle lost herself for a moment in the deep yellow-orange hues of her own power, a cathartic burning of negative emotion that relaxed her, calmed her. Her eyes slowly slipped closed; her breathing relaxed.

"Miss Knightley..." a voice said hesitantly.

Her eyes flicked open again, the young man's voice dragging her back from the trance.

"*Captain* Knightley," she corrected him, irritated at his interruption.

"Sorry...Captain. I just wondered what you meant when you said we have power. Not magic. My parents always told me that what I had was magic. Fae magic. From my father's side..."

She stared at the young Welsh kid – what was his name? Her mind was momentarily blank. She closed her fist, extinguishing the frolicking flame, and shut her eyes. Deep breath.

"Well, your parents are...fucking idiots."

Yeah, Norbel would probably be pissed about calling her students' parents idiots.

Fucking idiots, actually, she thought. *Could have been worse.*

But if they wanted her to teach these kids, then she would do it her way. No sugar-coating the truth. Her thumb prodded the button on the stylus in her hand and a gently rotating hologram of the Earth appeared, hovering serenely above her desk. Brandishing the stylus wand-like at the image, lines started to appear, encircling the blue-green planet in all directions.

"Who can tell me what these are?"

A couple of hands rose hesitantly. She pointed at the terrified looking blonde with the flawless tawny skin who visibly gulped when she realized she had been chosen. She stumbled over her words as she lowered her hand.

"Ley lines, Miss...Captain. Sorry."

"They are indeed," Gayle nodded. The girl had a French accent, but that didn't help with any form of name recognition. "However, I bet that none of you know the real significance of them."

Uncomprehending faces stared back.

"Earth. Air. Fire. Water. The powers of the Fae, born of light and dark but fueled by those four elemental forces, blah blah blah. *That* is the rhetoric about what we all wield. But the truth is they're not the *Fae's* power. They were there all along – the Fae just discovered how to draw on it, manipulate it. Now we do, too. We draw upon the primal energies of the planet and channel them."

Her eyes scanned the faces of her students, who were all still looking blankly at her. Incomprehension was clear in their glassy-eyed stares. To Gayle, this was further proof, if any was needed, that she was in no way cut out to be a teacher.

"Okay, let's try this..." She paused for a moment searching for a good analogy that would put the point across. "Think of the elements as a weapon. Like, say, a gun. The gun already exists; it's just that the Fae figured out how to fire it. How to pull the trigger."

Evidently, she hit the correct comparison. The dawn of realization flooded the features of most of the kids. Gayle cast her look toward the Welsh boy. Dylan, was it?

Damn, I have got to learn these kids' names!

"Power...*not* magic," she said more softly this time. "Have none of you ever wondered exactly how we do it?"

One girl put her hand up. She looked like she had been dragged to class through a bush or two, her red hair wild and untamed. As Gayle looked into her eyes, she saw a hard edge she recognized. Rosario returned her stare with unflinching confidence.

Now why do I remember her name?

"Anger, Captain," Rosario said quietly. "We channel anger."

Interesting answer.

"Not the answer I was looking for, but as you brought the subject up, yes...anger works," Gayle nodded. "So do love, happiness, fear, even hunger. Any emotion will suffice if it's strong enough. I can see in your eyes that you have the fire, Rosario...am I right?"

A tentative narrowing of the hazel eyes before the young girl nodded. Gayle recognized the same inferno that burned deep inside herself.

"Show me," Gayle instructed.

The girl didn't hesitate to lift her hand and ignite it. The flame danced, tinged a burnt sienna. Gayle was impressed; the girl already had some semblance of control.

"Show of hands," she said to the class at large. "How many of you can create fire like myself and Spitfire here?"

Six members of the class raised their hands, a few less confidently than the others. Gayle felt her eyes drawn to the back of the class, to a young Latin face obscured behind a cascade of ebony curls, but she wasn't sure why. The girl stared back at her teacher with stunning chocolate-colored eyes. There was something there...a shyness, but also a flinty firmness.

Let's call her Raven...

"And those of you who can control the air? The wind?"

She watched Raven, somehow knowing the girl's hand would stay aloft. Some new hands rose as others fell.

"Water?" she asked.

Most of the class responded, Raven's hand still among them.

"And earth?"

The final element, and Raven's hand was still up, raising some truly interesting questions.

Four for four.

"Different emotions feed different abilities. Earth and water, they are the tools of positive emotion. They are grounded. Love, happiness, hope, pride, empathy...desire. The more positive the feeling, the stronger your ability to manipulate those energies.

"At your age most of you may not have experienced the negative emotions that give you the capability to use fire and air. At least not to a powerful degree. Anger, fear, jealousy, sadness, doubt, shame..." Her eyes flicked toward Raven, gauging her reaction. "...grief and guilt."

The young girl's face twitched visibly at the final two.

"Fire and air are immensely powerful, but they are flighty. Disconnected, ungrounded. They are difficult to harness and even more challenging to control."

Gayle turned, gesturing toward the still rotating globe and its latticework of ley lines.

"Ley lines focus and channel elemental power, allowing those of us who can do so to manipulate it. The closer you are to a ley line, the stronger you'll be. Think of them as...powerlines, and yourselves as appliances."

Time for another demonstration.

She nodded to the quiet girl with the long, ice blue hair sitting in the front row.

"You had your hand up for water, yes?"

The girl took the questioning tone as a nudge to identify herself, which she did immediately.

"Andrea Campbell, Captain. And, yes...water and air."

"Okay, Andrea, let's see what you've got," Gayle said, nodding toward the glass of water on her desk.

Andrea hesitated for a moment, nervously glancing from teacher to glass and back again. She stretched her hand out slowly with a look of intense concentration. The water started to gently swirl, forming a tiny waterspout that rose from the glass and began to meander across the desk. Gayle watched for a few moments, impressed by the girl's proficiency.

The other students were so entranced by the hypnotic dance of the whirling fluid, they failed to notice Gayle move surreptitiously to the wall near the door and place her hand on a small touch-sensitive switch panel.

"Nice control. You've got some skill. But...as I said earlier, you're plugged into the ley line that runs through London, and like any appliance that is plugged into a powerline...I can turn you off."

She gently brushed her finger over the switch and watched

the waterspout abruptly collapse into a puddle of water, surprising the cadets. All except Andrea, who simply looked confused.

They need to walk before I let them run.

| 27 |

THE HUNT

– Zarra Anderson –

– Tuesday – Mont Tremblant, Pack Nation –

The night air hung pregnant with the possibility of danger. The wind shifted haphazardly, making it tricky to track their prey while remaining hidden. It didn't bother Zarra. If they were careful, everything would be fine. Her companion, however, found the situation untenable, a fact he wouldn't stop hinting at.

"Wind has changed again," Alex muttered.

"Yup," Zarra responded under her breath.

She was hunkered behind a fallen tree on the ridge, surveying the forest below through binoculars. She'd been patiently doing this for the past hour, much to her partner's annoyance. Alex had been padding back and forth relentlessly, his tail flicking with impatience. For the twentieth time in as many minutes, Alex drew a deep breath and exhaled in an exaggerated show of his exasperation.

"What?" she finally hissed at him.

"We *know* they're both down there. We can take them now. Especially if you'd just—"

"Not happening," she cut him off. "So, let it go."

She was trying not to get angry but keeping things professional with Alex was wearing on her more than she'd expected. Four days in and she was increasingly wondering if

158

they *could* see this job through without coming to blows.

Not for the first time, she questioned why, even for three million credits, she was here doing this all over again. It seemed so long since they had been close. Today, both had quite different sentiments about what happened five years ago in Sawtooth Forest, a fact that meant they would likely never see eye-to-eye regarding it.

"Fine, but still, we can end the hunt right here and now. It's a cave. They're trapped. Cornered. It's a situation we can take advantage of."

"Really?" Anger bubbled in Zarra's retort. "We have *no* clue what they're doin' in there. They armed? Did they set traps? Is there another exit or entrance?"

"They're just hiding out in a cave. If you'd just—"

Now he was really pissing her off. She made a decision that, in hindsight, she probably wouldn't have made if she wasn't tired and annoyed. She poked the proverbial bear.

"What *you* do is tracking," she stated matter-of-factly. "Not hunting."

"What?"

"You heard me right. You ain't no hunter, honey. You're a tracker...and that's all you are."

"I beg to *differ*," he shot back, obviously offended.

"Alex, I've spent the past few years workin' as a freelance bounty hunter... The key to a hunt is patience, something you are in short supply of," she said condescendingly. "Look at you...all ready to charge in there half-cocked. I've seen colleagues – good friends – killed, simply because they didn't respect the patience of the hunt."

Her eyes stayed glued to the binoculars as her verbal attack pressed on.

"For starters, we're not goin' anywhere while this wind is whippin' around. It's intermittently gusting toward the cave, meaning they'll know we're comin' before we get there...losing the element of surprise.

"Additionally, if you spent a little more time observing and less time yammerin,' you'd have noticed something else..."

Alex sniffed the air again, his brow furrowed in confusion.

"I don't..."

"Change blindness. You've been concentrating on our targets for too long. Broaden your horizons."

She watched him tilt his head, focusing his senses. His nostrils flared as he directed his attention toward the other scents being carried on the breeze.

"I think we found one of your missing persons," Zarra whispered.

"Shit," he growled. "Young male... How the hell did I miss that?"

"Like I said – impatience. Makes you careless."

After it became evident that Kareena was in no hurry to move on from the clearing in which she had settled two days prior, Vanessa and her partner backtracked to the cave that Zarra and Alex were now surveilling. Zarra and Alex speculated about why they had taken this detour, but now it was starting to make sense.

"We need to get down there," Alex said. "Now!"

"Did you not listen to a word I just said?" Zarra sighed.

"We have a responsibility—"

"Alex—"

"We can't just leave him down there. I saw what they did to his family—"

"—it's too late," her voice softened. "I know death when I smell it."

His nose twitched one more time, and his head dropped as he detected the same faint aroma that Zarra had already identified.

"Dammit," he said quietly.

Zarra knew how Alex felt, because she felt it, too. The sense of failure. Rescuing the two missing persons the incubus had taken prior to his kidnapping Kareena hadn't been part of the deal. She hadn't even known about them until Alex had briefed her on the history of their assignment a few days ago. The reward was for Kareena, and neutralizing Vanessa and the incubus. In all honesty, Zarra hadn't really thought about the young man that had gone missing at all.

Did she feel guilty about that?

Kareena was the mission.

Vanessa and her partner were the mission.

"A succubus and an incubus..." Zarra muttered thoughtfully.

"We don't know the Wolf is an incubus. That's purely speculation."

"*Your* speculation!" she retorted as she finally put the binoculars down and looked at him. "But...the male is definitely the controlling influence here. *He* raided the Lodge and *he's* callin' the shots on this hunt. He's an incubus, I'd stake my goddamn life on it. What I'm strugglin' with are the hows and the whys."

"How and why what?"

"How does a Vampyrii succubus hook up with a Werewolf incubus in the first place?" Zarra mused. "How do they even find each other, especially with someone as protected – or sheltered – as Vanessa Balthazaar? Why venture so deep into Pack Nation territory just to kidnap some random girl? Then why simply release her and start hunting her all over again?"

"Entertainment? Why does it need to make sense?"

"Because they're not killing for sport. At least she's not," Zarra reasoned. "Vanessa never went to Domaine Saint-Bernard. That bloodbath was all his. It's possible that if she'd have known what he was doin', she'd never have gone along with it."

Zarra paused for a moment as she followed her own developing train of thought.

"We know Vanessa links to Lyssa Balthazaar, and we know how Lyssa links to Damian. Given Kareena's connection to Damian, too, I've got to think that takin' her *wasn't* an accident...she was targeted. He deliberately separated her from her family and friends. But why?"

"So, you're saying what?" Alex interjected. "That the others at Domaine Saint-Bernard were just collateral damage?"

"Wrong place, wrong time."

"So why even kill them at all if he had already split Kareena from the group?"

"For pleasure," Zarra said instinctively. "He enjoyed the

torture and the killing, but he didn't prolong it. Which, if he had a choice, I think he would have. He was on a timetable, which implies a plan. And if there's a plan, then I want to know what it is before I make any rash moves."

"Okay, if all that is true," he said, begrudgingly accepting her logic, "then I guess we do it your way. Proceed with patience."

"So, it is possible to teach an old dog new tricks," Zarra chuckled, but immediately regretted her choice of words.

"You would know," Alex snapped, his tone resentful. "I'm not the oldest dog you turned tricks with, am I?"

Okay, she thought. *So, this is where shit goes sideways.*

She cursed her own greed and the temptation of the huge payday that had put her in this position. This was precisely why she had been hesitant to accept the job in the first place. Matters of the heart were rarely easy bedfellows with professionalism.

"Come on then." Zarra lowered the binoculars and turned to face Alex. "Let's do this."

Alex had been waiting for this moment and was at the ready without hesitation.

"From that day in Sawtooth," he began, "when I saved your life—"

"*Saved* my life?!" Zarra snarled. "You *ruined* my fuckin' life. You were selfish—"

"Selfish? Really?" Alex said with a bitter laugh. "The moment I made that call, I blew my cover. I did that to save you because I loved you."

"I *know* you loved me," irritation tainted her tone. "But for fuck's sake, Alex, I didn't love *you*."

The moment the words slipped past her lips, she regretted them. Wished she could take them back. Suddenly, Zarra felt like the bad guy in all this. She hadn't meant to be so heartlessly insensitive; only to make him understand the truth about what they had been to each other.

"You were a comrade in arms..." she said, striving to find a fairer, less cruel, way to explain her point of view. "A friend."

The damage, however, had already been done. Alex's tone

was shaded in anger as he responded without pause for thought. "You never gave us a chance..." he growled. "As soon as your wounds healed, you were in bed with Damian. Never a thought for me."

"Gimme a break," Zarra said, rolling her eyes. "It was *months* before anything happened between me and Damian."

"And it was over in months, too. I warned you, but you wouldn't listen."

Touché.

His verbal counterpunch landed squarely, making Zarra wince internally. Her brain, however, was now struggling mightily to keep up with her mouth. Every word she reflexively uttered just seemed to be one more thing she wished she could take back. As a result, she found herself further escalating the tension between them, rather than defusing it.

"I didn't need your advice then, and I don't need this shit now."

"I saved your life."

"Which doesn't give you a controllin' interest over who I sleep with." She sighed heavily. "This job was a mistake. I knew it was too much to expect you to be professional."

"I *was* being professional," Alex muttered. "You started sniping at my hunting skills."

Ouch!

She reached into her head for a snappy comeback, but there were no words. Finally, her brain caught up. She had to reluctantly admit...he had a point. While Alex had been a source of irritation for her over the last four days, it *was* her snide comment that started this argument.

More than that, she was the person responsible for the pain he was feeling, an emotion for which she had empathy. Being rejected by someone you love when they're in love with someone else...hurt. Personal experience had taught her that. After all, wasn't this similar to what Damian had done to her? Rejected her because *he* had been in love with someone else.

Zarra closed her eyes, her mind flitting back to another long unresolved personal matter. She was starting to think that she was carving out a niche for herself in being an expert on hypocrisy. It was something she hadn't thought about in a while, yet it was always there. A nagging feeling of unfinished business.

She took a deep breath and opened her eyes again to look across at Alex, recalling how close they had once been. The good times they had shared so many years ago.

Accept some responsibility for something, Zee! Just for once, accept it, the little voice in the back of her head admonished her. *It's not his fault you hurt him.*

And just like that, the fight went out of her.

"Okay, listen," she said softly, attempting a conciliatory tone. "I'm sorry for what I said. Can we at least try to get along for the duration of this job?"

She was met with stony silence.

The conversation apparently ended for now, she lifted her binoculars and once more trained her line of sight in the direction of their prey. She still couldn't see them, but every sense and instinct she had told her they were there. What those traits couldn't tell her was what they were up to.

It was a riddle that needed to be solved before this temporary partnership imploded beyond their ability to fix it.

| 28 |

TWO STEPS BEHIND

– Alex Newman –
– Tuesday – Mont Tremblant, Pack Nation –

The evening wind gently ruffled his ebony fur as his nostrils twitched, searching the breeze for its hidden secrets. When nothing presented itself as a threat, he crept forward, keeping his body close to the ground. Slowly, cautiously, he padded quietly into the shadow of the cave. While he remained alert for the unexpected, there was one thing he *knew* he would find in here.

Death.

The air was thick with its lingering stench, threatening to overwhelm his senses. Yet as he edged further in, his confidence grew. Zarra had been adamant that she wanted to wait for Vanessa and the incubus to leave the safety of the cave prior to investigating. Kareena was the priority, and Zarra's focus right now was on gathering as much new information as they could about what their opponents were up to. She was also firmly of the opinion that they should be the ones picking their battleground for any potential showdown. It was important not be lured into a situation that put them at a disadvantage.

Alex wasn't entirely happy about it, but he could see her reasoning and didn't totally disagree. Still, venturing into the darkness gave him a sense of trepidation.

Is this a trap?

The adrenaline surged through his veins as he considered the possibility. He needn't have worried, however. Their quarry was evidently long gone.

"Clear," Alex growled quietly.

He battled the impulse to push deeper into the cave alone. Zarra's words had stung his ego, but deep down he knew she was right. He could be impatient, or impulsive, depending on how you looked at it. Patience, then. He waited; muscles primed to respond to the merest hint of danger. Zarra entered the cave, stepping carefully so the soles of her boots made barely a whisper on the stone floor. Her Freelancer was cradled in a firm two-handed grip, safety off.

She crouched alongside him and paused, focusing her attention on what lay ahead. He scanned for the slightest noise, tilting his head curiously back and forth, but the only sounds to be heard were the rhythmic dripping of water on stone and the calm cycle of Zarra's breathing.

"What the hell is that?" she sniffed.

"Death," he answered succinctly.

"I know what death smells like. I pointed that out to you earlier. I mean the *other* smell."

He focused, sorting through the scents his nose was processing. She was right...there was something else. A very faint aroma, fragrant to the nostrils yet almost completely obscured by a cocktail of far more unpleasant scents. It took him a moment to correctly decipher what it was.

"Cedarwood?" She beat him to the recollection.

"Yes, but more than that," Alex said searching his memory. "Cassia and...something else... Galbanum maybe."

"How the hell do you know that?" Zarra whispered in astonishment.

"No idea. I must have smelled those things before, somewhere...but I don't recall the context..."

He cautiously pressed on, Zarra close behind. As the cave curved naturally to the left, the light from the entrance diminished noticeably until Zarra finally signaled for them to stop. She gestured toward her eyes, then pointed at Alex, and then around the corner. The instruction was clear – her eyes couldn't see in the dark, but his could. With a nod, he stalked around the bend and into a comfortably-sized chamber, which he quickly surveyed to confirm its abandonment.

"Clear."

Zarra moved into the space, leading with her Freelancer. Her finger flicked a button on the side of the weapon, activating the tiny but powerful integrated flashlight. She made a quick move, splashing light across the walls and floor in a figure-of-eight motion to confirm Alex's assessment.

"Keep an eye out for traps," she said, turning on the dual LEDs on her headset to aid in a more thorough sweep of the room.

The light revealed several discarded items, amongst which lay the source of the terrible aroma. The body of a young man lay naked, face down on the cold stone floor. The smell told them he had been dead for a while, but Zarra crouched and went through the formalities of checking for signs of life anyway.

"What the hell happened here?" she muttered.

Alex shifted back to Human form and retrieved his own headset from his pack, moments later adding his illumination to hers. Between them, they cast eerie double shadows across the gruesome scene. As Zarra gently rolled the young man over, Alex found himself surprised to see that there was a distinct lack of any bodily injury.

"He wasn't tortured..."

"If he wasn't tortured, then why was he trussed up?" Zarra gestured toward the ropes still wrapped around the victim's wrists and ankles, and the canvas hood held fast by coils of rope around his neck.

The knots on the rope were too tight to tease open, so as Alex held the young man's head steady, Zarra carefully cut through the loops with her boot-knife. Finally, and with a deference that Alex knew the man would never recognize, she gently peeled the hood away to reveal a youthful face and a shock of shaggy blonde hair. If he was out of his teens, it was only barely. Whispering a silent prayer, Alex tenderly laid the young man's head to rest on the floor.

"Ritual." He quietly voiced what his brain was thinking.

"What sort of fucked up goddamn ritual is this?"

"I'm not sure, but...doesn't it strike you as *kinda* ritualistic? The smells you detected earlier... He reeks of both."

"But why?"

Alex had to admit that was a very good question. He searched his memory, looking to find the answers he knew were in there.

"Cassia...is an anointing oil, if I remember right," he said slowly. "And galbanum...a ceremonial perfume? Maybe he was some sort of sacrifice. There's another scent, too. Something..."

He inhaled deeply, trying to detect the source of the new yet familiar smell. His nose led his focus to a shallow wooden bowl sitting on the floor near the body. Picking it up he sniffed at the residuals and then tasted a little off the tip of his finger. Recognition dawned.

"Caramaru," he murmured.

"I'm not familiar with that..." Zarra shook her head and took the bowl from him.

"It's a powder made from catuaba bark and a *really* powerful aphrodisiac. Especially for Lycans. Hard to come by..."

"So, this was...what? An orgy?" she said with a measure of disbelief as she inspected the young man's neck. "There's more goin' on here. I can feel it. Look at his neck – he's been bitten. Twice."

She was right – a pair of bite marks were clear. The first set had a small radius and the distinctive twin puncture wounds of a Vampyrii bite. The other bite was wider with multiple puncture sites. It was a bite pattern Alex knew intimately. Zarra had apparently been following the same line of thought.

"It doesn't make any sense," she mused. "Obviously, the Wolf bite came first because we know what happens vice versa. So, surely this was *always* gonna end in his death..."

Something still niggled Alex about those anointing oils. Something he felt he should know.

"I need to make a call back to base."

"Now?" Zarra raised her eyebrow. "We're too far out and we're too low down. Signal will never reach..."

She paused, silently pursing her lips and thinking.

"What?" Alex said impatiently.

"Becka is close by," Zarra said. "She could pass on a message. Might have to wait for the response, though."

She was right. Without satellite communications, and with the mountains and the trees between them and command, the only way to get a message to Damian was to use *Diana* as a relay.

"Let's do it," he nodded.

Outside the cave, Alex kept watch while Zarra pulled the long-range comms antenna out of her pack, opening the tiny umbrella-like array with practiced efficiency. From career soldier to professional mercenary, he had to admit – she *was* very different from the woman he had known. It was an impression he had been getting for a while now, but little moments like this brought a stark clarity to the feeling. After a couple of final checks on the setup, Zarra pressed the button on her earpiece.

"Becka," she said. "You listenin'?"

Silence, but Zarra patiently waited for her partner to get to the radio. A moment later, her patience was rewarded as Alex's sensitive hearing heard the tinny response through Zarra's earpiece.

"Always, Zee," Becka replied. "What ya need?"

Zarra flicked her eyes toward Alex as she threw him the second earpiece. He snatched it out of the air with one hand and, after toggling it on, placed it into his ear.

"Lonewolf has a message he needs to relay to Alpha. Can you do that and relay the response back to us?"

With the earpiece now in and active, Alex heard the response as clear as crystal.

"Roger. What's the message?"

"Becka," Alex started, "I need some information on Werewolf culture and the use of cassia, galbanum, and cedarwood—"

He hadn't even finished his request when Becka interrupted.

"Lycan birthing ritual," Alex heard Becka chuckle gently. "That answer your question? It's not practiced much these days. Mostly practiced by just the older clans. Traditionally, the mother is purified and cleansed prior to the birth by bathing in a water and cedarwood oil mix. Burning the wood supposedly then stimulates the birthing process. Once the child is born, he or she is anointed with cassia for good health, and galbanum for prosperity. I thought you'd know that being a Lycan yourself, Alex?"

"My upbringing was not very...religious," Alex answered. "But you're right – I knew those things sounded familiar."

"That doesn't answer the question, though," Zarra mused.

"What question?" came Becka's inquisitive reply over the radio.

"The question," Alex vocalized, "of why they would capture him, string him up, force-feed him aphrodisiacs, anoint him, and *then* both bite down on him leading to his predictable death."

"You're chasing a succubus and an incubus – both feed off sexual energy. Maybe this is just their way of getting kicks?" Becka hypothesized.

"I considered that idea," Zarra sighed. "But why the whole birthing ritual if this was just for sexual amusement?"

They stood in silence for a moment. Alex didn't have a good answer to that question. Nor did he have an answer for the next one.

"And what," Zarra mused with a tilt of her head, "makes Kareena St. Claire so special that they'd chase her halfway to New Victus?"

With that said, another question popped into Alex's head. "And why did they stop chasing Kareena just to do what they did here?" he asked. "What made *him* so special?"

| 29 |

THE FACULTY

– Lana Fordham –
– Wednesday – London, England –

After squaring away her affairs at the farm, Lana travelled down to London, dropped her luggage off at Gayle's place as arranged, and headed to the Academy. The plan was to rendezvous with Gayle on the grounds behind the Palace to meet with Captain Reynolds.

Gayle was already there waiting for her, standing on the path near the edge of the landing field, watching as the cadets tackled a formidable looking assault course in the rain. Or was she watching the man supervising them, stopwatch in hand?

The cadets had just approached a low strung zigzag of barbed wire under which Captain Reynolds was directing them to go. One by one, they all crawled through the thick mud, emerging on the other side covered in filth.

"You know, I've lost count of the number of times I've had to wade through mud and belly-crawl through muck and filth. And that's not including my sex-life," Gayle chuckled as Lana approached. "So...I called her, just like you wanted."

"What did she say?"

Gayle tilted her head to one side, bit her lip, and rolled her eyes a little in a sign of capitulation.

"Yeah, so...you were right. She's not angry with me."

"Told you." Lana grinned smugly.

"Well, not angry for *that* anyway. She did take a justifiable jab at me for not contacting her sooner, for which I apologized."

Captain Reynolds turned and noticed them watching from the gravel path. Gayle beckoned to him. At first he didn't move, but then Gayle pointed to the high heels on her boots and to the waterlogged grass and shrugged. With an almost imperceptible shake of his head, he started to make his way toward them across the sodden grass.

"How's she doing?" Lana asked quietly. "She was waiting for the cybernetic implant when I last spoke to her a week ago."

"The surgery went well. I said we'll go visit her next week..." Gayle let the statement trail off; the implication was not lost on her friend.

"Oh, *we* will, will we?"

"Is that okay?" Gayle asked with a hint of nervousness. "I mean we're cool...but I really don't want to go on my own."

"I'll come. A visit is overdue anyway. She still in Stoke Mandeville?"

Gayle sighed with obvious relief. "Yes, she is. And thank you."

Captain Reynolds closed the last few yards between them and smiled warmly.

"Captain Fordham." He extended a firm handshake. "Welcome to the faculty."

"Thank you, Captain. Feels good to be back."

"Your answer had seemed pretty definitive," he said with a smile. "I didn't think you'd change your mind."

"I can be quite persuasive," Gayle interjected.

"I don't doubt it," Captain Reynolds replied.

And so, it began.

"What's that supposed to mean?" Gayle served.

"Nothin' at all," Michael volleyed.

"I told you I was going to be professional from now on. We just talked as friends and I laid out the reasons why we need her."

"I didn't imply you did anything otherwise..."

And on it went.

Dread started to knot Lana's stomach. Was this to be her true role here? To provide a buffer zone between them? If so, then the job promised to be an exhausting endeavor at best. She interrupted their to-and-fro sniping with a question.

"Where's *Artemis*?"

"Huh?" Gayle grunted.

"Where is *my* dropship?" Lana clarified.

A look crossed Gayle's face like she had just realized the mistake she made in arranging to meet here.

"I mean, I see *Minerva*," Lana gestured to the left-hand side of the field where the insect-like dropship of the 136th sat dormant, "but *Artemis*...appears to be missing."

"Ah'm sorry..." Michael nodded. "The *Artemis* is at Brize Norton being—"

Before he could finish, Gayle leapt in a little too loudly.

"—repaired," she said. "Don't get mad!"

"*Repaired!* What did you do to her?" Lana was horrified.

"Nothing, I swear!" Gayle protested; hands spread in supplication. "After Valletta, she'd been sitting on the landing pad for a while, and it turns out...that Torbar's team may have borrowed a few parts here and there..."

While Gayle had a soft spot for the transport, as her pilot, Lana had a personal bond with the dropship. *Artemis* wasn't a thing to her; she was an entity with a distinct personality.

"You let them strip her for parts?" Lana said, a hint of anger creeping into her voice.

"In my defense," Gayle protested, "we weren't using her. And just think...*Arty* gets shiny new parts!"

Lana was just thinking how Torbar was going to be getting a very unpleasant visit from her at some point in his near future when she clocked Captain Reynolds' confused look and the pieces started to fall into place. Gayle had accepted the post a week ago, and only started the role in anger just two days prior. There was no way that she had been here long enough to allow any kind of cannibalization of *Artemis*. Additionally, Gayle never would have let it happen.

On the other hand, Captain Reynolds had no attachment to

the dropship; he wouldn't have thought twice about allowing Torbar to take the parts he needed for *Minerva*. He also wouldn't have realized the emotional impact to Lana.

Which meant one thing – Gayle was covering for Captain Reynolds. She had taken the responsibility upon herself for the violation of their dropship, knowing that she would bear the brunt of Lana's inevitable anger.

Interesting.

She *knew* she had detected something in the way Gayle spoke about him when she came to the farm. The way that she slipped into calling him 'Michael' instead of by rank. Standing here now, witnessing the two of them together, Lana could feel it. The chemistry was palpable, even if the two of them seemed oblivious to it themselves.

Gayle Knightley could be impulsive, that much was undeniable, but she also didn't waste time on the trivial. It was one of the things that made her such a good leader. Over the past year, a series of events had attacked key parts of her psyche, shattering that bedrock of confidence. It was painful to see her friend so broken. The decision to come back here had been, in part, to help Gayle find herself again.

Yet, it was possible that Gayle already had what she needed right here. Many things in life could be remedied by having a good friend by your side, to have your back and support you through the tough times. Whether by luck or management, Gayle working with Captain Reynolds could prove to be the best remedy for what was ailing her.

Lana smiled, attracting the attention of her best friend. Gayle mirrored her smile, but with a look of confused suspicion.

"What?" she asked slowly.

"What 'what?'" Lana replied innocently.

"The grin." Gayle's glance flicked from Lana to Michael and back again. "You're not...angry?"

Lana shook her head and decided to keep her thoughts to herself. For now. "No, no. Just...get me my ship back in one piece, please."

"She'll be shiny. Good as new, I promise," Michael reassured her, going along with Gayle's obvious fabrication. A look of gratitude mixed with relief flitted across her friend's face. Lana gestured toward the cadets.

"Have they been at this since oh-eight hundred?" she asked.

Michael nodded in response.

"And here I thought *I* was going to be the bad cop in their lives," Gayle chuckled. "You do realize I'm teaching them this afternoon?"

"They're kids, they should have energy to burn. I wanna see what their limits are, how far I can push 'em." Michael kept his eyes on the cadets. "Plus, it shows me the team players from the mavericks, which is always good to know."

Lana watched Gayle bristle at the 'M' word, but she didn't think he was sniping at her, simply making an observation. As she watched, it quickly became evident that the class was split into two distinct groups – those that were completing the obstacle course on their own merit and those that were running it as a team.

The latter group approached an eight-foot wall standing across the course, slick with mud. The only way past it was to go over it, a feat with which a couple of the cadets were struggling. The more athletic members of the group took it upon themselves to help the strugglers climb over before scaling the slippery wooden surface themselves.

Teamwork.

Conversely, a black-haired girl came sprinting up to the wall, sprang upward, grabbed the top of the barrier, and easily hauled herself over it. As she hit the ground, she was already focused on the next obstacle.

"I see your point," Gayle murmured.

"I never said anything about this bein' a competition," Michael said simply. "The key to their survival out there will be teamwork. I want 'em to get that mindset early. Puttin' their individual achievements to the back of their mind. Then, hopefully, they'll start to trust each other. I think trust is important to workin' together, don't you, Knightingale?"

Lana noticed the deliberate use of Gayle's call sign.

"Total agreement. And with that in mind..." Gayle said segueing into a new subject, "what I'm proposing is that all three of us teach classes to the students that play to our strengths. I'll do the powers bit, Rogue takes them for combat tactics and physical education, and Fordith does the hand-to-hand combat classes. She's way more qualified to teach self-defense than either of us. Lana's got black belts in seven different martial arts—"

"Eight actually," Lana interjected.

"See? Eight, actually," Gayle finished.

Lana smiled as she watched Captain Reynolds' eyebrows raise in surprise. "I musta missed that in your file, Captain Fordham."

"It's a hobby, really. I pursued them outside of the service mostly." She shrugged. "Karate, Wushu, Shaolin Kung Fu, Ju Jitsu, Muy Thai, Judo, Taekwondo, and Akido."

"Akido?" Gayle commented. "That's new."

"I felt I needed to learn how to whack people with sticks. I'm currently studying Capoeira."

"Ralf's preferred style..." Gayle said quietly.

"Scrapper," Michael stated softly.

A small gesture, but one that Lana could see meant a lot to Gayle. The team had always used each other's call signs in casual conversation, and while Captain Reynolds had obviously never been part of that team, he did know them from their files. Knowing Ralf Schneider's call sign had been 'Scrapper' was a minor detail, but sometimes the small things made a huge difference.

"After watching how graceful it made his clumsy, German ass look," Lana nodded, "I figured I needed to try it myself. Anyway, if you want me to do this, I will...but I'm really not a teacher."

"You think *I* am?" Gayle laughed.

She had a point. "No," Lana chuckled. "*You* are about as far away from a teacher as I can imagine anyone being."

"There you go then." Gayle smiled sheepishly. "The precedent is already set. Oh, and...I'm working on a fourth member for our little faculty. To take on the firearms training long term."

"Do we need a fourth?" Michael asked.

"Yes," Gayle said firmly. "I want these kids to have the best in *every* aspect of their training."

Gayle was looking directly at Michael, her eyes locked with his. Lana had seen Gayle brow-beat people into submission before, but this was something very different. Her look was asking, not demanding. Michael nodded his approval, and Gayle smiled in return. A genuinely pleased smile.

"Thanks," she said softly. "I just wanted all of us to be on the same page."

"Can I ask who you have in mind?" Michael asked.

Gayle hesitated and bit her lip. "Do you mind if, just for the moment, I don't disclose that? I just...I'm not sure how my invitation is going to be received yet, so... Trust me, as soon as I know, I'll tell you."

Lana had a feeling Michael probably already knew who she had in mind.

"I trust you," he said, nodding promptly.

"Thank you."

"Okay then, if we're all done here, ladies..." Michael paused to allow either of them to interject if needed. "I need to go wrap up my class and hit the showers. I'll catch up with you at the daily debrief later, Gayle, and I'll see you in the morning, Captain Fordham."

"I look forward to it, Captain."

She waited until Michael was out of earshot before turning to Gayle with a sly grin. So many questions, but somehow, they all got encapsulated into one catch-all query.

"What," she said with amusement, "was that all about?"

"What?" Gayle said blankly.

"When you came to the farm, you talked about Captain Michael Reynolds. What you didn't talk about was *Gayle* and Captain Michael Reynolds."

"There is no Gayle and Michael."

"Oh, but you want there to be."

"Fuck off," Gayle snorted.

Lana laughed, shaking her head. "You can deny it all you want. But just so we're on the same page...I think he likes you, too."

Gayle said nothing in response. Her eyes flicked downward as she reached a hand up to brush away a strand of hair that had fallen across her face.

"I did *not* make a good first impression. Nor second. I still feel like I'm on the back foot."

"He doesn't strike me as a man who bears grudges," Lana shrugged.

"I hope not..." Gayle said wistfully.

| 30 |

ALONE

– Kareena St. Claire –
– Thursday – Mont Tremblant, Pack Nation –

She sat cross-legged in the clearing that had been her home for the last five days, trying to get a handle on her new abilities and form a plan about what to do moving forward. She wanted to go home, to Domaine Saint-Bernard, but she knew that wouldn't be possible. As time passed, she realized that she would probably never go home again. Everyone there was dead

She was alone.

She closed her eyes and reached out with all her senses. Senses that had once threatened to overwhelm her, she was now learning to control.

No.

Control was not the right word, not yet. Utilize was a better description for it.

Her former captors had tracked her here and loitered for a couple of days, acting like proud parents making sure that their offspring could survive in the wild without them. She had no idea what they had done to her, but she wasn't so deluded as to think that they were anything but the people who murdered her family. As it became clear that Kareena had no immediate intention of leaving the clearing, they eventually moved away and disappeared for a few days.

Now they were back.

Even at this distance, she could sense something different about them. He was unmistakable. The disgusting odor of malignant death still lingered on him, but she was more subtle. The faint whiff of musk, the remnants of intimacy with her partner. She loved him – it radiated from her like a beacon – but now there was also a sadness. Kareena tried to reach out with her abilities to find out why.

That was a mistake.

The thoughts crowded her mind again. The same sensory overload as before, it had her retching and vomiting as her head spun with new unfettered sensation. It was like her sense of smell and taste had been turned up to one hundred. Her eyesight was pin sharp, her hearing so hypersensitive the tiniest sound threatened to pitch her brain into a migraine. Her body was one huge delicate sensor array, and her brain needed an upgrade to cope with the information it was being sent. Or maybe it had been upgraded already. Maybe it just needed a reboot.

This new sense, the one she was using to pinpoint her pseudo-mother, was almost impossible to describe. She had taken to calling it her 'aura-sense'. If she closed her eyes and concentrated, she could *feel* all the living things around her. Every single one of them. It had taken a while to realize it was this perception that was making her vomit every time she stood still. Once she figured it out, though, she started to understand it, and found she could use it, if only in a passive way.

Using it aggressively...that was proving troublesome.

She took a deep breath, centered herself and calmed her mind as best as she could.

Don't force it. Let it come to you.

Her mind flashed to the others, the ones who were tracking her former captors. She had detected their presence earlier in the day, albeit at the extreme range of her senses. Yet despite the distance, she could read them with clarity.

One male and one female. They loved each other but not like her former kidnappers did. No, that wasn't quite right. One of them did...the male. She didn't feel the same, but there was also something else between them, something darker in color. Not hatred... Regret maybe? Kareena wished she had experienced more in her young life in order to be able to identify such emotions more distinctly.

They had been cautious to mask their tracking. Always downwind. She would never have known they were there without her newfound ability, and she was sure her former captors had no idea they were being shadowed. She sensed no animosity from them. Quite the opposite in fact. They felt...safe.

Kareena suddenly experienced a keen need to know who was following her and why.

She made a decision.

It was time to engineer a meeting between them.

| 31 |

NIGHTMARES

– Lana Fordham –
– Friday – London, England –

Tea.

What she *really* needed right now was a steaming mug of tea – two sugars and a splash of milk.

Third day back and she was trying hard to establish her old routine, including her early morning jog around the Academy estate. The golden shades of autumn colored its well-maintained gardens, providing a gorgeous backdrop to her exercise regime. Alas, this time of year in the United Kingdom also delivered frigid temperatures and a deceptively light drizzle, saturating a shivering Lana from head to toe as she jogged toward the Palace that promised shelter, a fresh towel, and a hot 'cuppa.'

"You're wet," Gayle muttered, barely glancing up from the tablet she was reading as Lana padded into the Officer's Lounge dripping a mixture of rain and sweat onto the polished wooden floor.

"Rain or shine, gotta keep in shape," Lana responded as she headed for the kettle and the assorted collection of colorful mugs. "You really should join me if you want to keep fitting into your CombatSkin."

Gayle sat sideways in one of the lush burgundy leather armchairs. Her legs were draped over one arm and dangling,

182

but in response to Lana's statement, she lifted her right leg by straightening it.

"Bad knee. Can't run."

"I'm sure a little light jogging wouldn't hurt," Lana retorted while pouring the hot water over the teabag and stirring.

"You sound like my physio." Gayle pouted, still not averting her gaze from her screen.

"Maybe you should listen to both of us then."

Her friend lifted a hand and made a 'yadda-yadda' gesture with it. Lana rolled her eyes and turned her attention back to the contents of her mug, fishing out the teabag and reaching for the milk.

"Anyway," Gayle continued, "I *never* gain weight no matter what I eat or do. It's my superpower."

"Lucky you," Lana grumbled, stirring in a pair of heaped teaspoons worth of sugar.

"Speaking of CombatSkins, we'll need to sort one out for you now that we've got them on order for the kids."

"No effing way," Lana protested as she slumped into the armchair opposite Gayle, being careful not to spill her tea. "I am not wearing one of those...unflattering skin-tight monstrosities."

"*Excuse* me," Gayle said, finally looking up from her screen. "I look fucking great in mine. Anyway, it's not negotiable. They will be required wear for combat missions."

"Screw that," Lana muttered and sipped from her mug.

Between the delicious beverage and the wood crackling in the fireplace, she started to feel a warmth spread through her. She sighed contentedly. Gayle's attention was firmly back on the screen she was holding, a serious look on her face.

"You okay?"

"Mmm," Gayle murmured distractedly.

"Come on," Lana pushed. "Spill it."

Gayle put the tablet down. Her face flickered with a look of conflict. Lana knew the expression. She was debating whether to come clean or just dodge the subject again. The former sentiment won out.

"I had this bright idea while lesson planning. The A-to-Z of vampires. First lesson is this afternoon."

Lana nodded in agreement with the plan. "Move through the species alphabetically?"

Gayle nodded.

"That sounds like a sensible approach. So, you're starting with A for..." Lana trailed off as she processed the thought to its logical conclusion and realization dawned. "Ah. 'A' is for Adze."

"Yeah," Gayle said flatly, biting her lip.

There was a lull in the conversation for a moment and Lana searched for the right thing to say. "Still having the nightmares?"

Gayle shook her head slightly, paused, and then changed it to a small nod.

"No...yeah. Sometimes. Not as often lately. But sometimes when I do, I..." she took a deep breath and exhaled it slowly. "You know, Lana, I don't know if I could ever face them again."

"You've just got to remember that *you* came out of Valletta alive," Lana leaned forward. "*You* survived."

"But that's the whole problem. I survived, but I don't *remember* it at all. Nothing after the initial attack. I've listened to Amanda's recount of what happened. I've read the reports, but...it's not real to me because I don't recall it. Not any of it until I woke up onboard Lizzie."

The HMS *Queen Elizabeth*, one of five aircraft carriers in the Royal Navy's fleet. The oldest of the five, but the one that generally supported HFA operations. She had been their base of operations for the Malta mission.

Gayle had been in a fugue state when they brought her and Amanda Forrester – the only survivors of the disastrous mission – back to the carrier. She was mostly unresponsive, and if she did respond, she was...confused. Seeing her like that horrified Lana, but after a few days, this state gave way to something even more distressing. Depression, uncontrollable weeping, and grief. An overwhelming sense of shame that she had somehow survived when her team – her friends – hadn't.

Then...the anger.

When Gayle visited her at the farm, Lana felt apprehensive about who she would see. To find her friend almost back to normal had been a relief. She could still see the scars, and not just the physical ones, but there was real progress in her becoming whole again.

"You'll remember. In time." Lana tried to put some measure of comfort into her words.

Gayle simply looked at her. "Do I want to? If what I see in my nightmares is even half true...they're memories I don't want, Lana."

"I'll take the class for you—" Lana hadn't even finished the sentence before Gayle was shaking her head.

"No. It's mine to teach," she said decisively.

"Why don't you start with something more...benign? Shadow-wraiths are cool."

"Then it would be a shitty A to Z, wouldn't it?" Gayle shook her head. "No, I'll do Adze."

"You're sure?" Lana asked.

Gayle nodded and took a deep breath. "Yeah, I gotta face up to it sometime."

"Okay, then I'll be there with you," Lana said firmly.

"You don't have to—" Gayle began, but Lana cut her off with an even firmer interruption.

"No arguments," she said. "Give me twenty to wash up and change and then we'll go over the lesson plan together. Okay?"

Gayle's look conveyed both her gratitude and relief. "Thanks," she responded, almost apologetically.

| 32 |

ADZE

– Gayle Knightley –
– Friday – London, England –

Okay. Suck it up and accept your fate, Gayle. You're a teacher now.

"There are dozens of old movies and TV shows that talk about Vampires. From Buffy the Vampire Slayer through Twilight, to Underworld and its sequels. Believe me...I've seen them all."

The cadets looked at her blankly. To be fair to them, Gayle had always been in a geek-minority – old films and TV were a hobby of hers. At least they'd gotten the Harry Potter references in Monday's class.

"Regardless," she said swiftly moving on, "all *you* need to know is that they're all bullshit. If you think, like I did at your age, that you can research what you're going to face by watching TV and movies...you're *woefully* mistaken.

"You know monsters are real, but in your minds they're abstract concepts. You've never seen one in the flesh. Since the Purification and the erection of the Bulwarks, the United Kingdom is a monster-free zone. No Werewolves. No Vampires. Just Humans and a handful of Fae. Our borders are carefully monitored to keep it that way.

"This class is aimed at trying to make the abstract into something...tangible."

She waited for a moment, making sure they were focused on her.

The class held their collective breath.

Now that I have your attention...prepare to have your minds well and truly blown.

"Vampires," she said slowly, "are the tip of the iceberg, and they're not even a single species in themselves. The term '*vampire*' does not refer to a creature – it's a *genus*. A type. Like the word dog or cat, it describes the animal but not the breed. Here's something to think about...there are over *forty* different types of Vampire alone."

She paused for effect.

"That's more than forty types of just *one* of the monsters you actually *know* about. And this is the *first* five minutes of your *first* lesson. Just take a moment to contemplate what else you don't know."

Twelve youthful faces all stared at her with eyes wide, more than a hint of trepidation and fear etched on their features.

Good. They should be afraid.

Her job was to slowly expose them to the truth of the world they lived in. To get them ready to survive in it. If they weren't afraid, then she wasn't doing her job properly.

"We live in a world inhabited by gods and monsters. Where every inch is fought for with tooth and claw. Where humanity is outgunned and outnumbered to a *hilarious* degree and where *we* are the thin line that protects them.

"While I *will* help you hone your skills and maximize your potential, there are creatures out there who are stronger and faster than you will *ever* be individually. Your strength will lie in being a team."

One hand rose hesitantly.

"Yes, Ms. Jiminez?" she nodded toward the young girl with the long jet-black hair, the one for which she had already decided on the call sign 'Raven.'

Isabella Jiminez hesitated for a moment, seemingly looking for the right way to phrase her question.

"Did this...all of this, frighten you when you were—?"

"No," Gayle interrupted quickly. "But it should have."

She took a deep breath before continuing.

"We didn't know any better," she said softly. "But you...you get the benefit of having had us blaze that trail for you. We found the potholes in the road you're about to travel, and we can teach you how to avoid them.

"So, here's your first lesson...every single one of the races we're going to teach you about should be treated with *respect*. Because every single one of them has the power to kill you in a *heartbeat*."

She felt her jaw tense and clenched her fist tightly, feeling the clammy sweat of fear on the palm of her hand. Where was Lana?

"No, I wasn't scared of them then," Gayle continued, shaking her head. "The 137th Hunters *were* that thin line of defense, and we were fucking *good* at it. We vanquished monsters, slayed beasts, and went toe to toe with beings that thought they were gods. But...*we* never gave them the respect we should have. We thought we were invincible. Losing – on the rare cases it happened – felt like an aberration. Our invincibility was an illusion."

Shattered in one single, bloody day.

She swallowed the lump in her throat before continuing, trying to hide the crack in her voice.

"I will not allow you the liberty of such illusions. Death is *always* one tiny mistake away. One tick of the second hand. Out there you don't get second chances. You only get one."

She walked around behind her desk and faced the class.

"So...Vampires. They do *not* sparkle, and if any of you even mention how garlic would be an effective weapon...I'll send you out there armed with nothing but a few cloves and a bottle of holy water and see how long you last."

An uneasy ripple of laughter went around the class. Gayle didn't smile. She waited until she was sure she had their attention before clicking the stylus to change the image on the screen at the front of the class.

"Especially," she said as the first image appeared, "if you're facing one of these."

Gayle didn't look at the screen, she didn't need to. Their

horrific visage was burned vividly into her memory, a vision she revisited almost every night in her sleep. Roughly human-oid, the monster stood tall and willowy with skin the color of midnight and giant almond-shaped eyes that swam a milky white. A flattened nose with oversized nostrils loomed above a nightmarish mouth filled with rows of sharp, piranha-like teeth. As if that wasn't terrifying enough, a pair of curved fangs, three inches long, protruded menacingly from the upper jaw.

"Today, we start your Vampire breeds with A..." she took a breath, "for Adze."

A bitter anger surged inside her.

"There are *many* monsters in this world. All shapes and sizes," Gayle continued in a low tone. "But these...these are the ones that should be giving you nightmares. The ones that should be scaring you *shit-less*."

Because they scare the shit out of me.

"With that in mind..." She prodded the stylus again.

Gayle had dimmed the smart-glass windows prior to the class beginning and, as the lights went out and the screen went dark, the room was plunged into a sudden twilight. A murmur of surprise went around the class as she waited patiently for their eyes to adjust to the new ambient light level. A palpable sense of fear filled the room as the tension ratcheted up a notch. Each of the cadets wondering what was coming next.

This was her strategy.

In order to respect this monster, you *needed* to be afraid of it. A lesson Gayle had been taught in the cruelest of ways. Even knowing what was coming, she could feel her heart racing, her breathing quickening. The tiny stylus felt slippery in her sweaty palms. She adjusted her grip and tried to squash the feelings deep inside her. Memories threatened to surface and overwhelm her.

Had this been a dreadful mistake?

Maybe she wasn't ready to face this demon just yet.

She was starting to wonder how to perform a graceful exit from this strategy with her dignity intact when the classroom door slowly creaked open. In the dim light, Gayle made out the figure of Lana as she slipped through the door and into the darkened room. A subtle nod of solidarity in Gayle's direction as she headed to the back of the room buoyed Gayle's confidence.

"For Adze, sunlight is exceedingly painful; they avoid it at all costs, nesting in dark places. Look around the room – can you see your classmates?" she asked in a low voice. "Make out their features?"

She walked slowly and quietly between the desks toward the rear of the room, returning Lana's nod as she approached. Her friend brushed a finger across the small glass control panel next to her on the wall, and the already tinted windows darkened further still. Only the vague featureless silhouettes of the cadets could be seen now.

"How about now?" Gayle asked quietly as she walked, her heels tapping rhythmically on the floor. She could feel her students following the sound of her footsteps and extending their other senses to compensate for their impaired visibility.

Excellent.

"*This* is your nightmare scenario – a light level so low you can barely see. Where you must rely on your other senses to compensate. To an Adze, this is akin to broad daylight. Their eyes are designed for this. They see better in these conditions than we do during the day. *This* is their comfort zone, their *preferred* battleground.

"Now, if you'll turn your attention to the display screen..."

It was Teyah who screamed first, but she wasn't the only one. Each member of the class either shrieked, screamed, or gave a high-pitched, cursed exclamation. Dylan and Florian both fell out of their seats. Wesley pushed backward on his chair so fast he tumbled to the floor in an undignified tangle of legs – both his and the seat's.

Glowing in the twilight at the front of the class was an Adze. Its milky, oversized eyes drew their immediate attention to its face and the nightmarish fangs that glistened with saliva. The sharp claws capping its long gangly arms went almost completely unnoticed.

The life-sized holographic representation started a slow, menacing advance, its horrifying head turning from side to side, regarding each student as it walked by. It moved with a discontinuous staccato that looked like a stop motion effect. Teyah and Alexandre, who had been sitting at the front of the class, stumbled out of their seats terrified, backing hurriedly away. Behind her, Gayle heard Lana inhale sharply at the sight of the harmless, yet unnervingly accurate, depiction of the nightmarish monster.

Gayle felt herself shaking. Her heart thumping hard against her ribcage as unwanted memories flooded back. She jumped almost imperceptibly as she felt Lana's hand squeeze her shoulder softly. A gesture of solidarity and comfort.

You can do this.

"Obviously," she said, her throat dry, "they don't glow in the dark when they hunt you in real life. They'll be hidden in the shadows and you won't see them till you feel their claws tearing your flesh, their teeth sinking into your throat. *Then* you'll see their ugly fucking faces..."

She stopped as a boiling sea of anger started to bubble within her. She took a calming breath.

"There is *one* other thing that stops this from being a completely accurate representation of what it's like to hunt Adze..." she paused as she triggered the next surprise. "Adze are *never* alone."

They dropped from the ceiling and crawled out from beneath desks. A dozen or more of the terrifying creatures invaded the classroom with seemingly murderous intent, their claws and fangs flashing in the shadows. Gayle could feel the terror in the room. Her own heart was racing, her hands shaking. Enough was enough – she froze the holograms in their tracks, leaving them as chilling portraits of impending death.

She knew that there was no way these collections of photons could physically hurt her, but it still took a phenomenal act of courage for Gayle to walk through them to the front of the room.

"They are the ultimate pack hunters. They bait you, draw you in, and surround you before you're aware of how foolish you've been. That lone rogue Adze you were hunting has fifty friends all waiting in the shadows.

"They're agile, extremely swift, and light on their feet. They make no sound when they move. In Africa, they call them 'Kifo cha Kimya' – *'The Silent Death.'*"

"If they're so silent," Teyah asked, a quiver of fear still evident in her voice, "then how do they co-ordinate attacks like this?"

Gayle was impressed and made a mental note about the young girl's ability to think analytically under pressure.

"Good observation. Look at their mouths – what do you see?"

"Teeth," said Darius. He sounded surprisingly calm. "Lots of teeth."

"Look closer," Gayle answered simply.

The superior ability to think, evaluate, and adjust strategy on the fly was, in Gayle's opinion, the trait that had separated her own team from Torbar's. The 136th Terminators had all been ex-military, regimented and set in their ways. Gayle would not spoon-feed these kids the answers; she wanted them to process the information and draw their own conclusions.

Being smart. That would be their edge.

"Wide mouths...odd jawline," Darius mused.

"With fangs that long, how does it talk?" Teyah offered her thoughts. "How does it eat?"

"Like a snake?" Darius shrugged.

An emerging rivalry was becoming evident for the role of squad leader. Her heart ached as she flashed back to her training days and the competition between herself and Gabriel.

"Gold stars to both of you." Gayle nodded, motioned to Lana to raise the light level a little, and then gestured toward the closest hologram. "The lower jaw *can* move independently from the top jaw. Gives them a sizeable bite radius, but as far as we can tell, it removes their ability to manipulate their lips and tongues to form meaningful sounds like a language."

"No words at all?" Teyah asked.

"All we've ever heard from them is hissing, like snakes,"

Lana said, moving to join Gayle at the head of the class. "So, that said, if they don't talk, then how *do* they communicate?"

"Telepathy?" Darius theorized.

"One theory," Gayle nodded. "It's hard to know for sure. But before the '*Treaty of Nexus*' banned it, dissection of deceased Adze showed an area of the brain that is significantly more developed than its Human equivalent. Many scientists believe it is a telepathic transmitter-receiver. However, there is another competing hypothesis...if anyone wants to hazard a guess."

"The nose, or lack of one," Andrea Campbell chimed in, "flattened with oversize nostrils, suggests a larger than normal olfactory sense."

"That's quite the observation, Andrea..." Gayle said with a twitch of her eyebrows.

"My mother is an evolutionary biologist and my father is a geneticist," Andrea shrugged. "I've studied a little of both myself."

Gayle already had a firm hunch about where *her* specialist skills would lie.

"Some think they communicate via smell, or maybe by releasing pheromones or body chemicals," she nodded. "There *is* a precedent for it in our own biology as hybrids. I'm sure some of you know what I'm talking about."

A few of the students started to look distinctly uncomfortable, and it reminded Gayle that this was a subject she would need to discuss with Michael as a matter of priority. Teenagers and pheromones. Nobody had been there for Gayle and her team when they were going through this, and it led many of them down a dark and self-destructive path. These kids would get all the help they needed to understand their biology and avoid the same fate.

"Though *our* ability to produce pheromones..." she said, hoping to alleviate the guilt in the room, "is mostly involuntary."

"What we *do* know," Lana moved the subject along quickly, "is that the Adze perform more like insects. They don't build houses or run governments. They only operate rudimentary technology that they inherit or steal. They don't create art or pursue science. They have a hive mentality..."

"...and, like insects, they all revolve around a queen," Gayle stated.

"Or a king," Lana finished.

"True," Gayle nodded. "Adze culture doesn't seem to distinguish between a patriarchy and a matriarchy. The strongest leads, regardless of sex."

"Kill the king or queen and the rest of the Adze in that hive generally become uncoordinated and easy pickings," Lana continued. "Problem is hives often contain hundreds, if not thousands, of Adze, and they ferociously protect their leaders with their lives."

"So how do you beat them?" Teyah asked curiously.

"You don't," Lana shrugged. "The mega-hives of Africa are long-established now, and far too large. They're totally off limits. If you want to wipe one out, it requires airstrikes and artillery...the big guns. Occasionally we may be called in to mop up the stragglers, but most often our job is to tackle 'start-up' hives."

"What's a start-up hive?" Payge asked.

"Sometimes the king or queen might be challenged," Gayle explained. "A fight for leadership ensues and the loser is evicted from the hive. Often, they will go on to establish their own start-up hive. We can nip these in the bud before they grow too large."

Gayle closed her eyes. Valletta was supposed to have been a start-up hive.

"We call them 'bug-hunts,'" she finished. "But they are *not* jobs to be taken lightly."

Gayle shuddered as she glanced at the hologram of the Adze. A part of her was proud for facing her fear today, yet she was afraid that the nightmares would haunt her more than ever tonight. With a touch of a button, the holograms disappeared and the lights in the classroom came back up.

"Okay, so..." she said, trying to convey a strength she didn't truly feel. "Let's learn how to kill one of these revolting bastards, shall we?"

| 33 |

CROSSROADS

– Zarra Anderson –
– Saturday – Mont Tremblant, Pack Nation –

Zarra raised a hand, bringing them to a halt.

"Trail splits," she said quietly.

They had worked diligently to close the gap to their quarry over the last few days, but this latest turn of events only added to the questions that were rattling around in Zarra's head regarding Kareena and her pursuers. She knelt to closely inspect the ground.

"They ain't far ahead..." she muttered. "Our girl is still headin' south-west, but the others are now headin' southeast. Why ain't they followin' her anymore?"

"How far from the border are we?"

Alex padded closer to allow Zarra access to his pack containing the handheld GPS tracker, which she quickly removed. With a few deft strokes of her fingertips, she brought up their current location on the tiny screen.

"Fuck, we're close..." she muttered with a shake of her head. They were less than five miles from the border with New Victus. "We need to intercept her before she crosses over."

"No," Alex snarled. "We turn east and follow our targets. That's the mission."

"No, Alex, it's not. I'm gettin' paid to bring Kareena home. The termination option for the other two is a side package."

"Our mission is to track and eliminate the rogue."

"Maybe that was your *original* mission," Zarra retorted, feeling the anger rise in her again, "but events since then changed things somewhat, dontcha think? You really believe Dane gives a rat's ass about some errant sex-Wolf and his Vampyrii slut right now? From the moment he saw what happened at Domaine Saint-Bernard, this became a rescue mission for Kareena St Claire. That's why I'm here."

Alex didn't answer and Zarra felt a tiny surge of victory.

"Fine. But we do this quick. Get her safely with Becka on your ship and then we double back and pick up the scent on the others again. You've seen what they're doing, we can't leave them running free."

"Fair enough," she nodded. A little more cash in their pockets was fine with her. "I'll help ya eliminate them *after* we get Kareena to safety."

She shut off the GPS tracker and slotted it back into his pack.

"Let's go then." Zarra broke into a jog, tracing the direction that Kareena had headed.

The young girl was no soldier, she had no concept of stealth. Her flight took her on a haphazard path through the forest leaving a trail of broken undergrowth in her wake. A thought crossed Zarra's mind – was it too indiscriminate? Did she *want* to be followed?

After an hour, Zarra slackened their pace. Kareena had slowed herself and was now only just ahead of them. What sort of state, mentally and physically, would they find her in? Hungry and exhausted certainly. Scared maybe. Apprehensive at best. It was imperative to keep her calm when they finally confronted her.

Alex stopped abruptly in his tracks ahead of her, head tilted, ears upright like a pair of furry radar dishes. They twitched as he scanned forest, listening intently for something. Zarra looked at him quizzically, indicating she wanted to know what he was listening for.

"I thought..." he growled hesitantly.

Zarra strained her own ears, but all she could detect were

the sounds of nature common to the forest. Nothing out of the ordinary.

"...a repulsor-lift or something," Alex continued. "Like the engines on the *Diana*, but a long way off."

"Can't be *Diana*," Zarra mused. "Becka shouldn't be anywhere near here. Commercial flight maybe?"

She could see his amused mockery of her suggestion even on his canine features.

"Over this airspace? With repulsor-lifts?"

"Point taken."

Commercial aircraft here were still old-fashioned jets; neither Pack Nation nor New Victus had expensive repulsor-lift technology. They also never flew this close to the border due to the multitude of concealed anti-aircraft stations hidden on both sides. The possibility of creating an international incident was high if their flightpath erred even a little.

"Maybe I imagined it..." Alex shook his head as if to clear it. "Anyway, I propose that I circle ahead to get out in front of Kareena. Let her run straight into me, then you move around the rear and—"

"—and that's a real bad idea," Zarra interrupted. "Alex, she's an eighteen-year-old girl who has been savagely, possibly sexually, assaulted. She's been chased for days through miles of forest by her abductors...one of which happens to be a Wolf. What d'ya think her reaction is gonna be when you spring out of the undergrowth in front of her?"

She watched Alex think for a moment.

"Yeah," he growled slowly, "maybe you should take point on this one."

"Ya'think?"

"Just go."

"Stay close an' wait for my signal," Zarra ordered. "Do *not* break cover till I give the all clear."

He didn't respond, just started stalking slowly in the direction of Kareena.

"I mean it, Alex!"

They were dealing with the psyche of a young girl who was already in a delicate state. This was no time for Alex to display his impulsive side. He regarded Zarra, his face contorted by a disgruntled snarl.

"I'm better at this than you give me credit for, Zarra."

"Fine," they didn't have time to argue. "Call Becka. Get her to relay a message to Damian. Tell him to call Lyssa Balthazaar, let her know where we are and the anticipated co-ordinates of her sister's crossing point into New Victus if they continue movin' south-east. Maybe they can intercept them if we can't."

For a moment she thought Alex was going to protest, but he simply nodded then disappeared into the forest.

The hunt had been Zarra's life for the past four years. She knew how to stay hidden from her quarry. Keep her distance, stay upwind. Don't be seen, heard, or smelled. She had diligently obeyed all the rules. Why, then, were her instincts telling her that Kareena was *allowing* their approach? Engineering it. Had she slowed down because she knew that her former captors had given up their pursuit? Did she know that Alex and Zarra had been following her? All questions for another time; her current priority was to get Kareena to safety.

She circled discreetly so that she was ahead of Kareena and found a modest clearing on her trajectory that she felt would make for a suitable meeting spot. It wasn't long before Kareena broke casually through the tree line and into the glade. Her body language was subtly defensive, but the lack of surprise on the girl's features confirmed Zarra's earlier hunch.

It was unquestionably the girl from the photographs she had seen in Domaine Saint-Bernard. She was naked as a newborn, allowing Zarra to also do a cursory inspection of her condition. Slender, perfect flawless skin, perky in all the right places, not a blemish on her... A tiny smidgen of envy set in, but then Kareena *was* half her age, not even out of her teens. The perfection of youth was to be expected...

Yet the closer Zarra looked, the more it seemed like something was...wrong.

If anything, Kareena looked *too* perfect. She wasn't *just* slender, she was athletic. She wasn't *just* perky and blemish-free, she was muscular and toned. And while Zarra was nursing multiple tiny wounds to her face and hands where errant flora snagged her on her way through the forest, Kareena's skin was utterly flawless. How was it possible that despite days of running naked through the forest, she had not sustained so much as a scratch?

Kareena was observing her with the same scrutiny, evaluating her. Was she trying to decide if Zarra was a threat from which she needed to run? Zarra stood motionless, trying not to make any gesture that could be misconstrued as a threat. She held her hands outstretched and open, demonstrating she had no malicious intent, whilst summoning up her warmest and most soothing voice.

"Kareena St. Claire? My name is Zarra. You can trust me, so please, stay calm. I'm just here to help you. Just to help, okay?"

Her words and tone seemed to have the desired effect. Though Kareena didn't alter her defensive stance, she did at least refrain from fleeing. It was a promising start.

"I know ya been runnin' for over a week now. Runnin' from the people who did this to you. I'm here to ensure your safety. To bring you back..." she almost said home, but after seeing what had happened to the girl's parents and family, she avoided lying to her, "...to somewhere safe."

The girl eased her stance a little but still didn't say a word. She appeared willing to listen, but her face still held a guarded look and her eyes darted around assessing escape options. The kid-gloves needed to stay on, at least for now.

"Kareena, please try to stay calm. I need to tell you that I work with a partner," Zarra slowly beckoned in the direction of the woodland with her hand. "He's still in the forest, out of sight. He won't come out till I tell him to. Only when I'm totally sure everything here is cool. I'm tellin' you this so there are no nasty surprises. He's a Wolf...but he is *not* the one who did this to you. You have absolutely nothing to fear from him. Do you understand?"

Kareena hesitated, her eyes flicking toward the tree line momentarily. Finally, she nodded abruptly.

"I know," she said quietly. "I knew you were coming. Knew

you were following me."

"We came to rescue you," Zarra said softly.

"My mother would talk of the Wolf, how you would protect us. But you didn't." There was a tone of accusation in Kareena's voice. "Where were you when the other Wolf attacked us?"

"I'm sorry we weren't there then," Zarra apologized. "But we're here now."

"Are you..." Kareena hesitated. "Are you taking me home?"

Zarra didn't want to lie to her. The girl was intuitive, and her instinct said that honesty was the best policy here. She needed to establish a level of trust that would allow Kareena to come willingly with them and board *Diana* without her, so that she could be taken to safety while they hunted down Vanessa and her paramour.

"Kareena," using her name again to establish familiarity. "Honey, we can't take you home. I think you know why. Your parents, I'm sorry, but they're gone. Those that did this to you...they..."

"I know," Kareena said sadly. "I know. I was just...hoping."

"I'm so sorry, honey," was all Zarra could say.

"*They* called me 'Honey'..." Kareena started.

"Who did?" Zarra asked gently. "Your parents?"

"The monsters. She said she wanted children..." Kareena continued. "They said I was *their* daughter. They called me Honey. They told me my sister Autumn was dead...but I've never had a sister..."

"Kareena," Zarra addressed her by name again, trying to pull her from her reverie. "None of that was real..."

Kareena's eyes flicked to Zarra's, but the girl seemed to look right through her.

"They said they would give me a brother..." she said quietly. "I always wanted a brother..."

"Please...come with us," Zarra pleaded gently.

"Come where?" Kareena's eyes snapped into focus again. "Where will I go?"

"Right now, Kareena, my *top* priority is to get you to safety."

"Safety..." Kareena started hesitantly. "Something is coming..."

"I don't understand..." Zarra said with gentle confusion.

The tree line burst open abruptly, and a huge black Wolf charged out into the clearing, scrabbling to a halt to face Zarra.

"Goddammit, Alex..." Zarra turned on him angrily.

"Remember that noise I heard earlier?" he growled and looked up. "It's back. We got incoming!"

She heard it, too – the low whine of repulsors, much lower pitched and quieter than *Diana*'s. Her head followed the others and the moment her eyeline hit the sky, she saw it come into view. A dark gunmetal grey and while it was shaped in a configuration and size comparable to *Diana*, that was where the similarity ended.

Zarra had always loved her own ship and its sleek lines, but this was on a different level of design. It looked like it was one cohesive skin – no welds or visible panel joins. The canopy was iridescent, like an insect's eyes. It pivoted in a way that Zarra immediately perceived as threatening, the long tail tipping upward and the snout down. As she thumbed the releases for her pistols and began to draw, she saw Kareena break into a run in her peripheral vision. Her guns were almost clear of their holsters and she had thumbed the safeties off when it happened.

A low-pitched noise, like a large drum being hit just once. There was no projectile, but something seemed to hit the ground between the three of them. It felt like a bomb blast going off, but without the fiery explosion. Just a wave of concussive force that threw Zarra about fifteen yards through the air like a ragdoll. She was out cold before she hit the ground.

Consciousness came back to her with a nasty headache and a ringing of the ears, and even through her shuttered eyelids, the sunlight stabbed at her like tiny daggers. Her brain hurt.

She groaned and tried to sit upright, but her stomach muscles screamed in protest, so she slowly rolled over onto her front instead. Everything hurt down the front of her body where she had taken the impact of whatever weapon she had been hit with. It felt like every inch of her skin was bruised.

Something was oozing down her face from her nose; she could feel it on her lip, and a quick flick of her tongue confirmed the presence of blood.

What the hell just happened?

| 34 |

FEMINAM LUPUS

– Kareena St. Claire –
– Saturday – Mont Tremblant, Pack Nation –

She ran.

She seemed to be doing a lot of that lately.

As a little girl, she had always loved to be outdoors. She hated being cooped up inside, so come rain or shine, she would be chasing adventures in the forest. Like a pioneer or explorer, she would obsessively catalogue the flora and fauna with her own ingenious names. Like *rangleplants* and *sticky-grass*. Who needed to know their real names when it was so much more fun to invent them? Days were far too short for her inquisitive mind. There was too much in this world to discover, and not enough time to see it all.

So, she ran.

Around the lake, through the forest and along the dirt tracks. Up the mountain and down again. She chased the deer and followed the river. It filled her with joy. Inspired a passion that delivered vivid experiences and overflowed her brain with endorphins.

To run was to be free, to feel, to experience.

Then the monster came, and she ran for her life. A flight fueled by terror; a heart beating out of her chest and a feast of adrenaline surging through her veins.

After her rebirth, it had been a journey of freedom and discovery. An exhilarating headlong dash through the forest while learning to see from a new perspective.

When she met Zarra, for a fleeting moment she almost believed that her flight was over. Of course, she was wrong. Running was a part of her life, always had been. It was as inevitable as the sunset. This time, it was different again, though. This time *she* was the hunter. This was *fight*, not *flight*.

And it was exhilarating!

Make no mistake – though the flyer was chasing her, *she* was the one on the hunt, leading them unwittingly toward the perfect moment for her to strike. No longer was she the helpless young waif of a girl being pursued by scary monsters. Now *she* was the thing that her pursuers should be afraid of, and she could sense that fear coming off them in palpable waves.

She relished the feeling of being the woodland's newest apex predator.

The queen of the forest.

She felt bad for Zarra and her Wolf friend. She truly wished they had been able to help her. She desperately wished she could go home, see her parents and her friends again. But death had come for them that day, and Kareena had been forced to grow up quickly over the last week. She knew there was nothing to go back to and she was grateful to Zarra for telling her the heart-breaking truth. Most people would have lied in order to placate her, but with that simple and honest gesture, she had earned Kareena's trust.

I hope we meet again, Kareena thought sincerely, though she knew it was unlikely.

Kareena knew that the flyer was there for her. She was the target, not them. Zarra and her friend would simply be collateral damage. She tried to repay their honesty and trust by leading the attackers away. The thought flushed her with a peculiar sense of pride. They'd come to rescue her, but now she could be *their* protector.

The flyer had given immediate pursuit, as expected. Kareena instinctively knew she couldn't fight them until they relinquished the high ground. She had to find a way to remove that advantage. She rushed headlong through the trees, hunting for deeper cover that would force them to face her on her terms.

The aircraft carried eight plus the pilot; she could see them all as clear as day with her new senses. They were soldiers, but they were anxious. Afraid. Of her certainly, but also of something – or maybe someone – else. Her mind was filled with questions.

Who were these people?

Why were they so terrified of failing?

Why, when she was so close to freedom, was she now being chased all over again?

You only went to this much effort when something was important. Or valuable. So, which was she? Important? Valuable? Or both?

Their auras were familiar...

Vampyrii.

Kareena heard stories about them but had never seen one until the hood was torn from her head and she saw those elegant, razor-sharp teeth, scarlet with her own blood. She mimicked the motion she had seen her captor use – flicking her tongue across the tip of her own canines. The points felt sharp. Honed to a perfect edge and designed for...what?

She still didn't truly understand what had been done to her in that cold, dark cave. She knew she had been bitten by Wolf and Vampyrii both and was forever altered. Her body, her senses, *everything* was different now.

Human no more.

The density of the forest had increased to a point where the canopy shaded her from direct sunlight. This was the spot; they would *have* to come to her now. She stopped, turning her face upward, eyes firmly closed. Her body tensed, but her breathing was slow and methodical. She reached out with her senses. Searching.

She didn't have to wait long.

Noises in the leaves above her, a rustling. She opened her eyes to see dark metallic objects tumbling toward the ground like ripened fruit. She was no expert on munitions, but she recognized grenades when she saw them. They bounced off the forest floor in a circle around her, a pattern designed to hem her in. Instincts kicked in, and powerful leg muscles propelled her some twenty feet straight up into the branches from which the grenades had just fallen.

She grasped the closest limb, anchoring herself with those still unfamiliar claws. Tiny, diamond-hard daggers extending an inch or so from each fingertip. As the grenades started to detonate, a surge of triumph flooded her brain. She had dodged their trap.

Her victory was short-lived.

There was no explosive devastation as the grenades detonated. They weren't bombs; they were devices designed to disorient in a multitude of ways. Strobing flashes of light, a cacophony of high-pitched noises, and a thick, billowing toxic smoke. It felt like being trapped in a thundercloud during a storm. Kareena winced as the assault on her senses made her head spin. She lost her grip, tumbling toward the ground as she screwed her eyes tightly closed and squeezed her hands over her ears.

Then something unexpected happened.

Instinct took over once more, but this time it wasn't just claws that manifested themselves. The noise abated as there was a change in her ears and, as she kept her eyes firmly closed, her other senses took over. She tilted her head up in the direction of the flyer and watched the soldiers confidently begin their assault, rappelling from their flyer on thin strands of cord. They expected to take Kareena with minimal resistance, safe in the knowledge that their devices would have rendered her confused and distressed. Such confidence was woefully misplaced. Their careful camouflage and their combat tricks meant nothing to her. With her new senses, she could see through their smoke just as well as they could with their fancy electronics.

Kareena was at no disadvantage. On the contrary.

The living energy of the forest was laid bare to her, ebbing and flowing. It's movement through the trees, from the tip of each root to the fan of each leaf, played out in a pleasant pastel cerulean. Each blade of grass underfoot pulsed a slightly darker shade, almost indigo, where her footfalls had compressed their delicate structures. Through this prism, Vampyrii were beautiful to behold. Like a neon light in the darkness, they shimmered a bright gold on the multi-hued symphony of blue.

She didn't stop to comprehend exactly what she was seeing or how she was seeing it; it just felt second nature to her now. As her adrenaline flowed, her perception of the world shifted. She was moving faster, processing thoughts and visuals with astonishing celerity. The Vampyrii were moving in slow motion by comparison.

The first one hit the ground, poised for combat. He looked straight at her through the smoke. Evidently the inorganic nature of metal didn't register on her new senses, but she could tell by his posture and the distinctive curve of his finger that he was brandishing a weapon. A pistol of some sort. She saw the twitch of his forefinger and the tell-tale jerk of the recoil on his hand.

She dodged left, as the projectile tracked past her right shoulder. Her legs easily propelled her across the distance between them in one mighty jump as she screamed, something unintelligible and starkly terrifying. The song of her defiance, the roar that signified her arrival as a predator.

Kareena knew she was *not* a killer, but she felt a furious bloodlust begin to rise within her. A dark side of her that hadn't been there before. A beast that frightened her as much as it exhilarated her.

She crashed hard into the Vampyrii soldier, all brute force with little elegance. Her claws tore easily through his body armor like it was wet tissue paper, piercing his chest and reaching the hard bone of his sternum. Yet the beast inside her pushed further still, punching through his ribs like they were dried twigs. Suddenly, his heart was in her hand. She crushed it, horrified at her own actions.

That was simply the coup-de-grâce. Her left hand had slashed through his windpipe severing vital arteries. He was already promised to death as Kareena felt the final beats of his ruined heart pump raggedly in the palm of her hand.

As the last vestiges of his life slipped slowly away, the little girl within screamed with guilt and misery, momentarily seizing back control. Tears welled in her eyes, forcing their way past her screwed up eyelids to meander slowly down her cheeks. There was blood on her hands now. They had turned her into a killer, like those who had butchered her parents, her family.

This is your life now, the beast within growled. *Deal with it and move on.*

With that, Kareena was lost. She had seen the term 'out of body experience' in books she read over the years, but today she truly understood what that meant. Kidnapped by a dark part of her psyche that was now free to prowl, to hunt – and she reveled in it.

Her head snapped around, another enemy drawing the attention of her sinister alter ego. In her mind she screamed and begged for the violence to end, but dark-Kareena was already in fluid action.

Performing a low, supple pivot, she lashed out with feral grace, her claws slashing easily across the midriff of the female soldier who had been advancing on her. The soldier collapsed to her knees holding tightly to the wound before slumping sideways, her guts oozing through a series of parallel cuts torn through fabric and flesh in equal measure. Her death would be long, and painful.

The 'danse macabre' continued, another target and more instinctively choreographed countermoves. A low slide across the forest floor and an upward slash of the right hand that carved through the thigh of her next opponent severing the femoral artery. A fountain of blood sprayed free as her left hand drove into his neck and likewise sliced through his carotid.

She knew the names from a medical textbook she had found in one of the random boxes of goodies Uncle Thomas had brought back from one of his road trips. She had poured over the book repeatedly, thinking that perhaps there would be a future where she could learn medicine, to use this knowledge to benefit her little community. Now she was using it to be a better killing machine. The change to her physically was one thing, but to her mind and her values? Altering the things that made her what and who she was...that truly terrified her.

She cracked open her eyes. The strobing of the lights had thankfully subsided and the world now seemed oddly mundane. Just a few wisps of smoke and the distressing sounds of the wounded and dying. She stared at her blood-stained hands; crimson life gleamed on her arms soaking her almost to the elbows. She slowly looked down at her body to find it mottled with flecks of red, a flawless canvas splattered with the art of a killer.

What have I done?

On the ground sprawled the ruined bodies of seven Vampyrii. Seven visceral examples of her lethal and bloody handiwork. How was it possible that she couldn't even remember performing such an inhuman endeavor?

She fell to her knees alongside the closest as a sob wracked her throat. His face was a bloody mess of lacerations from her sharp talons, yet he was still alive and moving. She reached out and gently touched his face, feeling the blood slick on her fingertips.

"I'm so sorry..." she whispered hoarsely.

Lying next to him was another victim who had not been so fortunate. She lay in a gathering pool of her own blood; her shattered helmet lay a few feet away stained in gleaming burgundy. Her blonde hair matted and blood-soaked from the fatal injury inflicted to the nape of her neck. Through the torn and shredded remains of the flesh, Kareena could see the broken and mangled spinal column and knew without a shadow of doubt that it had been her hands that had inflicted such trauma without a pause for thought. The body twitched subtly, but the golden glow of life had already ebbed from her.

What have I become?

Something stung her left hip, a sharp pinprick just below her hipbone. Then another in the shoulder.

Seven victims.

There had been eight soldiers.

Her eyes flitted to the source of the pain in her thigh, a tiny dart jutted out from where its needle-like point had gained purchase in her flesh. As her hand scrabbled to yank it free from her skin, she could already feel the effects of the tranquilizer flooding her bloodstream and making her head swim dizzily. She winced as the nasty barbed end took with it a tiny hunk of flesh and skin, leaving a bleeding wound that instantaneously started to heal. Likewise, the dart in her shoulder resisted removal but eventually relented in the same self-mutilating manner.

The beast within her screamed with rage, trying to fight the influence of the drug. For a fleeting moment, she felt the effects start to subside, but even as her metabolism fought off the lethargy-inducing invaders in her bloodstream, her overlooked target hit her with yet more tiny darts. A shadowy abyss beckoned.

Dark-Kareena, however, had one last card to play.

Amongst the leaves and the pooling blood of her victims, a potent surge of endorphins dispatched her on a pleasure trip the likes of which she had never known. Almost orgasmic but more intense. She threw her head back in a mixture of pleasure and pain, her mouth agape and her eyes bulging. Kareena wondered what was happening, what madness was this, but then the transformation began.

She stared at her hands, watching them change their structure and appearance into what would have been an excruciating symphony of metamorphosis if not for the pain-killing, pleasure-inducing drugs pumping through her system. Bones cracked, grew and shrank, shuffled and reorganized. Her flesh stretched and contracted, muscles tearing and then mending themselves. It was then, as she watched the matt of soft fur grow swiftly across arms that were changing to forelegs in front of her disbelieving eyes, that she realized what she was.

But it was too late. Too many darts had now pumped their sleep-inducing payload into her body, and it was the sand and stone colored she-Wolf who fell to the ground unconscious.

| 35 |

TAKEN

– **Alex Newman** –

– *Saturday – Mont Tremblant, Pack Nation* –

Alex felt like his brain was trying to force its way out of his skull. A throbbing repetitive pounding made all the worse by the incessant ringing in his ears. He cracked his eyes open to witness a world that was spinning wildly, a disorientating shimmer of green and blue. It took a moment to recognize the sights as grass, trees, and sky blurring into one smeared canvas. It threatened to overwhelm the limited extent of what his senses could manage to process.

I'm gonna vomit...

He took a deep breath and squeezed his eyes closed again, trying to protect his scrambled mind.

A gentle hand caressed the soft fur of his neck. He didn't flinch. Her scent cut through the turmoil in his head, letting him know that the touch was safe and that she was alive. He forced his eyelids open a fraction and this time his view was filled with Zarra's worried face. She was mouthing something silently at him. He watched her closely, trying to read her lips. He couldn't make out all of it, but the last bit he recognized.

"Alex? Are you okay?"

He watched her shift position, grimacing with pain. There was blood on her face. He sniffed subtly – it was her own

blood. A nosebleed, already drying to flakes. He tried to articulate words, but they wouldn't come readily. She mouthed his
name again, then pointed at him before gesturing toward each
side of his head.

"Fix ya ears," she seemed to say.

Fix my ears?

It took a moment for his addled brain to catch up, but after
a moment he nodded his understanding. He closed his eyes
again, concentrating, willing the transformation that was
usually instinctual. Pain surged through his bruised and battered body, but as his fur began to recede, the endorphins
kicked in. Despite the numbing of his pain receptors, he
couldn't remember ever having suffered through such a trau-
matic change before. Shifting like this was not a panacea for
everything, but it was handy for healing minor injuries and
dispelling most aches and pains. With his now-Human ears,
he could finally hear again.

"Welcome back," Zarra said as she handed him the canteen
from her pack. He took a grateful gulp of the tepid water, observing her as he drank. Along with the bloody streaks on her
face, she was moving gingerly and in a very tentative manner.

"You look like how I feel," he croaked with a wry smile.
"Maybe you should—"

She cut him off with a dismissive wave of her hand. "I'm
fine. Battered and bruised...but fine. Look worse than I feel,"
she said with a forced smile.

Always the brave soldier, Alex thought, but didn't vocalize
the sentiment.

"How long?"

"Not sure," Zarra said thoughtfully. "Ten minutes, maybe
less. I'm a little fuzzy myself, to be honest."

"Sonic cannon," he muttered.

"Yeah. Whoever they were, they wanted Kareena alive. Are
you okay? You were closer to the hit than me."

"Just...sensitive ears." Alex rubbed his head, the headache
resurfacing. Apparently changing forms could only help so
much. "Other bounty hunters?"

"Nope. Job was mine, no competition," Zarra said shaking

her head in annoyance. "Two million credits...gone."

"Where is she?"

"She ran. I assume they've taken her by now," she said angrily.

Alex knew Zarra well enough to know it wasn't the lost revenue that she was angry about. Her anger came from a purer source.

"Can we track the ship?"

Zarra shook her head. "I called Becka the minute I came to. Ship must have been runnin' stealth because there wasn't a whisper of it on *Diana*'s sensors. Only one type of tech I know of that's that good..."

"Fae-tech," Alex finished.

Zarra nodded. "Ship flew in from the north," she said looking skyward for a moment, "so I assume – unless they turned around – that they're still headed south toward New Victus..."

"How the fuck did they find us?"

"All I got is guesses," Zarra shrugged. "I'm sure they weren't trackin' us, which means they're either trackin' Kareena somehow or..." she paused in thought for a moment, then tilted her head and continued. "Or it's the incubus."

"What makes you think that?"

"Everything that's happened...*he's* the catalyst. Vanessa, Kareena...neither of 'em ends up in this forest if not for him. That dropship made its move as soon as the two parties split. Coincidence?"

He shook he head, trying to clear it, but his brain wasn't up to analytic thinking. "So, what do we do now?"

"If you're feelin' well enough, I suggest we back-track and try to pick up the trail of Vanessa and her friend before they move too far afield. If he *is* in on the plan to snatch Kareena, then I, for one, want answers."

He watched as she pulled out her sidearms one by one, checking them to make sure that they still worked after the blast. He recognized the custom weapons and whistled in appreciation. She looked at him and smiled.

"F21 Freelancers. We didn't get *those* in the Army."

"The perks of mercs," she said with a chuckle. "When it's

your own cash, you can afford to buy the best."

"They as good as their reputation?"

"More reliable than most men I've dated." She snapped them back into their holsters, satisfied that they were still fine. "They've never let me down yet."

"You dual wield?" Alex nodded toward the fact that she wore one on each hip.

"Hell, no. I'm a hopeless shot with my right hand. But if I come up on a bounty looking badass, full of confidence and a sidearm on each hip, it makes them think twice before messin' with me. Sometimes...image is more important than reality. Most targets come peacefully if you show the right amount of swagger."

"And if they don't?"

"Well," she tilted her head as she replied, "then I shoot from the left hip and know I got a backup weapon on my right. It's been workin' out okay so far."

Alex pushed himself to his feet and adjusted the fit of his combat suit where it had ridden up a little on him post-transformation. Zarra handed him his pack from where it lay on the ground.

"You shifting back?" she asked.

"Four legs are better than two," he replied with a nod.

She ignored the subtle hint in the seemingly benign comment and started walking back into the forest in the direction from which they had come.

"Come on then, Furball," she said. "We got bounties to collect."

For the first time since she had dropped from the *Diana*, it truly felt a little like the old days.

As he shifted to his canine alter-ego, a toothy grin spread across his snout. This was *never* going to be the romance that he had once dreamt of – that ship had left port long ago – but maybe it *was* possible to at least ease back into the comfort of friendship.

Maybe.

| 36 |

BRIDGES

– Gayle Knightley –
– Saturday – London, England –

Gayle's cheerful state of mind turned immediately sour as she yanked open her front door from its sticky frame and saw her father standing behind her sister. Allyson smiled sweetly as Gayle's eyes flicked abruptly from her to their father and back again. She found herself emotionally torn. He had gone behind her back, a fact she was still angry about, yet she missed talking to him. A large part of her wanted nothing more than to put this mess behind them.

But she wasn't ready. Not yet.

She glared at her sister, who looked back with a blank stare of mock innocence. Gayle's own expression was far more overt.

I know what you're doing!

"Hello, Allyson," she said curtly. "Dad."

"Hi, Sis. Can we come in?" Ally replied nonchalantly.

Gayle didn't say a word, simply turned on her heel and strode back into the house leaving the door, which she had been tempted to slam, open for them to follow. She curled up into one of the lounge's over-sized armchairs and heard the front door close with a gentle click before Allyson entered the room slowly.

"Gayle, I know you're still angry at Dad—" She got no further before Gayle interrupted.

"Why on earth would I be angry?" she laughed bitterly. "Oh, you mean about having my dad and my uncle gang up to rail-road me into doing a job I really don't want to do and am not in the least bit suited for?"

She cast an accusatory look at her father.

"And then," she continued, "rather than just come face me alone, he drags my sister down here to try and placate me."

"We were hardly conspiring..." Jaymes said diplomatically.

Gayle was having none of it. "I don't want to hear it, Dad. You may be king of the diplomats up in Nexus City, but here you're just a dad dealing with a disgruntled daughter. I learned how to bend a narrative from watching you and Mum, so don't think you can pull that trick with me."

She knew her father was a great ambassador, but there was no way he could negotiate a truce between them by using the same tactics he used to suspend hostilities between two warring nations. This was parenting, and in parenting the rules were distinctly different. Especially when your child was old enough to stand up to you. This was her house, and it was her father who was in the wrong here.

Probably.

"And while we're on the subject," she added, "was Mum in on this, too?"

"Your mother...she..." he uncharacteristically stumbled over his words. "Well, she advised me to stay out of this."

"You should have listened to her."

"That...is very true," he admitted with a sigh.

He stood in the doorway, head bowed, and did something Gayle had rarely seen him do.

"I *am* sorry, Gayle."

He turned to move back toward the hall, then paused.

"What I did...I promise it came from a place of love. Perhaps today is not the right time for this." He glanced at his watch. "I have a meeting with your uncle this afternoon so...I'll leave you girls to it. Love you, Allyson, I'll see you at home later."

He hesitated for a moment; a small smile lifted the corners

of his mouth.

"Or at the SkyPort tomorrow afternoon," he finished.

Despite her annoyance, Gayle *almost* giggled. Her father knew his daughters well enough to understand that a Saturday night out would more than likely end up with the consumption of far too much alcohol in London's bars and clubs. The end result being that they would be getting their heads down just as the sun was coming up.

"Okay, Dad," Allyson said and kissed his cheek as he walked by.

"I love you, Gayle," were his final words as he looked back at his eldest daughter.

"I know," she replied and waved indifferently.

And with that, he left.

The sisters stared at each other as the front door squeaked in its frame and the gentle clunk of the latch indicated the departure of their father. Gayle felt a pang of guilt at having dismissed him in such a brusque manner. She was also self-aware enough to realize that she was blowing this a little out of proportion.

But he was the one person whom she had trusted not to go behind her back. She couldn't help but feel betrayed, even if he had done it with the best of intentions.

"Gayle," Allyson started, "I really do think..."

Gayle cut her sister off with a gesture.

"I don't want to hear it," she said with a sigh. "Dad and I will make up eventually, but for now, all I want to know, Allyson Evelyn Knightley, is are you here to bicker and fight? Or shall we indulge in playful shenanigans across old London town tonight?"

Allyson grinned wickedly.

| 37 |

THE PRISONER

– Sebastian StormHall –
– Saturday – Vermont, New Victus –

"What makes her so special?" Sebastian mused.

"We're still awaiting the DNA analysis," Dr Shauston commented, pushing his glasses up on his nose with his finger as they both looked at the unconscious figure of the mystery girl through the one-way glass. "That should tell us more."

The weight of urgency pressed upon him...time to find answers was running out. The girl was merely a package, and soon he would be contacted about making the promised delivery. At that juncture he would have no choice but to hand her over without any appreciable delay.

"Do we even know *who* she is?"

Shauston shook his head. "We know only that she is a Vampyrii-Wolf hybrid, which in itself is unusual—"

"But not unprecedented," Sebastian interrupted. "We've seen such individuals before; all it takes is for the Wolf to bite first. But I was specifically directed toward *her*, and I want to know why."

"I can wake her up. Maybe she can enlighten us. At least to who she is."

Sebastian shook his head. "No, Doctor, leave her under for now. I don't want to take the risk of her learning anything about me that she could relate to anyone else. Wait till I'm gone and then let her come around in her own time. See what she knows. Ask nicely...interrogation is not an option."

"She may not talk without...coercion."

"She will be in the hands of our benefactor very soon, Doctor. A good-natured conversation we can get away with, but if our patron were to discover that we actively interrogated our guest..." Sebastian let the sentence hang.

Benefactor.

In the early days of the War, the partnership had been a boon to his fortunes, both financial and political. He wouldn't be Grand Chancellor without her assistance decades ago, but she had been trading on that favor for years now. Truth was, it had been a *long* time since their arrangement had been beneficial toward Sebastian and his aspirations. It was a dynamic he intended to change.

To do so, however, would take careful planning. There would be a time for bold action, but for now he continued to whisper in the shadows. Biding his time. He didn't want her to know that he was looking into what her plans for this mystery girl might be. Hence, for this endeavor, the only people who had seen the girl were the soldiers who had captured her, and Dr Shauston. The circle had been kept deliberately small and trusted, which presented its own challenges, such as the aforementioned delay in getting any swift testing done through the laboratories. So be it. Sebastian knew he would rather err on the side of cautious secrecy than impatiently tip his hand.

"Just do what you can in the time we have. I exposed a valuable intelligence asset to hunt her down and lost seven of my Elite Guard apprehending her. The former, especially, is a resource I cannot easily replace."

"As you wish, Grand Chancellor."

Shauston left the observation room without further comment, and Sebastian stared at the girl through the observation window. There was a familiarity about her that Sebastian couldn't quite put his finger on. She lay quietly secured to the bed, blissfully unaware of his scrutiny. He grasped the shaft of his cane, an unnecessary accoutrement, but he found that using it gave the impression of prestige and made people assume he was less spritely than he truly was.

Perception was everything.

Lifting the cane, he softly tapped the silver head of it against the glass, as if trying to attract fish in a tank. He narrowed his eyes and muttered under his breath.

"Who *are* you, little girl?"

| 38 |

ELEGANTLY WASTED

– Allyson Knightley –
– Saturday – London, England –

Allyson knocked back her sixth vodka-and-lemonade.
Or is this the seventh?
She had lost count probably around the same time she lost her inhibitions. Gayle had been nursing a glass of cola all night, so Ally took it upon herself to be the designated drunkard by demanding each of her drinks be a double. The lemonade mixer was purely a token gesture.

To distract Gayle from her mood, she had led them to the nearest venue she knew could provide the holy trinity of music, food, and alcohol. A little place called Barnun, not far from the Academy. They stuffed their faces with pizza and danced till their feet hurt.

At first, all she could entice out of her sister was a smile here and a chuckle there, but after a while, Gayle started to loosen up...and laugh. Ally didn't care that she was *mostly* snickering at the idiot she was making of herself with her flirtatious advances toward women in the bar, all of whom politely declined. All that mattered was that fun was being had, and Gayle was finally embracing it.

Mission accomplished.

Eventually, Gayle could witness Allyson's humiliations no longer and guided her to a more private cubicle. Ally had drunkenly sat down a shade too hard on the wooden bench and was rubbing her rump as Gayle slid into the seat opposite.

Which brought her back to her seventh vodka-and-lemonade.

She frowned...

Or is this the eighth?

Ally shrugged and took a quick swig from her glass, putting it back down a little too abruptly. The clear liquid sloshed out of the tumbler and onto her hand. She giggled as she licked it off.

"Why don't they put cushions on these benches?" she slurred in confusion. "And where are all the hot gay women?"

"I'm afraid I'm not up to speed on where the hot lesbians of London hang out these days, Sis," Gayle laughed and shrugged.

"Lesbians of London!" Ally guffawed. "Now I know what LOL *really* means!"

She threw back the last of her drink and then reached for the bottle to refill her glass. As she drained the last of the contents she stared dumbly at the bottle, noting it too was now empty. She frowned and looked at Gayle.

"We're gonna need more vodka. I'm gonna get a bottle."

"We don't need another bottle." Gayle raised an eyebrow. "It's getting late..."

"But the night is young!" Ally protested as she signaled to the bartender to send over the requested bottle. "And Sweden's finest awaits!"

Russian vodka was exceedingly rare and prohibitively expensive these days, far beyond the means of the Knightley sisters. The Swedish-sourced version was much cheaper and more readily available, which was a shame because it was said that some Russian vodkas were better than sex.

"I *really* need sex." Ally leaned forward and stared too closely at the tabletop.

"I know we're close as siblings, but that's where I draw the line."

"I'm serious, Gayle!" Ally whined. "It's been *ages* since Dannielle. It's been like..." She lifted her hand and counted off the months slowly on her fingers.

"Ally, I really don't need—" Gayle started to protest.

"—Two," Ally interrupted. "Two *months* since I've had sex. I've been using a lot of batteries, and *not* the rechargeable ones. My non-sex life is not good for the environment, Gayle. I'm contributing to a global catastrophe simply because I'm not getting laid."

"I'm sure the world will be just fine. Can we change the subject, please?"

"Oh...fuck. I'm sorry, Sis. I totally forgot. I guess this is a sore point for you." Allyson felt mortified for a moment, before her mind sank into the gutter again. "Which, incidentally, is what I've been suffering from lately."

"That's really not funny," Gayle said, unamused.

Ally couldn't help but giggle uncontrollably. The more she tried to stop, the more irrepressible it became, till eventually even her sister found it infectious and laughed along, too. Their laughter drew the attention of a nearby group of guys who proceeded to eye up both of them with lascivious looks. Gayle cocked an eyebrow at them and shrugged apologetically.

"Sorry, fellas. I'm not interested, and she doesn't do dick."

Which only made Allyson laugh even harder, till she started to slide down the bench under the table.

Gayle reached across and grabbed her sister's shirt, using it to haul her back up onto her seat as the men turned their attention to the other ample opportunities in the bar. Allyson's giggles subsided, and she looked across the table at Gayle. She knew that Barnun had been a frequent haunt of the 137th Hunters; she had even been here with them on more than a few occasions. It was why she had pushed for them to come here.

This place, and this booth specifically with its pair of three-seater benches and its scruffy wooden table, would be a source of discomfort to her sister, but also a place full of happy memories. Drunken celebrations of life and mission successes without casualty. Ally knew that everywhere she looked, Gayle would see mental snapshots of her comrades smiling, laughing, and flirting. Being at their best. Living their lives to the fullest. Gayle, though, had already seemingly made her peace with working at the Academy, so Allyson reasoned that there was no point in hiding from the feelings this place would generate. That maybe it would do Gayle some good to recall the happier times. To help her push past the pain that had recently been overwhelming her.

For a Fae-Human hybrid, life was all about emotion.

And trying to control it.

Sad, happy, angry, or horny, it didn't matter. Their abilities were fueled by their feelings, and in order to harness their power to the maximum, Gayle and her team were taught to experience them to their fullest. To revel in them. To feed off the rush. Ally had an inkling of what that felt like, but she'd never had to stoke the emotional furnace to facilitate her job as a cop, and even less so now as Security Chief. Yet, it was a high that she understood could lead down a very self-destructive path if one wasn't vigilant. Lines could so easily be crossed, a consequence she knew Gayle recognized from bitter personal experience.

Maybe...bringing Gayle here had been a terrible mistake.

"Does being here bother you?" Ally gestured around the bar at large.

Gayle didn't answer straight away, but her eyes flicked around the room as she considered her response.

"No..." she said eventually. "Maybe a little. There are a lot of memories here."

"Good ones though, right?" Ally slurred, furrowing her brow.

"Yeah." Gayle nodded and smiled sadly. "Good ones for sure."

Excellent! Then my plan is going superbly!

Flushed with success, Allyson's drunken mind decided that maybe a change of subject was in order, so she clumsily segued into another topic that obviously needed her brand of expert assistance.

"So," Allyson said slowly, "are you and Dad gonna make up?

Because it's a *drag* hearing him go on about you, and how his favorite daughter hates him... He's a very sad man, Gayle. Seri...ously."

The last word was broken in two by a subtle hiccup, underscoring just how far down the drunken path Allyson had meandered.

"I don't hate him," Gayle reiterated. "I'm just...angry."

"You said you weren't angry." Ally looked confused. "Just hurt and...even more hurt than...hurt. Like, personally hurt."

"I think the word you're looking for is be—," Gayle started before Allyson interrupted proudly and triumphantly.

"Betrayed!" she shouted a smidgen too loudly. "He's a betrayer!"

Gayle said nothing, just shrugged.

"He just cares about his little Songbird," Ally said, her face suddenly serious. "We were *all* worried. I cried for...fucking ages. And Mum... Have you noticed Mum never really cries? Do you think that's a Fae thing 'cause if so, I did *not* get that bit of her at all. Cause I cry like a motherfucker. I cried when Danni left me. I cried like..." The sentence trailed off as Ally sighed.

"I thought you broke it off with Danni?"

"Fuck Danni!" Ally muttered angrily. "Bitch!"

She took another swig from her glass and then slammed it down on the table again, sloshing more of the vodka onto the worn, smooth surface.

"I thought you said you broke it off as it just wasn't working out?" Gayle said with a hint of confusion.

"I'm full of shit, Gayle. A liar. Bullshit flows from these lips like water from a tap..." she slurred.

"You wanna tell me what really happened?"

Ally picked up her glass and knocked back the remains of the alcohol contained within to give her the courage to reply honestly.

"You were *so* sad, Gayle. Like so *very* sad, and I didn't want to give you my sad, too. Danni...she never really liked me. It was just my Fae...ness."

"Fae-ness?" Gayle asked.

Ally nodded.

"Yeah. You know how when you first sort of meet a Human and they get all gooey about the amazing sex cause of the pheromone thing? Then there's the whole superpowers thing and the 'Ooo, can you do this and that and...whatever.' But after all that novelty wears off..."

She could feel herself on the point of tears, and she really didn't want to cry over this again.

Fucking vodka!

"You know," Allyson finally continued, "I fell in love with her. I fucking loved her, and I know that because of, you know, the..." She flattened her hand out, soaring it through the air in a flying motion, and just said, "*Whoosh.*"

Gayle stared at her sister and nodded with a bemused look that indicated she truly had no idea what Ally was talking about.

"Well, it was all the pheromones. That's all. I never met her parents, you know. Like she was ashamed of me. Of me! I'm the daughter of two fucking famous ambamadors." She stumbled over the word. "*And* I'm a Chief of Security, dammit. With a badge and a gun and shit, and *she* was embarrassed to be with *me*?

"She said she wanted to be with someone normal. With a normal job and with normal sex things. Apparently, I'm not normal enough for normal people. She thought I was a freak."

"Forget her," Gayle said softly.

"Yeah, fuck her for making me feel like that," Ally growled.

"Is that why you started dying your hair again?"

Ally grabbed a handful of her long black locks and stared at it. She could already see her natural blue creeping through again, manifesting as cobalt streaks. She nodded and pursed her lips.

"Yeah, but it never takes."

"I like the blue."

"Well, I figured that now I got the responsible job in Nexus, I'd better start looking profeshnial..." She furrowed her brow at her pronunciation but decided not to try correcting it. "But I guess since Danni's gone, maybe I'll just let it go back to normal."

"Love sucks," Gayle muttered.

"You have no idea, Sis." Allyson laughed.

"I've been in love!"

"Pffft!" Ally spat her vodka out as she laughed again. "Torbar? Pffft! That, my dear older sister, was just a bunch of fucking."

She sighed, reached for the bottle of vodka, and haphazardly sloshed a new shot into her glass.

"What you need, Gayle, is to get back in the saddle. Find someone worthy of your...pink hair. What about whaziname...?"

"Who?" Gayle looked confused as she knocked back the dregs of her glass.

"Captain America? The captain dude. The one you work with and say you don't like, but secretly kinda do," Allyson finished.

"I don't like Michael!" Gayle pulled a *'you're crazy'* face at Ally.

"Aha!" Ally pointed her finger accusingly. "Lies. See... No... You *can't* lie to me, Sis. My superpower calls bullshit on you. Besides, Lana told me."

"Oh, great." Gayle slumped back in her chair. "So, now I'm fodder for gossip."

"She only told me because she worries about you. All I'm saying is that sometimes opposites attract. I mean for me and Danni, pffft, but for you two, who knows? He's Human and you're Fae. You're a Brit and he's American. You've got pink hair he's got...some hair." Allyson's drunken ramble started to stumble as she ran out of examples of their inherent differences that were somehow supposed to prove they were perfectly matched. "You're short and...he's what? Six-two? Six-three? It's *really* hard to tell from the pictures."

"Pictures?"

Allyson grinned knowingly and nodded. "Lana sent me pictures. I know he's not my type, sex-wise, but even I can recognize...he is a *tall* glass of handsome..." She tried to whistle but found the alcohol had robbed her of that particular skill. "You should totally fuck him."

She watched Gayle close her eyes, and then her brain caught up and realized what she had just said. A wave of mortified embarrassment warmed her cheeks.

"Oh, shit. Sorry... Again," she hastily apologized. "I mean..."

What do I mean?

"How about you try to find that thought while I go visit the bathroom?" Gayle said eventually after taking a deep breath.

Ally watched Gayle walk across the bar, utterly oblivious to the admiring glances she was drawing from the men she passed. The world felt a little off kilter suddenly and she stared at her drink, trusting the liquid over her own brain. The vodka was level, ergo so must the world be. She placed her head on the table, pressing her ear against the wet, wooden surface and stared sideways at the shot glass, giggling. She could kind of see through it, but it distorted her view. She could make out the shape of Gayle's phone, but it was all upside down and magnified.

What can I do to fix things for Gayle?

Suddenly she had an epiphany. She focused her eyes on the small flat communications device and a devious thought crossed her mind.

Gayle's phone!

Reaching across the table, she snagged it and stared at the screen, expecting it to unlock at a glimpse of her face.

It didn't.

Ally frowned. Though she and Gayle were separated by two years in age, they looked like identical twins. Apart from their differing hair colors – and the recent scar on her sister's neck – anyone would be hard pressed to tell them apart. So why wasn't the facial recognition fooled by their similarity?

Prodding the touchscreen with her finger, she was rewarded with a number pad and a prompt for an unlock code.

Old school. I really shoulda known...

A six-digit number was all she had to decipher to gain access. She put her vodka-addled brain to the task.

Gotta be her birthday! Ally thought triumphantly, confident of cracking it on the first try. Day, month, and year.

Access denied.

Come on, brain!

Screwing her eyes shut and rubbing her forehead she tried think what else it could be. Maybe it was a name? After all, the keypad had the alphabet on it too, where the numbers corresponded with letters. Gayle only had five letters; Allyson had seven, so they were out. Carrie-Anne had ten letters, but Carrie on its own had six. She tried it but struck out again.

That left their parents' names, both of which had six letters. She tried their mother's first, spelling out her name with the number keys. Seven for the S, three for the E, another seven for the R and so on till she had spelled Serlia.

Access was once again duly denied.

She paused then prodded five, two, nine, six, three, and seven.

'Jaymes.'

The phone beeped in her hand and the lock screen vanished to show a picture of herself, Gayle, and Carrie smiling in the sun at the family farm. Her feet tapped a delighted jig on the floor as she hurriedly scrolled through the contacts list to find what she was looking for.

Captain Michael Reynolds. Rogue.

Ally glanced at the bathroom door expecting Gayle to walk out at any moment and stop her dastardly plan before she could put it into action, but there was no such intervention. She selected his number and then, after a moment when she probably should have let her conscience talk her out of the act, she hit the '*call*' button.

| 39 |

TRUE NATURE

– Kareena St. Claire –
– Sunday – Vermont, New Victus –

For a fleeting moment she thought that maybe it had all been a terrible dream.

She awoke in comfort, on a bed. She was clothed, warm, and it was blissfully quiet.

The first sign that the nightmare *was* real, was her first deep breath. The air tasted recycled and antiseptic, missing the familiar scents of the forest and lake. No wind caressed her face, no comforting sounds of nature reached her ears. Just stillness and the hum of electric wires.

She eased her eyes open and stared at the ceiling.

A soft light greeted her. Not daylight, but a gentle artificial light from panels around the room. Three of the walls were windowless and a calming beige in color, the fourth was a huge mirrored surface. Her eyes flicked around the room as she sat up slowly, pivoting her legs over the side of the bed to place her feet warily on the floor. She glanced down at the bed, a slim mattress atop a welded frame fixed firmly to the polished floor. Across the room was a tiny sink and a toilet.

It looked like a cell but felt more sterile than that.

Like a laboratory.

Am I being watched? Observed?

She stared at the reflective wall, wondering if it was a two-way mirror. Her thoughts were quickly distracted by her own visage. She tilted her head and watched in fascination as the stranger across the room mimicked her actions. She didn't know this doppelganger in the mirror. Whoever it was, it wasn't Kareena.

Yet it looked like her.

She ran her hands through her long blonde hair; it didn't look any different. Her skin, likewise, looked as unnaturally smooth and unblemished as it had since her transformation. The dreary loose-fitting clothes were not hers, though. Elasticated pants and a baggy button-up shirt in a matching color – they looked like pajamas.

She hopped off the cot and walked slowly toward her image, her stare never wavering. A thought occurred to her and she teased down the left-hand side of her pants. Her fingers lightly caressed the skin just below her hipbone where she had been hit by the tranquilizer dart. No missing flesh, no scar, not a single blemish to mark its former presence. The sensation and the feeling of euphoria, had it *all* been a figment of her imagination?

Had she imagined the transformation? If not, then what was she?

Human?

Wolf?

Vampyrii?

Something else?

Her tongue flicked across her canines; sharp points grazed its flesh. She opened her mouth, spreading her lips apart so that she could clearly see her teeth in the mirror, the proof that it was *not* a dream.

Fangs. Retracted, but still sharp and lethal.

Oh, God...I killed people!

The memory hit her like a thunderbolt. Images in her head of the things she had done. The torn chest, the ruined throat, the shattered spine, a heart beating its last in her firm grasp. An endless sea of blood, on her victims, on the ground... On her own hands. Tears flooded her eyes as her breathing became erratic.

No, it's not true. I don't have the claws! See, it's a lie, just my imagination! It never happened!

She stared at her hands as the memories filled her mind and watched in horror as her elegant fingers started to slowly transform into long curved talons. Sharp enough to easily inflict all the damage that she saw in her mind.

No!

A plea rather than a denial. Kareena screamed at the monster in the mirror, lashing out, etching the shiny surface with deep jagged gouges. Tears flowed as she slashed at the mirror repeatedly, acting out her fear, her anger. She felt the contents of her stomach start to rise and fled toward the toilet, sliding to her knees before it. Awareness of the empty state of her belly came into focus as she dry-retched uncontrollably into the sterile bowl.

When the panic subsided, she lay on her side, curling herself into a ball and sobbing.

Who am I? What kind of monster have I become?

A voice broke her reverie, filtering into the room from a hidden speaker. "You're safe now."

As she looked around the room, searching for the source of the voice, the scarred, mirrored wall shimmered and turned to glass. A man with greying hair and a full beard smiled kindly at her. His white coat told her his profession even before he introduced himself.

"I'm Doctor Shauston. I've been looking after you since you arrived here. Are you hungry?"

Kareena stood slowly, approaching the previously mirrored wall. She nodded suspiciously but made no verbal response. She could see but couldn't sense him. How had he done that? Why was he hiding from her? Despite his caring words, she didn't trust him. However, she also couldn't deny her hunger. She shuddered, remembering vividly the last time she had turned down the offer of food.

"I'll get something sent in for you. Can you tell me your name, my dear?" he asked in a soothing tone.

She ignored his question. "Where am I?"

"Safe," Shauston said, deftly dodging her inquiry. "You

should know that you're being held in that room—"

"So, I *am* a prisoner?" she hissed.

"—for our mutual protection," he finished, gesturing toward the deep gouges she had left in the glass wall. "Do you blame us for making sure you can't hurt anyone else?"

She briefly averted her eyes from him in shame. Still, there were so many questions that needed answers.

"Why have you brought me here?"

"Because you're unique." Shauston grinned, an expression Kareena found sinister.

"What am I?"

His eyes pierced hers as he leaned into the glass.

"That," he said simply, "is a very good question, isn't it?"

Despite his empathic demeanor, this man did *not* have her best interests at heart. She could feel it in her gut. The ingratiating tone of his voice and the creepy look on his face told her everything her new senses couldn't. She couldn't trust him. As much as she wanted answers, she wanted them on her own terms, not his. She backed slowly away from the mirror, surveying the room, evaluating her escape options.

There were none.

"Let me go," she pleaded with a whisper.

"I'm sorry, my dear, but that is not an option," he said with a shake of his head. "Food will be here shortly. Rest, and later we will start our examination of just who you are. Won't that be exciting?"

A statement more than a question, and one she vehemently disagreed with.

"Who are you?" she hissed.

"Nobody you need to worry about," he answered, cryptically adding. "You won't remember me anyway."

A chill ran down her spine as new questions regarding her fate spiraled through her mind and she realized that, once again, she was in trouble.

| 40 |

FAMILY MATTERS

– Michael Reynolds –
– Sunday – London, England –

"Is this a bad time?"

On his doorstep in the glow of the streetlights, seemingly oblivious to the persistent drizzle, stood the surprising figure of his commanding officer.

"Not at all, General. Please...come on in," Michael politely lied.

Norbel nodded and walked past Michael into the hallway, where he paused.

"I apologize for the lateness of the hour."

"It's really not a problem. I was up late doin' student evaluation reports. Can I offer you a drink, General?"

"Thank you. Water will be fine." Norbel nodded his head politely in a gesture of gratitude.

Michael returned to the lounge, glass in hand, to find Norbel looking with interest across the rather barren bookshelves populated with just a few battered paperbacks leaning haphazardly against each other.

"Not much of a reader, Michael?"

He had heard the general refer to Gayle by her name on several occasions, but then they were family, so that was hardly unusual. But this was the first time Michael could remember

Norbel referring to him by anything other than rank and surname. Why the new level of familiarity?

"I enjoy reading, General. My limited library is more a result of constantly movin' around. We didn't have space for much in the way of personal possessions on the ships I grew up on. Since then, I've been in the army, so..."

"Well, maybe now that you are settled here, you can grow your collection somewhat. And please, call me Norbel. This is not a work-related visit. Tonight, I am here as a concerned uncle."

So, this was about Gayle.

"Of course. What can I do for you?"

"It is about my niece Allyson," Norbel said and then took a sip of water from the glass. A wry smile spread across his lips as he saw the surprise in Michael's expression. "You were perhaps thinking this visit was to discuss Gayle?"

Michael chuckled and nodded. "I have to admit, hers *was* the first name that crossed my mind."

"Gayle is the one niece I am *not* unduly concerned about. She is going through a process, that much is true, but she would not be the niece I know and love if she did not rail against us helping her. I know the heart of that girl, and she is undeniably strong. She simply needs to find that strength once more.

"Her current course *is* the path she should be on. She objects because this was not her choice. The trick with Gayle is to hold your ground until she decides that it was her idea all along. I know yourself and Captain Fordham have your concerns about her, but trust me, she is exactly where she is supposed to be right now."

"Well," Michael admitted, "first – and second – impressions aside, I think we have established a good workin' relationship. We still have our moments, but I actually find myself warming to her...to workin' with her."

If Norbel noticed the slip, he didn't show it.

"It is a good thing that you are...getting acquainted with each other. I brought you to the Academy because I knew that you two would be compatible. You complement each other exceedingly well."

Norbel's statements made it sound more like match-making a romantic relationship than forming a working partnership.

"I think we'll make a good team movin' forward." Michael nodded, trying to emphasize the work aspect.

Norbel smiled. "I have no doubts. However, as I said, it is Allyson for whom I am here to ask your help."

Michael gestured toward one of the armchairs for Norbel to sit, while he perched himself on the edge of his barely used sofa. The house now felt homier, but it certainly wasn't truly lived in or reflective of his personal tastes. Decorating had been a perfunctory exercise in choosing items from a catalog and having them delivered. It didn't *feel* like home yet, but he was sure that would change over time.

"As you may be aware, my niece was recently made Security Chief for Nexus City," Norbel continued. "The upcoming Nexus Summit will be her first challenge. You were the Head-of-Security at the Army base in Miramar if I recall correctly."

Michael nodded. "That's correct."

"Allyson's time with the FSE International Police made her an accomplished detective. However, her new role as Nexus Security Chief is a sizeable change of responsibility for her. A new direction.

"A few days ago, Nexus Security received an anonymous bomb threat."

So, that's what this is about.

"A conference of that magnitude is going to attract that kind of attention," Michael commented. "From what I hear about your niece, I'm sure she has it under control. She has a reputation for professionalism."

His phone started vibrating, reverberating against the glass surface of his desk. Despite being curious about who might be calling at this late hour, he ignored it and let it go to voicemail. He would pick up the message after his guest left.

"Allyson was always the more...professional of the three sisters. It is not her attitude with which I concern myself."

Norbel hesitated. "It is her experience. To speak frankly for a moment, there are many who consider her appointment a case of nepotism. That myself or her parents had some sway in the matter. This is untrue. Allyson was appointed on her own merit."

He paused and looked Michael in the eye.

"However, if something were to go wrong at the Summit then those who maintain that mistaken opinion would have, in their minds, ample evidence to justify their criticism. I would prefer to avoid that scenario. It would put my mind at ease, and that of my sister, if you might do me the favor of looking over her security arrangements and evaluating them for me. To ensure nothing is...overlooked."

"No problem." Michael frowned. "But I'm not sure why you need me to do it. Surely you could look over the plans yourself?"

Norbel tilted his head and looked a little sheepish. Then came the epiphany.

"You don't want her to know you're checkin' up on her."

"The HFA do not have a seat at the Summit; thus, I have no vested interest in the security arrangements apart from personal. If I request a copy of the security designs from Allyson's office, she will *know* that I am vetting her work. I already have one disgruntled niece, and I would like to keep my relationship with Allyson on good terms. Thus, I wondered if you might request the information yourself on the grounds that you are doing a review for the NAA contingent."

Michael considered Norbel's appeal. He understood the general's concern but hated the idea of subterfuge. On the other hand, it wouldn't hurt to have a second pair of experienced eyes examine the plans that Allyson had drawn up. There was only one flaw he could see in Norbel's plan.

"General, I don't have any valid NAA credentials. Not anymore." he shrugged apologetically.

"Yours is not the first favor I have asked for today," Norbel laughed softly. "Ambassador McAdams is in the process of renewing your credentials as we speak. You should have your official status restored by morning."

In hindsight, Michael should not have been surprised that Norbel had seemingly thought of everything. During their first interview, he had come across as being a man who was always thinking one step ahead. A master puppeteer, adept at pulling strings.

"Okay, General. As soon as the clearance comes through, I'll contact Nexus Security and make the necessary arrangements."

Norbel stood in a smooth, efficient motion. His business now complete, it was evidently time to leave.

"Thank you, Michael. Your assistance in this matter is *much* appreciated. I knew bringing you on board was an excellent choice."

Though there was gratitude in his tone, Michael couldn't help but feel that the flattery was somewhat forced.

"No problem, General."

As Norbel stood on the doorstep, he spent a moment looking up at the night sky. A hesitation before the inevitable request that Michael knew was coming.

"Suffice to say...I would like this kept between us," he finally said quietly.

"Of course," Michael immediately replied. "G'night, General."

Turnabout is fair play as they say, and Norbel had been true to his word in keeping Michael's own secret thus far.

"Good night, Captain."

Norbel turned, walking away into the night without so much as a glance backward. Michael watched him for a moment before closing the door and heading back to the lounge. Midnight had come and gone, and a wave of fatigue swept over him. He yawned; bed beckoned.

He shut down his computer, turned out the lights, and plucked his phone up from the desk on his way to the bedroom. As he climbed the stairs, he remembered the call he had received earlier. A swipe of his finger on the screen showed him a pair of notification bubbles. One missed call from Gayle Knightley, and one voicemail message.

He picked up the phone and tapped the button to retrieve

his voicemail.

| 41 |

MESSAGES

– Lana Fordham –
– Monday – London, England –

With a gentle creak, the door to the Officer's Lounge eased open and the face of Michael Reynolds poked through the gap, scanning the room. Evidently, he was looking for Gayle because when he spotted her, he smiled and pushed the door wide open.

"Afternoon, Captain," Lana offered as he entered.

He nodded at Lana and sat down on the sofa positioned parallel to the armchairs that cradled herself and Gayle. Initially he said nothing; just sat. Thinking. Finally, he leaned forward, putting his phone down on the low coffee table between them and scratched his chin. He looked uncomfortable.

"Hi?" a bemused Gayle offered in a questioning tone.

"Captain Knightley...Gayle," he said slowly. "Could we maybe speak in private?"

"Whatever you want to say, I'm sure Lana is okay to hear it."

"Are you sure? It's...it's about your phone message," he said cryptically.

Gayle tilted her head and gave him a bewildered expression. "What phone message?"

"The one you left for me on Saturday night."

"I didn't leave you a phone message on Saturday night."

Lana quietly observed the exchange between Michael and Gayle, each one now looking as confused as the other.

"Well...you did because I have it on my answering service."

"I don't think so," Gayle responded with a cast iron certainty. "Because I was out on Saturday night, and what's more, I *didn't* get drunk. Which means I remember everything that happened with perfect clarity."

"Well, I can play it if it'll jog your memory..."

"By all means, make a fool of yourself."

"You're *absolutely* sure?" Michael clarified while looking at Lana.

"Oh, yes," Gayle grinned. "Lana and I are both really looking forward to the hilarity that will ensue."

There was an undeniable chemistry between these two; Lana had felt it the moment she first saw them together. What intrigued her right now, though, was that both seemed so sure that they were somehow about to embarrass the other. But while Michael appeared to be trying to spare Gayle any humiliation, she exuded confidence that he was about to make a fool of himself.

For one of you, this is going to backfire spectacularly, she thought to herself in amusement, and settled back to enjoy the show.

Michael hesitantly pressed the touchscreen on his phone a few times to access the message.

"*Heyyy...Mike...?*" The voicemail started out sounding more like a hesitant question.

Suddenly Lana understood. She could see why Michael had been fooled by the drunken voice emanating from the speaker – it sounded eerily like Gayle Knightley. From the look on Gayle's face, realization had dawned for her, too.

"Oh, fuck," Gayle muttered, closing her eyes and preparing for the humiliation to come.

Lana, conversely, started to giggle.

"*I've been thinking...*" A pause. "*About you and Gay...me! You and me! I think that you...we?*" Another pause as the person speaking tried to hop back on her train of thought. "*We make a really cute couple. I mean, you and me. So, I was thinking that maybe you two should just do it. And by you two, I obviously mean you and Gayle. You and me, 'cause I'm Gayle. And by 'do it' I don't mean...y'know...sex. Just dating... Fuck it..."* The voice went from a normal volume to a secretive whisper. *"I mean, if you want all the sex with me...Gayle, then that would be good, too. The sex."*

The 'x' got drawn out in a clearly drunken manner and was punctuated by what sounded like a combination of a hiccup and burp. The caller giggled and then 'shushed' herself before continuing in what suddenly became a distinctly upper-class English accent.

"It has been a long time since I've had sex." The last word was whispered again. *"And I really miss it."* An audible sigh. *"I know this is pretty forward of me, but I know she won't say this. So, I'm making the first move...'cause I'm a strong woman and I can do that."*

"I'm going to fucking kill her..." Gayle murmured quietly as she shrank into the chair and put her arms over her mortified face.

"But this is not about the sex...this is about a connection, Mike. You and Gayle, you got something...and sometimes you gotta just explore this shit...because you don't want to waste time with the wrong girl. You like girls, right, Mike? I mean who doesn't like girls? I like girls... I mean me, not Gayle. Not... Okay, I think maybe I'm maybe confusing you because what I mean is that I am Gayle and I'm a girl and I think you like girls...unless you're gay! Which is totally okay with me because so am I. I mean, I'm not gay...I'm Gayel." More giggling at her own joke. *"Anyway, I mean, I have experience with that 'cause Gayle's sister is the other type of gay. The lady type..."* The last part was said in an almost conspiratorial manner.

"Anyway..." The word was drawn out and slurred. *"I just wanted you to know that if you want to, then that would be great. So, just call me sometime when it's maybe convenient for you. Maybe not a work night...'cause we have to think of the children!"* she muttered thoughtfully and then burst into giggles that took a while to subside.

"So, this is?" Michael asked taking advantage of the lull the giggle-fit had provided.

"It's Allyson," Lana somehow managed to squeeze out through tears of laughter.

"My soon-to-be very dead younger sister!" Gayle exclaimed.

"*Okay, so I gotta go 'cause she's finished in the toilet...*" Allyson whispered urgently.

"Oh, my God..." Gayle muttered under her breath.

"*...but yeah, call me, okay? For dating and maybe sex. All the best...*"

"All the best!" Lana choked with amusement as she doubled over in the chair and clutched at her stomach.

"I will murder her in creative ways. I will strangle the life out of her in cold blood." Gayle was curling herself up into a mortified ball on the chair.

"*...Gayle. Knightley.*" The recording continued for a few more moments even though the official message was apparently finished. "*Fucking nailed it,*" was the quiet end to the voicemail.

"So...your sister, then? Not you?" Michael leaned back on the sofa and grinned at Gayle, the look of the victorious.

"Dead. Woman. Walking," Gayle mumbled from within her protective ball.

"Shame. Frankly, I was lookin' forward to all the sex," Michael stated matter-of-factly, which just caused more peels of hard laughter to be torn from Lana's already agonized stomach.

"Oh, fuck you!" Gayle shot back.

"I thought that was what the phone message was about..." Michael parried almost immediately.

"Can't...breathe..." gasping for air now, Lana could not stop giggling.

Something had happened in this room though; the dynamic had shifted somehow for the better. As Gayle unraveled herself from her ball of shame, Lana could see the look in her eyes. As embarrassed as she was, she could also see the funny side, and she was looking at Michael with an expression that Lana hadn't seen on her friend's face in a long time.

| 42 |

THE CABIN IN THE WOODS

– Zarra Anderson –
– Tuesday – Mont Tremblant, Pack Nation –

Alex's plan: Consider the last known direction of their targets, extrapolate how far they might have travelled in the intervening time since that last contact, and then plot a course to intercept them.

As plans went, it was not the *worst* idea.

Naturally, Zarra vetoed it immediately.

She knew from experience that it would likely be a colossal waste of time. Shortcuts backfired far more often than they succeeded. Alex's strategy was basically the hunting equivalent of crossing your fingers and hoping for the best.

Her own plan was to backtrack their path and attempt to reacquire the trail again. Her way *would* take more time, that was undeniably true, but she also knew that it was the best way to make sure that they actually *found* Vanessa and her partner. As usual, it was a course of action that tested the limits of Alex's new-found devotion to the art-of-the-hunt. Zarra was just beginning to tire of his subtle whining when they detected the now familiar stench of decay from the cave of the male victim.

It was a powerful beacon to guide them in, but they didn't revisit it. They had no desire to bear witness to that atrocity again. The distinctive scents of their quarry were, by now, very weak. However, the path Vanessa and her partner had taken was still unmistakable if you knew the tell-tale signs. They weren't moving with stealth, and while their head start was significant, they didn't appear to be in a hurry. Zarra and Alex pushed the pace to close the distance between them.

Zarra was not a detective...had never wanted to be. She hated mysteries, preferring her hunts to be neat and tidy. Job done and money in the bank. However, there was an element of problem solving in every hunt, and this one was revealing an infuriating complexity that was only getting worse. As they jogged through the forest, Zarra's mind was a-buzz with unanswered questions.

Who was the incubus, and how had he known about Vanessa Balthazaar?

Why had they fled into the forests of Pack Nation? Had Domaine Saint-Bernard always been a part of the plan?

Who was Kareena St Claire, why was she so special, and who had taken her?

Who was the boy in the cave? Was he linked to Kareena somehow?

If she thought about it too much, her head started to hurt. Too many questions. Not enough answers. Then, on the third day of their pursuit, they found something that created a whole new set of queries.

As Zarra jogged, Alex moved ahead, his Wolf-form far more capable of swiftly covering this terrain. The forest was his element. It was his whispered voice in her ear that first alerted her to his new discovery.

"Zee, I'm about a half-mile ahead of you. There's a clearing in the trees. Not natural. Some kind of cabin. Place reeks of death."

Zarra tabbed the button on her comms device hooked over her ear. "Wait for me to get there," she whispered back. "We'll sweep it together. Any sign of 'em?"

"Negative. They passed through here on their way to wherever they're going, but...they've also been here before. Weeks ago."

She upped her pace to a brisk run. She might not cut quite

as easy a path as the Wolf, but she was nimble enough to not have a problem. She would be with him in just a few minutes.

"Weeks? Scents usually dissipate in days."

"Yeah, well it's not *their* scents I'm getting...just his. He was here a while."

"The incubus? Alone?"

"Yeah, but not alone," Alex confirmed. "It's faint. There's something else here. Some*one* else I think..."

"Any sign of our airborne friends?" she said.

"Not a peep."

"Okay, I'll be there shortly." With a gentle tap on her earpiece she closed the channel.

A few minutes later she was crouched with Alex in the brush at the edge of the clearing, hidden by the foliage. There was evidence that the log cabin sitting in the center of the clearing had been built from the trees that had previously grown here. Stumps littered the area and unused logs were strewn haphazardly around the site. To the west, there was what appeared to be an access road, but it was heavily overgrown now. It would have been an idyllic forest retreat, somewhere to get away from it all to enjoy the tranquility of nature. That had clearly been a long time ago.

Zarra surveyed the clearing, evaluating the tactical options as a matter of habit. There was a pick-up truck of some kind parked under a covered veranda to the left of the cabin. It leaned heavily to one side where time and corrosion had resulted in the collapse of its suspension. Out front, a similarly decrepit tractor sat alongside a wood pile and a tree stump with a rusted axe embedded in it. From her vantage point she could just about make out the front door. It looked slightly ajar.

She signaled to Alex with a subtle wave of her fingers that she was going to advance across the clearing toward the front of the cabin. Another hand-signal indicated she wanted him to circle around and cover the rear. He nodded his understanding and stalked away through the bushes, his body keeping low to the ground.

Easing her Freelancer quietly out of her holster, she

thumbed the safety off and dialed up the setting for standard rounds with a practiced flick of her finger. She broke cover, staying in a crouch low to the ground as she quickly and stealthily headed for the cover of the tractor. She was suddenly struck by how quiet the forest was. Not a sound apart from the rustle of the wind through the trees. A dead zone. Her instincts started screaming at her.

Something's wrong here...

Their recent ambush was still fresh in Zarra's mind. The revelation that there were other players moving pieces on the board had been a surprise, especially since she and Alex were still trying to figure out what game they were playing. She hated surprises, especially ones that made her feel disadvantaged. While her senses couldn't detect immediate evidence of a threat, she couldn't ignore the prickling of the hairs on the nape of her neck.

"I'm in position," Alex growled quietly over her earpiece. "Cabin has a back door. It's closed – possibly locked. Can't tell from here."

"Check it out," Zarra whispered. "I'll take the front. Be careful."

She edged warily forward, darting swiftly but stealthily across the clearing. The scruffy grass kept her footsteps silent, so she tried to avoid the noisy gravel wherever possible until she was crouched behind the cover of the abandoned tractor. From the comprehensive amount of rust evident, it must have been an antique even before the War broke out. There was a gap between the motor and the chassis which allowed Zarra a clear, if narrow, view of the cabin's front door.

Everything seemed peaceful.

She moved slowly around the tractor keeping her back pressed closely against it, her senses fully alert. With a deep breath, she crept out into the exposed part of the clearing and headed for the cabin's front door. Her footsteps were light, like a dancer, but even so, she couldn't fail to hear the delicate crunch of the stone beneath her boots. Each deliberate tread took her closer, and with each footfall, her nerves jangled.

Something's VERY wrong here...

Zarra was barely halfway to the cabin when her instincts proved their worth once more. There was the crash of splintered wood from the back of the house as she heard Alex breach the back door. She cursed his lack of subtlety under her breath and dropped any concessions toward stealth as she broke into a run. She was about to step onto the porch when all hell broke loose.

Over comms she heard Alex's expletive-laden exclamation of shock, and from the darkened interior of the cabin there was a bloodcurdling inhuman shriek that made Zarra wince. An instant later, the front door exploded outward in a shower of wooden splinters as something incredibly powerful burst through it.

Despite the jangling of her intuition, Zarra was surprised by the streak of orange-hued fur with burnt sienna stripes. Its claws, teeth, and matted pelt were stained with the burgundy of blood. It had wide eyes that flashed with hate, and huge curved fangs. A saber-toothed tiger was the first thing that popped into Zarra's head as she awkwardly raised her Freelancer to protect herself. It was barely halfway up when the monster barreled into her.

She was winded as she crashed heavily to the ground. Razor-sharp claws sliced through the leather of her combat suit, grazing the wound that had only recently been stitched after the job in Havana. She winced, twisting her head away, frantically trying to protect her face from the creature's talons, which seemed to flash past her eyes in morbid slow motion.

Too close.

She cursed as she watched her weapon somersault through the air, knocked from her hand in the collision. The beast landed a few feet away and immediately scrabbled to turn and face her. Zarra twisted on the ground herself, trying to regain her footing and scramble backward as she tried to extricate her other Freelancer from her right hip. She was too slow, and her opponent was unnaturally fast. It slashed at her with its left foreleg and long, curved claws speared deeply into Zarra's right shoulder. The stitches tore; the wound reopened. She cried out in white hot agony as the claws sank deep enough to grind against her clavicle.

"Zarra!"

She heard Alex's deep growl of concern but couldn't see him beyond the nightmarish visage that was looming over her. Its eyes were almond-shaped pools of midnight aside a long lupine snout housing rows of jagged teeth behind those huge moon-shaped fangs. It was a jaw designed to rend flesh.

She pushed upward with all her strength, trying to keep the beast at bay, but she could feel its fetid breath heavy on her face. She realized that she had only one chance to survive. It was something she didn't want to do, but she had no choice. She had to...

A huge black shape flew past her vision, all fur and teeth, as Alex joined the fray just in time. He forcibly knocked Zarra's attacker off her and back across the clearing. Zarra struggled to her feet, clutching at her ruined shoulder. Now that she could see the creature clearly, she was shocked by the size of it. Alex's Wolf form was a powerful example of his race, but this new opponent was easily larger and far more lethal looking. Alex bared his teeth and snarled. Trying to warn off their attacker, urging it to cease hostilities.

A futile gesture.

Zarra stumbled backward, desperately trying to come up with a plan. Something that could help. Her mind started thinking about the gun still strapped to her right hip, but as she reached back, her hand found a different solution.

| 43 |

THE TAPESTRY

– Sebastian StormHall –
– Tuesday – Vermont, New Victus –

"Do you have her?"

The tone of her voice irritated him.

Sebastian did *not* like taking orders, especially from a woman. His relationship with this mystery benefactor was becoming increasingly uncomfortable.

"I have her. I hope she's worth the effort. I lost significant assets in the pursuit of her. Assets I cannot readily replace."

Her voice came back over the speakerphone, cool and calm, serene almost. "Tell me...have you ever seen the Bayeux Tapestry?"

"Should I have?" Sebastian asked, puzzled at the sudden diversion of topic.

"It was created in the 11th century and depicts the events leading up to the Norman conquest of England. Half a meter wide and almost seventy meters long and consisting of fifty separate scenes, all individually woven."

The answer did nothing to alleviate his confusion. If anything, it just made it worse.

"I'm sure you have a point..." The sarcasm dripped from his words.

"New Victus, here and now, is one small section in the center of a much greater and more complex tapestry. Concern yourself with *its* embroidery alone. Do not concern yourself with the whole."

"Because that's your job?" Irritation crept into his tone.

"It can be nobody else's." Not spoken with arrogance, but with a begrudging acceptance. Once again it left him wondering who this mysterious woman was.

After Damian Dane had humiliated him three decades earlier, she approached him with candied words playing directly to his bruised ego. Enticing words of a patron who had ideas far beyond his own. Why plot in secret to take vengeance on the man when a war could wipe out the scourge of his kind? Why settle for a seat on the Council of Blood when you could rule your own country? Follow *her* lead, and she would help *him* spearhead a new Vampyrii nation to a glorious future.

Her plan was far-reaching, requiring the meticulous manipulation of events over many years to stack the game board in their favor. From inserting operatives in the highest levels of the US government and military, to seeding his brethren around the globe, readying for what the world would come to call The Rising. Patience was the hardest part, but when they had finally tipped the first domino and watched the world tumble into chaos, it had all been worth it.

The Fae had been an unforeseen complication. Or so Sebastian had thought.

From time to time, she would say something that subtly implied she knew all along the Fae would rise to challenge them. That she was still playing a wider game to which Sebastian was annoyingly no longer privy. The 'tapestry.'

"So, if the Bayeux Tapestry details the events leading up to the Norman conquest of England," Sebastian said almost casually, "where does *your* tapestry lead?"

"To our future." There was no hesitation.

"And *you* know where that future leads us?"

"Yes..." A slight pause. "And no."

"Could you be any more cryptic?"

His sarcasm was ignored.

"There's no need for you to concern yourself with the future." Her tone implied a shrug. "All I need from you is to deliver the girl to me. As requested."

Requested?

It had *never* been a request. It had been a command, given from a superior to a subordinate, only phrased more politely. More politically. He had been willing to suspend his annoyance with this state of affairs while it benefited his rise to power. He had bitten his tongue, patiently observing a neutral silence as he hitched his wagon to her train and let events pull him along.

Now the impetus seemed to be waning. The moment had arrived to leave his long-time patron to her tapestries and start weaving one of his own.

His overture to Lyssa Balthazaar had not been bluster and lies – it was broadly the truth. The facts were plain: too much land to protect, too few soldiers to protect it, and too many enemies. For his New Victus to survive, it *would* need to contract its borders and neutralize those enemies...both domestic and foreign. His plan for Lyssa at the Summit was part of his own grand scheme. A scheme of which his patron knew nothing.

Sebastian smiled. "Tell me where you want the girl and I'll arrange it."

This is the last time – after this I will be free.

Her answer both surprised and unnerved him.

"Thank you, Sebastian. I'll forward the details to you shortly." He thought he heard a hint of amusement. "And don't worry, old friend. I will be in touch shortly for my *last* favor. After that...you'll be free."

The line went dead.

| 44 |

WHO HUNTS THE HUNTERS?

– **Alex Newman** –
– *Tuesday – Mont Tremblant, Pack Nation* –

Wisps of cloud floated lazily across a serene sky that blended exquisitely from a gentle powder blue to a vibrant azure. It was quite beautiful, and Alex idly mused that he rarely took the time to gaze upward with his Human eyes. Overall, his lupine senses were significantly more acute than his Human ones. Eyesight, however, was the exception. What he gained in field of vision, he lost in depth of color and clarity at a distance. An amazing sense of smell couldn't compensate for not being able to see the stars at night or make out the ethereal shapes of the clouds in the sky.

What the hell was that thing?

The adrenaline of the attack and his close shave with death was starting to wear off. He took a deep breath and tried to calm his heart which was thumping violently in his chest.

If *she* hadn't rescued him...

He turned his head slowly, eyes scanning for Zarra. She stood about ten feet away, swaying over the still-twitching body of their attacker. Her left hand pressed against her right shoulder as she wobbled on unsteady legs; clearly the shock of her injury was setting in. Alex twisted to get up, scrambling to his feet. Her eyelids fluttered as she looked at him sleepily. From between her fingers there was a flood of burgundy.

"Alex..." she slurred in a shaky voice with a weak smile. "How are your sewing skills?"

He caught her as her legs gave out and gently lowered her the rest of the way to the ground. Quickly shrugging off his pack, he snatched out the medikit and rapidly scoured it for something that would help. Finding a large gauze pad, he pressed it firmly against the oozing wound and reached for Zarra's blood-soaked hand, guiding it to the gauze.

"Press," he instructed her. "Hard as you can."

She did as she was told and Alex started unpacking other items from the kit, searching for anything else that would offer a better option going forward. In his mind, however, there was only one real solution.

"You're pretty cut up, Zarra. Maybe you should—"

"No." Even in her woozy state she cut him off firmly. "Just...get the needle... Stitch it up."

"But—"

"I said no, Alex." Despite a crack in her voice, she was vehement. "Sew it up."

"Are you sure about this? It's already been stitched up recently."

She nodded weakly, and he could see she was barely hanging onto consciousness. "If I pass out...just keep stitchin', okay?"

"It won't be pretty."

"Never is..."

"I'm going to have to cut some of the leather away, I'm afraid..."

"Do it," Zarra slurred drowsily, her eyelids drooping. "I was gonna spen' some of the bounty money buyin' one of those new CombatSkins anyway..."

He gently peeled the torn leather from her bloodied shoulder. It was an ugly wound, and he grimaced as he slowly revealed the extent of the injury.

"...Gonna get one for Becka, too..." Zarra whispered. "Leather is so...last year..."

She slipped into the embrace of unconsciousness that she had already been resisting for far too long. He turned back to the tiny medikit and started to rifle through it looking for the items he would need to suture Zarra's torn up shoulder. Needle, synthetic thread...

Where the fuck are the shears? Fuck it - improvise.

Alex extended a razor-sharp claw from his right index finger and used it to carefully slice at the blood-soaked leather. He tried to limit the amount of material he cut away, conscious of the fact that even though he needed a window within which to work, Zarra was still going to have to wear it once he was done.

He winced as he cleaned away the blood – it was worse than he had first thought. The creature's claws left five haphazardly overlapping slashes and a deep penetration wound. This was not going to be an easy fix. It was probably a good thing she was unconscious, as stitching her injury without any anesthetic was likely to hurt like a bitch.

He cursed under his breath. Zarra could have made this so much easier for herself.

With fingers that truly weren't designed with surgical skills in mind, he tried to tease the flesh and skin close enough together so that he could suture them. It took some doing, but in the end, he had stemmed the blood flow and pieced her together to his vague satisfaction. She would probably disagree, but then if she wasn't going to help herself, she would just have to accept what she got.

Her pulse was strong and her breathing normal again, so it was now just a case of letting her rest. Moving her in her current condition was not an option, and while the sky might be beautiful today, the sun was relentless. He fashioned a makeshift sunshade from some canvas he found near the wrecked pick-up and some wood that was lying around. It would offer a little respite to her as she recovered.

He gave her a shot of antibiotics to prevent infection, and then carefully went about bandaging the wound, using almost their whole remaining supply of bandages to encircle her chest and shoulder. Finally, he cleaned her blood off his hands using a little of the water they were carrying and started to repack the medikit, making a mental note of what they had left as he did so. The results of the exercise concerned him. It was depleted to say the least.

He bit his lip in thought. Maybe this was the right time to put a stop to this hunt.

As he slotted the medikit back into his pack, he contemplated pulling out the comms unit. Maybe he should signal the *Diana* for pickup and get Zarra back to proper medical care.

Alex hesitated. Their relationship was already on shaky ground. Zarra would be pissed beyond belief if he called time on this mission without consulting her first. It was a discussion he would have to have with her when she awoke, whenever that might be.

He looked up into the pale blue sky. The sun might be beating down on them now, but at this time of year the forest could get awfully cold after sunset. With her level of blood-loss, the overnight temperatures could be exceedingly dangerous.

Perhaps the cabin was an option? He dismissed the thought almost as soon as he had it. The stench of death in there was oppressive. Still, it might just be a case of any port in a storm should the need arise. He hadn't been back inside yet, but he suspected the creature had been hunting in the surrounding forests, bringing its kills back here to eat. That would explain the rotten smell that assaulted his nostrils.

What kind of beast was it anyway? Nothing that he was familiar with, but there were elements that reminded him of...

What the fuck!?

He stared at the corpse in confusion.

This was *not* the monster he remembered.

He recalled how strong and ridiculously fast it was. How close those lethal daggers of claw and fang had been to his exposed throat. Even in his Wolf-form, the monster had overpowered him with shocking ease. He had been forced to shift rapidly back to his Human form simply to gain access to his hands to defend himself. To try and stave off those claws reaching for his vulnerable neck. His Human strength was no match for his opponent's, though, and death had seemed a foregone conclusion.

Zarra had been his savior, taking the creature by surprise

with that rusty axe. How she had even managed it in her condition was some kind of minor miracle, a testament to the fortitude and persistence of the woman. Simply pulling the axe from where it had been embedded in the tree stump for decades couldn't have been an easy task with only one good arm.

And yet, that same axe that was now buried deeply into the back of the corpse's skull where Zarra had put it, confirming that this *was* the same entity that attacked them.

"I really should know better by now than to underestimate her," he muttered as he crouched next to the body of their attacker.

"Goddamn right, and don't you forget it," came the weak response from behind him. "Help me up."

"You need to rest."

"I'll rest when I'm dead."

Alex rolled his eyes as he walked over to where she was trying to push herself to standing by shifting to her knees and using her good arm to lift herself. Before she could do herself another injury, he crouched and put an arm gently around her waist to help her up. She was still weak, and it was noticeable how she leaned on him as he helped her, the grimace on her pallid face betraying the level of pain she was feeling.

"What the hell...?" she whispered as they approached the body of their attacker. "How is that even...?"

Lying on the ground was the body of a young girl. Blood stains covered her naked body like a crimson tattoo. Her sunset orange hair was streaked with shades of burnt sienna as it curled gracefully to her waist, the colors oddly complimenting the burgundy of the dried blood that matted it. She looked about the same height and age as Kareena but was fuller figured. She was, however, definitely another victim of their quarry. The tell-tale smells of the ritual were all over her.

"What the hell is she?" Zarra muttered, echoing Alex's thoughts.

"I don't know. She has – or had – fur at one point. I'm sure..."

"Definitely," Zarra confirmed with a tired nod.

"And she was strong. I mean *really* strong."

"And fast."

"Very fast. But...the eye shape, the teeth and those claws, they kind of reminded me of..."

"Adze," Zarra finished wearily.

"*That* was the scent I couldn't place," he nodded. "Not quite the same as Adze...but close."

Zarra, looking fatigued and pale, rubbed at her temples. He said nothing, knowing she would likely give heavy resistance to any suggestion that she should rest. Maybe a subtle hint could do the job a statement wouldn't.

"If you're going to be on your feet, Zee, we're going to need to sling that arm."

She grinned tiredly at him. "Put me down here, Alex."

He carefully helped her sit on the ground next to the body of the young girl.

"Sling?"

"Do it," she nodded. "And while you're at it, get on the comm unit. We need to call this site in so that Dane can get his people to come sweep it."

As he busied himself, she sat cross-legged, looking with great interest at the girl. With a grimace, she used her left hand to lift and guide her dangling right arm to her lap, and then reached out to tenderly turn the girl's head to the side. She stared sadly at the youthful face.

"What the hell did they do to you?" she muttered.

| 45 |

INTERCEPTED

– Lyssa Balthazaar –
– Wednesday – Albany, New Victus –

Lyssa opened the door to a miserable looking Mercy, the sadness in her eyes telling her everything she needed to know before so much as a word was exchanged. The shake of her niece's head simply confirmed that this was going to be news of the 'bad' variety. She gestured for her to come in.

Mercy trudged past her into the lounge and slumped into one of the comfortable leather armchairs. Despite her posture, she looked anything but relaxed, rubbing at the bridge of her nose as if trying to stave off a headache. She looked so tired, and Lyssa reminded herself that Vanessa was Mercy's aunt, too. No one was working harder to find her.

"Are you okay?" Lyssa asked as she sat down on the nearby couch.

"Not really."

Mercy said no more, but Lyssa knew what she was thinking. She had been resolute in her certainty that she could bring Vanessa back safely. Evidently her confidence had been misplaced.

She had failed, and she was feeling it.

"Merce, this is not your fault," she said empathically. "Just tell me what happened."

Mercy considered her words carefully and then sat up,

leaning forward in the chair. Her eyes flicked for a moment as she organized her thoughts, and then she started to speak calmly and methodically.

"Dane had been keeping us updated with the details of the hunt for Vanessa. Every transmission he relayed to us included a co-ordinate package. By plotting those co-ordinates, we could see that their heading was clearly bringing them back to New Victus. We extrapolated their course to find the likely stretch of border where they would cross, and I instructed our outposts in that area to discreetly increase our surveillance drone presence."

Lyssa knew this part already, but it seemed to be helping Mercy to treat this like an official debrief. She didn't interrupt.

"Last night, a surveillance drone operating out of the outpost in Pointe-au-Chêne spotted them in a clearing a couple of kilometers over the border. They appeared to be loitering on the Rivière-Rouge. Bathing and...things. Relaxing."

Fortunately, the posts along the Vermont stretch of the border were all controlled by House Balthazaar. All the commanders were trusted family members who Lyssa knew would not have breathed a word of this back to Storm.

"I was alerted just before dawn, so I took a team and we headed straight up there. I hoped they'd still be there by the time I arrived."

"I take it they were?"

Mercy nodded. "They hadn't moved. Looked like they were just enjoying the water and the sunrise. They were only a short way over the border and there are no Pack Nation patrols in that area. I decided the risk was low enough that we could attempt an extraction."

She paused, her eyes lost in the memory of the events that had transpired.

"So?" Lyssa prodded. "What happened next?"

| 46 |

SWEET ESCAPE

– Vanessa Balthazaar –
– Wednesday – Vermont, New Victus –

Freedom was bliss.

Truly.

For uncountable decades, her mind's edge had been dulled by a cocktail of drugs aimed at repressing her *true* nature. Now, for the first time in what seemed like forever, she felt alive. She felt *everything*. The delicate breath of the breeze brushing her skin like a lover's touch. Raindrops forming meandering rivulets across her body, caressing her every curve and crevice. Each blade of grass that tickled her flesh was a hedonistic delight. The pebbles and stones that dimpled her body as she lay in her lover's arms were a post-coital treat. Vanessa felt intoxicated, high on sensation.

This was where she belonged.

With him.

He had protected her. Warned her they would come for her. She was heir to the House of Balthazaar. A princess who had been hidden away from the world in a tower, so that her sister could enjoy the spoils of her position while everyone thought that Vanessa was ill. Or worse...that she was crazy.

Vanessa didn't feel crazy.

He didn't make her feel crazy.

For a moment she had swayed, taken in by the words her

niece had used to try and twist her mind. Words of family and of safety. But *he* had dispelled their witchcraft and helped her find her true nature once more.

All because *he* loved her.

It had all started with six simple words, blinking on her computer screen with a metronomic urging.

> *Hello, Vanessa. My name is Thynan.*

She knew she shouldn't reply. Lyssa would be angry with her. Her sister had been *very* careful not to allow her unfettered access to the outside world. But Vanessa was a dreamer, and she was painfully lonely. She had always kept faith that one day her prince would come. Curiosity got the better of her.

Weeks passed. They talked openly, exchanging intimate secrets. He used words like 'fate' and 'destiny.' She worried they would be discovered or that he would be taken from her.

> *Don't worry*, he would say, *this is our secret.*

The day he called her his 'soulmate' made her heart flutter, and her tummy spin. Text on a screen, hard-edged letters that captured her heart like elegant handwritten poetry. Words that made her weep, as she read them repeatedly.

Was this love?

How could she know?

She would lie awake at night, a tangled mess of her own insecurity, craving his digital voice to calm her heightened state. He talked sweetly of forests and lakes, of mountains and valleys, of running wild and abandoned. One day soon, he would share it all with her.

> *First*, he said, *I need to see the real you.*

On his urging, she stopped taking the pills, and the starving demon within her resurfaced. She found herself ravenous for late-night sessions of intimate prose that made her squirm, as he brought her pleasure by proxy far too many times to count. Satisfaction eluded her, however. She craved more than just charged words and her own wandering fingers.

Why could they not meet?

With fear and sadness, he revealed his true nature.

At first, she was horrified. Wolf and Vampyrii was forbidden. Yet Thynan had known all along what *she* was, and if he didn't care then why should she? Destiny had *chosen* them to be soulmates.

Their first meeting was a physical and spiritual coming together. Words went unspoken as they feverishly made love in the shadows of a forest glade on a soft bed of grass. Their moans a symphony of unfettered desire. Her clothes lay forgotten on the ground, torn and ruined, a metaphor for her former life. As they basked in the afterglow, he presented her a ring. A band of gleaming silver inset with dazzling stones of pure sapphire – a symbol of his love and devotion.

Vanessa understood why her sister had secreted her away at House Balthazaar's largest military base in Vermont, but even trapped in her gilded Burlington cage, she had dreamt of what it would be like to be freely and truly loved. To Thynan, she was a treasure to be prized and cherished. She loved these sensations, these wonderful surging emotions. He had given her everything for which she had ever wished. Her wildest fantasies made manifest.

Freedom, children, and undying love.

What woman could want for more?

"Lover?" his gentle baritone made her shiver.

"Yes, my love?"

"We can't stay here."

She sighed, not wanting to leave this perfect place, the memory of the morning still fresh in her mind. She had never killed before. It was a novel experience, a new world of powerful sensation. An adrenaline-fueled high and, as the intoxicating aroma of the blood on their hands lingered in the air, his gentle touch was electrifying. The sex had been nothing short of transcendent.

As the sun breached the horizon, they tenderly washed the blood of their victims off each other. His hands roamed her body, arousing her, and she eagerly returned the favor. Her fingers drifted lightly across every inch of his muscular frame. Caressing his face, thick neck, and broad shoulders, drifting slowly downward toward her ultimate target. She couldn't help herself; she felt her excitement building as she used her tongue to sensuously clean his stomach and thighs.

The hunger consumed them, and she devoured him with abandon, grazing him playfully with her fangs. He may not have been the Wolf at that moment, but he howled like one all the same as he threw her to her back and took her roughly in the shallows of the river. The water flowed around their over-heated bodies, and the tiny sharp stones cut a pattern of ecstasy into her skin.

She squirmed as she remembered how her body had stiffened and shuddered, her legs wrapping tightly around his waist as she drove him deeper into her. Desperately squeezing him, teasing him until the onrushing storm of emotion overwhelmed her.

She had waited centuries to experience that feeling, dreamt of it so many times. Once Thynan showed her how to feel this, she wanted nothing else. It felt like an avalanche of pleasure that nothing in the world could stop. His timing had been perfect. She felt the urgent twitch within her, and simultaneously, her own fireworks began.

Breathlessly they collapsed back into the Rivière-Rouge and let the waters cool them. She remembered how she had giggled when Thynan mentioned the irony of the river's name, the cascade now running red with the blood of their victims. People said killing was wrong, but she didn't feel that way. It had exhilarated her, excited her to a peak of something she had never felt before, and while she knew at some point she would crash back to earth, she wanted to savor the experience for as long as she possibly could.

"I don't want to leave." She slurred her words, the endorphins still tickling the pleasure centers of her brain.

"We have to, they'll be coming for us," Thynan said softly. "We killed a lot of people, 'Nessa. They won't let that stand."

"They came to capture me, to take me home. It was self-defense! Lyssa will understand."

"You killed your kin. I'm sorry, my love, but your sister will *not* understand."

Her mood shattered into a thousand tiny shards of disappointment. He was right. Thynan was always right. What she

had done was ethically and morally wrong. It was unforgiva-
ble. How could everything be so clear...yet still so confusing?

Why did I do that?

She sat up slowly, opening her eyelids a fraction. The sun
was peeking over the treetops, bathing her nude body in its
lovingly warm embrace. It was beautiful but hurt her sensitive
eyes if her gaze lingered for too long. She closed them again,
memorizing and internalizing the view she had briefly witnessed.

"Where will we go?" she asked in a husky voice. The
memory she relived had reignited the passion deep in her
belly.

"The soldiers, they knew where to find us..." he growled,
deep in thought. "The question is how?"

"Does it matter?" Vanessa purred.

"You want to be free...don't you?"

She heard his question and her heart surged.

"Yes." She bent down and kissed his lips as he lay beside
her in the burbling waters. "More than anything in the world."

He reached up and held her face gently in his hand, cupping
her chin between his powerful fingers.

"Then...we still have work to do."

She melted into his arms, kissing him passionately. She
was his. He had changed her life. She had run away from
home...for him. Today she had killed members of her own family...for him. There was nothing that she would not do.

For him.

| 47 |

BETRAYAL

– Mercy balthazaar –
– Wednesday – Albany, New Victus –

"She turned on us."

Mercy had flown directly to Lyssa's home in Albany to deliver the bad news that she knew would be hard for her aunt to hear. The truth would hurt, but Mercy also knew that lying to Lyssa did her no favors. The look of anguish and despair that spread slowly across Lyssa's face as she came to terms with the painful realization of her sister's betrayal, and likely fate, cut Mercy to the core.

"Tell me what happened," Lyssa whispered flatly, without a hint of the emotion Mercy knew was tearing her apart.

"I consulted with Sergeant Maysun and we decided that, rather than spook them into going on the run again, we would discreetly circle around them at a distance and deploy the retrieval squad in two groups. Drop four upstream and four down.

"We coordinated the two teams to close in while I ran air support. We approached with care; our strategy was to attempt to separate them so that we could reason with Vanessa. If we could reach her, then we hoped she would talk her partner into a surrender. Failing that, if we had to take him down by force, then I didn't want Vanessa caught in any crossfire.

But...she put herself between us and him...and then they attacked *us* first."

That had been the plan. A hope that they could resolve this without the need for violence or bloodshed. It was a hope that was dashed the moment Mercy saw Vanessa and her paramour together.

"Lyssa...Vanessa was a stranger. I'm not sure she even recognized who we were. Who *I* was." She shook her head slowly. "Without her medication, her condition is running unchecked, and clearly he's encouraging it."

"I was afraid something like this would happen if she ever got out." Lyssa closed her eyes. "I hated keeping her under house arrest, but I dreaded what would become of her if..."

"We searched everywhere for a cure. Left no stone unturned. We had to face the fact that the succubi mutation *is* rare and incurable. You did everything you could to keep her safe."

"Did I?" Lyssa sounded unconvinced. "Or by keeping her secluded did I simply fan the flames of her desire to be free? Maybe I could have done something differently, something that would have kept her safe. I never meant to drive her away."

Silence lingered between them. Mercy knew there was little she could say to dissuade Lyssa from trying to shoulder the blame. Responsibility was core to her character. Instead, she shifted the emphasis of the conversation away from introspective recriminations.

"I'm sorry, Lyssa, but I think she's lost to us now. We just may have to accept that. It was hard to reconcile her as being *our* Vanessa. Naked and covered head to toe in the dirt of the forest. Her spark of innocence was gone."

"How many people did we lose?"

"Five dead and three wounded," Mercy replied quietly. She had known each of them. "Kristen, Skellen and Maysun are in intensive care. Their wounds are...pretty severe."

"Gods!" Lyssa whispered in dismay.

"It happened so fast, Lyssa. It was disturbing to see Vanessa as a...a predator. And the Wolf...he's big. Like a force of nature, but he'd been trained, too. Ex-military maybe. He knew *exactly* what he was doing. I've never seen a more efficient killer. The way he shifted between forms so fluidly in combat...he made us look like amateurs. Half of the team was already down by the time they made the switch to...to something more lethal. By then it was too late.

"I opened fire from the dropship, but they were already heading into the forest again, deeper into Pack territory. Then they were gone. I landed in the clearing and picked up our people. Brought them home."

She slumped back into the armchair. She didn't say any more. She didn't know what more *to* say. Only one thing sprang to mind.

"I'm so sorry."

Lyssa was one of the strongest people she knew. The only person she had ever seen stand up to Sebastian StormHall and the only one who had the nerve to risk everything establishing a dialogue with Pack Nation by fronting a face to face meeting with Damian Dane on his own turf. Lyssa was a great leader for their House. Yet a large part of what made her great was her sense of family. Today she looked at Mercy with tears welled in her eyes. Not many people saw her like this. Mercy felt oddly privileged.

"It's not your fault. This whole mess is the result of decisions I made before you were even born."

"But today...I could have landed," Mercy said, searching desperately for something she could have done differently. "I could have fought..."

"It's not *your* fault," Lyssa repeated. "You did the right thing. It's saddening that I have lost good people today, and I will grieve for them. True and loyal members of our House. But if I had lost you... I'm glad you're safe. You have nothing to apologize for – the responsibility lies with me. No one else."

Lyssa rose from her sofa and padded barefoot across the lush cream carpet to the brilliant white mantelpiece where there was an array of different sized and shaped picture frames. Mercy had always liked the aesthetic in here, minimalist and modern with a variety of distinctive textiles and textures. Light and airy, with rich burgundy colored drapes and rugs that contrasted harmoniously with the cream and white décor. She lifted one of the frames containing a photo of Vanessa, sighing as she stared at it.

"I should have found a different...better way. A gilded cage is still a cage. You can see the sadness in her eyes; she just wanted a chance to be a real person. To experience the world as we do. To love and be loved."

She placed the picture carefully back on the mantle and ran a hand wearily through her hair, flicking the white stripe up over her head temporarily before it fell forward again, unnoticed. Mercy hated to see her aunt like this, so tired and stressed. While she may have been talking about her sister, the words Lyssa had just spoken echoed of a truth about herself, too. Mercy knew that the responsibilities of leadership were a gilded cage of their own. It seemed unfair for someone who had done so much for their House, for their kind.

One day she would be famous as the woman who led the Vampyrii race out from the darkness of the StormHall era, Mercy was confident of that. But for now, she was forced to work tirelessly in the shadows doing things that would likely hand her a death sentence for treason if she were caught. Quite the burden weighed on the slender shoulders of Lyssa Balthazaar.

"How can I help?"

"You've done all you can. There's nothing more we can do about 'Nessa now. It's down to Dane's hunters...and I will have to prepare myself for the worst. If they're not going to come peacefully, then..."

Lyssa said no more. She didn't have to. Dane's people would no doubt try to bring Vanessa back alive, but after seeing Vanessa and her paramour in action personally, Mercy had her doubts that it would be possible. Lyssa took a deep breath and seemed to tap a fresh vein of strength.

"I do, however, have another job for you," Lyssa said. "If I'm going to be the delegate for New Victus at the Nexus Summit, I'll be damned if I'm trusting my security to one of Sebastian's lackeys. I want you to come with me as part of my delegation party. With that in mind, I'd like you to go to Nexus ahead of the Summit and make sure everything is above board."

"Of course."

Maybe it was the wrong emotion to be having right now, but the nature of the job *excited* her. She hadn't travelled outside of the boundaries of New Victus in decades, her recent hop across the Pack Nation border notwithstanding, so to be able to go and experience somewhere new was a mouth-watering prospect.

"When would you like me to leave?"

"Early next week," Lyssa said with a wry smile. "I'm just finalizing arrangements. On your way there, though, I'd like you to do me a favor. A favor I want kept off the record. I've arranged permission for you to go somewhere I *know* you've always wanted to go."

"Sounds intriguing..."

A warm glow started to spread through Mercy as Lyssa laid out the details of her plan. Even after being confronted with such bad news about Vanessa, Lyssa was addressing the bigger picture. Putting personal issues aside temporarily to keep the wheels in motion on her long-term plan. Mercy wasn't sure if she could do the same thing if she were in her aunt's position. It was truly inspiring.

She left Lyssa's home feeling *much* lighter in spirit than when she had arrived.

| 48 |

ON THE RUN

– Michael Reynolds –
– Saturday – London, England –

The sun was fresh in the sky as Michael worked through the early morning element of his regular fitness regime – a brisk run around Hyde Park. He enjoyed the sound of his footfalls pounding the pavement, a regular left-right metronomic backbeat to the cheerful dawn chorus. It was oddly tranquil. He had this idyllic oasis in the middle of London all to himself.

Or so he thought.

"Hey!" Gayle Knightley said jauntily with a warm grin as she appeared alongside him, matching his stride.

She may have been several inches shorter in height, but those long legs evidently made up the difference.

"Hey."

"You know...you got some serious pace." Gayle sounded a little out of breath. "Been trying to catch up with you...for a good few minutes."

"I usually run alone..."

As much as he had found himself warming up to her lately, he wasn't keen to share his morning routine these days. Either Gayle didn't get his subtle hint, or more likely just didn't care

"Oh...don't mind me," Gayle panted cheerfully.

Michael glanced over at her, his eyebrow arched.

Her sneakers matched the hue of her hair, which was

drawn back into a simple yet elegant plait, while a pair of dark wraparound sunglasses hid her emerald eyes. The snug white sports top with red side-panels flaunted the pale skin of her toned midriff and bared her arms, which Michael realized were decorated with a modest collection of tattoos.

"Ain't you cold?"

"Nah," she replied, her breathing starting to settle down. "For an early London morning in October, this is pretty mild."

"I thought you didn't run? Due to your bum knee?"

"Meh. Doc says I need to rehab, but as you can see...s'fine."

Any other time the body-art would have been his primary topic for a follow-up question, but the mention of her injury had unconsciously drawn his gaze down toward her legs and the matching pair of Lycra gym shorts that hugged her thighs to a couple of inches above the knee.

He had read the reports and knew the details of her injury. Gayle almost always wore long pants, or her CombatSkin, so for the first time, Michael could see the long surgical scar where the doctors had repaired the joint. Roughly five inches running vertically from just above the kneecap to just below it. The knee itself didn't look that much different to the one on her left leg. Maybe just a little more swollen.

"What was the injury? If you don't mind my asking."

"Dislocated and broken patella, compound fracture of the fibula, broken fibula, and a torn ACL. The bingo win of lower leg injuries." She shrugged her shoulders as they bounced in time to her running. "It was pretty bad...now it's just not pretty. Fortunately for me, Fae medical science is fucking good. Lana's been bugging me to start running again, so I figured I'd get back to it this week. This is day four of my new regime."

"You're sure it ain't too soon?" Michael asked with a note of concern.

"You sound like Allyson when I started wearing heels again!" Gayle snorted. "Honestly, it's taken me a while to trust it enough to run. I was afraid it would give out."

"Well, it seems to be holdin' up just fine."

Gayle nodded.

The two of them were now running in step, Gayle matching his foot falls in perfect synchronization, her arms pumping in rhythm with her legs. She looked like a professional runner, or at least someone who had done this regularly for years. Yet she was obviously a little out of condition. Her breathing was a touch labored, her face flushed, and a sheen of perspiration covered her brow.

As they ran together in comfortable silence down the tree lined pathway parallel to South Carriage Drive, Michael realized that rather than still being annoyed at Gayle's intrusion, he was appreciating her company. He had never trained alone in the past, always having the company of either Alex or his fellow soldiers. Here in London, he had been forced to go solo with his daily ritual out of necessity. It felt natural to once more have a running mate.

"I didn't see you in Hyde Park earlier in the week. You run at a different time?"

She glanced in his direction and smiled. "Nope, always morning. But I usually head into the Palace early and run around St James instead. Been doing that since my days as a student here at the Academy."

"So, what brings you here this mornin'?"

"Ally has a place close to the park. Lana has been using it since she came back to the Academy, and I stayed over there last night."

"Knightsbridge?"

"Yup."

"I live in Knightsbridge, too."

Gayle glanced at him again, this time with a sly smile.

"No kidding!" she grinned.

"But then you knew that already..." Michael shook his head.

"Just like you already knew how fucked up my knee was," she laughed. "I read your file too, y'know."

Michael found himself wearing a smile of his own, though he wasn't entirely sure why.

"Where in Knightsbridge is your sister's place?"

"Trevor Street. Lana and I had dinner in town last night and it was getting late, so I stayed over with her rather than head home. You're Montpelier Walk, yes?"

He nodded and noticed that they were approaching the right-hand pathway that led to the Hyde Park playground. He would normally have left the park by now, heading home for a shower before starting his day proper. Yet as he was enjoying the amiable flow of conversation with Gayle, he decided to carry on for a fourth lap of the park. Just three weeks ago he had strongly doubted that they could work together, let alone pursue extra-curricular activities in each other's company.

He mused at his subconscious choice of words. It was becoming increasingly difficult to deny the fact that he was finding himself attracted to her in more than just a physical way. His mind flashed to the drunken message Gayle's sister had left him. Maybe she was on to something. He snorted with laughter, which of course drew the attention of his new running mate.

"Care to share?" she said with a confused laugh of her own.

"Just thinking about the message from your sister."

"Oh, fuck," Gayle sighed. "I was hoping we'd have forgotten all about that."

"Well, I'm flyin' out to Nexus this afternoon to meet with her. NAA want me to run an eye over the security arrangements for the conference," he admitted. "I'm sure that message will more than likely come up during my time there…"

"Well, I hope you embarrass *her* as much as she embarrassed me!"

"I'll see what I can do," Michael laughed. "I am imagining a whole lotta awkward."

"It'll be fine," she shrugged. "Ally's a lot like me…only with less cursing. You two will get on like a house on fire. Like you've known her for years. Trust me. If it helps, it's her you have to thank for the turnaround in my attitude."

"There's been a turnaround?"

"Fuck you, Captain Reynolds," Gayle laughed. "I've been on my best behavior and you know it. Anyway, that day we first met…she was the one who talked me down off the ledge. I told her what an idiot I'd been and how badly you fucking hated me."

"Hate is a mighty strong word," Michael protested. "But...I did have serious misgivings about whether we'd be able to effectively work together."

"But now you're realizing that I'm not so bad after all, right?" she asked with a tiny note of something in her voice.

Hope?

He turned his head to look at her, an acknowledgement of her question and her tone. He found her looking squarely at him awaiting his response. Unfortunately, this meant that neither of them was looking where they were going.

The pothole was shallow, but it was enough. Gayle wasn't ready for her right foot to drop that inch or two further than usual, which led to a stumble, and then a fall. With a yelp she began a decidedly ungraceful tumble, breaking her rapid descent with the exposed palms of her hands. Her momentum carried her into an awkward forward roll, which started with her surgically repaired joint crashing hard onto the asphalt. She ended up sprawled on her back on the grass, holding her knee and grimacing in pain.

The correct phrase for the tumble in UK parlance, as Michael would find out later, was 'arse-over-tit.'

Michael stopped running and quickly backtracked the few yards to help her.

"Fuck, fuck, fuck..." Gayle was muttering under her breath, her trembling hands clasped tightly around her kneecap. Her sunglasses lay broken on the ground and there were tears running down her cheeks.

Pain? Frustration?

He crouched next to her and placed his hands gently on top of hers.

"Let me take a look," he said softly.

She looked at him with eyes that betrayed both anger and fear. Anger that she had had such a stupid accident and fear that she fucked up something that had been so long healing to this point already. Her hands trembled beneath his.

"It's gonna be okay. Trust me."

Reluctantly, and with a sharp intake of breath, she uncovered her damaged knee. It was covered in blood, but as far as

Michael could tell, it wasn't badly wounded. She had a pretty severe graze from the asphalt, but much of the blood seemed to be the result of the wounds on the palms of Gayle's shaking hands. It was, however, starting to swell.

"It's fucked, isn't it?" Gayle said with a hint of dismay and fear. "Oh, shit...it's fucked."

"It ain't that bad," Michael reassured her. "Can you stand?"

She shrugged and accepted Michael's outstretched hand and the invitation to help her up. For someone with his strength, pulling the slender form of Gayle to her feet was an effortless task, and in a moment, she was standing next to him, balancing on one leg like a wounded flamingo.

"Okay, let's try walkin' on it."

She nodded and took a deep breath. Biting her lip to suppress the pain, she gingerly lowered her right foot onto the pathway and gradually began to transfer her weight. A moment later she gave up with a yelp and went back to standing on her left leg.

"Nope, nope, nope," she winced.

Michael looked around the park, evaluating the best course of action.

"Okay, so my place is just behind us," he said eventually. "I reckon I carry you there, we get some ice on that knee of yours, and..."

Gayle interrupted him before he could finish.

"I'm not some fucking damsel-in-distress," she snapped. "You're *not* carrying me anywhere. I'll walk it. I'll fucking hop if I have to."

If Michael had learned anything over their few weeks working together, it was that there was little point in arguing with her. There were strong-willed women...and *then* there was Gayle Knightley. She had a habit of making sure things were done her way.

Fine. Let her figure this one out herself.

"Come on then," he said as he encircled her waist with his arm.

Her skin felt soft under his fingertips and as she started to slowly and tentatively hop back down the pathway, he did his best to support her. They managed about twenty meters or so before Michael finally stopped biting his tongue, hoping that by now Gayle might be more amenable to his plan.

"You had enough yet? Can I please pick you up now?"

He could see the protest about to spew forth from her mouth, so he leapt in with his counter argument before she had the chance to shoot him down again.

"Look, I get it, okay? But I'm lookin', and I don't see a damsel-in-distress," he stated firmly. "You're wounded — it's that simple. Do you think you will be the first wounded soldier I've carried out of a combat zone? This ain't about gender. If you were a man, I'd be sayin' the exact same thing.

"Approach it objectively... Who knows what stress and strain you're puttin' that knee under trying to be the brave lil' soldier? You could be makin' it worse. You ain't that heavy, and the faster we get you resting up, the better. Believe me, if the roles were reversed and you could carry me, I'd let you do it in a heartbeat. So, please, climb down off your high-heels for a moment and let me help you."

Gayle looked at him carefully with narrowed eyes. "Are you comparing Hyde Park to a combat zone?" she said.

"That's what you took from all that?"

"Fine," Gayle sighed. "I'm in too much pain to argue."

He didn't waste time, simply swept her up into his arms. She was lighter than he thought she'd be. Gayle reached up and put her arms around his neck to secure herself, causing Michael to swallow involuntarily. Her face was now so close to his he could smell the mingling of her sweat and perfume. They stared into each other's eyes for a moment. Neither spoke. Eventually he broke the awkward gaze, looking away and clearing his throat.

"You okay?"

She nodded and smiled at him in amusement, fluttering her eyelids. "My hero!"

It was said in jest and she followed up by leaning in to kiss him playfully on the cheek. However, Michael was turning his head back to reply to her when, by happenstance, their lips met.

HUNTERS

He froze.

So did she.

What was supposed to be a joke had now turned into something far more uncomfortable. Neither moved, both hesitating and wondering how to extract themselves from this predicament. The kiss was now lingering far longer than it was ever meant to, moving from awkward to embarrassing. Gayle giggled.

"I'm sorry..." she said quietly as she retreated from their locked lips.

"Don't be," Michael said, realizing he meant it.

Gathering his composure, he backtracked them along the pathway to the road crossing at Rutland Gate. Once they'd crossed Kensington Road, it was a short distance to his home on Montpelier Walk.

An awkward silence hung between them as Michael tried to process his thoughts and he assumed Gayle was doing likewise. Or perhaps she was just focused on suppressing the pain from her damaged knee. It was hard to tell.

His front door recognized his approach and unlocked.

"You mind...?" Michael asked, nodding toward the door.

Gayle unhooked one of her arms from around his neck to reach for the door handle, wincing slightly as she did so. As the door pivoted open, he turned sideways in order to get them both through the frame and into the hallway. Gayle giggled, causing Michael to furrow his brown in confusion.

"What's so funny?"

She looked at him demurely. "Does this mean we're married now?"

Michael glanced back at the threshold and chuckled softly, suddenly realizing what she found so amusing.

"Not yet," he said.

"Yet?" she arched an eyebrow and grinned.

He pushed the front door closed with his foot. Gayle's playful nature evaporated, the coquettish look replaced quickly by one of apprehension as he navigated the hallway and carried her into the lounge. She bit her lower lip, and her eyes animat-

edly flicked from her bloodied leg to her strange new surroundings. A twinge of disappointment colored his mood.

*Is all this flirting simply a game to distract herself from her
pain?*

Moving carefully so as not to jar her injury, he lowered her
gently onto the sofa in the lounge, and as she got herself comfortable, he headed into the kitchen to grab some ice from the
freezer which he wrapped tightly in a hand-towel. After a
quick phone call, he grabbed his first aid kit and a bowl of water before heading back to the lounge.

"I'm pretty deficient in the first aid supplies department,"
Michael said as he entered. "But I'll clean up your knee best I
can and wrap it up in ice, okay? I already called a cab to get you
home."

"Thanks."

He pulled up the matching ottoman and sat down, beckon-
ing for her to pivot her leg over to him. He carefully removed
her footwear and gently placed her foot on his lap so he could
reach her knee.

"How's them hands feel?" he asked as he took some sterile
wipes from the first aid kit.

"Never had any complaints..." she said playfully.

He raised an eyebrow at her.

"They sting." She rolled her eyes. "I'll survive."

"Here." He handed her a couple of the wipes. "Clean up
your palms while I take a look at that knee."

It was then that he noticed his small artist pad, sitting on
her lap opened to a few pages in. Gayle had her head tilted and
was, to Michael's embarrassment, inspecting the gentle pencil
lines of the sketch that detailed a portrait that looked uncannily familiar to her.

"Is this *me*?"

Michael nodded. "Sorry," he said quietly.

"Don't be. It's...it's beautiful. Is that how you see...?" She
paused before continuing. "I didn't know you could draw."

"I sketch to keep my hand in, but painting is my real passion." He shrugged. "Anyway, you kinda have a thing for art
yourself, yeah?"

Michael nodded toward her body-art as he carefully lifted her leg, placing her foot between his thighs. The position kept her knee flexed a little as he started gently rubbing at it with the wipes, cleaning off now drying blood as carefully as he could.

"I like tattoos, but I can't draw." She shrugged. "Art takes talent, and in that arena, I have none."

"I recognize the unit crest on your shoulder," Michael said as he continued to dab at her knee. "Does the dragon on your back have any meaning?"

"I used to dream about dragons when I was a little girl..." Gayle said wistfully. "I was talking to Ghost about it one day, describing a particular dragon, and she drew if for me. It was a gift... How's the knee looking?"

He knew a change of subject when he saw one. Ghost was otherwise known as Maggie Brennan, one of her former teammates. Lost in Valletta during the Malta operation.

"Lookin' good," he said reassuringly.

The skin underneath appeared a little sore, but apart from that there were no serious cuts. Just grazed and likely bruised.

Gayle sighed heavily. "Used to be my legs were my best feature."

"From what I can see, they still look pretty darn good to me."

He had responded without thinking and as he heard the words coming out of his mouth, he was suddenly aware of how flirtatious they sounded.

"Why, Michael Reynolds...are you trying to seduce me?"

There was a coy, playful nature to her riposte, and for a moment Michael wondered where all this was leading, not that he objected to the return of the flirtatious nature of their banter. She closed the sketch pad and put it aside, looking at him with a impish glint in her eyes. Not in a million years had he ever before contemplated sleeping with a fellow teacher, but as he sat there holding her knee in his hands and saw the look on her face, the idea suddenly became a reality. Gayle burst out laughing.

"I'm just fucking with you. I wouldn't repay your kindness

by shamelessly taking advantage of you."

"Takin' advantage of *me*?" Michael exclaimed. "You're the one sittin' here bleeding. Or was all this a ruse to get into my house and...what?"

"Lure you to bed? Handsome, if I wanted to fuck you, we'd be horizontal by now."

"I doubt that," he shot back.

"Really?" she raised her right eyebrow and cocked her head. "Have you not heard about my reputation?" She laughed. "Firstly, if you're right, then I, being an evil seductress, have brilliantly engineered a situation where I'm vulnerable, scantily dressed, in *your* house, and I have my foot on your crotch."

She wriggled her toes suggestively as if to illustrate her point and suddenly he realized she was right.

"But, and here's the kicker...I'm half Fae and if I really wanted to, I could..."

She stopped herself mid-sentence, blushing. Michael looked at her closely and saw that she was now averting her eyes from his.

Embarrassed? Or ashamed?

What did that mean?

| 49 |

FALLING FOR THE FIRST TIME?

– Gayle Knightley –
– Saturday – London, England –

Prior to her being 'invited' back to the Academy, Gayle was convalescing at her family home near Ely. It was a peaceful atmosphere. The perfect place to rest and lick her wounds.

To grieve.

She had a home in London but found it hard to return there. The city held too many memories, both good and bad. Memories with which she was struggling to cope in the aftermath of Valletta. However, over the decade or so she lived there, the place had been decorated to her tastes and contained her belongings. It *was* home.

When she returned to it after her uncle made her the offer she couldn't refuse, she found that changes had been made. One of her spare rooms was now a rehabilitation gym, and a hydro-therapy hot tub replaced her previously functional bath. Norbel had seemingly never doubted his ability to manipulate her into returning, so took some liberties to get this work completed prior to their meeting. If she hadn't been angry already, this tipped her over the edge into full-on fury.

Over the weeks, however, much of that anger dissipated. She lay back in the bath and let the vigorous water jets massage her body.

Say what you like about working for the HFA, but the perks are pretty good.

The more she thought about it, the more she realized that the defusing of her temper had much to do with her new partner. Even she wasn't too stubborn to realize that Michael Reynolds was a positive influence on her.

The hot water was bliss swirling around her aching knee. She idly tried to flex it a little. After the initial bout of fear, Gayle was now confident that she hadn't damaged the knee permanently. There was clearly bruising and swelling, which was probably why it felt stiff. To be honest, though, it was the palms of her hands that hurt more, but they would heal soon enough.

Eyes closed, she relaxed into the supporting comfort of the water and cast her mind back a couple of hours to Michael's place.

What in God's name had that been?

Other than confusing.

There was something going on in her head. Something new. Something she had never truly experienced before...and it was befuddling the hell out of her. She took a deep breath and forced herself to think things through logically.

She found herself easily and naturally flirting with him, and she enjoyed it. Immensely. Additionally, the flirting was *not* about getting sex, which historically *had* been the case in her life to this point. At no time during their encounter had she been that way inclined despite her teasing him otherwise.

One image wouldn't leave her mind. She kept cycling back to that battered artists pad and the sketched profile image of her done in monochromatic shades of red. He drew her with her head tilted upwards, eyes closed as if bathing in sunlight. The line of her face looked beautifully elegant, yet haunted. Sad. She recognized herself in it immediately, stunned by how he captured not just her image, but her feelings, too. Her soul. No one had ever looked at her like that before. Had so intuitively understood what was beneath the surface.

Now that image haunted her.

She had genuinely been enjoying his company so much that when the car Michael requested arrived to take her home, she was more than a little disappointed. Why hadn't she made the effort sooner to really get to know him outside of work?

The epiphany hit her.

This whole thing had been a set up. The whole timeline of events dating back to the previous evening had been subtly manipulated by her own subconscious to bring her to this point.

She *had* been on a night out with Lana, she hadn't lied about that, but the evening of dinner and a few drinks in SoHo finished early enough for her to have gone home. So, why hadn't she just headed back to her own nearby place in Chelsea? Why had she instead gone to stay with Lana at Allyson's house?

It was not a spur-of-the-moment decision, either. If it had been, then why had she already packed an overnight bag with her workout clothes in it? Why had she timed her run in Hyde Park to deliberately coincide with when she knew Michael would be on his? For heaven's sake, she even *waited* near the park entrance in the guise of doing warm up stretches, until she spotted Michael run past. *Then* she joined him on the run.

So, the big question was...why?

Was it sex she was after? That would fit her profile.

But if that was the case, she'd had ample time to seal the deal, so to speak, when they had been alone together.

So, if it's not for the sex...then what am I looking for?

One way or the other, she was afraid of the answer. Either she was slipping subconsciously back into old patterns again, or she was experiencing something that was a *long* way outside of her comfort zone. Taking a deep breath, she sank beneath the warm water, fully submerging her head.

Due to the Fae blood that burned hot inside her, Gayle had been sexually prolific.

Some porn stars have had less sex than me... Not sure that's something to be proud of.

She slowly exhaled, blowing leisurely bubbles in the warm water. Finally, she emerged, feeling the cool air on her face once more.

But if it wasn't purely sex, then was it love?

If she was brutally honest with herself, love had been an elusive partner, not that she had been looking. There were always other things in her life. Training, her fellow students, the competition, the missions, and then...the loss. Love had never been a part of her grand plan.

Well, maybe she thought she was in love once...but that hadn't turned out so well. Mistakes had been made. But maybe now she was ready to expand her horizons a little. Maybe start looking into something new.

She sighed and felt the warm water wash over her body as she cleared her mind of speculation and thought back to that morning. His hands caressing her leg, his fingertips on her soft skin.

The accidental kiss.

A serendipitous confluence of events that led them to a place she felt they both wanted to go.

The memory of that touch of his lips started her down a rabbit hole of fantasy. A fantasy that would soon blissfully make her forget about her aching knee in a far more enjoyable way.

| 50 |

EMBARRASSMENT

– Michael Reynolds –
– Saturday – Nexus City, Iceland –

As Michael stepped out through the hatch of the Airbus A600 Skyliner, he took a grateful breath of fresh air. After the recycled oxygen of the two-hour flight, a lungful of the frigid atmosphere was most welcome. He shivered and glanced around with interest; the Icelandic scenery was just as majestic as he had expected it to be. A fine mist hung in the air against a backdrop of snow dusted mountains, showcasing blue-grey volcanic rock and low-lying hills that looked like they had been plucked from the pages of a fantasy novel. A peek of green vegetation here and there gave the vista a splash of color.

However, it was the city, laid out before him, that was the real selling point of the trip for Michael. Dozens of cultures thrived here, each bringing their own architectural sensibilities to a metropolis that was quite unlike anywhere else in the world. A unique collection of different styles that all blended seamlessly together and sat in perfect harmony with the landscape surrounding it.

Welcome to Nexus City.

He would have liked to savor the view for a few moments longer, but the other passengers were queuing up behind him.

Reluctantly, he shouldered his satchel and carefully descended the stairs to the pristine asphalt of the landing strip and the outstretched hand of an uncannily familiar looking young woman with a tight ebony ponytail. The insignia and rank pins on her tailored black jacket told him she was a captain in Nexus City Security, but it was the striking resemblance to her sister that informed him this was Allyson Knightley. He took her outstretched hand in a firm shake.

"Captain Reynolds, it's a pleasure to *finally* put a face to the name," she greeted him, in a manner considerably more professional than the last time he had heard her now familiar voice.

"Captain Knightley, thank you for receivin' me," he smiled warmly.

"Please, call me Allyson. For the record, my title is Chief. *Captain* Knightley is my sister."

She gestured toward the SkyPort terminal building, indicating the direction they should walk.

"Allyson it is then. Please, call me Michael. It's good of you to make the time to see me on such short notice."

"Honestly, it's the least I could do." She took a deep breath. "I thought that maybe I owed you an apology..."

He regarded her with a playful look of mock confusion. "Does this mean that we're *not* gonna be havin' all the *sex*?" He whispered the final word, mimicking her voice message.

Allyson blushed. "I thought that might come up. I have no excuse, other than to state – for the record – that vodka is *pure* evil. Nexus City Security is dedicating a special team to expunge it from this world in order to prevent things like that from ever happening again."

"You really want to rid the world of vodka?" he chuckled.

"No...you're right. That's crazy talk! How would I embarrass my sisters without vodka?"

Gayle had been right. Michael found it remarkably easy to fall into the same rhythmic banter with Allyson that he had established back home with her sister that morning. There was a feeling of familiarity talking with Allyson. She had the same sense of humor as her sister, but without the underlying bitterness. A glimpse of what might be perhaps?

"We've all done stupid things when a little drunk."

"A *little* drunk?" Allyson laughed, but her face quickly turned more serious. "Honestly, being the chief here and with this being my first Summit...there's a lot of stress. Then dealing with Gayle and...family stuff...I really needed the release that night. I am sorry you were on the receiving end of my alcohol-impaired judgement."

"Truthfully, it was worth it to see the mortified look on your sister's face."

"Oh, she relayed the extent of her humiliation to me in an extensive phone call laced with much profanity and *multiple* promises to kill me as I sleep."

Allyson ushered him into the arrivals area of the terminal building, and they walked slowly toward the Nexus Conference Centre link and its security checkpoint. The staff there diligently checked his satchel as he passed through the body imaging scanners. Once cleared, Allyson led him at a deliberately leisurely pace along a wide promenade. A tunnel fashioned of wooden arches and curved glass windows allowed stunning views of the city and the landscape to either side.

"Security seems pretty tight," he commented as they walked.

"I hope so. That's what you're really here for, right? I was surprised that the NAA called you in for this."

"I served under Ambassador McAdams back when he was a general at Fort Miramar." Michael shrugged. "I admire the man immensely, but he can be a little...paranoid. I ran security there for two years, so I guess I'm a known quantity to throw a second pair of eyes over your plans. From what I've seen so far though, you seem to have it all under control."

"God, I hope so." Allyson took a deep breath. "I ran smaller security operations for conventions and things back when I was a cop but this...is magnitudes bigger. I've tried to scale up everything I learned in London, tried to think of everything, but I'm not too proud to believe a review by another expert wouldn't be beneficial. I'll pull up all the strategies, maps, procedures, and paperwork when we get to my office, but just to give you the abridged version..."

She brought them to a halt and gestured back down the tunnel.

"The SkyPort is the only practical way in and out of Nexus City—" she started.

"No overland connection?" Michael interrupted.

"Technically, yes," Allyson replied. "You *can* drive here...if you have a vehicle with serious off-road capability and enjoy long bumpy rides in the country. Realistically, though, no one ever does."

"What if they did?"

"Well, as I'm sure you know, Iceland, and ergo Nexus City itself, is divided into three distinct territories. We have no control over what happens in the New Victus or Pack Nation sectors; their borders are their responsibility, not ours. While we do try to work closely with NVSec and PackSec on matters of general security, we simply have to trust they do their jobs. Relations with PackSec are pretty good, actually; NVSec...not so much.

The FSE sector, however, is one that we *can* control. All roads come in through security checkpoints in the perimeter wall, which is monitored from camera towers with overlapping fields of vision."

"Sounds good," Michael agreed. "But in my experience, if someone is really determined, they'll find a way past a barrier."

"Agreed," Allyson nodded. "Which is why we are concentrating security efforts around the SkyPort, Conference Centre, and the WCC."

"WCC?" Michael queried.

"World Council Chambers. The Nexus Conference Centre is a sprawling campus of smaller buildings, the centerpiece of which is the primary diplomatic chambers known as the WCC. That's where the Summit will take place, hence the extra security."

"Understandable."

"Every visitor coming through the SkyPort is scanned for weapons, explosives, the usual drill. No one gets in without diplomatic papers or an entrance visa. As for stowaways, there are more cameras watching the SkyPort than we have on the perimeter walls. We watch every plane, flyer, skyship, and dropship that lands here."

"I noticed that the SkyPort is walled in."

Allyson nodded. "Twelve feet high with motion sensors at overlapping intervals extending another twenty or so feet above that. So, even if you do get in as a stowaway, you need to come through a security checkpoint to get into the city. Nobody hops the wall without us knowing about it."

"What about Fae? I've never seen it, but I know they can fly."

"The old stories of fairy-folk? Tiny people with wings? All true." Allyson smiled. "When we were children, Mum used to do the fairy thing sometimes to entertain us. In truth, though, they rarely actually do it, and the Fae are at the bottom of our potential threat list."

"But let's say there's an evil Fae, hell bent on getting into the city," Michael pushed. "What stops them from flying over the wall?"

Allyson pointed toward the trio of sizeable radar-type dishes spinning lazily atop the SkyPort Control Tower.

"We call them the 'Triplets.' They can pick up objects as small as a housefly. They cover Nexus City airspace in real-time through three-hundred-and-sixty degrees, down to a height of around twenty feet..."

"Which overlaps with the motion sensors on the wall," Michael finished.

"Exactly."

"Can they be hacked?"

"The radar or the motion sensors?"

"Either. Both," Michael said. "Or the cameras."

"It's hard to stop a truly determined hacker and as they're all computerized systems...yes, technically they could be hacked," Allyson admitted. "But we work very closely with the Advanced Computer Centre in Belgium on detection and countermeasures. In the event of a system infiltration alert, we immediately lock the city down till we're satisfied the threat is neutralized."

"If I recall correctly, doesn't the Conference Centre have its own landing pad?"

"Only ambassadorial flyers can land there," Allyson sighed. "It's not big enough to serve anything commercial or chartered – those need runways, so they have to use the main SkyPort. Unfortunately, most ambassadors have personal fliers and flit in and out whenever the mood moves them. It's a pain in my arse. Excuse my language."

"I work with your sister," Michael laughed. "Believe me, I hear *much* worse on a daily basis."

"Gayle never met an expletive she didn't fall in love with." Allyson reciprocated the laugh and looked sideways at Michael with a twinkle of something in her eye. "Speaking of whom..."

There was a moment of silence between them before Allyson seemed to find the right way to broach the subject of her sister.

"Genetically, being a hybrid has its perks. It also has its downsides. Because our abilities are fueled by our emotions, those feelings can bubble right under the surface for us. Carrie, our younger sister, and I don't use our abilities day-to-day, so it's not a big problem for us to...control our feelings. Gayle, though..."

"She's been embedded in a world where she has had to use her powers regularly, and to an extent that I never have. She's been forced by her career choice to leave a paper-thin layer between the world and what she feels. It makes her prone to anger, excitement, saying and expressing what she feels. It *also* makes her straightforward to read if you know what you're looking for."

Michael hesitantly half nodded. "Can I ask where you're goin' with this?" He understood what she was saying but wasn't sure what the point was. Allyson smiled.

"People think that Gayle is angry all the time, but what she is right now...is scared. Her role in the Hunters defined her, and now the Hunters are gone. She's trying to redefine a life without that touchstone. She's scared that she's responsible for killing her friends. She's scared because she's been put in a position where she is accountable for those kids. She's scared because she feels like she's damaged goods. She's scared because she feels like she's alone."

Allyson paused before continuing, her voice softening. "She's scared because she has feelings for *you* which she doesn't understand."

Michael didn't quite know how to respond to that, so he didn't say anything. As he gathered his thoughts, he was suddenly aware of how stupid he was probably looking. Allyson laughed.

"Too much too soon?"

"I'm just not sure what to say..." Michael admitted.

"Sorry." Allyson shrugged. "Being forward runs in the Knightley family genetics. I don't know you well, Michael. I just know what I see in my sister and what I hear from Lana. And she tells me that there's *definite* chemistry between you and Gayle. Now, I'm not telling you this because I want you to jump my sister's bones, despite what my ill-conceived phone message may have intimated. I brought this up because...if you are in any way interested, it's worth giving her the time to heal. To figure things out. That's all I'm saying."

She paused for a moment, studying his face for a reaction. Her slow smile told him that she found what she was looking for.

"You're not that difficult to read yourself," she said with a glint in her eye. "Lana was on to something. Honestly, though, I just wanted to put more *eloquently* what I was trying to drunkenly express the other night.

"Now, if you'd like we can go back to the matters of security?"

"Please." Michael laughed and breathed a small sigh of relief.

Her words had given him much to think about, especially regarding his own thought processes over the last couple of weeks. He couldn't deny that she was right – there was *something* there. Every time Gayle was around, he had to catch himself to stop from staring a little too long at her eyes, and when she left, he loved the way the scent of honey and lemon lingered as a gentle reminder of her presence.

"Okay, where were we...?" Allyson started walking again.

"Private landings."

"Right, yes, thank you. So, if a flight is being tracked into the Conference Centre landing pad, we ensure that a security team member is there to meet it to manually sweep any passengers and crew before they're let into the city. Personal luggage is not allowed into the World Council Chambers at all."

"No exceptions?"

"No exceptions," Allyson confirmed. "We had special diplomatic attaché cases designed and built using proprietary Fae tech to protect against duplication. Only these can be used to ferry documents in and out. They are all uniform and uniquely ID-tagged and are run through a specially designed scanner upon entry to the Center, and again at the WCC.

"You'll see two types. Silver diplomatic exchange cases, and black personal cases. Both are almost identical, but the personal cases are biometrically coded to the carrying diplomat only, whereas the exchange cases are pre-biometrically coded to both the sender and the recipient. We handle that coding on request and distribute the cases accordingly.

"So, for example, if the Pack Nation ambassador wants to exchange confidential documents with the Australasian ambassador, then they will submit a request to my office for a silver case. We'll biometrically profile it for both ambassadors and send it to the Pack Nation embassy."

"And no one else can open it?"

"Only Fran and I...Francesca Romano, my deputy. We have security override profiles on every case. But if a case is stolen, and someone tries to force it open, then the contents of the case are destroyed using some fancy incineration tech the Fae built."

"And you said no other luggage is allowed in?"

Allyson nodded. "Yup. We cracked down on that. You'll only see these black and silver cases in the Conference Center and all of them will have gone through our scanners to get in.

Any other luggage is taken off the plane and forwarded directly to the appropriate sector or embassy. It doesn't come through here."

She gestured to their new surroundings – a vast hexagonal atrium with a clear crystal dome that bathed the room in natural light.

"Welcome to the SkyPort MagLev terminal," she said. "MagLevs run directly to each of the three major factions and operate on totally independent underground lines. Each faction has two – one direct to their embassy and the other to a civilian terminal. It's quiet today, but this place will be *heaving* closer to the Summit."

"Trouble spot?"

"Could be," Allyson admitted. "This and the arrivals lounge are the only places where the factions mingle freely until they reach the Conference Center, so we have had flare-ups in the past. That's why we have a security office over to our right."

His eyes followed the direction she was pointing, and he immediately spotted the Nexus Security officers in attendance.

"To the left of that is the secure entrance to the Nexus Conference Center itself," Allyson continued. "Everybody is security checked again on the way in. Then you have the individual border controls for the three main factions – Pack Nation, the Federation, and New Victus.

"I take it you know your Nexus history at least a little?"

Michael nodded.

"Those border control stations are where my security remit ends as regards to Pack Nation and New Victus. We have zero jurisdiction over there – that's their sovereign territory. The FSE sector, however, is a different matter. To the north, next to the SkyPort, is the area the FSE generously – though some would say foolishly – agreed to allow other nation-states to place their own embassies. We colloquially refer to it as 'Embassy Alley.' There's an independent overland MagLev that runs directly there from the SkyPort which we also control. Pretty much all the other factions' diplomatic parties filter through our gates. Some are friendly, some not so much. For instance, NordScania I trust, whereas the Free Traders Association..."

Allyson trailed off but her point was clear. She looked at him thoughtfully. "We'll take a walk through the Conference Centre to the WCC, and then I'll show you Embassy Alley while we wander back to my office. Then I'll run you through the rest of our security arrangements."

"You know...you're nothin' like your sister." Michael shook his head and smiled.

"Yeah, she wasn't exactly the spirit of co-operation from the jump, was she?" Allyson chuckled.

"I'll tell you one thing y'all do have in common. Both of you give an *awful* first impression."

"But I give a better second one, am I right?" Allyson laughed. "You have siblings?"

"Yes. Alex, my twin." A stab of melancholy caught his thoughts. "Like you and Gayle, we're...nothin' alike."

"I feel there's a story in there somewhere," Allyson said, noting the change in his tone. "How about we go talk families and security matters over a beer or three?"

"You sure that's wise?" he frowned.

"You don't like beer?"

"Aren't you on duty?"

More of her light laughter ensued, a sound that Michael realized was almost identical to her sister's, though Allyson seemed to give of it more freely. She looked at him with a mischievous look in her eye.

"I'm the Chief of Security and it's a *really* quiet day. Consider me clocked off duty and all yours. Beers and shop talk. You have any better offers?"

He had to admit, he did not.

| 51 |

HYPOCRITIC OATH

– Zarra Anderson –
– Sunday – Mont Tremblant, Pack Nation –

Zarra understood that her physical prime was behind her, but thirty-seven was hardly old age. She was in great shape – probably the best of her life – but even so, this hunt was beginning to take its toll on her. Even if she hadn't been coming off the back of six months of hard work, the terrain, the injuries, and the blood-loss would have led her to this point anyway. She was beyond the limits of her endurance, and fatigue was setting in fast.

Zarra yawned, the fifth in as many minutes.

The cabin-clearing had been their pseudo-home for two days as she rested to regain some of her strength and allow her shoulder to start the healing process. In all honesty, Zarra knew that they had probably moved on too early. A couple more days would have been beneficial, but the trail was getting colder by the minute and to delay any longer was to risk having no chance of completing the hunt. It had become now-or-never time, and she was not the kind of person to quit a hunt.

Which presented her with a dilemma.

She had seen the work of this incubus firsthand. He was dangerous. While he was free, innocent lives were at stake. Zarra had taken on dangerous hunts before, and she knew that success *always* lay in being patient and picking the right moment to make her move. The question then became; when *was* the optimal time? Because to confront him and Vanessa rashly, without a plan or a strategic advantage, was suicide.

There were too many variables stacked against them, giving their quarry the upper hand. The incubus obviously knew the terrain, as evidenced by the hideaways they had already found. He also had a plan; his actions were decidedly not random.

Vanessa was the wild card.

Was she just along for the ride? Or was she an active part of this murderous spree? The evidence suggested she was mentally unstable and Zarra had no idea how she would react if confronted. Either way, she *was* still a Vampyrii *and* a succubus, and as such represented a clear and present danger. Even if Zarra was fully healthy, her odds in a fight were even at best.

Something which Alex was constantly needling her about.

"You know our chances would be a lot better *and* you'd be fresher if you'd just—"

She interrupted him before he went any further.

"Leave it be, Alex," she hissed, pain and fatigue having left her exceedingly short tempered.

The fire warmed her as she lay on the soft grass and stared up through the canopy of trees at the stars. At least this hunt was giving her the opportunity to appreciate the beauty of a night sky for once, something she didn't get to do very often these days.

Alex mumbled to himself, but Zarra's sharp hearing picked up his snide comment as clear as crystal.

"What's *my* problem?" She almost laughed in disbelief. "Honestly, are you kiddin' me? What the fuck is *your* problem?"

"After what happened at the cabin, I really thought that we were finally starting to put our history behind us. But the smallest comment sets you off."

"Smallest comment? You've been consistently buggin' me about this since day one, *despite* my tellin' you to leave it alone every goddamn time. I don't need your constant reminder of what I've become. Let me just be what I am…what I want to be right now."

"You're so much better now," Alex said. "Look at you, how far you've come. You were wasted in the army."

"Gildin' the lily only works if you like goddamn lilies. Yes, I am fuckin' good at what I do, but it isn't what I *wanted* to do. You think I enjoy being a freelance peacekeeping agent?"

"You seem to," he shrugged.

Zarra laughed almost hysterically. "You just don't get it, and you never will because that life was never yours. You were just fakin' it."

"That's not true," he rebutted. "I fought alongside you. I wasn't pretending."

"The fighting was real, I'll give you that, but I joined the army because, for me, it was a calling. For you it was just another assignment."

"I fought alongside you," he repeated, as if that argument trumped all.

"You were a spy. That's all. You should've let me die on that forest floor instead of…"

"And there it is." There was a note of smugness in Alex's tone.

"Don't you dare…"

"You want to know what *my* problem is? My problem is that since Sawtooth, you've been—" he started, but she cut him off.

"I've been what? Ungrateful? Angry? Guilty as fuckin' charged! I am *all* of the above."

"It's been five years…"

"So now there's a statute of limitations on bein' angry at someone for ruining their life?" She sat up and stared at him.

"I didn't ruin your life. I saved your life."

The rage bubble burst inside her. He didn't understand what he'd done. Never had in the five years since the incident and probably never would. This argument was inevitable every time they spoke. She was surprised it had taken this long to happen this time around.

"Did you?" she shot back, her voice trembling with anger. "You ripped my life away from me, Alex. My friends, my family, my career...my home. All of it gone. *You* put me in a position where I had to start from scratch, and I *hated* you for it."

She knew what was coming next. This was where he threw it all back in her face. Exposed her as a hypocrite. It was the one part of the argument for which she had no rebuttal because she knew he was right.

"If that's true, then why did you save *him*? Why did you do precisely what you're saying I should never have done?"

There it was.

Black pot, meet black kettle.

She closed her eyes and sighed.

"You're right," she admitted angrily. "I did do the same thing, and you know what? He and I have barely spoken since because I ruined his life just like you ruined mine. So, please... Please, Alex, just give it a fuckin' rest. Okay?"

An awkward silence descended between them. It was a few minutes before Alex spoke again, this time in a softer more conciliatory tone.

"You know...he *would* forgive you."

"Would he?" she said softly. "Even if he did, would it make a difference? Alex...I've forgiven you for what you did. I truly have. I remember lying on the forest floor beggin' to be saved. I didn't want to die. But if I'd known the price I was going to pay..."

Her voice trailed off as she paused to take a deep breath before looking at Alex and continuing.

"My understanding of your motives, and my forgiveness of your actions, doesn't change how I feel. Not about my life as it is now. I'm a hypocrite, and it's me that I can't forgive. And if I can't grant myself forgiveness, then how can I look him in the eyes and ask for his?"

Silence again as Alex considered what she had just said. Finally, in an even softer apologetic tone, he addressed her again.

"If I could take it back...I would."

Her shoulder ached as she looked across the fire at him and smiled. The orange light of the flames cast shimmering refractions on the shine of his fur as he lay on the ground, ears flat against his head and his big canine eyes looking sorrowful. Zarra laughed gently and a little sadly.

"No, Alex," she said knowingly. "You wouldn't."

Hypocrite. The word echoed in her mind as she realized that she was truly no different than Alex.

"And honestly...neither would I," she whispered into the fire.

| 52 |

LETHAL WEAPONS

– Gayle Knightley –
– *Monday – London, England –*

"Don't believe everything you see in old Hollywood movies. Dual pistol-wielding is impractical and stupid, and holding your gun sideways is for showboating idiots."

Gayle held up her sidearm for the class to see. The burnished silver highlights on the matte black finish glinted in the sunlight that was peeking through the dark clouds to briefly stream through the glass roof of the Academy's shooting range.

"The Beretta 20-20 *Firestorm*," Gayle continued. "My personal weapon of choice. A bespoke version of the Beretta 92FS-X semi-automatic pistol. It's Italian-made, lightweight, with negligible recoil. Unlike older weapons, the magazine..." She popped out the slide magazine from the butt of the handgrip and showed it to the class. "...uses new technology in the form of micro-bullets. Seventy rounds. Explosive tipped.

"Micro-bullets are a fraction of the size of regular rounds, but are made of a denser material, so their weight ratio and impact are comparable to a conventional bullet. The extra magazine load makes it a little heavier than most handguns, though modern materials help keep the weight down. The micro-bullet entry wound is smaller, yet penetration is better, and the explosive tips will do the rest. The *Firestorm* is an excellent close-range weapon for effective one-shot kills.

"This one has a biometric handgrip which operates as an electronic safety - only two people in the world can fire this weapon. It's pretty much, pound-for-pound, the best handgun money can buy."

She eased the magazine back in and slid the weapon back into the holster strapped low on her right hip.

"On this range you'll be taught to handle a wide variety of weapons. This," she gently patted the holstered weapon, "is what you aspire to, but as rookies you'll be starting at the bottom. You'll be learning with the Gen 4 – Glock 19. It's a thirty-year-old weapon that was built in such huge numbers that you'll still find them knocking around today."

Gayle gestured to the score of matte black handguns that were laid out neatly on the table in front of her. Behind the guns were a row of small black boxes, the carrying cases for the weapons that contained their user manuals and care kits.

"There is one of these weapons for each of you. You will *not* be having access to any ammunition for the weapons outside of this gun range. To do so is a serious breach of Academy rules and will end with your expulsion. Is that crystal?"

"Clear, Captain!" came back the response in unison,

It was apparent some of the more excitable students were eager to experience these weapons. To hold their textured grips in their hands. Other members of the class were more uneasy with the concept of handling an instrument designed specifically to kill. The responsibility of life and death in the palm of their hands rightfully terrified them.

They would need these weapons, though.

It was vitally important that these kids learn how to protect themselves when their powers failed them. Gayle gestured toward the by now familiar sight of the Power Access Dampener and made a show of turning it on, immediately depriving them of their ability to use their gifts.

"While we're here, the PAD stays on at all times. You will not be using your powers on the gun range. At least not for the foreseeable future..."

Gayle paused, momentarily distracted by the entrance of General Norbel in the company of a woman she didn't know. Yet she instinctively recognized her immediately for *what* she was. The hairs on the back of her neck stood to attention. It was a dull London afternoon, overcast with thick grey clouds covering the sky, yet this pale-skinned mystery guest was wearing dark sunglasses.

Vampyrii.

Here, in the Academy.

"In the future, I will teach you to use your abilities to enhance your shooting," she continued hesitantly, "but *not* until you prove yourself proficient in using firearms without them."

The stranger's presence triggered something within Gayle, something deep down in her gut. She had spent years fighting Vampyrii and their kin all over the globe, and now here was one on her turf. Her adrenaline surged, pumping her heart a little faster. She found her hand drifting reassuringly toward the grip on the *Firestorm* she had just re-holstered. Her mind started to re-evaluate her decision to activate the PAD.

"Today, though, is all about gun-care. You don't fire a gun till you prove to me you can look after it. So, go get a gun and a case. Find an empty lane and use your manuals to figure out how to strip and re-assemble your weapon. I'll move between you, correcting your inevitable fuckups.

"Right, hop to it..."

Gayle finished distractedly; her attention now almost totally focused on evaluating this enemy in their midst.

The stranger looked muscular, carrying herself with confidence. A soldier then. At the very least, someone with combat training. Identical height and build to Gayle, but it was the woman's face that drew her attention. The stranger looked like no Vampyrii Gayle had ever seen before. She was...pretty, in a no fuss, low maintenance kind of way.

Pretty was not an adjective Gayle had ever used in relation to a Vampyrii before, but she couldn't deny it was true. The woman's face was framed by a tumbling cascade of auburn hair, while her lips were full and drawn into a wide smile, flashing perfect teeth, fangs retracted.

She looked...happy.

Gayle had seen Vampyrii with dozens of expressions from furious to gloating but had never seen a genuinely *happy* Vampyrii before.

"Is that who...what I think it is, Captain?"

While most of the class were still more fascinated with the guns they'd been given, Andrea's attention had been drawn to the new arrival in much the same way Gayle's had. She'd wager that the young Scottish girl was probably the only cadet who realized what this stranger was. Gayle didn't even glance at her student – her eyes stayed glued to the potential fox that had been invited into the proverbial henhouse.

"Yes," she answered quietly. "She is *exactly* what you think she is."

"But...how?" Andrea said with a furrowed brow. "I thought..."

Gayle didn't answer but knew what her student was thinking. Everyone knew that the United Kingdom was surrounded by a coastal defense system colloquially referred to as the 'Bulwarks.' Essentially, it was a huge wall built around the tiny island nation with gun emplacements and monitoring stations to prevent an invasion. It had been a study in post war paranoia, and despite calls to have it dismantled, it persisted to this day.

Technically, it was possible for a Vampyrii to be allowed beyond the Bulwarks if they had the right access visa. She remembered that StormHall himself had visited once, many years ago.

But it was rare.

Very, very rare.

"What's a Vampyrii doing here?" the young girl asked with her soft burr.

Gayle shook her head slowly and shrugged. "A *very* good question. Keep it under your hat, will you, Andrea? Now, get back to work while I go find out."

She headed toward Norbel without a backward glance to Andrea, forcing a false smile onto her face to cover the suspicion she truly felt. As she approached them, the Vampyrii woman smiled at her with a look of recognition. Her smile, unlike Gayle's, contained a genuine warmth. A sentiment Gayle had truly not expected.

"General." She nodded at her uncle as she approached, but her eyes were firmly fixed on the stranger. "Can I help you with something?"

What she really wanted to say was, '*What the fuck are you doing here with a Vampyrii?*' but for some inexplicable reason what actually passed her lips was cordial. Polite even.

Michael Reynolds must really be rubbing off on me.

Gayle glanced at the badge swaying from the visitor's lanyard. The name surprised her. Assuming the non-capitalization of the House name wasn't a typo, the newcomer was half-blood. A half-Human hybrid like Gayle herself. That kind of heritage was generally frowned upon in Vampyrii culture...which meant this woman was either expendable or someone very special.

If she were to put money on it, Gayle would bet the latter.

"Mercy balthazaar, may I introduce you to..." Norbel started before he was interrupted.

"Captain Gayle Knightley," Mercy said with barely contained excitement, thrusting out her hand. "It is *truly* an honor to meet you."

Gayle hesitated for the briefest moment before accepting the handshake. Mercy's grip was unyielding, and she pumped the hand enthusiastically. Gayle could tell that the sentiment was sincere which – considering how many of her kind the 137th had killed over the years – was genuinely surprising. She had expected to be greeted with a modicum of hatred, or at least a healthy dose of dislike.

Unfortunately, while she managed to keep her opening gambit polite, she couldn't prevent a smidgen of something a little more biting from shading her next question.

"House Balthazaar. Long way from home, aren't you?"

"I had business to attend to with General Norbel. I'm on my way to Nexus City to oversee the New Victus security arrangements." A purely professional reply.

"Ms. balthazaar is not scheduled to depart for Nexus until

the morning," Norbel commented. "I was hoping perhaps you could show her around London this evening."

Clearly an order.

"I haven't been outside New Victus in almost thirty years." Mercy smiled. "And this is my first time visiting the UK."

Even if she was a foreign dignitary, a tour of the Academy seemed irresponsible. Showing her the innermost workings of the facility that trained the most elite forces the Federation had for taking down Mercy's kind was borderline negligent. And now letting her loose in London...

He must have a good fucking reason.

"Yes, sir," Gayle agreed flatly.

"Excellent." Norbel smiled. "Unfortunately, I have business to attend to, so I shall leave Ms. balthazaar in your capable hands."

"Thank you for your time, General." Mercy bowed her head in a farewell.

Norbel reciprocated the gesture before gracefully exiting the gun range. There was an awkward moment of silence until Mercy took the initiative and nodded her head toward the students.

"Gen 4 Glock 19s," she said. "A nice weapon, although maybe a little basic."

"Kids gotta start somewhere." Gayle raised an eyebrow. "You're familiar with it?"

"I am. We have a great many of them in New Victus. They were a popular weapon with law enforcement and security forces."

"Which you, of course, took when you conquered the country."

The comment brought a pause to the conversation as Mercy seemed to be internally debating the merits of getting into a political debate with her new chaperone. Eventually, she decided to keep the conversation light.

"I usually carry a 92FS-X myself, though...not a custom *20-20 Firestorm* like yours." she gestured towards Gayle's holster.

The 92FS-X had only gone into production about six years ago in Italy, and as such, should have been off limits to anyone outside of the FSE. They weren't inexpensive, either. Most military and security forces used either the cheaper Beretta 2010A *Sureshot* or Glock 25s.

"I didn't think you could get those in New Victus."

"Black market," Mercy said simply. "May I?"

She didn't make a move, but Gayle understood what Mercy was referring to. Gayle recognized that the weapon was coded so that only she could fire it, yet her instincts were screaming at her not to willingly hand over a weapon to a Vampyrii. With gritted teeth and in the interest of playing nice, she pulled her gun from its holster and made a show of unloading it before handing it to Mercy to inspect. Her unspoken message was clear.

I'll go along with this little charade, but I sure as hell don't trust you!

"Now this..." the Vampyrii said with admiration, "...is a gun. Seventy-round magazine and biometric safety in the handgrip..."

She turned the gun over in her hand like it was a precious heirloom, eagerly inspecting it from all angles. She paused as she looked at the bottom of the handgrip, squinting at the inscription there. Her eyebrows shot up.

"This...this was Zephyr's weapon?" she asked with barely hidden awe.

"It was a gift. How did you know?" Gayle gave her a curious look and held her hand out to accept the gun back.

Mercy placed the pistol gently in her hand with reverence.

"House Balthazaar runs a private intelligence gathering service, some of which we pass to StormHall and his cronies, but much we keep for ourselves. The 137th Hunters are as infamous in our culture as they are famous in yours, and I have to admit, you and your squad has been a fascination of mine for a long time. A hobby even. I know all of your team members."

"Knew," Gayle stated pointedly.

"Yes...sorry." Mercy blushed, embarrassed. "My condolences on the loss."

Genuine again – it seemed to be the sentiment of the day. Gayle was suddenly in a position where she was having to refocus everything she had ever known about Vampyrii through this new Mercy-sized lens. She was compelled to do an on-the-fly re-evaluation of her view of Vampyrii as a race, obliging her to visit upon the idea that not everything was black and white.

She found herself wanting to explore this new world view in more detail.

"Thank you," Gayle said graciously. "How about I wrap up with the students and then I can take you out and show you some of the sights of London at night?"

"I would like that very much," Mercy grinned.

Another genuine smile.

| 53 |

SHADES OF GREY

– **Mercy balthazaar** –
– *Monday – London, England* –

Mercy was overwhelmed by a complex spectrum of conflicting emotions that were difficult to reconcile.

She was stood in the middle of the sumptuous Hunters lounge, surrounded by tactile memories of the 137th. A group of people she admittedly idolized to a certain extent. Zephyr's gun had been just the tip of the iceberg. This room was full of Hunters memorabilia. Everywhere she looked provided more fodder to the fangirl in her.

Framed photographs of the team hung haphazardly all over the walls, full of familiar faces taken in happier times. The shelves in the kitchen area were stacked with mugs of all different colors, shapes, and sizes, no two the same. Mercy had spent the past few minutes trying to work out which mug belonged to which team member. Standing here surrounded by all this history was...surreal.

And not a little awkward.

It was plain that Captain Knightley was uncomfortable with Mercy being there, that much had been obvious from the moment General Norbel introduced them. However, Mercy thought that she had felt that stance soften a little as they conversed. She fervently hoped that was the case. Spending an evening in London with *the* Gayle Knightley was the stuff dreams were made of. So many questions she wanted to ask, so much she wanted to know. Whether Gayle would answer was another matter entirely.

Still, if you don't ask, you don't get.

"Is this your car?" she asked as Gayle walked back into the room.

"Hmmm?"

"The photo." Mercy gestured toward the framed picture of the white convertible hanging on the wall. "I recognize Tank and Rio...and...is that Ghost?"

Gayle glanced at the photo and smiled sadly.

"Yeah, that's Jaylen, Gabe, and Maggie," she confirmed. "And, yes, that is my car."

"Ford Mustang?"

"2011 GT500. Gabe found her for me. Not easy to get hold of American muscle in the UK these days, but Gabe always had a source for everything." Gayle sounded wistful. "She was in rough shape when I got her, but Jaylen and Mags helped me fix her up. Mags especially. She worked her magic with a very broken V8."

"Is she all original parts?"

"Not quite. Mostly though. Petrol engines are banned in the city, so in order to drive her in London I had to fit a secondary electric motor and batteries..."

"Ah, a *hybrid* then?" Mercy smiled and nodded knowingly.

It was common knowledge that Gayle was half Human and half Fae, but Mercy felt like she knew Gayle more intimately than most. In more detail. She had studied the Hunters and their infamous captain over the last five years and she knew how thorough they were in their preparation. Knew how they had competed with Captain Torbar's 'Terminators.' How they had sought to hone every edge they had. They had lived by the ethos of 'know your enemy,' and while Mercy didn't think of herself in those terms, she knew that Gayle would have studied Vampyrii in detail. Strengths, weaknesses, capabilities, and even culture. She would absolutely know what the uncapitalized spelling of Mercy's House-name meant.

Oh, Captain Knightley, we have so much in common. If you'll just see past my race.

"You could say that, yes." Gayle shrugged, choosing to by-pass acknowledgement of Mercy's reference to her hybrid nature.

"You still have her? The Mustang, I mean?"

"Yup, she's my pride and joy. So, I have been thinking. Maybe we should..." Gayle stopped mid-sentence as Mercy turned to face her.

Mercy smiled and gestured toward her eyes. "Contacts," she said by way of explanation.

While her chaperone had been changing into something more conducive to an evening exploring the city, Mercy had slipped in a set of contact lenses to disguise her tell-tale Vampyrii eyes. Now no one would be any the wiser as to her origins.

"Hazel suits you."

"Thanks," Mercy smiled. "I know this is an...inconvenience for you. So, wherever you decide to take us tonight, I really don't want to draw any unwanted attention for you to have to deal with."

Gayle looked casually understated. Snug black jeans topped with a cream roll-neck sweater that hugged her figure and extended down over her hips. She sat in one of the chairs to pull on her black suede boots. Despite her friendly demeanor, it was clear that she didn't trust Mercy. Not yet. In return, Mercy's military instincts evaluated her host.

Tight clothes and hair tied back, so nothing to grab. Flat soles, in case she has to run. Calf-length boots, probably hiding a knife, and she's still wearing the Firestorm on her hip. She may not be expecting trouble, but she's prepared for it.

"I was thinking that we'd take a stroll down the Mall towards Trafalgar Square. From there, we can walk down White-hall to Millbank, past Parliament, and cross over the Thames at the Lambeth Bridge. Do a little sight-seeing. Weather is brisk tonight, but not too bad for this time of year, so we can have dinner at Tamesis Dock. It has a nice view of Westminster Palace, good food, variety of menu options, and more importantly, it has a bar."

"So...sightseeing, food, and alcohol," Mercy summarized.

"In a nutshell."

"My kind of evening." Mercy smiled and nodded enthusiastically.

Gayle gave an amused chuckle and tilted an eyebrow at her. "You don't get out much, do you?"

Mercy shook her head slowly and sighed.

"Since StormHall started this war, our kind has been pretty much confined to the United States. We're not welcome anywhere else in the world. It's kind of like being under house arrest."

"You called it the United States," Gayle said with curiosity. "Not New Victus."

"Believe it or not, some of us never wanted this. StormHall's egotistical claim that *he* finally gave us a home does not take into account the fact that many of us felt we already *had* a home. New York City was my home. The United States was *my* country, my nationality, and I was proud of it. The Stars and Stripes was my allegiance."

"So, when war broke out, why didn't you fight for it?"

"House Balthazaar is small," Mercy sighed. "Mostly normal people, families with children. If we had fought back, StormHall would have wiped out our bloodline. It was about our survival. We have no love for him or allegiance to his banner."

"I never realized there were Vampyrii with that attitude."

When General Norbel had made the offer of an evening in London with Gayle Knightley as her guide, Mercy had been excited, but also filled with a healthy dose of trepidation. Would this evening be one of friendly co-operation or a difficult night of animosity? It had certainly seemed like it would be the latter. Now, she felt a surge of delight, realizing that Gayle was genuinely interested and not just making polite conversation.

"It is not...widely known," Mercy said with a shrug, "StormHall did a superb job in covering over the cracks in his regime. Making the world think we're a truly united nation. But many of us feel differently in private; mostly the older Progenitor Houses. Those that are left anyway. They *all* sat out the War and were...*persuaded* by StormHall to keep their mouths shut about it. We may not have been able to fight StormHall back then, but we weren't going to bloody our hands for his cause."

"But you're a soldier," Gayle said. "I can see it in you. You've fought."

"I have," Mercy admitted. "But not in *this* war. Not for him."

"Where have you seen action?"

Mercy laughed. "I'm one hundred seventy-eight years old. At this point, it's easier to list where I *haven't* seen action."

"Point taken." Gayle smiled.

"Talking of attitudes..." Mercy paused trying to find a diplomatic way to address the next topic. "You obviously weren't pleased to see me, or rather my kind, at the gun range earlier. If tonight is a problem for you, then..."

Gayle was already shaking her head. "It's not," she paused and took a deep breath. "A year ago I might have felt differently."

"After the death of your teammates?" Mercy asked bluntly, immediately regretting it.

To her credit, Gayle raised an eyebrow but considered the question anyway. After a moment, she nodded.

"To some degree, yes. But lately I've been...re-evaluating many of my life choices. Finding a different way to consider things. It's an ongoing process." Gayle sighed, her face changing subtly with a moment of reflection. Finally, she smiled. "Let's keep the subject away from that tonight, shall we? In the interests of...diplomacy."

She thought Gayle almost said 'friendship' but changed the word at the last moment.

"Agreed." Mercy breathed a sigh of relief. "I apologize for bringing that up. I know I stated it at the gun range, but...I have great admiration for yourself and the 137th Hunters. I truly meant no offense."

"You mentioned back at the Academy that your interest in the exploits of my team was almost a hobby for you... Which, I have to say, I find mind boggling!"

Gayle smiled as she plucked up her tan leather jacket and pulled it on, careful to extract her hair in the process. Mercy was struck by the normalcy of the endeavor. Could the two of them ever actually be friends?

Maybe. Once Lyssa carried out her plan.

"Gathering intel on the HFA forces was my favorite part of my job," Mercy confessed.

Gayle smiled. "We were basically just guns for hire."

"You guys were *much* more than that," Mercy shook her head vehemently. "I remember being confused when I first started gathering intelligence on you. One month you'd be fighting with the NAA on the West Coast, then next in New Africa with the FSE."

"We're an Alliance unit, not affiliated with any of the world nations specifically," Gayle shrugged. "We just went wherever we were sent and did the job at hand."

"Oh, you didn't just do a job. You guys were...artists!"

Gayle laughed out loud and shook her head at Mercy's compliment.

"I'm serious! I had a grudging respect for Torbar's Terminators, but Knightingale's Hunters always triggered my imagination. You took on the craziest missions, used the most unorthodox tactics, and always came across more as a family than just a combat unit. That struck a chord with me because Lyssa has always fostered an attitude of family in House Balthazaar. I have to say...I dreamt about being a 'Hunter' more times than I'd care to casually admit."

"I'll take that as a compliment," Gayle said quietly, her face inscrutable.

"It was intended as such."

The Academy was draped in shadows as the evening drew in and the two of them walked leisurely through the Palace. Mercy noticed that Gayle was limping slightly, favoring her right leg as she performed the role of tour guide. As they made their way toward the front gate, Mercy couldn't help but bombard Gayle with questions for which her host generously provided open and interesting answers. Such as how the Palace had been rebuilt after fire ravaged it during The Rising.

As they headed down the Mall, past St. James Park, the two conversed amiably about the differences between living in the

UK and New Victus. This time it was Gayle who was asking most of the questions.

"I've always wanted to see New York," Gayle said wistfully. "Is the city anything like it looks in the movies?"

"New York City? No, not anymore, not really," Mercy said sadly. "You watch a lot of old movies?"

"Too many. Anything pre-Rising, not that there is much since. I haven't felt the urge lately, but I used to scour little shops all over London to buy DVDs or Blu-ray disks for my collection."

"Old school." Mercy laughed; Gayle shrugged.

"Before the War, the world was apparently going digital..."

"I remember," Mercy nodded.

"The collapse of the infrastructure means that's all gone now. So much was lost. But I like something I can hold in my hands anyway. Films, books, music... I love browsing my shelves, seeing the amazing cover art..."

Gayle shrugged and Mercy looked at her with a grin.

"I've studied 'Knightingale' the soldier for many years, but I'm finding Gayle Knightley the person far more fascinating. I would not have pegged you for a collector."

"My dad and I used to watch old movies and TV when I was a kid. Mostly science fiction and fantasy, comic book movies, that sort of thing. This world can be a crazy place, so whether it be Middle Earth or Westeros, or the far reaches of space on the bridge of a starship...sometimes you just need a place to escape to. Especially when things get tough."

A hint of sadness colored Gayle's reply. Mercy decided not to push on that subject.

"Have you seen the film 'I Am Legend?'" she asked instead.

Gayle grinned and nodded effusively. "Will Smith movie. Based on the book of the same name by Richard Matheson." She winked. "A guilty pleasure."

Mercy laughed and nodded. "Much of Manhattan looks like that movie now," she sighed. "House Balthazaar maintains a few square miles around Hearst Tower, but most of the city is uninhabited, overgrown, dilapidated. To run parallels with the film even further, there are many Trampyrii that live on the streets, too."

"Trampyrii?"

"A Human who was only half-turned, or was enslaved during the War, and then lost their sire."

"Oh, I'm familiar with that. There are still a fair amount of them in the FSE living in care homes," Gayle commented. "But I've never heard them called that before."

"Not a surprise. Trampyrii are another of StormHall's dirty little secrets. He counts them in the New Victus population numbers, when in reality, they shouldn't be. It's a portmanteau of 'transient' and 'Vampyrii.' They wander aimlessly around, with no real will of their own. New York City has thousands of them. We have no way to cure them, so where we can, we encourage them to be...something more. Try to instill in them a purpose, even if it is just performing the menial tasks associated with a city's amenities. Street maintenance, trash collection, that kind of thing."

Mercy heard the edge of bitterness creeping into her voice. Evidently Gayle did, too.

"They make you angry."

"No. *They* don't make me angry. What StormHall and his followers did to them makes me angry." Mercy shook her head as if to clear it. "Changing the subject... London looks absolutely how I expected it to. It's stunning."

"I guess I take it for granted," Gayle said softly as they approached Admiralty Arch. "I didn't want to come back here after...well... After."

As they emerged from the other side of the archway, they crossed the road and Gayle brought them to a halt.

"My father used to tell me that prior to the War this area would be heaving with traffic and bustling with people all going about their daily business. Even at this hour, the roads would be so busy you would need the help of the traffic lights to cross en-masse. Now, though, there's room to breathe...and admire the view."

Mercy followed Gayle's finger as she pointed across the road.

A sprinkling of rain had turned the sidewalk into a natural

mirror, reflecting the gorgeous palette of autumnal oranges and pinks. The setting sun turning the famous landmark, Nelson's Column, into the central spire of a giant pseudo-sundial, casting its long shadow across the Square. The National Gallery, with its famously recognizable dome, elegant fountains, and varied resplendent statues, formed a striking backdrop.

They stood in silence, drinking in the ambience. Trafalgar Square was tranquil tonight. Just a young couple walking home arm in arm, whispering promises of the intimate evening to come. Mercy's sensitive hearing picking up their lovers' banter. Finally, she turned to her chaperone.

"Thank you for showing me this."

"Oh, we're not done just yet." Gayle chuckled. "Come on."

They talked amiably as they walked along Whitehall, Mercy quizzing Gayle with a hundred questions about the sights, and Gayle answering as best she could while highlighting things she missed. Mercy felt like a child again, beaming with delight at every famous landmark they found on their stroll. The more time she spent with Gayle, the more it just felt like two girls on a night out. The icy façade of distrust – borne of years of fighting – was beginning to thaw.

"One hundred seventy-eight..." Gayle said quietly, as they walked on from where they had been staring up through the windows of the Banqueting House, admiring the finely painted ceilings.

"Excuse me?" Mercy asked, confused.

"Your enthusiasm for this, the sightseeing. Surely you'd have seen everything in the world by now, in that kind of a lifespan?"

"I wasn't lying earlier; this *is* my first visit to London."

"It just seems so...improbable." Gayle shook her head.

"Maybe," Mercy laughed, "but remember we've been confined to North America for the past thirty years. Even Nexus City is out of the realm of possibility unless you're a StormHall supporter; The Collective rigorously control *that* access."

"The Collective? That's StormHall's political party, right?"

"Right," Mercy nodded. "You'll never find a more sickening group of sexist, racist, and xenophobic individuals on the planet, and Sebastian StormHall is their elected leader. The Collective hold the majority of seats on the Blood Council and, thus, control the Night Quorum. Pretty much every Vampyrii you'd meet if you went to Nexus City would be a member of The Collective."

"Can't you vote him out?"

Mercy laughed bitterly. "If only it were that easy," she said. "StormHall got a law voted through decades ago that declared, while New Victus remains on a war footing, all civil elections are suspended. Suffice to say, New Victus has been on a war footing for thirty years.

"Anyway, putting politics aside for tonight, even if I had visited London before the War...I'd hardly remember it well. Pop culture has painted a picture of our kind having long and perfect memories of everything we witness in our lives. Truth is our memories fade, just like yours. I know that I've been to Paris in my life, but I don't really remember it. Couldn't even tell you when. 1930s maybe...between the two World Wars certainly."

"How far back do you remember?"

"With clarity?" Mercy paused to consider her answer. "I remember The Rising. I don't think any of us would forget *that* moment in history. I remember some details from before that, but the further back I go, the hazier it gets. You get to a certain age and you don't feel the years anymore. Vampyrii age slowly. This is the equivalent of me in my Human thirties. I don't know if any of this makes any sense to you."

Gayle stared at her for a moment and then smiled. "No," she said, "I think I get it."

They walked on in silence through the quiet city. A couple of cars passed by, but none of the black cabs and red buses made famous by all the old London-based movies. When they arrived in Parliament Square, the view opened up and took Mercy's breath away.

Across to her right was St. Margaret's Church, dwarfed by the familiar shape of Westminster Abbey sitting magnificently behind it. Finally, a red London bus passed them, breaking Mercy's eyeline, as it passed by down George Street toward

Westminster Bridge. As her eyes followed it, she took in the sand-colored shape of the architecturally glorious Westminster Palace and then the most recognizable sight of all – Elizabeth Tower stood proudly before them. Mercy felt her mouth drop open.

"I never thought..."

"I know you have bigger shit in New York City, but Big Ben is...iconic," Gayle commented in an almost reverential tone.

Mercy felt like she wanted to weep with joy, but that was just one of a mix of emotions surging within her, the strongest being anger. StormHall had taken so much from them so many years ago. How many Vampyrii would *never* have the opportunity to see the world? To experience these things?

London was now ticked off her mental bucket list, but there were places to visit and histories to see that were impossible to get to, impossible to experience, all because of StormHall and his war. And what about places like Moscow? Did the Russian capital even exist anymore?

She glanced at Gayle and considered her comparatively short life. She was just twenty-eight years old, and it made Mercy furious to consider how the course of her life had been dictated by the selfish actions of one man with a personal vendetta. Gayle had been born into a world where her choices were limited, where her genetics had dragged her into a decade of fighting against Mercy's own kind. Fostering a hatred for the monsters that Mercy represented.

Yet Mercy saw a woman undergoing profound change. Someone who was already letting go of her preconceptions.

"Captain Knightley..." She hesitated but pushed ahead. What she was about to do *felt* right. "I know business is off the table for tonight, but...I would like to come back here before the Nexus Summit."

Gayle tilted her head and looked at her apprehensively.

"Look, Mercy," she started, "as much as I can see that you're enjoying it here, this is a one-off. We can't have—"

Mercy interrupted, shaking her head vehemently. "No," she said forcefully. "You misunderstand. Not sightseeing. I need to talk to you about something important."

"Talk to me tonight."

Mercy shook her head. "I can't. Not yet," she sighed. "I need to talk to Lyssa first. I'll need her approval before I bring to you what I want to say..."

"Well, we can certainly talk to General Norbel and see if we can get you permission," Gayle said. "I mean, he did it this time, so maybe—"

Mercy interrupted again, shaking her head. "No," she said firmly. "Only you."

"Why me?" Gayle asked.

Mercy bit her lip and looked back up at Big Ben. "Because I trust you. Meeting you simply confirmed what I knew from following your career. You are a good and honorable person. I don't mean this to sound too forward, but... I already now consider you a friend."

Gayle looked confused by the shift in the conversation.

"I'm flattered, truly." Gayle smiled. "But Mercy...I don't have the power to grant you a visa. That needs to come from someone at Norbel's level."

"Then we find another way. Maybe you could come to Nexus." She hesitated before continuing. "It's important. I don't trust General Norbel. But I trust you."

Gayle said nothing. Mercy knew the family connection between her and General Norbel and that she had just cast aspersions on the character of Gayle's uncle.

She couldn't put her finger on what it was about Norbel she disliked. Maybe that he was simply *too* perfect. It felt unnatural. Gayle, by contrast, had many flaws. She didn't hide her scars, emotional or physical. It exposed her as a person, made her seem more...Human. Mercy appreciated that.

She also realized the position in which she was putting the young captain.

"I know what I'm asking of you. I do. Please, just think on it, and come visit me in Nexus during the Summit. I believe you'll be very interested in what I have to tell you."

"I'll see what I can do," Gayle answered noncommittally.

"Thank you." Mercy had made her pitch. Now it was up to

Gayle. "Okay, how about we get back to being two girls enjoying an evening in London? Lead me to your boat-restaurant thing."

Lyssa would probably kill her for setting this up, but Mercy had a good feeling about Gayle Knightley. She also had a bad feeling about the Summit. She trusted her instincts, and right now they were telling her that House Balthazaar would soon need all the friends it could get.

| 54 |

CATCHING UP

– Allyson Knightley –
– Tuesday – Nexus City, Iceland –

"So, Dad blackmailed me into coming to the gala."

"He hardly blackmailed you, Carrie," Ally said distractedly, engrossed in the paperwork on her desk. "You wanted a favor; so did he."

She loved her sister dearly, but she had more important things to do right now than shoot the breeze. Her desk was littered with reams of paperwork and her inbox had dozens of emails that needed urgent responses. It was not a trivial job, fettling the city for the upcoming Summit. The infernal gala that Carrie was talking about was just complicating matters.

While the Summit itself was a gathering of the world's diplomats and leaders, the gala would include their families, too. Wives, husbands, and children. In some ways, it was a more complex undertaking, while also requiring a softer touch. Her days had become a blur of dealing with the hundreds of questions being asked.

Where can I land my flyer? How many family members am I approved for? Should I bring my own vehicle or will transport be provided? Can I bring my own security? The list seemed to be endless, and each question needed an answer and her security approval, if appropriate.

Ally knew that this job would entail some bureaucracy but

had never imagined the ocean of red tape and paperwork in which she was currently drowning. Another stress headache was on the horizon. She could feel it coming. Times like this, she missed the simplicity of working cases as a London cop.

"You look rough," Carrie commented.

Ally dropped the tablet she was holding onto the desk and fixed her younger sibling with a withering look.

"And I love you, too, Carrie. Now, what can I do to expedite your exit from my office?"

Carrie smiled and scratched her head but continued to lean against the door frame.

"I thought maybe we could take a stroll together, grab a bite to eat, talk. Honestly, it looks like I came here just in time, because *you* look like you need a break, Sis."

Ally was about to argue the point when she realized that she was reading the request for a permit to bring Ambassador Neary's assistant's pet cat through quarantine...for the third time. Carrie was right. She was tired, and truth be told, her progress on the pile of paperwork had slowed to the point that she was now just wasting time.

"Fine," she said with a sigh. "I'll take a break to grab some lunch...but *you're* buying."

She stood slowly, stretching the kinks out of her back. Carrie reversed out of the doorway and into the corridor allowing Ally to exit, and the two of them started the short walk toward the building's food-court.

"You can't swing us a free lunch with your position here?" Carrie shot back.

"Yes. Nexus is an oasis where we all eat for free." Sarcasm oozed from Ally's response.

The food-court *was* complimentary to Nexus personnel, and Carrie would indeed eat at no cost simply by virtue of being with her sister. Still, Allyson found she was enjoying the banter. It was a welcome break from the monotony of the day.

"But they pay *you* the big bucks while I'm just a poor journalist..." Carrie whined before Ally interrupted.

"A poor journalist who can afford to buy a personal flyer *and* brought it up here *and* parked it on the conference center

Skypad despite her older sister telling her not to."

"Dad pulled a few strings..."

"Again, despite me telling him not to." Allyson shook her head. "For fuck's sake – does nobody in the family listen to me anymore? I *am* the Chief of Security here. How do you think it makes me look when you guys swan around making up your own rules?"

"I'm sorry, Sis." Carrie sounded genuinely apologetic. "I just thought that if I can twist Dad's arm up his back to get me to see Ambassador Alzim over the next couple of days then I can just fly straight from here to NordScania."

"Oh, no." Allyson stopped in her tracks. "No. No. You are not going to leave me to go to the gala dinner all on my own. It's bad enough Gayle's not coming, so now I have to be Dad's surrogate showpiece. No. You're going to be here for that, too."

"Fine. I'll be there," Carrie huffed.

"What do you need from Ambassador Alzim anyway?"

"A visa. For a story," Carrie replied cryptically.

"Story?"

"I'll tell you when I've firmed up the details," Carrie said, dodging the question before changing the subject. "On the up-side, how many times do you get access to all the world's ambassadors in one room? Just think of the doors it could open."

"Unbelievable..." Ally commented under her breath with a shake of her head as she started walking again.

"What?" Carrie protested. "If you're going to strong arm me into coming to this thing then I'm at least going to work it to my advantage. Anyway, talking about Gayle..."

"What about her?"

"Don't you think it's time we staged an intervention, to get her talking to Dad again?"

Ally closed her eyes as they entered the food-court. The mingled aromas of different types of foods assaulted her nose. Her empty stomach rumbled.

"I tried," she said with a yawn. "It was a somewhat failed attempt, to put it mildly."

They joined the short line for the hot food counter. Allyson chose the simmering aromatic lamb balti with a huge naan bread to accompany it. Carrie kept it simple with a thick slice of the lasagne and a leafy salad on the side. They both selected bottles of water from the drinks counter and then Allyson flashed her ID at the young man operating the checkout. He waved them through without charge.

"What do you mean 'tried?'"

"Dad and I visited London," Ally continued as she peered around for a free table to sit at. "Gayle wouldn't talk to Dad at all, except to tell him to leave."

"How's she doing? I haven't spoken to her in a couple of weeks."

"She's doing okay. Better actually," Ally commented off-handedly as she pulled out a seat at an empty table and sat down.

"Better?" Carrie asked as she followed suit.

Allyson tore off a chunk of the naan bread, shaping it with her fingers, and used it to pick up a chunk of the succulent lamb with a generous helping of the balti sauce. She scooped it into her mouth with a groan of delight. As the spices hit her taste buds, she forgot all about her busy schedule and bliss-fully lost herself in the flavors.

"God, that's good," she mumbled with the food still in her mouth. "Gayle's working with this guy. Captain Michael Reynolds. He's American, ex-military. I met him last week. I like him. I think he's having a *really* good influence on her."

"In what way?"

Ally looked at her sister with a grin. "I think our big sister is kinda smitten."

"Oh-my-god. Really?" Carrie gasped as she forked a bite of the lasagne into her mouth.

Ally laughed and nodded. "She didn't seem as angry as she was when she first came back... Or when she felt she'd been shanghaied into the Academy job. Don't get me wrong, there's still a long way to go, but something *has* fundamentally changed. I think it's him, and Lana agrees with me."

"Lana... Lana Fordham?"

Allyson nodded as she eagerly took another mouthful of the Indian dish.

"Gayle roped her into coming back, too," Ally explained. "I tell ya, Carrie, the turnaround is astonishing. As much as our Gayle *wants* to hate being back at the Academy, I think it's absolutely the best place for her."

"So, Dad and Uncle were right then," Carrie said.

Ally nodded again as she swallowed. "Yeah, and Gayle is already well on her way to figuring that out. You know what she's like. Stubborn bitch most of the time, but she comes around eventually."

"We should visit."

"I've just been," Ally protested.

"Yeah, but when was the last time all three of us had a girl's night out?" Carrie was undeterred by her sister's lack of enthusiasm.

Ally had to admit, it had been a while. The results of the Malta mission had left Gayle distant and insular, putting a kink in the previously close relationship they all shared. She couldn't pretend to understand what her sister was going through. Some of the injuries she sustained were pretty gruesome and were going to take time to heal, but the mental scarring was where the real damage had truly been inflicted.

And those wounds started even before Valletta.

Gayle had gone to her sisters and confessed that she had a problem. She needed help. She started therapy with Dr. Griffin the week before the mission and had been openly optimistic about her progress after the first couple of sessions. What subsequently happened to the 137th sent her into a tailspin which both her sisters had worried she wouldn't pull out of.

Allyson could now say, with a degree of certainty, that Gayle had managed to arrest that particular nosedive.

"Maybe you're right. It could be fun. Just keep me away from phones," Allyson laughed.

"I sense a story in there somewhere." Carrie looked at her with a sparkle of bemusement.

As they finished their meals, Allyson regaled her with the tale of her trip to London, the drunken night with Gayle, the voicemail message, and the ensuing embarrassment of meeting Michael Reynolds. At one point, Ally thought her sister would choke on her lasagne, so hard was Carrie's laughter.

From the corner of her eye, she noticed a newcomer walking into the food-court. One that instantly triggered Allyson's instincts. Pale skin and striking ice-blue eyes that contrasted beautifully with the burnt orange of her long, plaited hair. She was dressed professionally, black pant suit over a snow-white sweater, but this wasn't any Vampyrii diplomat that Allyson recognized.

So, why are her eyes locked onto me? Why is she heading over here?

The stranger arrived at the table and extended her hand, grinning broadly from ear to ear. Not the inherently fake smile she witnessed from most of the New Victus ambassadors she had met thus far. This one was as sincere and unpretentious as they come. Whoever the mystery woman was, she was genuinely happy to be meeting Allyson.

"Chief Knightley?" said the woman with the dazzling smile. "I'm Mercy balthazaar. Your sister Gayle told me so much about you. Can we talk?"

Allyson reciprocated the gesture, shaking Mercy's outstretched hand while wondering what details her older sister had disclosed about her.

| 55 |

DEBRIEF

– Lyssa Balthazaar –
– Thursday – Albany, New Victus –

She opened the door to see the face of a woman she barely recognized. Lyssa couldn't recall Mercy looking this happy in a long time; a broad smile dominated the face of her friend.

"Welcome back," Lyssa said with a grin of her own.

"Thanks!" There was a definite spring in her step as Mercy bounced in through the open door.

"Looks like *someone* had a good time."

Mercy nodded and walked past Lyssa into the sunken lounge. She promptly collapsed into the same large, comfy armchair in which she had been sitting when Lyssa dispatched her on the excursion. The look on Mercy's face told her just how different circumstances were a mere eight days later.

"I had a *really* good time," Mercy sighed happily.

"You *do* know I sent you on business, not pleasure?" Lyssa teased.

"Of course," Mercy laughed. "And thank you. It was so good to get out of New Victus and go somewhere...new. Now I see the appeal of your trips north. The other appeal, anyway."

Lyssa smiled and sat down on the opposite sofa. Seeing the glee on her niece's face distracted her momentarily from her own burdens.

"So, tell me all about it. Did you do as I asked?"

The mood shifted a little as Mercy's face turned more serious. Evidently the trip hadn't been all fun and games. Lyssa braced herself for bad news.

"Have you ever met General Norbel?" Mercy began. "You communicated with him to organize my visit, but you never *met* him...face to face, I mean?"

Lyssa shook her head. "No," she admitted. "We exchanged correspondence and had a video call or two...but, no, I never met him face to face."

Mercy was confirming what she already knew. They had been over this ground before Lyssa sent her niece to London.

"So, barring a couple of video calls and some emails, all you know about General Norbel is his reputation?"

"Yes," Lyssa said slowly, wondering where Mercy was going with this. "He's Fae and, like most of his kind, is somewhat...enigmatic. He's leader of the HFA and has been since the start; we know that much. It's said he was the leading influencer behind stabilizing events after the War and bringing a semblance of peace to the world."

"Which is why you wanted me to sound him out about an alliance?"

"Yes," Lyssa nodded. "If we're going up against Storm, then we're going to need more allies than just Damian Dane. General Norbel could be instrumental in getting us the ear of the FSE and the North American Alliance.

"Again, you know all of this..."

She paused for a moment. Mercy's line of questioning was obviously leading to a reveal. Lyssa narrowed her eyes and stared at her niece.

"Where are you going with this?" she prompted.

"I didn't ask him," Mercy said flatly.

"I'm sure you had a good reason."

Mercy simply sat, contemplating how to say what needed to be said. Lyssa recognized her process. The distant look and the flexing of her hands, rubbing her fingers idly together. After a few moments she sat forward and looked Lyssa squarely in the eye.

"I didn't...like him," she said quietly with a shake of her

head. "Something was off. I trust my gut, Lyssa, and he's *not* our man."

Vampyrii didn't have the special psychic powers some fictional accounts attributed to them, but Lyssa *had* learned long ago that their extended life experience generally made them excellent judges of character. Over the centuries, you developed a keen sense for when someone was not being genuine; maybe not in a rational sense that could be articulated, but more as a feeling deep in your stomach. It wasn't fool proof but was right more often than it was wrong.

If Mercy thought something was amiss with Norbel...then something *was* amiss with Norbel.

"I met him on arrival; we sat in his office and engaged in small talk. The more we talked, the more it just didn't feel right... He was perfectly nice, said all the right things, but he seemed to be looking through me. I can't explain it any better than that."

It was clear that Mercy was struggling to articulate what she meant, so Lyssa tried to help.

"Did he seem like he was lying?".

Mercy shook her head. "No. I'm sure he wasn't." She pursed her lips in thought for a moment before continuing. "It's more like he simply didn't care. Which seemed odd. I mean, how often does a Vampyrii request a secret audience with the leader of the HFA and then risk traveling to London? You would have thought he would be, at the very least, intrigued by what I was coming to talk about. Yet he just seemed politely ambivalent to my presence, like he already knew why I was there. Or maybe that I just didn't matter, like I was just a blip on his daily routine somehow... It's hard to put my finger on what it was. I just...he's not the right person to trust. Not for what we want to do. For what we *need* to do."

With that she slumped back in the chair again and Lyssa did likewise. She couldn't help but feel disappointed.

"So, what did you tell him? Didn't he wonder why you'd come all that way?"

"I bull-shitted some talk about how important the New Victus announcement was going to be at the Summit. That we were looking for political allies and that we knew he had a personal connection to the FSE Ambassadors." Mercy shrugged. "I tried to make a show of how important it is to us."

"Did he believe you?" Lyssa asked with a hint of concern.

"I think so."

The back of the couch cradled Lyssa's head as she stared at the ceiling in thought. To overthrow the Storm regime would be a dangerous undertaking. She knew that if she led House Balthazaar into the uprising, then the other Progenitor Houses would follow – she had already sounded them out. But...they would only join Lyssa's rebellion if the numbers were balanced, and Storm and his allies currently outnumbered them in terms of manpower. It wasn't even close. Even with Dane's allegiance bringing Pack Nation into the fray, the numbers game still heavily favored Storm. They wouldn't risk it while they were at such a disadvantage.

She had been counting on establishing an alliance with the FSE and the NAA. Bringing them on board would tip the scales hugely in their favor. Without them, Lyssa wasn't sure what to do next.

"We're screwed then," she sighed.

"Did I say that?" Mercy replied with a lightness of tone.

Lyssa looked back at her niece with narrowed eyes. There was a sly look on Mercy's face, and a grin that implied there was a little more to the story.

"Mercy... What did you do?"

Mercy leaned forward again, conspiratorially.

"Norbel isn't our way in," she said cryptically. "But I think I found someone else."

Lyssa leaned in to join the comically private huddle.

"Who?" she whispered.

"I met Gayle Knightley," Mercy stated, as if that answered all Lyssa's questions.

"*Captain* Gayle Knightley?"

"Mmm-hmm." Mercy grinned like the cat that got the cream.

"I take it she lived up to your expectations?"

"When General Norbel introduced us...I almost *wet* myself

in excitement," Mercy giggled. "But it was pretty clear at that point that the Captain did not want me there at all."

"Awkward."

"Very. Especially when Norbel offered her services to me as a chaperone around London. *That* really did not go down well at all. She was polite, but you could tell that she really saw me as the enemy."

"Honestly, that's probably to be expected. We're all simply Vampyrii to her. An adversary she has fought against countless times."

"True," Mercy said slowly. "But what I *didn't* expect was to see that attitude change. Yet it did. By the end of the evening, she was treating me like...a friend. Almost. Lyssa, she's not someone who is tied to a rigid thought structure. She flows with the information presented to her... It's so fucking obvious now why her team was so good in the field.

"She makes decisions based on the facts that are true in that moment, and she's not afraid to shift her viewpoint appropriately. What made her such a good commander in the field – her ability to adapt to different tactical situations – also serves her in life. While she saw me as an enemy in their midst on initial encounter, she shifted that view over the course of the evening. She accepted me for *who* I am, not *what* I am. As Mercy, not as a Vampyrii. To her, that was something I just happened to be. It was refreshing.

"It was also very encouraging. We need allies that are going to accept us and fight alongside us. I'm telling you, Lyssa...she's the one."

With that Mercy sat back in her chair again, as if what she had just said was the answer to everything. Lyssa, however, had questions.

"She's just one person, though, Merce. And she's only a captain in the HFA. She has no pull in the FSE or the NAA. In fact, according to latest intelligence, the Federation brass doesn't even like her that much. She doesn't even have a team anymore. How is she 'the one?'"

"Because," Mercy said with that smug grin again, "she is also the daughter of *both* of the most prominent Federation

Ambassadors. She's our in."

"Okay. Granted there is that connection, but Ambassador Serlia Knightley is the sister to General Norbel. We can't keep him out of the loop," Lyssa countered.

"True," Mercy conceded. "But I don't trust him to be the person *leading* that loop. I think that if we make our case to Captain Knightley and her parents, the Ambassadors, then we have a much better chance. I feel like General Norbel won't take us as seriously as we need him to. Gayle will."

"*Gayle* now?" Lyssa teased.

"I liked her." Mercy almost blushed. "I consider her a friend."

"The question is, does Gayle reciprocate that sentiment?"

"Honestly...I don't know. I think I made an impression. A good one. I asked her if she would come to Nexus City before the Summit so we could talk."

"Did she agree?"

Mercy made a screwed up face that indicated immediately there had been no such agreement.

"She was hesitant about it. But I don't think it's about me. We had dinner together on this boat place on the river, and we talked. She didn't say anything overtly, but I got the impression that she's feuding with her father at the moment. I think her reticence about going to Nexus was because she doesn't want to see him, rather than anything to do with me."

"That doesn't sound promising." The pessimist in Lyssa found a way to be heard.

"Which is why I also have a plan B," Mercy said slyly. "I know her sisters *will* be at the Nexus Summit Gala. Both are cut from the same open-minded cloth as Gayle. The middle sister – Allyson – is the Chief of Security at Nexus. Anyway, I figured that we might see if we can apply some pressure there, too. You're going to the Gala, aren't you?"

"I am," Lyssa nodded.

"Good. I've laid the groundwork for you. Go meet the ambassadors. In the meantime, I'll keep an open dialogue with the sisters. Meeting Gayle has given me faith that these are the right people to get us the help we need."

"I hope you're right."

"Am I ever wrong?" Mercy cocked her eyebrow and tilted her head as if to challenge her aunt to come up with a time. "I have a good feeling about this. Trust me."

"Okay, point taken." Lyssa forced herself to relax and smile. "So, forgetting the work stuff, tell me about your trip."

Mercy's face lit up like a Christmas tree at the memory of her previous couple of days.

"Oh, my gods, you'd have loved it. London, the Academy, Trafalgar Square, Big Ben, Nexus City... I'm not sure where to even start!" Mercy exclaimed.

"Start at the beginning. Tell me about London."

| 56 |

PHOTOGRAPH

– Lana Fordham –
– Friday – London, England –

There was a murmur of noise from the dojo as Lana approached it. She had expected that their first Kendo training session might generate some buzz. It was, after all, their initial step on the road to using a Katana blade. But this sounded more like the rumble of a multifaceted argument being raged between the more outspoken members of the student body. Lana sighed wearily before entering.

What the hell has gotten into them today?

The class was split into two groups who stood facing each other, barefoot and wearing their kendogi with the skirt-like-hakama over the top. Considering the confrontation being had, Lana was glad she hadn't given them access to shinai yet. The likelihood of them whacking each other with the bamboo sticks, despite not donning the protective armor, was high.

The debate was raging so hard that none of them had noticed Lana pad barefoot into the room. She stood at the back, quietly trying to get an understanding of what was causing such a heated discussion between the two factions. Two words kept cropping up.

Captain Knightley.

"Okay," she finally broke her silence. "That's enough. What the hell is going on in here?"

Guilty looks surrounded her, but eventually it was Darius who voiced the thoughts of the group in his privileged Jamaican accent.

"Well, it's about Captain Knightley... She errr..."

"Get to the point, Mr. Williams," Lana said impatiently.

"It's just that Captain Knightley is..." Darius continued, still searching for the right words.

"...not exactly as advertised," Rosario angrily found them for him.

Lana looked at the Canadian girl. The call sign Gayle had given her was 'Spitfire,' which was surprisingly apt. Rosario was often angry and held strong opinions on just about everything.

"We've all heard the stories...about her being a badass, but so far..." Dylan chimed in. His sing-song Welsh baritone seemed out of place coming from his teenage mouth.

"...all we've seen is angry with an undercurrent of..." Darius continued.

"...couldn't give a fuck," Rosario finished.

Lana held up her hand to bring the cadets to a silence. "Curb that language, Ms. Hudgins! I take it from the argument that you don't all feel that way?"

It was Teyah Matthews who spoke out on her teacher's behalf while shaking her head.

"Some of us...want to *run* before we can walk," she said in a mildly accusatory tone but named no names. "While the rest of us think that it's better to learn the basics first."

"That's our point!" Rosario butted in. "She's not even teaching us the basics. After that first class of "This ain't magic, it's power," she hit that button and we've not been using our powers ever since. Not even talked about them!"

"It's only been three weeks," Teyah argued.

"A wasted three weeks!" Rosario shot back.

"There's plenty of time," Teyah sighed.

Rosario, who was clearly the instigator of this little mutiny, was about to retort when Lana decided to nip this in the bud. As the young girl opened her mouth, a glare from her teacher stopped the words in her throat before they emerged.

"Okay, all of you...simmer down."

The class settled into a quiet attention; Lana scanned all their faces before continuing.

"Captain Knightley is, without doubt, the best person to teach you how to be Hunters. Those stories...they're all true. Most of them actually *undersell* her achievements. I know because I was there."

She paused for a moment to let her statement sink in.

"She was the leader of the 137th while you were learning your first words. Over a decade of experience in some of the hottest combat zones on the planet, fighting the worst kinds of monsters. Three hundred and ninety-one missions, with only a single casualty."

"Until Bloody Valletta." Rosario put the quiet conclusion to the statement that Lana was making.

Lana nodded. There was no point in hiding the truth. "Until Valletta."

She swallowed hard and thought about that fateful day and her lost teammates and friends.

"You drop Valletta into the conversation like you know what happened, Rosario, but you have no idea. None of you do. Because if you knew what Captain Knightley went through that day, what she did...then this conversation wouldn't even be happening." Lana felt a surge of anger and took a deep breath. "The fact that she's here at all, trying to teach you how to be Hunters, is nothing short of a miracle."

"Maybe if you could tell us what *did* happen that day, Captain Fordham?" Payge chipped in.

"That's classified for a reason, Ms. Anderson. All you need to know is that Captain Knightley knows that there is a lot more to being a Hunter – to being a *good* Hunter – than just how to manipulate your genetic abilities."

She understood the palpable level of disappointment in the room and did empathize with the cadets. It was plain to see that, although Gayle had made huge strides in the past few weeks, she was not quite herself yet. Her confidence was missing. The 137th had breezed through close to a decade of missions with only one casualty. They had gone as far as to chalk that one up to a folly of inexperience. A fluke result from early in their careers.

We got over-confident. Cocky.

One terrible night in Valletta taught them a harsh lesson.

Consequently, there were now *two* Gayle Knightleys. The maverick super-soldier from the mission archives who had led the 137th Hunters to such an impressive reputation. And the one who was nursing a healthy dose of survivor's guilt. The one who was now playing everything safe in a determined effort to make sure that these cadets never suffered from the same false bravado and overconfidence that her own team had.

Neither was a healthy way to train these kids.

Lana would have to deal with this head on, with Gayle herself. In the meantime, she also had to resolve the issue with how these kids saw their infamous tutor. A tiny epiphany gave her an idea of how to cope with this particular issue.

"Up on your feet, one-three-eight. You're coming with me."

She led the confused group of students out of the dojo and barefoot through the Academy, ignoring the whispered theories regarding their ultimate destination. They were still confused when Lana escorted them into the combat briefing room and instructed them to sit down and watch the large tactical display monitors. As they sat and continued to speculate in low tones, she spent a few minutes searching through the servers for the files she was looking for. When she found them, she paused and turned back to the group.

"One day, the combat logs will be opened to you. The plan for your training is to give you access to certain things as and when they become relevant to your progress. As Cadet Matthews neatly stated, you've only been here for a few weeks. It is far too early for you to be seeing classified information just yet."

She watched as the class went through a wave of different emotions. First there had been the obvious supposition that Lana was about to break the rules and show them the mission logs anyway. Disappointment then flooded the room as they realized that was not the case. Then the room bounced back to a level of puzzled anticipation. Surely their teacher hadn't just brought them to this room to tell them that?

"I can't show you the combat logs and video, but what I can show you is the video that was recorded during the original team's training sessions. I'm going to show you who Gayle Knightley is, who the Hunters were, and why you have such a long way to go before you're ready to emulate them."

She triggered the file, and on the screen a high definition video started to play. The first shot immediately tore at Lana's heart.

The screen was dominated by the handsome smiling face of Gabriel Oliviera – call sign 'Rio.' His sparkling white teeth contrasting brilliantly with his richly tanned skin and jet-black hair. It was evident from his movements and proximity that he was the one setting up the camera. As he finished and started to back away, the periphery became viewable, immediately bringing tears to Lana's eyes.

The 137th Hunters.

Not all of them. In the camera shot, she could only see Gabriel, the perfect russet skin of Chloe Barbier, and the big, brash, blonde-haired, blue-eyed energy bundle that was Jaylen Johnson, who dwarfed her petite French teammate. All were dressed in workout clothes and sneakers suiting their individual and distinct styles.

"Rio, do we *have* to record this?" Out of shot, but easily recognizable came the voice of Gayle Knightley.

"You said it yourself, if we're going to be better than the 136th, then we need to practice and see where we're going wrong," Gabriel said to the camera.

The background was also familiar, not just to Lana but to the assembled students. A ripple of murmurs went around the group as they recognized the tree line from the Academy grounds.

"Yes, of course I want to beat Torbar's tossers, but I brought us out here onto the grounds so we could get away from the fucking cameras in the gyms."

It seemed somehow apt that the moment she cursed was also the moment Gayle came into view on the screen. She was wearing the same tight black workout leggings and the white and red trimmed sports top she always wore, showing that toned six-pack Lana had always envied. Her hair was shorter than it was today, but still tied up from her face. Lana was stunned by how young she looked. This was a Gayle Knightley not scarred by defeat and loss.

"Is he settin' up that goddamn camera again?" Jaylen's distinctive Texan twang was heavier than the one they were used to hearing from Captain Reynolds.

Lana knew that Jaylen's aversion to cameras was due to her insecurities regarding her weight – she often self-deprecatingly referred to herself as 'The Texan Tank.' Yet she was one of the most objectively attractive women Lana had ever met, sporting devastatingly photogenic looks coupled with infectious joie-de-vivre.

She jogged into view, with her usual baggy, sky-blue football shirt over her long black leggings, and her tousle of blonde hair tucked beneath the grubby baseball cap she always wore. She was a strikingly powerful figure of a woman. She glared at the beautiful Brazilian who was carefully backing away from the camera.

"It is the best way, Tank," Rio said as he walked, gesturing back toward the camera. "We record, we review."

Broad, muscular, and tanned, Rio was a handsome figure of a man and he knew it. He groomed himself to perfection and showed off his physique with shirts so tight they looked sprayed on.

"Okay, folks, listen up," Gayle called the group together. "Dodgeball training, combat protocol, so call signs only from now on. Rio and Tank against myself and Misty. As we're not wearing combat suits, let's keep it decidedly non-lethal, please. Misty, Rio, and I are water. Tank, you're on the mud-balls. All clear?"

The group nodded and Chloe sighed.

"Problem, Misty?" Gayle queried.

"So, Rio and Tank just get wet, while we get muddy?" Her French accent had a husky quality, as if she smoked too much.

"Only if they catch you," Gayle laughed. "I intend on going

back to the Academy spotless."

She reached for her wrist where she wore an oversized sports watch and hit a button on it. There was a distinctive 'beep' – the start of the stopwatch.

"Fifteen minutes starts...now."

The group was in motion before Gayle even finished her sentence. Rio conjured a swirling globe of water the size of a baseball in the palm of his hand. With a flick of the wrist, he sent it briskly toward Knightingale, who was pre-emptively ducking and rolling to avoid it. The water passed safely over her head as she prepared her own counterattack. A moment later, a wind-assisted watery sphere of her own creation sped toward her opponent.

Rio backpedaled, narrowly avoiding her retaliation as another ball of water appeared in his left hand. With a thrust, he sent it whirling toward the second globe Knightingale had directed his way. The two collided in mid-air, dispersing each other in a rainbow-casting spray of droplets.

Tank was also on the move, stalking Misty while keeping a watchful eye on Knightingale's battle with Rio. She wasn't a pure water summoner, but with her earth abilities she could create mud, an orb of which started to churn in her right hand. She twisted as she ran, throwing it behind her in Misty's direction. The French woman dodged right, watching the mud sail harmlessly past her shoulder. Tank's opening volley had simply been a distraction. It was her follow up throw that was about to hit Misty squarely in the face.

Knightingale saw the threat to her teammate, however, and as she dodged another water-ball from Rio, she gestured with her hand toward Misty. A micro-gust of wind interrupted the flightpath of Tank's second shot, diverting it to impact harmlessly into one of the trees behind them. As it oozed leisurely down to the ground, it left no doubt as to the mess it would have made to its intended target.

"Merci, Knightingale!" Misty called out.

"Pas de problème!" Knightingale replied with a grin.

"La tête haute!" Misty pointed behind her squad leader.

"Hey!" Jaylen shouted indignantly. "No fair with the

French!"

On screen, Gayle laughed uproariously as she twisted away to avoid Jaylen's mudball.

Lana smiled. This was a Gayle Knightley these kids hadn't seen yet. The one unburdened by loss. Eighteen years young, bright, fun, and vivacious with the title of Squad Leader only recently bestowed upon her. A role she relished and took great pride in. *This* was the version of Gayle she wanted the students to see and relate to; the one not too different from them.

Not a word was spoken as the cadets sat enraptured by the video on the screen. It wasn't all about military training; it demonstrated to them the skill with which their powers could be used. Gayle and her peers had used exercises like a simple game of dodgeball to learn and practice their craft. Conjuring perfect spheres of water or mud and then using their other abilities to enhance their actions looked so simple. Yet it required a level of skill that these kids could thus far only dream of.

Standing at the back, Lana felt tears welling up in her eyes, threatening to run down her cheeks. As painful as it was to watch such memories play out in high definition, she also realized this was something she needed. Even before the events on Malta, the team had been in a rough place. Lana wasn't sure why things started to slide. She supposed that losing Valerio eight years prior had been the tipping point. It was the mission where the Hunters lost their carefree edge, when they realized that this wasn't a game. In some ways, they grew up that day, each finding solace in something different, whether that be the bottom of a bottle or in each other's beds.

Was this the destiny for these kids, too?

Lana watched the frivolity unfolding on the screen, each of the four Hunters on the film deftly dodging and weaving. All of them moving seamlessly from offense to defense while expertly wielding their abilities with the precision of a scalpel. She suddenly realized that these kids, whose eyes were glued to the monitor in wide-eyed astonishment, would spend their careers trying to compete with the team they were watching.

The video brought a clash of emotions to Lana. The joy of

seeing her friends during a happier time, railing against the resurfacing of grief and the intense sadness of their passing. She missed them all deeply, including that part of Gayle that had been lost in Valletta, too.

She wiped away the tears that were in her eyes and took one final look at the screen. It was time to stop living in the past. To cherish their memories, but ultimately say goodbye. Nobody could take their place, though these kids were being charged with attempting it.

They were awfully large shoes to fill.

A noise drew her attention and she glanced at the door, just in time to see a dash of pink hair disappear back into the corridor. She took a deep breath and closed her eyes.

Fuck.

| 57 |

CONFESSIONS

– **Michael Reynolds** –
– Friday – London, England –

Found her, he thought with a small measure of triumph.

To be fair, though, she hadn't really been hiding; simply sitting on the wall near the landing pads watching the ground-crew work on one of the dropships. He could hear the gentle whine of the repulsor-lift engines as they idled away, changing pitch slightly as the engineers put it through its pre-launch checks.

The evening was mild, and bar a small breeze from the east that rustled the leaves of the trees, it was still and pleasant. The sun was setting, slowly bathing the landing area in the soft pink and orange hues of twilight and giving the landing pad lights the beginnings of purchase over the impending night.

He stood for a moment and watched Gayle as she sat hugging her knees. Her hair was being whipped by wind as she nibbled on the thumbnail of her right hand. She was wearing simple black yoga pants and a snug white gym top with red trim. A pair of plain white sneakers completed the ensemble. That, along with the gym bag and water bottle sat alongside to her, led Michael to conclude that she may have been on her way to the Academy gym when she had passed the briefing room.

For a moment or two he debated interrupting her reverie, but eventually decided that he needed to make sure she was okay. She didn't look at him as he approached, but she did smile slowly.

"I wondered if you'd come over to say hi." Wry amusement was evident in her tone.

"I wasn't sure if you were havin' a private moment."

She turned her head slowly and looked sideways at him, her smile still in place. Genuine, not faked or forced. He knew because her eyes told the same story. Michael found himself reciprocating the gesture with a smile of his own.

"Oh, I realized a long time ago that when you join the Academy, privacy is a dim and distant memory. Actually...be kind of nice to have company tonight. I assume Lana sent you?"

For the first time since he had met her, Gayle Knightley looked genuinely vulnerable. Not in the injured way she had been after their run a few days earlier. That had been a moment of fear, after which her regular bravado quickly reasserted itself. This evening, though, she seemed openly disarmed in his presence.

"Are you okay?"

"Yeah..." she said quietly. "The video caught me by surprise is all. I just...I miss them. I thought I'd come down here and...I dunno."

He didn't push her; she would talk in her own time.

"The other morning... Thank you. You were really...gentlemanly. So...I just wanted to say thank you."

They hadn't spoken about that morning since it happened. He wanted to talk to her about it – he had questions with no answers. But he didn't have a lot of experience in communicating openly about things like this, and after a couple of days, he felt awkward bringing up the subject.

"How's the knee?" he said, side-stepping the topic uppermost in his mind.

"Getting there. The doc said yoga would help, so I won't be your running mate for a couple weeks."

"I can wait." he smiled.

"I'm sure you can." She threw him a sly sideways glance.

"But I know that you *really* want to talk about the kiss."

She let the last word linger as if teasing him with her knowledge of his state of mind. He couldn't help but let out a laugh and was quietly pleased to see that it made her smile a little broader as she tucked her hair behind her ear.

"I've read your file, and there's nothin' in there about mind reading."

This time it was her turn to laugh. "I don't need to be psychic. As I said, you're a gentleman, and that kiss is the proverbial elephant in the room."

"It was just an accident..." he said in an unconvincing tone.

"Sometimes things happen for a reason, Michael," she said cryptically. "I've been thinking about it quite a bit. I wanted to talk to you about it, but, well...things just seemed a little..."

"Awkward," he finished her sentence for her with his own thoughts.

She nodded in agreement. "I'm willing to bet that you've never...dilly-dallied with a co-worker, teammate...whatever you want to call what we are. Am I right?" she asked with a tilt of the head.

"Dilly-dallied..."

"Had relations with," she clarified.

"Oh, I understood the meaning. Just never heard it called that before."

"Welcome to Blighty, guv'nor." She laughed at her own bad mock-cockney accent, a sound that felt melodious to Michael's ears and he couldn't help but be caught up in the infectious nature of it.

He laughed as he answered her question.

"No, I can safely say I have never dillied nor dallied with someone I work with professionally."

"Yeah, I could tell," Gayle nodded. The levity faded from her voice. "On the other hand...I have."

She gestured subtly toward the landing pad and the tall, dark-haired man barking orders at some of the ground crew as they prepped the dropship.

"Captain Torbar?" Michael said with a hint or surprise.

Gayle nodded and sighed. "That was a big – *huge* – fuck-off mistake."

Michael wasn't sure how to respond, finding himself a little perplexed by their conversation. Ten seconds ago, they were enjoying flirty banter and he had been wondering where it was leading. But now he felt like they were at a fork in the road, and he wasn't sure which way Gayle was heading.

"When I took the Captaincy of the Hunters, it was the best day. The *best*. Graduation from the Academy after all our hard work. But the day before, Alastair Torbar and his squad graduated. He got his captain's badge just twenty-four hours before I did, but it meant that his squad – the 136th Terminators – got first dibs on everything. We *knew* we were the better squad, but that didn't matter. Torbar and his guys were the starters; we were the bench."

She had drifted away into reverie now and Michael wasn't sure where this was going, or what the relevance was to the conversation they were having. One thing he knew, though, was that Gayle Knightley had demons. Allyson had warned him on his visit to Nexus and it was all over her psych evaluation. It was obvious to anyone who spoke with her at length – there were scars from wounds that were more than simply physical. Whatever happened in Valletta had crushed her whole world.

He said nothing. If it helped her on the way to putting the pieces of her life back together, then he was happy to sit and listen.

"Torbar was a fucking dickhead about it. Loved to tell me how he was technically my superior due his 'length of service.' Just because his captain's pin had one day's more tarnish on it. Looking back now...it had to be like that. Our edge was the grudge we held about being placed second best. It drove us to excel, and we made life difficult for him. My squad outperformed his on every metric and every test. But we weren't the perfect little soldiers and that drove our superiors crazy.

"After graduation, I found one more thing I could do to wind Torbar up. Sex. I thought I could wrap him around my little finger. Fuck him so good he'd be begging me for more because that was my experience with men. They were easy, predictable."

She paused to take a deep breath.

"Stupid. I was so fucking stupid. He's half Fae, same as me, and while I can twist a Human inside out with my pheromones, he was utterly immune. He strung me along for almost three months before coming clean. I was so fucking angry. At him...but mostly at myself.

"You see, by that time it wasn't me playing games anymore. It wasn't me trying to get one over on him. I thought I had fallen in love with the motherfucker. Head over fucking heels. First love.

"That heartbreak – that pain – fueled my mission to destroy him. My squad, my friends, my Hunters...they followed me into that holy war. Every mission, every training exercise, every chance we got...we *destroyed* them. We forced the brass to sit up and take notice, that we were the better squad. Not them. Not Torbar and his Terminators.

"*My* Hunters.

"All because I felt slighted by him turning my own game against me."

She stopped for a moment and stared out onto the landing pad. Captain Torbar was ushering the dozen members of his team into the now fully prepped dropship. The ground crew were scampering away as the engines upped their pitch and the wings began to pivot into the take-off position. With his squad aboard, Torbar started to walk up the ramp himself. He glanced back toward the wall where Gayle and Michael sat and threw them a casual salute.

Gayle lifted a hand to her own temple and threw an identical salute back at her rival. The smile on her face was still genuine, but her eyes conveyed her sadness. Michael thought he saw the roll of a tear on Gayle's cheek, but it could just have been a trick of the light.

"Truth is..." she continued eventually, "there are two dropships on that pad. The *Minerva* – named for the Greek goddess of war – and *Artemis* – the chariot of the 137th Hunters and named for the Roman goddess of the hunt. *Artemis* hasn't left this launch pad in anger in over ten months, while *Minerva* is off again to carry her squad to a mission God knows where."

The tail of the *Minerva* dropped down into place as the ramp retracted and the wings completed their pivot. As the engine note rose and the *Minerva* lifted itself gracefully off the asphalt, Gayle turned to face Michael again. Her face was a study in serious reflection.

"Michael, you've read my file. I have made some epically bad decisions at really important moments. Decisions that recently got my squad — my friends — killed. You want to talk about that kiss? I like you. I like you a lot. I'm not going to hide that fact. I wanted to kiss you, so in that moment, I *decided* to kiss you.

"But I'm asking myself...was that simply me making another bad decision?"

She hopped down off the wall before he could respond. He wasn't entirely sure what he wanted to say anyway.

"Gayle—" he started.

"Let it go, handsome," she interrupted with a smile. "Maybe just go back to being professional and I'll do my best to reciprocate. New me."

As she walked backward away from him, she pointed up to the dropship that had now taken flight and was receding into the dark umber of the night sky, heading east to places unknown.

"You know, *Minerva* wasn't just the goddess of war. She was also the goddess of wisdom. Torbar might be an arrogant bastard, but he makes smart choices. One of which was to *not* fall in love with me.

"Good night, Captain."

She turned and walked slowly away from Michael toward the main building, a limp evident in her gait. He didn't try to follow her.

He sat for a while contemplating what he had just heard — her confession. That's what it felt like. He recognized that none of what was said was actually about their kiss. It was really about something wildly different. Blame. There was a lot of self-hate in her words. Broken confidence and second-guessing. Michael ran his hand through his hair, and sighed.

| 58 |

THE EMPIRE

– Sebastian StormHall –
– Friday – Pacific Ocean –

Sebastian *hated* flying.

His already pale knuckles were a shade lighter than usual as he gripped the straps of the seat harness as tightly as he could. The flyer was shaken violently by yet another surge of turbulence. He cursed under his breath and fought to keep his late dinner firmly in his stomach where it belonged. From his vantage point in the co-pilot's seat, all he could see was the dark interior of the low-level storm clouds, occasionally brightened by flashes of lightning. He knew one of those jagged lightning bolts couldn't take down a flyer like this, but the conditions still frightened him.

Ironic, really, considering his House name. Grand Chancellor StormHall scared of a little thunder and lightning.

To be fair, it was more than that; it was the illicit nature of his current endeavor that put him on edge. Not that he wasn't used to a little subterfuge and illegal shenanigans in his career, but normally he had flunkies to carry out this kind of work for him.

When his mystery patron asked for a favor, however, it was hands on. No one else must know how he found his path to the power he enjoyed. He glanced at the pilot, a Trampyrii slaved to StormHall's will. He would no more tell anyone about this trip into the Pacific than he would make decent conversation for the flight. The man was a blank slate, nothing more than a biological autopilot.

The flyer started to descend and before long they had mercifully broken the cloud cover, not that that helped with Sebastian's fear. It was pitch black over the ocean; only the regular flashes of lightning from the clouds illuminated the scene enough for him to see fleeting glimpses of the cold black rolling waters beneath them.

He hated this trip; it was fraught with danger. Travelling alone in a stealth-flyer across NAA-held territory down the west coast was bad enough, but now they were flying in enemy airspace toward an illicit rendezvous with what could hardly be considered an ally. This was purely a business arrangement, set up by his benefactor. One that had profited him hugely over the last few decades.

The flyer dipped, banking slightly to starboard and right on schedule. The distant lights of a large ship came into view ahead of them. Sebastian pried his hand from the straps and reached forward to the control panel to send an encrypted landing code to his contact. Almost immediately the response was received, allowing the flyer to approach without being shot down.

Still, Sebastian held his breath as they rapidly closed the distance to the ship, but no missiles rose to greet them. As they got closer, he could make out the enormous silhouette of the Japanese Imperial aircraft carrier, the *Akagi*.

StormHall had lived through World War II, and he knew that the original *Akagi* had been destroyed during the Battle of Midway. This new namesake was twice as big as the *Gerald R Ford* class carrier the NAA operated. The ship's apparent power prompted many questions. Where had they gotten the resources to build such a behemoth? How many of these ships did they have?

Sebastian had no idea of the Japanese Empire's military strength or what their political motives might be. They were a reclusive society, one of the world's most secretive nations. It was rumored that they were in an ongoing war with Zǔguó, but Sebastian hadn't been able to verify those rumors, let alone discover what they might be fighting over. He knew that they controlled much of the Pacific Ocean, and had clashed with the NAA near Hawaii and with Australasia from time to time.

Beyond that...nothing.

His pilot expertly dropped the flyer the last few meters to gently settle on the rain-soaked deck of the *Akagi*. Through the window he could already see his contact and a work team approaching the flyer. Sebastian clumsily unbuckled his harness and awkwardly extricated himself from the cockpit to head back into the cargo hold.

"Drop the loading ramp," he ordered the pilot. "And keep the engines running. I won't be long."

The pilot nodded in response and flicked a toggle-switch on the control panel. Sebastian heard the whine of the motors as the loading ramp started its descent. As the gap widened, the tall slender figure of the man he had come to meet came into view.

"TechMaster Takahashi. Yoroshiku onegaishimasu," he announced over the sound of the downpour beating against the deck.

It was a false pleasantry. He performed the obligatory bow, and had it reciprocated by the TechMaster.

"Grand Chancellor StormHall. Your flight was pleasant?"

The polite opening question, but Takahashi's eyes betrayed how he *truly* felt about having Sebastian on his ship. Neither of them wanted to prolong the meeting, so Sebastian lied in response to move things along more briskly.

"Very much so," he said with a curt nod. "I have your payment."

He gestured back to the large cargo crate in the back of the flyer, roughly eight feet in length and about six feet tall. Contained within were the four specimens that had been requested in payment for the item that Sebastian's benefactor told him to procure.

"You understand how dangerous they are? Precautions must be taken."

The look on Takahashi's face said, '*Do you take me for an idiot?*' but his reply was simple, and polite.

"The utmost care will be taken in handling them."

"You have the item I requested?"

The Japanese man nodded and gave a subtle hand signal. One of his subordinates hastened forward, proffering a small case in his outstretched hand. Takahashi took the case from him and stepped forward slightly into the rain cover provided by the rear fuselage of the flyer. He unsnapped the fasteners, lifting the lid of the small jet-black box. The item inside was tiny. Nestled in the center of a square of protective foam lay a tiny microchip.

"It will function as required and be undetectable."

"I'm sure it'll operate perfectly," StormHall agreed and took the tiny box into his own hands, snapping the lid shut again. "As always."

"Our business is now concluded," Takahashi said curtly. "I wish you safe travels, Grand Chancellor."

As the tall Japanese man turned to leave, Sebastian called out to him, drawing his attention back to him momentarily.

"Will the Empire be attending the Nexus Summit this year?"

Takahashi turned and regarded him, his face stoic. He glanced at the crate that his deck crew were unloading and then back at Sebastian once more. Finally, he opened his mouth to speak.

"I see no good reason for us to attend," he replied, and then reiterated his goodbye. "Safe travels, Grand Chancellor."

It was clearly a dismissal. A sentiment that rankled StormHall. He was the leader of a powerful nation, but rather than being treated as a dignitary with respect and courtesy, all he ever got from Takahashi was barely disguised disdain behind a polite façade. Alone on the deck of this powerful vessel, he was not in a position to demand to be treated in the manner he expected. Here he was little more than a visiting foreigner performing illicit business.

That was the status quo for now, but that *would* change.

He didn't bother to reply to Takahashi, the man had already

JON FORD

turned his back and stalked away. Sebastian wasted no time, passing through the now empty cargo bay and returning to the cockpit of the flyer. He strapped himself into the co-pilot's chair once again and steeled himself for the return flight.

Within moments, the flyer was lifting gracefully off the deck and once more ascending into the storm. As the rain lashed the windows and streamed off to the side, he looked at the small case sitting on his lap. Unfastening the clasps, he levered the top open and took another look at the small microchip sheltered in its protective foam and smiled.

This was the last favor he would do for her.

Now he was free to pursue his own agenda.

| 59 |

BAGGAGE

– Lyssa Balthazaar –
– Saturday – New York, New Victus –

The StormHall International SkyPort.
Gods, it makes me want to vomit.
Most Vampyrii respected heritage and tradition – it was in their blood – but renaming an airport for self-promotion felt like a purely egotistical endeavor. She begrudgingly understood the logic of rebranding their country, but the cities and states remained as they had always been. This might now be New Victus, but New York City was still New York City and Chicago was still Chicago.

And to Lyssa, this would always be the John F. Kennedy International Airport.

Lyssa lived through the Kennedy years. Voted for him. She had liked and respected the man for his handling of the nation during his relatively brief tenure, and whether the country had changed names or not, he was one of the most influential figures of its history. This renaming was a not-so-subtle nod toward the fact that Storm thought himself better than one of the most popular presidents in US history. It was a small thing in the grand scheme of reasons why Lyssa hated the man, but another reason, nonetheless.

The word 'International' was a study in irony. Pre-Rising, it had been one of the busiest hubs for foreign travel in the US.

Since Storm's ascent to power, however, Vampyrii international travel was blocked. Borders all over the world were closed to them without special visas. The only place flights could legally frequent was Nexus City, and to get there required diplomatic papers.

She glanced at her watch. He was only fifteen minutes overdue, but being kept waiting on a frigid evening in Queens wasn't doing anything for Lyssa's mood. She wasn't angry — simply wearily resigned to these little power games he liked to play. Just this once it would have been nice if he could have kept to the pre-arranged schedule. As if on cue, her sensitive hearing picked up the distant sound of engines and she cast her gaze up to the low clouds that obscured the night sky.

The huge silhouette of *Blood Storm One* emerged from the cloud layer, its running lights blinking and its landing gear extricating itself from the fuselage as it approached the runway. Crimson in color with black trim, the aircraft had enormous repulsor-lift engines suspended beneath the enormous wings where the General Electric turbofans had once been. It originally flew under the name *Air Force One*, before being converted and re-liveried when Storm came to power.

She watched it leisurely descend, gently touch down, and taxi toward the apron near Terminal 4, where her House's private flyer, *Spirit of Independence*, was parked. A small crowd had gathered near the SkyPort to witness the plane's arrival, hoping for a glimpse of its head-of-state passenger. She shook her head gently in dismay at the reverence some of the population seemed to have for this detestable man.

As it taxied to a rest, Lyssa was struck by how the Boeing 747 dwarfed her relatively petite LearJet 117.

It's like seeing our egos side by side, she thought with wry amusement as she started to stride toward the new arrival.

The engines dulled their roar and started to cycle down as the ground crew hurried to push the boarding steps up to the hatchway. The stairs kissed the fuselage as she approached and waited for permission to board. It was granted moments later by a black-suited bruiser with muscles to spare, who Lyssa recognized as one of Storm's personal bodyguards. He nodded his approval for her to board the plane, and she mused on the absurdity of him wearing mirrored sunglasses at night. He stopped her briefly at the top of the steps to perform the inevitable body-search, undertaken efficiently and professionally with not a hint of lasciviousness. Finally satisfied, he stepped aside.

The aircraft's interior was a statement in opulence, her footsteps disappearing into the thick luxurious carpeting as the bodyguard escorted her wordlessly through the cabin. They passed lines of huge, comfortable looking seats, usually used by Storm's entourage, until they reached his on-board office. The door opened as they approached, and she was greeted by the false smile of the Grand Chancellor himself.

"Sebastian," Lyssa said by way of greeting.

"I apologize for my tardiness," Storm began. "I hope I haven't inconvenienced you too much."

"I'm just here to collect the documents for the Summit, Sebastian. Then I can be on my way and you can go greet your adoring public."

She felt like she had fulfilled her quota of time in his presence with his last visit to her five weeks prior. If he found her abruptness in anyway disrespectful, however, he didn't show it. He motioned for his bodyguard to leave the room and then gestured toward the crystal decanter sitting secured on a cabinet nearby.

"May I offer you a drink?"

Lyssa glanced at it. While the deep-burgundy color suggested it contained the blood on which the stories falsely suggested their kind gorged, knowing Storm, it was likely to be port. He had a taste for the drink. She shook her head, saying nothing, and hoped that the bodyguard would return promptly, which he did a moment later carrying two narrow, silver attaché cases. At first scan, they looked identical, until Lyssa noticed each carried a tiny flag motif on the lid. One was that of the North America Alliance, the other the banner of Pack Nation. He placed them onto Storm's desk alongside a third attaché case that looked similar but was black in color.

"The silver cases are official diplomatic envoy cases, distributed to us from Nexus Security," Storm explained, finally getting down to business. "They are numbered, security tagged, and must be checked through Nexus Security upon arrival in the city. They are the only cases allowed into the WCC."

"I've read the security protocols," Lyssa said wearily.

Ignoring her, he rested his hand on the silver case bearing the flag of the NAA. It resembled the old Stars-and-Stripes but incorporated the Canadian flag where the stars used to be. The remaining five stars, representing the remaining states they controlled, were distributed evenly around the maple leaf.

"This case contains our proposal to the NAA for the New Victus withdrawal from the western states. You will present this to Ambassador Brady at the Summit."

He moved his hand to the second case. The Pack Nation flag on this one had an emerald green background with two howling wolf-heads back-to-back over a large golden circle. Dane had once told her that it represented the Sun and the Moon and the duality of their nature.

"This one is for Ambassador Sabadini," Storm continued. "Our proposal for a ceasefire and withdrawal along the Pack Nation border."

She couldn't help but hear the undercurrent of disdain in Sebastian's tone when he mentioned the Pack Nation ambassador's name. Lyssa walked to the table and brushed her hand across the tiny black-glass panel on the front of the NAA case. A biometric scanner for the lock, perhaps?

"Don't trust me with them?"

Sebastian gave that ingratiating smile that he used to woo political favors.

"The cases are biometrically coded to the respective ambassadors. Once we placed the proposals in there and locked them, the only people who can open them are the relevant ambassadors. These plans have been agreed to at the highest levels of the Council of Blood. They must be delivered in the official security-cleared attaché cases."

Finally, he gestured toward the matt-black case. This one

had the flag of New Victus emblazoned on it. She had to admit that while she hated what the flag stood for, she did admire its design. The background was tri-color, starting midnight black at the top and gently fading into a blood red band just over halfway down. That, in turn, met a stripe of brown that ran across the bottom fifth. Representations of the night, the blood, and the earth. A silver circle sat central to the flag itself, blended with a smaller, slightly darker, circle that was positioned just behind it to the right. Each had the silhouette of a face faintly etched on them. Solista and Nocturne, goddesses of the Sun and the Moon respectively.

"This one contains copies of what's in the other two, plus briefing documents. All you need to know is in here. This case will be blood-coded to your DNA...so if you would be so kind."

He nodded to his bodyguard who picked up the case and prodded a sequence on the tiny keypad before turning it and proffering it to Lyssa. She could see there was a small panel, maybe an inch square, perfect for her print. She placed her thumb on the panel and felt a short, sharp prick on her skin as the case tested her blood and stored her DNA profile. A tiny light on the top of the case changed from red to orange. The bodyguard, still not saying a word, indicated that she should proffer her thumb again. Same process, this time the light turned green and the locks within the case sprang open with a solid clunk.

"The case is now yours," Sebastian said simply as he returned to his desk. "Once you lock it again, even I cannot open it."

Lyssa glanced at the documents within, before pushing the lid down and hearing the locks close once more. She would read them later

"If that will be all."

Alas, the Grand Chancellor wasn't finished with her quite yet. As he returned to the fancy leather chair behind his over-sized mahogany desk, he eyed her carefully, steepling his fingers before finally talking.

"I thought you were on board with my proposals," he remarked with a tone that felt to Lyssa like he was setting her up.

She carefully considered her response. "I am. I'm more than happy to deliver this to the Summit."

"I feel it is in the best interests of our people."

She couldn't argue with that. There was a large part of her that simply wanted to rail on him, to tell him that this was just a fix for a problem he had created, but her mouth stayed firmly shut. Maybe a few weeks ago she would have given this man a piece of her mind. She certainly had not been shy expressing her opinion when he had visited her in Manhattan.

But something was not right.

You didn't live as long as she had without having a finely-tuned sense of when a situation was dangerous. Right now, she had the definite impression that she was a pawn being maneuvered in a larger game, one that she couldn't see. In Manhattan, there had been suspicions that this whole thing was a trap of some description. Now she was sure of it. The only questions left in her mind were what the nature of the trap was and how to avoid it. Standing there alone on his turf, her senses screamed at her.

Don't rock the boat, Lyssa. Just get out as soon as possible.

"I agree. I hope that the others at the Summit feel likewise," she said, deadpan. "Now, if you'll excuse me, my flight plan is already on record with the tower and I don't want to miss my departure slot."

She didn't wait for permission. She grabbed the cases, awkwardly holding two of them with one hand, and headed for the door, which was blocked by Storm's bodyguard. For a moment, she thought she might have to fight her way out, but then realized that Sebastian was not going to create a scene. Not there on his own plane, and not while he needed Lyssa to perform a task for him. This was simply another not-so-subtle powerplay.

"Have a pleasant trip, Lyssa. I will be waiting for you upon your return, after the conference..." a thinly veiled threat, "...to get an update on the success of our proposal."

She looked back at him. His face was inscrutable. She held his stare, refusing to back down. Finally, he nodded at the burly bodyguard who immediately stepped aside. Lyssa turned and walked back through the cabin to the hatch, her heart thumping hard in her chest. It didn't slow until she was sitting in the cockpit of her own flyer and the doors had been shut and sealed. She closed her eyes and put her head back against the headrest, trying to center herself. As she cycled deep cleansing breaths, she reached out blindly to take her headset from its usual spot and settled it on her head.

"Tower, this is bravo-alpha-lima-zero-one-niner '*Spirit of Independence*,'" she said into the mic. "I have a flight plan logged for a twenty-one thirty departure for Nexus City. Requesting permission for departure."

Over the headset, the light female voice of the control tower came back almost immediately.

"Bravo-alpha-lima-zero-one-niner, your plan is logged and approved. Taxi into position at skypad four and hold for instruction."

Calmer now, she powered up the engines and vectored her repulsor-lifts to roll her flyer smoothly forward toward the designated spot. No sooner had she reported in at the hold position than instruction came through clearing her for take-off. She throttled up the engines and the tiny Learjet lifted vertically to hover above the tarmac. Glancing toward *Blood Storm One* as she rose, the Grand Chancellor was visible as he waved from the open hatch of the plane to the small gathered crowd.

Lyssa smiled to herself. If the original namesake of this airport had been the one waving to the public from that top step, the crowd would be hundreds of times larger. Self-promotion could never compete with simply being popular; a sentiment that Sebastian Storm would never truly understand.

She angled the repulsor-lifts slightly backward and pushed forward on the throttle. The *Spirit of Independence*'s engines surged as the flyer leapt skyward, leaving Storm far behind. Yet, as fast or as far as she travelled, she couldn't escape the dark feelings that turned her belly with cartwheels of sick foreboding.

There was another shoe waiting, unseen, in the wings. And she was dreading the moment when it would drop.

| 60 |

SHARING THE NIGHT TOGETHER

– Allyson Knightley –
– Saturday – Nexus City, Iceland –

She missed her uniform.

It might not be a fancy piece of expensive designer military technology, like her sister's CombatSkin, but it was a professional ensemble suitable for any occasion. Black form-fitting jacket over a plain white shirt with long pants that hugged her hips snugly but flared enough at the bottom to allow easy removal of the comfortable boots. The sky-blue stripe down the legs, the Nexus Security patches on the shoulder, and the golden pins signifying her rank lent it an understated splash of color.

Her uniform gave her a sense of self-confidence that her evening dress simply couldn't duplicate.

She would have been a lot happier, certainly more comfortable, if she had been attending the Summit Gala in her capacity as Chief of Security. Alas, that would have profoundly disappointed her father. She knew he was proud of her achievements, but sometimes he wanted to simply flaunt her as his loving daughter. This evening was one of those times. So, as she stood before the large double doors leading into the ballroom, she was simply Allyson Knightley, the ambassador's daughter.

Deep breath... And relax.

She wasn't a fan of the banqueting rooms and their associated smaller, more intimate branch rooms. They were all a bit ornate and fussy for her, lacking in the simple, natural functionality of the Atrium. The two areas couldn't be more different, but then she supposed that was the whole point. One was built to be a peaceful oasis in a city of potentially stressful situations, while the other was designed to be a ritualistic home of pomp and circumstance. A place to practice '*the dance.*'

Which was diplomacy at its core.

She had once asked her father about diplomacy, and he had patiently tried to explain it in terms her eight-year-old brain could process.

"It's like performing a dance," he had explained. "You feel the rhythm of the music and you both try and move to it while not treading on each other's toes. Sometimes that means leading, while other times you follow."

"What if you don't know the dance?" she had asked astutely.

"Well, honey, what happens if you go to someone else's party and they are dancing to music you don't know? What do you do?"

"Then I try and learn the new dance."

"That's right, and by learning the dance it brings you a little bit closer together because now you have something in common. Now you can dance *together*. Now, let us imagine that someone came to your party and you were playing music that *they* didn't know...then what would you do?"

"I wouldn't want them to feel left out..." she had reasoned. "So...I would *teach* them my dance. Or find music we both like so we can dance to it together."

"That, my dear," he had said with a smile, "is the art of diplomacy."

"Well, that sounds easy!" she had giggled.

"Yes, but sometimes the dances are difficult to learn," her father had laughed with her. "Or sometimes it's hard to find music you both like."

While the memory brought back warm feelings from her childhood, it also brought the sickening realization of what the evening would hold in store for her.

Dancing.

Of course, that would only happen if someone *wanted* to dance with her. She glanced at herself one final time in the mirrors that lined the opulent corridor. Her hair was styled in an elegant plait that had taken her far too long to craft. Starting at the top near her parting, it then wrapped around her head to meet at the back and drop to mid-shoulder. She hadn't had time to dye her hair again, so there were striking hints of blue glinting through the ebony coloring. Not a problem. She'd noticed it when she was getting ready, so she had played to it, color-coordinating with a long blue and black evening gown.

She smoothed the dress down over her hips to remove the wrinkles, begrudgingly admitting that she looked pretty damned good. Oddly, this gave her a different type of confidence in contrast to how she felt in her uniform. She took one final deep breath.

Okay, let's do this.

Pushing the door open, she swept confidently into the ballroom, expecting to be the center of attention from the moment she entered. She was, however, essentially ignored, apart from a few admiring glances from men who really should have recognized her, but clearly didn't. Allyson paused for thought – was it because she was wearing makeup? Or because she was out of uniform?

Ally scanned the crowd trying to locate her parents. She quickly spotted Fran, looking immaculate as always in the same uniform that Allyson had eschewed for tonight. Fran was standing near the bar, supposedly surveying the assemblage in her professional capacity. Her scrutiny seemed to be fixed in one particular direction, however. Ally followed her eyeline, and spotted Jaymes and Serlia conversing jovially with a strikingly beautiful woman whose face hinted at a Native-American bloodline.

Allyson couldn't help but stare. She was a sucker for a bare back and a glimpse of leg, both of which were being provided by a crimson dress not too dissimilar to her own. She bit her lip to suppress the rising tingle of lust as she made her way over to them.

"Allyson!" her father beamed happily as he saw her approach. "Let me introduce you to Lyssa Balthazaar."

She recognized the name from her security briefings, and from Mercy's visit a few days before. But the woman holding out her hand to greet her was not at all what Ally had expected. Lyssa brushed aside her long raven hair with its distinctive white streak and flashed a dazzling smile at Allyson. Her eyes were a stunning ice blue, with the typically wide pupils of the Vampyrii. Pupils so deep you could easily lose yourself in them.

Wow.

She was suddenly acutely aware that she was staring.

"It's a pleasure to meet you, Chief Knightley."

"The pleasure is *all* mine," Allyson replied in a tone of voice that was far sultrier than she had intended, instantly provoking a tiny flush of embarrassment.

Lyssa's smile simply broadened. Her father, oblivious to the initial chemistry at play between the Vampyrii ambassador and his daughter, continued with his introduction.

"We were just talking about how excited we are that Lyssa is representing New Victus this year. Not that we have anything against Ambassador Lennix or, indeed, Grand Chancellor StormHall..."

Allyson watched Lyssa *almost* roll her eyes at the mention of the name. While she avoided such a political faux pas, she did hold her hand up to stop Jaymes in his tracks.

"Please, Ambassador, we both know that Sebastian Storm-Hall is..." Ally noticed the hitch between the two parts of the Grand Chancellor's surname, and she felt like Lyssa wanted to say something quite unsavory as she paused. Evidently, she changed her mind and went with something more diplomatic, "...not an easy man to deal with. Believe me, I have had my differences with him. As the current head of House Balthazaar, I originally opposed the War altogether."

"Originally?" Allyson seized upon the word.

"I am *still* opposed to the War," Lyssa clarified. "It has brought nothing but pain and suffering to our people. While the Grand Chancellor preaches his rhetoric of victory – that we now possess our own country to call home – I disagree with that shortsighted assessment. I feel he has irrevocably set back our race due to his own agenda."

"Yes, I heard that you refused a position on the Council of Blood," Jaymes said with interest.

"Not quite," Lyssa shook her head. "I have a seat on the Council but sit on the Earth Quorum."

"I'm not sure I understand the distinction," Jaymes said. "Details on internal New Victus politics are...not well known."

"The Council of Blood is divided into two houses. The Earth Quorum, and the Night Quorum, representing the two pillars of Vampyrii religion. The Earth Quorum is constituted of the heads of the twelve Progenitor Houses. However, as the elected leader of The Collective, the Grand Chancellor sits on the Night Quorum. I chose to sit in direct opposition to the Grand Chancellor. A fact that doesn't sit well with him."

"I expect not," Serlia chimed in. "It has also been said that where House Balthazaar leads, the other Progenitor Houses follow."

"I'm not really sure that's true," Lyssa laughed lightly. "Each of the Progenitor Houses have their own opinions and are strong enough to plot their own courses. I simply do what I feel is right for my House and am...delighted when they mostly follow my precedent."

"And that," Jaymes said with a smile, "is why I am thrilled that you're here. We need more people in this world who do what is right. It makes our job so much easier."

Allyson's exposure to Vampyrii as a race had been somewhat limited over the years, and as such, her views of them may have been somewhat colored by the stories of her older sister. They were the 'bad-guys.' Vicious killers. Monsters who were not to be trusted. Working in Nexus had been a first step on her re-evaluation of them, and now here was Lyssa. She didn't fit into any of the preconceptions, coming across as honorable, erudite, and gorgeous.

Yeah, I went there, she thought. *Gorgeous.*

"So, if you are in opposition to StormHall back in New Victus, why is it that he has sent you here as your country's representative?" Allyson asked with sincere curiosity.

"Now that," Lyssa said with a laugh, "is absolutely the right question to ask. Ambassadors, I think you may have rubbed off on your beautiful daughter here."

Where her father heard the whole statement, Allyson heard just the one word.

She thinks I'm beautiful.

"Oh, I won't take credit for my daughter's astuteness," Jaymes laughed.

"Well, if you won't, then I will," Serlia said with a sly chuckle of her own.

"Honestly, I was as surprised as you are," Lyssa confessed. "However, the Grand Chancellor has a proposal that I, for one, genuinely believe in. It is something that many will think out of character for him, but he is dealing with the reality of the situation in which we find ourselves. He felt that maybe his proposal would be taken more seriously if it were delivered by someone who is known to have a different viewpoint on world politics to himself."

"So, what is this proposal?" Allyson was honestly interested.

"*That* is something for the Summit, I'm afraid," Lyssa neatly sidestepped. "I can say no more in this public forum."

"As well you shouldn't," Jaymes agreed. "This evening is about getting to know each other, not for the proposing of agenda items for the meetings to come."

"You say that," Lyssa smiled. "But I'd wager that ninety-nine percent of the small talk around this ballroom is diplomats jockeying for position, ready for the meetings to open. Business is being conducted here as we speak and we both know it."

"She is right, my love," Serlia laughed.

Jaymes was shaking his head in amusement and mock dismay. "Oh, why couldn't the Grand Chancellor have given you the ambassadorial role for New Victus years ago, my dear? We could have avoided many a disagreement over all this time with you in charge."

"If wishes were horses, Ambassador," Lyssa sighed. "It pains me to see our race in a position I feel could have been largely avoided if someone different had been involved in the decision making. There are times when I wonder if I should have accepted a position on the Council of Blood back then, when I could have influenced events. But I refused on principle. It is one of my biggest regrets."

"Ah, Lyssa," Jaymes said with a smile, "Life is fond of throwing us curveballs..."

"...It's how we deal with them that makes us who we are," Allyson finished for him. "It's one of Dad's favorite truisms. We heard it *constantly* while growing up."

"I could not agree more," Lyssa nodded and laughed.

Jaymes reciprocated her gentle chuckle, "And, dare I say, you seem to be doing a wonderful job putting that regret behind you."

"You said you have a place on the Council now, though," Allyson commented.

"Yes," Lyssa nodded. "But my power on the Earth Quorum is...limited."

"And that is a great shame," Jaymes said with a legitimately sad smile that told Ally this was not just a diplomatic or political nicety – it was an authentic sentiment.

"We really must go and mingle," Serlia said with a sigh. "But this meeting has been genuinely enlightening, Ambassador Balthazaar..."

"Lyssa, please."

"Lyssa, then. I hope we can catch up later this evening once we have done the rounds, so to speak," Allyson's mother finished with sincerity.

"That would be lovely," Lyssa said graciously. "But I feel like I've taken up too much of your time already."

"Believe me," Serlia smiled, "it has been a pleasure."

"Until later then," Lyssa said with a small bow before addressing Ally directly. "Maybe, if you're not too busy, you could introduce me to some of the other ambassadors..."

"I...errr." Ally felt put on the spot.

"Oh, that's an excellent idea," Jaymes said excitedly. "We'll leave you in Allyson's capable hands. Until later then."

Allyson swallowed and bit her lip as her parents retreated to talk to one of the ambassadors from the NAA delegation, leaving her alone with Lyssa. Across the room, she spotted the lone figure of Ambassador Yetu from the NordScania entourage. She turned to Lyssa to find the young woman staring at her.

"Errr, I can, if you want to," she stammered nervously, self-conscious of the scrutiny, "introduce you to Yetu. I mean Ambassador Yetu. He's tall. Quite tall. And..."

"Actually, I've heard of a place here called...'The Atrium,' I believe. I've been told it's..." Lyssa stared deeply into Allyson's eyes, "...quite beautiful."

"Is it?" Ally found herself saying before her brain caught up with her mouth. She returned Lyssa's stare in kind. "Err, yeah, it...it is...breathtaking."

"Well, how about we both grab a drink from the bar and go take a look?" Lyssa said with a warm grin and a husky tone. "Together."

If she hadn't been sure before, the mutuality of the attraction was now a certainty. Ally wasn't totally sure how she felt about that, if she were honest. Her love life had never run an easy course, complicated as it was between her sexuality and her genetic heritage. Was this to be further obfuscated by the fact that the new target of her affection was Vampyrii?

She knew that she was attracted to Lyssa, which meant that Ally was probably already kicking out pheromones in her direction. At the best of times, it made it difficult to see the wood for the trees when it came to relationships. Like it had with Danni.

Were Vampyrii even susceptible to her unconscious pheromone assault?

She took a deep breath and nodded.

In for a penny, she thought and followed her Vampyrii suitor to the bar where plentiful drinks were theirs for the taking before Ally then led them to the Atrium.

As they walked barefoot along the beach of the artificial indoor lake, they drank freely, alcohol lubricating the wheels of conversation and dropping any lingering inhibitions. Allyson didn't introduce Lyssa to any of the other ambassadors that night, nor did they get together with her parents again. They were the sole focus of each other's attention.

By midnight, they were heading for Allyson's apartment, carrying bottles of champagne and wine with them.

Allyson awoke the next morning with a throbbing headache and the naked form of a beautiful, sleeping Vampyrii ambassador pressed up against her, snoring gently. She felt a momentary surge of panic.

What have I done?

She looked down at her peacefully sleeping companion and reached up a gentle finger to brush the streak of white hair out of Lyssa's face. The Vampyrii woman smiled gently in her sleep, and Allyson felt her anxiety start to ease. She settled back down into the soft pillow that cradled her head, and licked her lips. There was the faint taste of champagne mixed with something else that was definitely not bought from a bar. It conjured a memory that made her grin inanely.

Lyssa shifted gently and Allyson basked in the feeling of soft skin rubbing against her body. The silky inner thigh against her hip, the press of her breasts, the faint trace of a nipple against Allyson's skin. Lyssa was nestled into the crook of her shoulder, like the two of them had been designed specifically to fit together just like this. The intoxicating aroma of mint drifted up from the Vampyrii's tussled black hair, an unusual scent that suited her far more than some form of flowery fragrance would have.

Ally glanced at the clock next to the bed, subtly so as not to wake her lover. The time was early, way too early to be up and going to work just yet. A smile of contentment curled the corners of her lips as her eyes drifted shut again.

| 61 |

HUNT'S END

– Alex Newman –
– Sunday – Mont Tremblant, Pack Nation –

Epiphany.

Alex knew the meaning of the word but had never actually experienced it. Until now.

This Zarra was *not* the same woman he fought alongside five years ago. The well-trained and conscientious soldier was still there. She was still someone you knew you could count on in combat. Someone who had pushed herself to excel in every skillset – weapons training, marksmanship, self-defense, combat tactics, and more. Her time in the army had forged her into a capable weapon.

But now...

It took a while for him to truly see it, but since that day in Sawtooth, her new profession had driven her to the next stage in her development. Like a blade patiently sharpened with a whetstone, experience had honed her to a razor-like edge. She was no longer simply 'capable'...now she was *dangerous*.

A hunter.

He wondered how he had been so blind to her evolution.

She was constantly thinking ahead, her mind still sharp and her instincts on-point despite her injuries and fatigue. To Alex, it seemed like she had a form of combat-clairvoyance which, at least temporarily, saved their lives *again*. She'd seen the ambush coming moments before the trap was sprung. As the pain lanced through his bloodied leg, he wondered how they had so completely lost the upper hand and ended up abruptly fighting for their lives.

Zarra had been squirrely for a while, tentative, like she could instinctively sense something was off. Her warnings, however, had fallen on deaf ears. Their quarry was still upwind and making steady progress a day or so ahead of them. Their scents and tracks confirmed it. There was no rush. They could take their time, discuss their tactics, and choose their moment to intercept. Secure as he was in the knowledge that his lupine senses knew better than her ordinary Human ones did, Alex didn't anticipate any trouble.

Zarra did.

She first voiced her suspicion the day they crossed Rivière-Rouge. Evidence suggested that their quarry had lethally resisted an attempt by Lyssa's people to intercept them. The distinctive tang of Vampyrii blood hung ripe in the air.

A little further upriver they found evidence of a different, more intimate activity between Vanessa and her paramour. Seemingly, they lingered afterward, bathing in the afterglow as they cleaned each other in the river's waters. Their dalliance closed the gap between them, the scents much stronger now. Yet Zarra was deeply suspicious, commenting on how it almost seemed like they had doubled back for some reason — laid the trail twice.

Then the *really* odd behavior began.

They would split up periodically, circling back upon themselves. He always went clockwise while Vanessa went counterclockwise, creating a figure-of-eight when they met up again in the middle. The more they did it, the longer the circles became until their path was more oval than circle. When they met up again, they ended up retreading the long central path together where their scent trail was strongest. They undertook this exercise repeatedly.

Alex assumed they were hunting something; this behavior was simply some odd triangulation or herding motion. To Zarra, that didn't ring true.

"It feels like they're tryin' to catch us out..." she mused. "Like they *know* they're bein' followed."

Alex had disagreed. They had been careful, always keeping their distance and staying discreetly downwind. There was no *possible* way they could know. Perhaps it was just paranoia? A carefully choreographed way of avoiding any pursuit by Lyssa's people. Not that it mattered because the pair always completed their maneuver well before Alex and Zarra got anywhere close.

Days passed, and Zarra's suspicions grew as the circles became increasingly leisurely. Their pace slowed to a point where Alex and Zarra were merely a few hours adrift of them when they entered a small clearing in the forest, and Zarra abruptly stopped.

"Alex," she had whispered, her eyes wide. "Who do you smell?"

He paused, sniffing the air casually. "Vanessa and..." suddenly he realized what Zarra detected. "His scent is...fainter..."

"Shit!" Zarra exclaimed. "They *are* herding prey."

"What?"

"Alex, they're herding us!" She started frantically scanning the tree line. "The incubus...he's not here. We're getting the two scents because *he's* re-treading the track he already laid down, but his trace is less distinctive because he's not here anymore... Fuck! He's circling back behind us!"

The truth dawned on Alex a moment later as he heard the forest retreat into silence. The lack of ambient noise a forest displays when its inhabitants recognize a predator is amongst them. He turned just as the trap snapped shut and the ambush was upon them.

The incubus was a muscular mass of chocolate-colored fur, far larger than Alex had expected. Yet despite his size, he moved with astonishing speed. Alex was faster, but only just. He barely had time to dodge the monster's intended fatal first strike. Lethal claws targeted at his throat instead raked his flank, and white-hot agony overwhelmed him as he felt muscles and crucial ligaments being sliced by deep parallel wounds.

As the two of them circled each other warily, the incubus could clearly see that Alex was now severely wounded. With an intimidating snarl, it bared gleaming teeth slick with saliva, and waited patiently, cautiously searching for the right opening to finish Alex off once and for all.

Alex's regenerative abilities as a Werewolf would heal even *this* level of damage given enough time, but time was not on his side. Alex grimaced as he tried to move, feeling the limits of his range of motion. He stumbled. It was the tiniest of stumbles, his wounded leg refusing to cooperate, but it was an opportunity. The incubus surged forward. Alex pivoted on his three good legs, trying to protect the now useless wounded one.

A flurry of claw slashes and bites were unleashed as they matched each other blow for blow. On any given day, it would have been interesting to see how Alex's superior speed and agility would match up against the incubus's speed and strength, but his opponent had already neutralized Alex's advantage in that opening salvo. Hobbled as he was, a war of attrition was one that Alex knew he likely couldn't win.

Zarra was in a similar predicament in her struggle with Vanessa Balthazaar. The initial assault had knocked her Freelancer out of her hand and across the clearing where it lay uselessly on the ground. The other gun was still snugly holstered on her right hip, but she couldn't reach it as her hands were pre-occupied trying to prevent Vampyrii claws and fangs from reaching her throat. It was a frantic tussle of hand-to-hand combat —Vanessa's brute force versus Zarra's combat training and experience. Zarra was holding her own, but with her current level of injury and fatigue, it was only a matter of time before her opponent gained the upper hand.

The incubus used Alex's divided attention as an opportunity to launch another probing attack, forcing Alex to hop backward hastily. His own counter-slash was weak, a fact that his opponent would surely have noticed. He tried to get a sense of what the incubus was thinking, but the dark eyes were cold, unreadable. He had never done it himself, but Alex knew it *was* possible to lose yourself in your Wolf-form. He sensed no humanity in his opponent...only the beast. An icy grip of fear squeezed his heart. An unshakeable sense that fanged death was coming for him.

Across the clearing, Zarra continued her mêlée with Vanessa, who had broken loose and was regrouping to press a fresh attack. What she gained in enthusiasm, however, she lost in skill. Zarra dipped and pivoted, easily grasping Vanessa and using her opponent's momentum to her advantage. She flipped the succubus over her right shoulder, grimacing with pain as she did so, leaving her sprawling face down into the forest floor.

Zarra wasted no time, immediately reaching for her holster. Her injured arm, however, wouldn't cooperate as quickly as she needed it to. By the time the second Freelancer was in her hand, Vanessa had recovered and was lashing out, sending the weapon flying into the tree line. Another slash forced Zarra to parry weakly using her right forearm.

Alex smelled the blood before he saw it seep through the ruined leather. The pain on Zarra's features told the story of how significant the wound truly was. There was no way that Zarra could win this fight unless...

Unless she did something that she truly detested.

As this point, though, he didn't see how she had a choice.

He flashed back to the night he had kissed Alexa Reynolds.

| 62 |

THE KISS

– Alexa Reynolds – Call sign: "Zarra" –
– Five Years Ago – Sawtooth Forest, USA –
THE 215th RECONNAISSANCE BATTALION

Alexa Reynolds had *never* shared her brother's enthusiasm for the great outdoors. Twins they may be, but on this they differed greatly. Where Michael was drawn to the intricately simple art of nature, Alexa had always been more of a city girl. She acknowledged how beautiful it could be in the wilderness, but she'd detested camping trips with her parents as a child. Her dislike of the outdoors hadn't improved during her arduous Army survival training either. If anything, the lessons she had learned during her training had reinforced her opinion of the woods.

Take the Sawtooth Forest, for example. Her current whereabouts. The abundance of flora provided a thousand different hiding places for creatures who made a habit of living in the shadows. Places from which to spring a sneaky ambush. Meanwhile, the lush forest canopy made it practically impossible to be seen from the air, just in case you needed something important, like a medical evacuation for a serious life-threatening injury.

An injury like the shredded hole in her abdomen that was oozing her blood all over the forest floor at what was, frankly, an alarming rate.

She tried to lie still, focusing on each breath in an effort to stay alive even as she felt the life slowly slipping from her. The tiny breaks in the foliage allowed the passage of a handful of slender sunbeams that, at any other time, Zarra would probably have considered quite beautiful.

She shivered with cold and felt her body going slowly numb. Was this verdant hellhole to be her final resting place?

It even hurt to sigh.

She had no idea whether her squad-mates were all dead or running for their lives. Not that it mattered now. She couldn't help them either way. Her last moments were going to be spent alone, lying on a dirty forest floor, struggling to hold her stomach together while trying to reconcile the fact that she was about to die.

Her teeth chattered uncontrollably as she endeavored to divert the pain, to think clearly. How the fuck had it all come to this?

The 215th had been sent on a regular patrol detail through the Sawtooth Forest along the NAA border with New Victus. Alexa had been acting as rear guard for the column as they moved stealthily through the forest. Progress was fairly brisk; this path had been trodden twice a day for weeks now with little in the way of issue.

Maybe an element of complacency had set in. Maybe even a hint of bored disinterest. Either way, they weren't prepared for when the trees came alive and the shadows descended upon them with horrifying speed.

Adze.

Their skin gleamed like polished ebony, a black so dark it absorbed the light, making them look two-dimensional. Like paper cut-outs on a 3D backdrop. A gruesome illusion, these creatures were no paper monsters. They were inhumanly efficient killing machines, capable of delivering swift death by claw or by fang.

They dropped silently from the canopy, like feathers on a gentle breeze. Their staccato movement looked like they were moving between the ticks of the second hand, so unnatural and unnerving that the Human brain struggled to track their motion properly. They made you feel like you were fighting something that came from somewhere just to the left of reality. Somewhere out of the corner of your eye.

She had barely lifted the barrel of her rifle before it was knocked from her grip. The next thing she felt was agonizing, voice-stealing pain. Her mind lit up in a vivid kaleidoscope of colors. As her knees buckled, her hands went directly to her midriff and she felt the fabric of her fatigues warm and slick with her own blood. She stared down in shock at her crimson hands. How was it possible that there was so much blood so fast?

The world slid sideways in slow motion, as if the camera shooting her death scene was tumbling dramatically from its mount. It took her a moment to process that it was *she* who was falling sideways. She hit the ground hard, rolling onto her back on the soft, leafy forest floor. A bright light enveloped her, and for a moment, she thought that it was Heaven calling to her. An anger welled inside her...

No! I'm not ready!

She waited for the Adze to deliver the killing blow, the final strike that would send her unwillingly to the waiting afterlife.

It never came.

Sunlight. That's *all* it was. Not a stairway to Heaven – just a bright, brilliant, blinding pool of sunlight where she'd fallen. A temporary safety net from her impending death.

Adze were the night incarnate, nocturnal in nature. Their milky-white and oversized almond-shaped eyes were evolved specifically for seeing in the dark. Sunlight was exceedingly painful to them. Blinding, in fact. Here in this swath of golden light, she was as hidden to them as they were to her in the shadows.

Death would have to wait, but at the rate she was losing blood, the Grim Reaper wouldn't have to amuse himself for too much longer. She snorted and a blood-filled chuckle gurgled in her throat. A comical image of the Reaper sitting nearby, cradling his scythe and playing distractedly on his cellphone popped into her delirious mind.

It was so quiet.

That could only mean one dreadful thing. Eleven dead soldiers, and when she slipped away, she would make it an even dozen. No one would be any the wiser until their patrol failed to check in. No help would come for hours. Certainly not in time to save her.

Her vision started to darken around the edges, but Alexa refused to give up without a fight. She sobbed desperately as she struggled to battle the inevitable unconsciousness.

If she could only reach Eightball's pack. As the team's medic, surely he'd have something in there that could keep her alive until help came.

She tried to move her legs, but they wouldn't co-operate. She couldn't even wiggle her toes in her boots. She screamed in frustration and fear, a desperate plea for help. A plea that was unexpectedly answered.

"Alex?"

An urgent voice, snarling and growling her name. Her quiet forest suddenly filled with the sounds of wood cracking and snapping.

"Here!" replied a Canadian accent she recognized.

Of course. They mean the other Alex. 'Lonewolf.' Thank God he's alive.

So, someone in her unit had survived. She tried to call to him for help, but her vocal cords were drowning in the blood that was gradually filling her stomach.

"We got here as soon as we could," said the stranger. "Dane sent us the minute you signaled. I'm sorry, Alex... I'm sorry we didn't get here in time."

This new voice – what did he mean? Had Lonewolf called someone? Reinforcements? Why hadn't he told them? Who was Dane?

"It's not your fault, Kasey. By the time I'd caught their scent, it was too late. I got the transmission off to you only moments before..." Alex's voice trailed off as he came into view above her. Her eyelids fluttered as she looked at him.

Is he...naked?

"Zarra? Kasey, I think she's alive. Lexy? Alexa Reynolds, blink if you can hear me!" His voice was full of concern as he tried her real name rather than her call sign.

She blinked, slowly. Or, so she thought. She must have passed out momentarily because the next time her eyes crept open, she saw two shadows standing over her, mercifully blocking the sunlight.

"She's dying, Alex. There's nothing we can do. The wounds...they're too severe," the other man said with an undercurrent of sadness.

Kasey? Was that his name?

"No. She's a fighter," Alex said gallantly. "I can *save* her."

Yes! Fuckin' save me, Alex. Save me!

"You can't. I know you're sweet on her, but it's against the rules and you know it." Kasey sounded like an officious dickhead. "She's not been bitten."

Don't listen to him, Alex! Wait...you're sweet on me? You never said anything...

"She can heal these wounds," Alex said firmly. "One bite..."

One bite? What the fuck are you talkin' about, Alex?!

"Dane will have your fucking head if you do this!" Kasey definitely did *not* seem to be on her side.

Fuck him! Fuck him to hell!

"I don't care, Kasey. I can't let her die."

Don't let me die. Don't let me die here, Alex.

His face got closer. Much closer. Was he going to kiss her? Take advantage of her current predicament to get the kiss he had apparently always wanted? She didn't know if she was angry or kind of pleased. Fuck it. If the cost to save her life was a stolen kiss, she'd happily pay it.

He didn't kiss her.

His mouth headed for her neck and she felt his lips tease at the skin there, almost sensually. It tickled. If she hadn't been so close to death, she probably would have squirmed and giggled. The sensation changed to warm breath and something sharp, like the prick of a needle, pressing against her throat.

She panicked.

Then all she felt was searing pain and all she saw was dazzling white light before Alexa Reynolds finally slipped away.

| 63 |

CONTRACT COMPLETE

– Alex Newman –
– Sunday – Mont Tremblant, Pack Nation –

She had *always* been one of the most beautiful creatures that Alex had ever laid his eyes on.

When in Wolf-form, Zarra was effortlessly magnificent.

In direct contrast to his own midnight scruff, her exquisite snow-white fur was sleek and soft. She had a distinctive jet-black streak starting at her nose and running up between her dazzling azure eyes and those soft ears, before tapering off as it reached her shoulder blades.

Where Alex was built for brute force, thick at the shoulder and stacked with muscle, her slender canine physique was all about prodigious speed and agility. If Zarra was a formidable opponent in Human-form, she was much more so when transformed to animal. A lethal blur of sharp claws and even sharper teeth.

Vanessa, however, was no slouch herself. Changing to her Wolf-form may have helped Zarra with healing her injuries somewhat, but the transformation didn't mitigate them entirely. Even now, a dark crimson stain was spreading slowly across the white of her right shoulder. The odds – at best – were now even between them, but her opponent was more wary, measured. Vanessa began to circle guardedly, clockwise. Gleaming fangs and bloodied claws ready for the moment, she sensed a new avenue of attack against her now vastly different foe.

Alex had more pressing concerns of his own, though. He drew his lips back, baring his teeth and snarling, trying to intimidate the incubus across from him. His opponent, unimpressed, reciprocated the action with a savage snarl of his own, saliva dripping from his fangs. More than the size and strength of the incubus, it was the inactivity that concerned Alex the most.

His adversary was a thinker, a planner. *He* was the one who had painstakingly set this trap for *them*. He was the one who was now calmly evaluating Alex's injuries while waiting for Alex to make the first move. Anticipating and planning his counter strategy, he was counting on Alex's debilitating wounds to provide the opening for a killer blow.

Alex was not a tactical thinker; he tended to try and solve his issues with brute force. Even if he had been fully healthy, he wasn't sure he could take the savage stood before him. Not without a plan.

What would Zarra do?

His peripheral vision showed Zarra and Vanessa whirling around each other in a swift and nimble dance of deadly intent. The succubus slashed out with her talons, raking the air where Zarra had stood. Zarra's experience was paying off, though, as she deftly dodged the attack and slipped in behind Vanessa's defenses with an angry snarl. Her teeth sank deeply into the Vampyrii's right forearm, tearing through the flesh and leaving blood-red stains on the previously pristine fur around her jaw.

Vanessa screamed in pain, tugging at her arm frantically, trying to break free of Zarra's grip. She lashed out wildly with her left hand, drawing parallel lines of scarlet in the snow-white fur of the Wolf's flank. Zarra let go.

Without a sound, Zarra simply twisted her flexible torso away from Vanessa and reciprocated the attack with her own razor-sharp claws. She lashed out at the succubus's face, resulting in a trio of bloody slash marks and an animalistic shriek as Vanessa fell backward clutching at her ruined cheek.

Zarra wasted not a second, instantly on the offensive – not against the writhing and screaming succubus but coming gallantly to Alex's aid.

She launched herself at the incubus, approaching from behind with claws and teeth bared. He sensed her attack, but even his supernatural reflexes couldn't save him.

As he pivoted to defend himself, he put his neck at a vulnerable angle, and Zarra took advantage by burying her teeth deep into it as her claws sank into his shoulders. The forest echoed as the beast roared his pain.

He jerked and twisted violently, trying to dislodge his assailant, but Zarra's jaws were a vice. He shifted tactics, rolling onto his back, and tried to bring his own knife-like claws into play against Zarra's exposed underside.

With the two of them now locked in a mortal tussle, Alex couldn't help but notice how the incubus was at least double Zarra's mass. Yet, what she lost in raw strength, she more than gained in agility.

Sensing his shift, she preempted her impending vulnerability and immediately let go, twisting herself out of reach and landing nimbly on all fours between Alex and their aggressor.

She drew her lips back, baring her teeth protectively. Blood poured from the matted fur on the incubus's neck, his face drawn in a snarl of his own, but there was something in the beast's eyes that hadn't been there before. Respect. An acknowledgement that he now faced a real threat. He had been confident that in a match of basic strength with Alex, he could win, but now faced with a wilier and more skillful opponent half his size, he hesitated.

Zarra maneuvered to cover Alex's right flank, putting herself between the incubus and his disabled leg. He appreciated the sentiment, but even with Vanessa temporarily out of the picture, they were still on the defensive. Both were carrying significant injuries, and for all her veteran cunning and agility, Zarra was *still* at a relative disadvantage in Wolf-form. The odds favored size, stamina, and muscle.

Shifting forms helped Zarra partially heal her previously

ruined shoulder, but she was still much weakened by her ordeals. The blood-loss alone would catch up with her eventually, and one mistake would be enough to give the incubus an opening for the fatal blow.

There was, however, an equalizer in play.

Zarra's F21 Freelancer.

Alex saw it lying near the tattered ruins of her leather combat suit, maybe fifteen feet away. Zarra's eyes flickered briefly as she spotted it too, knowing as well as he did that the weapon would be the swiftest way to end this. With his damaged leg, there was no way he could get to it fast enough, but with a well-timed distraction, maybe Zarra could. All she needed was a moment.

He could give her that.

Pushing off as hard as he could with his good leg, he sluggishly surged toward the incubus who shifted easily to avoid the charge. Alex predicted the move and dodged his head to the right, opening his jaw and trying to inflict more damage to the neck that Zarra had just wounded. His jaws snapped fresh air, missing their target by scant millimeters. It didn't matter – the job was done. The moment was bought.

Zarra easily leapt the distance between herself and the Freelancer in a single bound. To use it, however, she would have to change back to Human form, something that suddenly became untenable due to Vanessa's recovery.

Her blood-covered face was contorted with rage as she charged toward Zarra with murderous intent. There was no dodging the speed of the surprise attack, her talons digging painfully into Zarra's neck and shoulder, eliciting a short, sharp yelp of anguish. She quickly counter-attacked using Vanessa's own momentum to throw her back to the ground, but the damage was done. The precious moment lost.

Alex suddenly had more pressing concerns. The incubus surged forward himself with a force Alex couldn't match. He felt like he had been hit by a truck as he flew bodily back into the bushes, the foliage snapping as he crashed through it. White hot agony flooded his system as an errant branch speared his already wounded leg. Desperately, he tried to push the pain aside and right himself before the inevitable follow-up attack.

That was when he spotted it.

Zarra's *other* Freelancer, the one Vanessa had knocked out of her left hand earlier.

The incubus was coming at him full tilt. Alex braced himself, but a split-second before the onrushing beast barreled into him...he flattened himself to the ground. His surprised adversary sailed through the air above him and crashed heavily into the sturdy tree trunk behind him with a loud crack. The incubus shook his huge head, momentarily stunned.

Alex made the easiest decision he had ever made.

He pounced for the weapon, changing form as he did so. As paw changed to hand, he landed sprawling on the forest floor with the Freelancer in his grip. He steadied his aim, held his breath, and gently squeezed the trigger. As the bullet fired, he marveled at how well-balanced the Freelancer felt in his grip. There was negligible kickback, and the shot sounded muted as it left the barrel, making Alex idly wonder if it contained some sort of suppressor. He squeezed off a second shot, adjusting his aim subtly.

Both hit their intended target.

Vanessa Balthazaar.

The first caught her in the chest, thudding solidly into her sternum. The second tracked slightly higher. It burrowed into her face on a faintly upward trajectory, striking her where her right eye met her nose. The mortal blow was dealt. Like a puppet having its strings cut, she collapsed to the ground without a sound.

It was the last thing he saw clearly.

Something heavy struck the side of his head, sending him sprawling in a spray of blood and dazed confusion. The Freelancer tumbled from his numb hands as pain unlike anything he had experienced before blossomed across his face. In turning the gun on Vanessa, he had left himself defenseless, giving the incubus the perfect opening. The follow-up strike would most likely be fatal.

His life for Zarra's.

It hadn't even been a decision.

The beast bellowed his grief for his fallen lover, and Alex waited for the inevitable final attack. But as he lay there, eyes closed, bloodied face pressed against the cold ground, the blow never came. Only the muted crack of the Freelancer.

Once. Twice. Three times. Then more in quick succession till his fading brain lost count.

Then silence.

Moments later, she came into view above him. He tried to focus on her, but his eyes fluttered as the darkness called to him.

"Hang in there, Alex. They're both down. Just rest and I'll call in Becka for extraction."

She sounded so calm. He tried to smile but his wounded features wouldn't cooperate. He stared at her, trying desperately to communicate his thanks with his eyes, but he couldn't keep them open. Heavy eyelids drifted closed as the pain finally overwhelmed him, pressing him into blissful unconsciousness.

| 64 |

PAYDAY

– Alexa Reynolds –
– Sunday – Montreal, Pack Nation –

"I'm sorry we couldn't bring Kareena back. We tried."

Being face-to-face with Damian Dane for the first time since he'd rejected her three years ago was bad enough; relaying such bad news made it feel so much worse. The dull ache of melancholy weighed on her chest. Though her apology was sincere, she was tired, wounded, and felt like the entire mission had been an unmitigated disaster.

"It's not your fault," Dane said flatly as he watched his medical staff working on an unconscious Alex in the back of *Diana*, a concerned look on his handsome face.

"He'll be fine," she reassured him. "Just flesh wounds, except for the leg which I think may be broken. It'll heal up just fine, though he may have a few facial scars to impress the ladies with."

A joke, even if just a small one. She saw Damian's lips upturn almost imperceptibly before the moment was gone, a fleeting glimpse of the man she used to know.

"He only has eyes for you, Lexy," he said simply and with a hint of sadness.

"Yeah, well..." She stopped before she said anything she might regret.

Damian was suffering. Of them all, *he* was the one most

personally affected by the tragedy at Domaine Saint-Bernard and by the loss of Kareena. Now was not the time to dredge up old heartbreaks.

"Sorry, I meant Zarra..."

"Actually," Alexa shrugged, "I've been thinkin'...maybe it's time to put Zarra away. Just be Lexy again."

Damian raised an eyebrow at her. "What happened out there?"

Alexa considered her response for a moment before giving him a small smile. "I...worked through some stuff."

The conversation hit a lull as the medical staff wheeled the unconscious form of Alex down the boarding ramp and onto the asphalt of the landing pad. The doctor in charge checked a few things momentarily, before nodding to his staff. They moved with practiced efficacy toward the nearby buildings, heading no doubt, for the medical complex. Vanessa's body and that of her paramour had been wheeled to the morgue earlier. Damian and Alexa were suddenly left alone together.

Alexa sighed and stood slowly from the cargo crate on which she had been sitting. Her sigh turned to a sharp intake of breath as she grimaced in pain. Her hand drifted to her right flank just above her hip, and she tenderly rubbed it as she rose.

"You need a doctor?" Dane said with a note of concern.

"No," Alexa shook her head. "I'm good. Just banged up. Transforming to Wolf fixed up the shoulder somewhat and back to Human helped with the other odds and ends. But you can only push a healing factor so far. Becka stitched me up on the way back and threw a dressing on it. I'm just feelin' a little battered and bruised, but...I'll heal in time."

"I can't believe you actually went Wolf. I'd like to have seen that again."

"Didn't have a choice," she yawned as she replied. "First time in two years."

Damian paused, biting his lip. Alexa recognized his thought process; she had seen it enough in the past to know he was wrestling with saying something he thought maybe he shouldn't.

"How'd it feel?"

She raised an eyebrow at him and smiled.

"Felt good," she admitted. "Transformative. No pun intended. I mean...I always loved the feeling, bein' the Wolf. But I *finally* realized, after some serious introspection, that my anger was never truly about what Alex had done to me. Some of it was anger at you. Broken heart an' all."

"I'm sorry. I—" Damian started, but Alexa cut him off.

"Ah, hush," she said holding up her hand. "In hindsight...I'd just been through a massive physical change and because of that I had to leave a life I loved. At the time, I thought that everything was going to be okay because I found you. You were my emotional crutch, and when you took that away...I was angry. And I held that anger for...a long time.

"It led me to do things that I wish I'd handled differently, and rather than shoulder the blame myself, I pointed the finger at others for what had happened to me. Alex mostly. I ran away. Changing my name was me tryin' to hold on to something...someone...that I used to be. The soldier. But I'm not that person anymore. I think it's time to embrace who I am *now*."

She closed her eyes, yawning again. Now that the hunt was over, she was becoming aware of how drained she felt. The toll it had taken on her physically and mentally.

"I'll wire over your fee." Damian changed the subject. "It'll be in your account within the hour. Full amount."

"Just the fee for the incubus. I failed to bring Kareena back, after all, and Vanessa ended up dead."

"Full amount, no arguments," Dane said firmly. "You cleaned up our rogue Wolf problem. It was Alex who killed Vanessa and not your fault Kareena got taken. You deserve all of it."

"Thanks," Alexa capitulated wearily, too tired to push the argument. "Have you spoken to Lyssa yet?"

He nodded slowly in response but said nothing. Alexa looked at the floor.

"I take it she wasn't best pleased that we shot her sister in the face."

"I haven't broken that piece of news yet," Damian admitted.

"Sorry," Alexa said with a sigh. "I'll write up a report on the flyer that took Kareena, too. Everything I can remember. I know you're gonna go lookin' for her."

"I owe her mother that much." There was a solemnity to Dane's voice.

Alexa said nothing. Talking like this with Damian *had* stopped feeling awkward, proving that burnt bridges could indeed be rebuilt with time. It gave her a spark of hope.

"What will you do now?" Damian asked. "You're more than welcome to stay a while and rest up. Recuperate before you head back out there to work again. Least I can offer you is a bed."

It was a genuine offer, but one laced with history and double meaning. Alexa smiled wryly, maybe it was time that she didn't let their sordid past haunt their conversations. She did consider for a moment how much she was looking forward to sleeping. Her body felt so battered that an extended hibernation *was* probably in order. But if this hunt had taught her anything, it was that she had unfinished business to attend to.

"Actually," Alexa said with a deep breath, "I figured that I might go and see Michael."

"In London?"

"You know where he is?" Alexa threw a quizzical glance at him.

"I keep tabs. Just like I did with you. He moved there a couple of months ago to take a job at the HFA Academy."

"Really..." Alexa trailed off deep in thought.

"You didn't know?"

"Mikey and I haven't spoken since... He was so..." She looked at the floor and shrugged. "Maybe it's been long enough. Maybe after all this time he will accept my apology. I figure I can only try. I mean *we're* good now, right?"

"We are," Damian nodded. "I'll get my ground crews to give your ship a once over and fuel her up."

"Thank you."

"Don't mention it. Just go and make things right." He

turned his look away from Alexa and out toward the distant New Victus. "Before it's too late."

Alexa wondered at the enigmatic tone to his voice. Was he referring to the lost time between himself and Eloise or her now missing daughter? Or was he channeling a deeper concern regarding something else entirely?

| 65 |

A DEATH IN THE FAMILY

– **Lyssa Balthazaar** –
– *Monday – Albany, New Victus* –

The acrid stench of tire smoke stung Lyssa's sensitive nostrils as she stomped hard on the brakes, bringing her Dodge Charger to a screeching halt inside the cavernous hangar. The engine had barely stopped turning over when she was out of the door and striding toward the unidentified flyer sitting quietly next to the much smaller *Tawaic'iya*. The rhythmic ticking of her car's cooling exhaust and the angry tapping of her heels on the smooth concrete floor were the only sounds to be heard. They echoed loudly around the huge, mostly empty space.

The flight from Nexus City had been long, but pleasant. The diplomatic flyer may have brought her back to the earth at StormHall International Airport, but her head remained firmly in the clouds. Filled with sensual daydreams of a beauty with tousled hair of ebony, with just a hint of azure. For the first time in weeks, she didn't feel like she was being suffocated under the crushing weight of responsibility. Her spirits felt unassailably high. The smile on her lips lingered as she relived the memory of a most unexpectedly delightful weekend.

Allyson Knightley had given her a gift.

It wasn't to last.

No sooner had she pressed the ignition button in her Charger, than an urgent – and apologetic – message from

Mercy torpedoed her mood with worrying news. The early warning radar system protecting their clandestine hangar at Lake Placid had alerted them to an incoming aircraft.

An *unidentified* aircraft.

The icy grip of fear seized her heart as she pushed her car to the limit, racing to intercept it. Her first irrational thought was that this was her greatest fear made manifest – that Storm had discovered her secret.

Her rational mind quickly reassured her that there was a more likely option.

The hangar had been constructed in the early days of the War with Pack Nation, but once the Fae stepped in and put a halt to hostilities, the place fell into disuse. Mercy had discovered it and diligently purged it from official records. To all intents and purposes, the place no longer existed.

If *Tawaic'iya* needed servicing, it was undertaken discreetly at one of the smaller, local airfields House Balthazaar owned, by a hand-picked group of trusted engineers. Mercy *always* oversaw the work personally before piloting the little flyer back here solo.

Thus, the location of this hangar was known only to herself, Mercy, and one other person.

The subtle military markings on the mystery flyer confirmed her relieved supposition. This was a Pack Nation troop ship.

As the ramp hit the ground, with a heavy metallic clank, Lyssa released the breath she found herself holding. It was Damian Dane who strode down the ramp.

Her fear gave way to anger – he had some explaining to do.

"For fuck's sake, Damian!" she called out as she crossed the hangar. "Is that a troop ship? Are you crazy coming here in that...that thing?"

"Lyssa..." Damian began, but she cut him off before he could continue.

"Do you have any idea how dangerous it is that you're in New Victus territory flying a piece of shit that size? And...coming *here*?"

"Lyssa..." Damian tried to interject softly again.

"How can you be so stupid? It's too big. Storm could have tracked it back here! His people could be on their way as we speak. What happens if—"

"*LYSSA!*" Damian said forcefully enough to interrupt her tirade.

Realization hit her like a sledgehammer as she put the pieces of the puzzle together. The troop ship, the quiet manner, the unsmiling face, and the sympathetic tone of his voice. But if all that wasn't enough, it was the look in his eyes that confirmed the horrible truth of why he had risked it all to come here.

"Vanessa..." her voice broke.

As he nodded gently, she felt her knees buckle and tears start to flow. She would have fallen to the floor weeping had he not caught her on the way down. He lowered her gently and held her close as they sat together on the cold concrete.

"I'm so sorry..." he whispered quietly.

She wept silently into his shoulder, there were no more words that needed to be said right now. Damian simply being here was enough; there weren't many people in this world with whom she could be so raw. There was safety to be found in his arms. He held her tightly, the comforting pressure of his embrace never wavering as he patiently let her process the shock of the news she knew he was there to deliver.

Lyssa didn't know how long they sat on the floor, lost in her anguish. Eventually, she became aware of his hand gently stroking her head. It was comforting, and with a few deep ragged breaths, her sobs subsided and her mood calmed. As he sensed her resurfacing, he spoke softly into her hair.

"Are you alone, Lyssa? Have you got anyone who can be here with you?"

She shook her head. "It's just me."

"You shouldn't be alone."

"I'm okay." Lyssa breathed and pushed him away slightly so she could look him in the face.

"You're not," he whispered. "I can stay..."

There was sympathy in his eyes. More than that, there was love. A love she knew that she could never truly reciprocate.

She shook her head.

"You know that you can't. You risked too much coming here like this already." Lyssa glanced at the flyer and swallowed. "Tell me what happened."

He said nothing, just helped her stand and guided her slowly back over to her car. He put his hands around her waist and gently lifted her up to sit her on the Charger's trunk. She looked at the ceiling of the hangar and opened her eyes wide, blinking away the tears. A deep breath to calm her quaking chest, to settle her racing heartrate.

"Please, Damian. Tell me," she prompted again.

She watched him draw a deep breath of his own before giving her what she was asking for.

"My people were tracking Kareena, your sister, and the incubus..."

"So, he was definitely an incubus?"

"We think so, yes. Since he's dead, too, it's hard to confirm immediately, but we'll test during the autopsy to be certain."

Lyssa nodded; it confirmed her own thoughts on the matter. Since Damian had revealed his suspicions that they were dealing with an incubus, she had been mulling over the subject of genetics. No-one had ever done any studies to verify how much DNA was shared between Vampyrii and Werewolf, but it struck Lyssa that there were far too many similarities between the two races to be purely coincidental.

"Did you manage to rescue Kareena?" Lyssa took a deep breath, dreading the answer.

Damian shook his head.

"Oh, my gods!" Lyssa felt sick, "Did Vanessa...?"

"No, no..." Damian interrupted. "Kareena isn't dead. Vanessa didn't..."

Lyssa let out a shuddering sigh of relief. She knew her sister had killed, but they were soldiers, and she acted in a twisted form of self-defense. Killing a young defenseless girl like Kareena would be something else entirely.

"They...let Kareena go. She was taken before my people could bring her back to safety."

"Taken?"

Damian nodded. "By an unknown party flying an unidentified dropship resembling designs they'd seen used by the Fae. The ship headed into New Victus."

"I'm sorry." Lyssa reached out and squeezed Damian's hand. "I can ask Mercy to start looking into it for you. Maybe our office has picked up something useful."

"Thank you." he smiled gratefully. "Anyway, after losing Kareena they doubled back onto the trail of your sister and her partner. They were tracking them when the tables were turned. Vanessa and her partner ambushed my people and... I'm sorry, Lyssa, but your sister was killed in the ensuing confrontation."

Lyssa closed her eyes, her head dropped. Her sister was dead. Vanessa's condition had always been a problem, but she never thought it would ever lead to this. She looked at Damian's old troopship.

"You brought her home?"

"I wish it had been alive, but yes. She's on the flyer."

"I want to see her."

"Lyssa...it's not pretty. There was gunfire...Vanessa took a headshot. There's some other wounds too. Just...take a moment to prepare yourself. There's no rush."

Lyssa nodded and closed her eyes.

Deep breaths.

Suddenly, she was acutely aware of how raw her eyes were. How ragged her breathing still sounded. Every inhalation, and every exhalation. Just a few hours ago she felt rejuvenated. Now, however, she felt tired. Exhausted. Allyson's gift had been to give her a break, but now it was over. The delicate shield her enjoyable weekend erected had been shattered by the news.

She prided herself on her ability to plan and prepare. She always knew that the most likely resolution to her sister's excursion would be one of tragedy. Hope had been a hard commodity to hold on to the longer it went on, especially after Mercy's report from their failed interception. The realization that Vanessa was not going to surrender peaceably brought with it an acceptance that this moment was coming. Lyssa had done her best to mentally prepare herself.

But now Vanessa was...gone.

Really, truly gone.

This was no longer a hypothetical exercise.

She shook her head to clear it, then glanced across at Damian who was quietly sitting next to her on the trunk. Waiting patiently, but also anxiously. Lyssa could tell by his subtle, yet uncomfortable fidgeting. Tiny movements, almost imperceptible unless you knew him well. The shallow tapping of his right foot. The rhythmic squeezing of his clenched fist, turning the knuckles white. Damian was a man of action, and right now there was nothing he could do but give Lyssa the space she needed to process her thoughts and feelings.

She knew that Vanessa had meant little to him. He didn't know her; they had never met. His knowledge of her was the result of a few oblique references during post coital relaxation. Yet, he had done his best to save her. And when he couldn't do that, he had taken the responsibility upon himself to be the one to come here and tell Lyssa in person. To be here with her when she needed someone.

His support meant the world to her. Damian was truly a good friend...

Fuck.

Was this to be her legacy as a person?

Despite Mercy's reassurances that it wasn't the case, Lyssa knew that she had been the one who drove Vanessa away. It didn't matter if it was Damian's operative who had delivered the killing blow; Lyssa knew that she had signed her sister's death warrant decades ago. Medicating her. Caging her. Lying to her.

Unfairly treating her like an inconvenience to her life, rather than as a true sister.

Vanessa had deserved better, but she couldn't turn back the clock.

Now, Damian deserved better.

He'd taken a huge risk coming here.

Not just for her, but for him. She knew the kind of trouble he would be in if he was caught in New Victus. She also knew the trouble he would be in back in Pack Nation, if his people uncovered their secret pact before it was the right time.

Yet, he had done all of this...for her.

She stared at his handsome face, realizing all she had done for him in return was bring him trouble and complications.

She wished that she had been able to make things right with her sister, regretting that now she wouldn't have the chance. Damian, however, she could do something about. She felt compelled to owe him the same respect he had shown her.

"Damian," she finally summoned up the courage to say, "something happened in Nexus City. Something I need to talk to you about. I—"

He held up his hand to stop her.

"Lyssa, stop," Damian said softly, shaking his head. "Ever since we met, I recognized that your one *truest* character trait is that you take responsibility for everything. *Everything.* StormHall's ascent to power, the War, your sister's situation... Even us. It's both your greatest strength and, unfortunately, your worst flaw.

"I know what Vanessa meant to you. I know the hurt you're dealing with. I also know that you're feeling responsible for what happened to her. Do yourself a favor...let it go. Let it all go, just for a little while, and allow yourself to grieve. That other stuff can wait. Anything you want to say to me...can wait."

She nodded.

"If you're ready, I'll take you to your sister."

He held out his hand, a gesture of both familiarity and condolence. She accepted it and he led her across the hangar.

As they got closer to the dropship and what was held within, all those feelings of guilt and responsibility started to ebb away. She gripped his hand tightly as the emotions she had been unconsciously trying to suppress pushed forcibly to the forefront of her mind. She swallowed hard, preparing herself as they walked slowly up the flyer's boarding ramp and into the small cargo compartment. Lyssa abruptly stopped when she saw the pod with the glass canopy, and her heart raced as she recognized it as a life support pod. Was her sister alive after all?

Hope faded as quickly as it surged. What else was Damian supposed to transport her sister's body in? A coffin? A box? Body bag? This was his way of giving Vanessa a little dignity. It was a sentiment Lyssa appreciated more than words could convey.

She placed her hand on the cool glass of the pod and stared down through its crystal-clear surface. Fresh tears started to flow in haphazard lines down her cheeks.

"Oh, 'Nessa..." she whispered.

It wasn't the horror she had imagined. There was some damage to her face; claw wounds to one side and a clean bullet hole where her right eye met her nose. Her eyelids were shut which disguised some of the damage done, and there was no blood in evidence. She still looked beautiful, with her elegant cheekbones and perfect skin.

"My people tried their best to make her look...respectable. I'm sorry I couldn't do more."

Lyssa said nothing, staring at her sister's peaceful looking repose. She wished with all her heart that Vanessa was just sleeping, but she knew the truth.

Goodbye, 'Nessa.

| 66 |

THE MOUNTAIN DWELLERS

– Jaymes Knightley –
– Tuesday – Nexus City, Iceland –

"God, I'm nervous. I *really* need this visa," Carrie muttered, her voice a quiver of excitement.

"I'm sure it'll be fine," her father said reassuringly.

"I hope so. My story is sunk without it."

They were walking slowly down Paragon Avenue. The tree-lined boulevard, more commonly known as Embassy Alley, ran from the Nexus Conference Centre all the way to the border with Pack Nation territory, and formed the longest and widest spoke of the city's wheel-like layout. Each embassy they passed brought its own unique architectural style and aesthetic to the area, drawing Carrie's gaze in a hundred different directions.

They sauntered past a few open areas on their stroll – empty lots currently being used as picturesque parks or communal meeting spots, complete with picnic benches and frolicking water features. These were place holders for the likes of the Japanese Empire or Zǔguó, should they ever decide to come join the global community here. There was only one prominent embassy that was not in attendance on Paragon Avenue. The New Victus embassy was ensconced in its own sector of the city, an area dominated by faux neo-gothic architecture constructed to give an impression of age and tradition where there was none.

The Vampyrii race may be ancient, but they had always assimilated with Human cultures around the world. This aesthetic was thus a choice, rather than a tradition. Though Jaymes suspected he knew who was ultimately responsible for the particular style preference.

The Pack Nation and FSE embassies sat proudly opposite each other at the points of their sectors. The latter building was a stunning blend of Human and Fae design showcasing gleaming organic spires of wood and crystal that dazzled with iridescent color. The former, a multitude of beautiful wooden lodges. A stunning array of natural colors and materials with a real texture to them. Both blended future technology with tradition in a way that was visually pleasing.

Jaymes, of course, had seen all these structures hundreds of times before. He and Serlia had been the Federation Ambassadors here for over a decade, and much of this had sprung up on their watch. It was a legacy he was immensely proud of. If a lasting peace was to blossom, then this is where the seeds of it would be planted. Today, though, he was finding a simple joy in watching the wonder on his daughter's face as they slowly meandered down the avenue and she absorbed the sights and sounds of this most eclectic of communities. A smile crossed his lips because he knew that what she was about to see was going to blow her mind.

"Oh, my God," she muttered as if on cue while stumbling to a stunned halt.

"Yes, it has that effect on most people," Jaymes chuckled.

"Is that...?"

"It is," her father nodded as he joined her upward gaze. "The NordScania Embassy is, indeed, a small mountain."

"But... How...?"

"The Trolls. They're earth shapers. They can manipulate and shape the very earth and rock upon which we walk. While it took months for our engineers to build the FSE Embassy, it took the Trolls mere days to conjure this magnificent construct for NordScania. One solid structure crafted from the granite of Iceland."

"It's…" Carrie shook her head, speechless.

"Getting Wi-Fi in there is a problem, but if a bomb went off in Nexus City, there would be no place safer."

Jaymes gestured to where Carrie was looking up at the large, elegant arched window of what appeared to be a single crystal-clear pane of glass, perhaps wondering where one acquired glass that huge. It was at least thirty feet tall and seemingly embedded into the rock that framed it.

"Ice," Jaymes said to answer the unspoken question. "The purest ice you have ever seen."

"It's *so* clear…" Carrie said, barely hiding her awe.

"Wait until you see inside," Jaymes said enigmatically.

He led her up the gently sloping path that meandered haphazardly to the enormous granite doors, each one hewn from solid stone and adorned with runes in Old Norse, a language he recognized but could not read. The translation was something he always meant to ask about, but his exchanges with Ambassador Yetu had been limited. Not due to any friction, but simply because the non-Human NordScanians generally kept to themselves.

They observed a pecking order based simply on the age of the race, and in those terms, humanity was the relative youngster. The Trolls outranked them having been around for far longer, and today's meeting was with Ambassador Yetu. For Carrie to be given the visa she needed to pursue her story beyond the Clypeus Mountains, she would first need Yetu's approval in order to get to the next level of NordScania authority – that of the Ice Giants. Specifically, Ambassador Alzim. It would be he who would make the decision to grant or decline the request.

The lobby was every bit as impressive as the exterior promised it would be – a symphony of crystal and stone. The floor gleamed like polished ice, but oddly wasn't slippery at all and the room didn't feel in the least bit cold. Everything was shaded in gentle hues of blue and grey, from the bright shades of cyan in the ice-made furniture, to the slate shades of the marble-smooth granite. The two-tone arrangement might have looked dull if it wasn't for the bright greens of the moss that dappled the walls and contrasted with the glinting veins of copper, silver, and gold accented with the occasional sparkle of a diamond or ruby.

"Knightley, friend," came the soft-spoken, reverberating baritone of Ambassador Yetu who was standing in the lobby, evidently awaiting their arrival. "Seeing you is pleasure and joy. Offspring, Carrie-Anne, of course. Most welcome, both."

He slowly bowed from the waist, yet even bent over, he still towered a good two feet or more over Jaymes and his daughter. It had taken a while for Jaymes to get a handle on the singsong manner in which the Trolls spoke. They had an odd manner with the English language. Yet what they said was always honest and straightforward, as if they had evolved past the need for lies and deceit. If only every race could be so uncomplicated, his job would be much easier.

"Yetu, friend." The diplomat in Jaymes tried to mimic the speech pattern to the best of his ability. Troll-speak wasn't easy, but he hoped the attempt would be appreciated. This was 'the dance,' as he often referred to it. "We greet you with happiness and peace. Offspring Carrie-Anne wishes to travel to Clypeus. Your recommendation to Honored Alzim, much appreciated."

Evidently, his Troll-speak was not quite up to par. Yetu laughed deep and loud, his belly jiggling delightfully in his mirth as his bulbous nose snorted. The old Troll raised his hands and clapped once loudly and then brandished his hands to Jaymes.

"Knightley, friend, no desire have I for you to speak like Troll child. Understand primitive English enough to make your conversation not difficult. Speak as usually speak. I will make no jest at your expense."

"Fair enough, my friend." Jaymes smiled. "I introduce to you my youngest daughter, Carrie-Anne."

"I'm extremely pleased to meet you, Ambassador." Carrie nodded and smiled, bowing her head slightly in deference to the Troll who clapped again in apparent joy.

"Delightfulness is mine, Knightley offspring. Delightfulness."

"I'm hoping that you can give your recommendation to Ambassador Alzim to grant me a travel visa to the Clypeus Mountains," she asked with a smile.

Jaymes recognized this expression as the one his little girl had often used when she wanted her father to convince her mother to do something for her.

Ambassador Yetu shrugged and grinned. "This I cannot oblige for Knightley offspring Carrie. I am sorry."

"May I ask why?" Carrie replied with a hint of confusion, a smidgen of annoyance creeping in.

Yetu picked up on the fluctuation in her tone, but it simply seemed to amuse him even more.

"Understand not," he laughed, his eyes glinting ice blue with humor. "I can make no recommendation when Alzim already ask audience with you. Knew request already."

"I... Are you saying...? Are you saying that Ambassador Alzim knew we were coming?" Carrie asked with a furrowed brow, mirroring the look that Jaymes knew was present upon his own face.

"I'm not sure I follow, Ambassador Yetu. You already asked Ambassador Alzim for us?" he asked.

Yetu shook his head, his nose wobbling slowly. "Not from me he hears. From Balent. And Balent from the Song. Alzim is to receive you and converse. Follow to your meeting where I lead."

They followed Yetu out of the lobby and down a passageway with a high arched ceiling. The walls were lined with a bioluminescent moss that provided natural light. As they strolled in silence, all Jaymes could hear was the gentle trickle of the stream that ran down the center of the corridor in the direction they walked.

The passage turned, sloping gradually downward in a gentle spiral. It followed the path of the stream until the two parted ways, and as the corridor continued onward, the water took a left turn under another rune-etched stone door. Yetu stopped and pushed the door open into a spartan room of ice.

Sitting within, on a colossal glacial throne, was the peaceful form of an Ice Giant. Seeing Ambassador Alzim never failed to astonish Jaymes, and he could tell from the awestruck look on his daughter's face, she felt the same way. Even seated, Alzim towered over them, looking like he had been sculpted from a block of living ice. To be in his presence took your breath away. Seeing him was like witnessing a force of nature.

"Welcome, Ambassador Knightley."

The deep voice reverberated soothingly, a bell-like quality to it.

"Ambassador Alzim. It is our pleasure to be here. Thank you for seeing us."

"I shall keep this brief," Alzim said, his English perfect, "I have approved a visa for your daughters. Their colleagues also. When the right time arrives, they may travel to the Dragontop Mount with our blessing, and our assistance."

"My daughters?" Jaymes was puzzled by Alzim's statement.

"Balent sent word. The visa is for all. They are expected and welcome. Balent looks forward to meeting the Songbird."

"Gayle?" Carrie asked in confusion.

Jaymes heard the shocked tone of his daughter's question, paralleling the surprise he himself was experiencing. Prior to coming here, he wasn't sure if Carrie's request would be approved or rejected, and he had readied himself to deal with either outcome. Yet, to hear that the visa had been approved for not just Carrie-Anne, but for Allyson and Gayle too, was something he was not prepared for at all.

Alzim, however, simply shrugged, as if he didn't care about such details. Which, to be fair, he likely didn't.

"The Dragon King listens to the Song of The Winds. It was his instruction to us to allow your party safe passage. I can tell you no more, as I have no more information to give. Balent will explain when the time comes."

"What do you mean by 'when the time comes?'" Carrie asked. "I was hoping to go straight away."

Ambassador Alzim looked impassively at her. "The time is not right. I'm afraid you must be patient."

Jaymes looked at his daughter who glanced back at him with confusion running rampant across her features. He could clearly see that she was about to push the point and argue her case with the Ice Giant sat before her, which Jaymes knew would be a mistake. Carrie-Anne had essentially been granted what she had come here for; to protest would risk having the permission revoked. He gave her a subtle shake of his head, trying to communicate the sentiment silently.

Please, just accept what you've been given!

She understood his unspoken plea, and pouted a little, but also gave the slightest of shrugs before sighing and graciously acknowledging the gift she had been given.

"Thank you," she said and bowed her head in deference.

Though he was grateful that Alzim had acquiesced to his daughter's request, he couldn't help but wonder...what exactly was it they were being thankful for?

| 67 |

NEW PROXY

– Lyssa Balthazaar –
– Thursday – Albany, New Victus –

"You know, StormHall is gonna be pissed when he finds out you're not going to be at the Summit opening," Mercy said slowly.

"Mercy...my sister's ritual..." Lyssa started, but her niece interrupted.

"I know. I know there's no choice."

"It's only for the few days," Lyssa added. "Once the ritual is done, I'll fly straight out. I left the diplomatic cases in the safe at the New Victus Embassy. You can pick them up from there. I just need you to hold down the fort and give the documents to the appropriate people on the opening day of the Summit."

"Here's hoping I don't get the cases mixed up," Mercy smiled.

"You won't. There are little flags on the top so you can't go wrong. Mixing them up wouldn't matter much, though. They're bio-metrically coded so only the proper recipient can open them. These are the only cases that are allowed in the Convention Centre and they'll be scanned upon arrival, as will you. So, no trying to smuggle weapons in or doing anything stupid. Security is *very* tight..."

Her mind drifted back to the night she spent with Allyson and a fleeting glimmer of light forced itself through her dark mood. However, thoughts of Vanessa's impending funeral ritual brought the black clouds rolling back in over that particular blue sky.

"...security is tight," she picked up again. "As it should be. If you need help or assistance, then contact either of the Ambassador Knightleys of the FSE delegation. They're not strictly allies, but I've met them, and I trust them. They'd help you."

"If they're anything like their daughters, then I'm in agreement. They were nice to me. The Chief of Security especially so." Mercy flashed a knowing smile.

Another fleeting thought of Allyson, her lips pressed against Lyssa's skin...

"You okay there, Lyssa?" Mercy said with a coy smile.

"Allyson Knightley... She's the errr... Security Chief. Yes?" Lyssa stuttered.

Mercy simply raised an eyebrow. "Yes. Very distinctive scent...like...honey."

"Mmm, yes... Oh..." Lyssa blushed.

"Yeah – oh," Mercy giggled. "I work in intelligence, remember? When I spoke to you in Nexus you sounded...giddy. Then you got back here, and while the good mood was gone, you were carrying her scent. Anyway, I am not criticizing. As I said, I really liked her."

Lyssa decided she didn't want to have *that* particular conversation right now. There was a time and place for girly gossip, and this wasn't it. She chose to ignore Mercy's leading statement and feigned ignorance to push forward with the topic at hand.

"The Knightleys are good people. I think it would be wise for us to make allies of them."

"For New Victus?" Mercy asked.

"Maybe," Lyssa mused. "But actually...more for us. While I can't fault Storm's plan and I'll back this play for now...I have that feeling, constantly in the back of my mind... Like I'm waiting for the other shoe to drop. And when it does, I want to be prepared. It can't hurt to have friends and allies. Just in case."

Mercy nodded and then looked at her aunt with a face that told Lyssa the subject was about to be changed before a single word was spoken.

"Lyssa...are you okay? I mean...about Vanessa."

Mercy wasn't usually one to stumble over words, but Lyssa knew what her niece was getting at.

"I'm...dealing with it," she admitted with a sigh. "Sometimes the life span we have is a curse. Vanessa was my sister for over two-hundred years. That's a long time to have someone in your life only to see them snatched away. You don't get over grief like that in a hurry."

Mercy nodded her understanding. "I have made the appropriate arrangements for the Blood to Earth ritual. I'm sorry it can't be the big affair that she deserves as a true born daughter of Balthazaar."

"Oh, gods... I'm such an idiot..." Lyssa suddenly realized how unfair she was being. "I'm so sorry, Merce. She was your family, too...and I'm sending you—"

"Stop it, Lyssa," Mercy interrupted. "Yes, we were blood kin...she was my aunt, too. But I didn't know her very well. I grieve for her, of course, but we were not close in the way you and I are."

Despite her forgiving words, Lyssa found she couldn't look her niece in the eye. She had been so wrapped up in her own grief, she hadn't stopped to consider whether Mercy would have wanted to be at the ritual, too.

"I'm here for *you*," Mercy said. "Whatever I can do to make this easier. I am more than happy to go to Nexus. Please, don't worry about it."

The two of them sat quietly for a moment. Lyssa lost in her thoughts and Mercy supportively being there, but not pressing her to talk. She thought about the ritual to come.

Ever since they discovered Vanessa's condition, she had known that her life and her death would be...abnormal. A life in a state of seclusion and a death that would pass almost unnoticed. A life that was the antithesis of what she deserved.

"She wanted simple things," Lyssa finally said quietly. "Love. Family. That she chose to follow that monster is my personal failure as her sister."

"You didn't fail her, Lyssa. You did all you could do under

the regime that StormHall forced upon us."

"Which is *also* my failure. I should have stopped his rise to power."

She was sliding into a pit of darkness, wallowing in self-pity.

"Allow yourself to grieve, Lyssa," Mercy responded as if she had been reading her thoughts. "But don't let it drag you down. The ritual is prepared, everything is ready for you. All you need do is turn up and recite the words, say goodbye properly to Vanessa. I can handle things at the Summit until you feel able to take over. StormHall may kick up a fuss, but I can handle him."

"Thank you, Mercy."

She took a deep breath and reached across to embrace her oldest and closest friend. Mercy returned the sentiment with crushing affection.

"I've been watching you run our House for the past century, and I couldn't have asked for a better education. I won't let you down."

She knew she could trust and count on Mercy – there was no one alive in whom she had more faith.

"Do you think Storm knows?" she asked Mercy. "About Vanessa?"

There was a hesitation before her niece replied with a certainty that Lyssa knew was false.

"No," Mercy shook her head. "How could he?"

Lyssa couldn't shake the feeling that something was wrong. A feeling deep down in the pit of her stomach. She trusted her gut; it was rarely wrong. But was it better to act now on a suspicion? As long as they were discreet, if she was wrong then no harm, no foul.

But if she was right...

She made a decision. To wait until it was too late would be folly. A folly that would lead to their extinction as a House.

"Mercy, I need you to do one last thing before you fly out to Nexus. I want you to contact Damian. Tell him I want to prepare the 'Exodus Initiative.'"

Mercy looked startled. "Lyssa, are you sure?"

She shook her head. No, she wasn't sure...but she wasn't going to leave anything to chance either.

| 68 |

SHOTS?

– Gayle Knightley –
– Friday – London, England –

"Well, thank fuck for that," Gayle stretched and exclaimed under her breath.

Finally, the end of the longest week ever in the history of long weeks. Ever.

Her muttered expression of gratitude drew an amused look from Lana, who grinned at her from across the desk. She had her pen held between her teeth as she finished shuffling the papers they had now completed grading into an orderly stack. Once the pile was neatly squared, she plucked the pen from her mouth and placed it, just so, gently on top,

"I honestly thought we were never going to finish," she chuckled wearily. "Were they as bad as you thought they were going to be?"

"The essays?" Gayle asked, gesturing at the papers.

Lana nodded.

"Better…I think," Gayle shrugged. "Norbel gave us that very same assignment at the end of *our* first few weeks at the Academy. I'm pretty sure our collective attempts back then were much worse."

"That was a decade ago!" Lana laughed. "You honestly remember that?"

"Fuck, no!" Gayle replied, looking at her best-friend as if

she were crazy. "I looked up our curriculum back then and re-trieved these from the archives. Why re-invent the wheel?"

"You do realize that Captain Reynolds, sitting in his office just across the way, is probably creating his own curriculum from scratch," Lana jerked a thumb over her shoulder in the direction of the door, "and here's you cheating the system."

"I mean, wasn't that the modus operandi of the 137th?" Gayle said with mock seriousness. "Work smarter, not harder. Gives us more time to play! Talking of which..."

Lana was already shaking her head. "No," she said vehe-mently. "I know that look."

"What look?" Gayle said innocently.

"The 'let's hang out and do something fun' look," Lana said. "But I am exhausted. Teaching is so much harder than I thought it would be. I'm honestly looking forward to a quiet might in. Takeaway food, comfortable clothes, crappy TV, and an early night."

"Boring!" Gayle scowled.

"I am prepared to live with that stigma," Lana laughed. "And on that note...I am going to head back to my office to fin-ish up before making my way home."

She scooted her chair backward slowly and gingerly stood. With a groan, she stretched to straighten out the kinks in her back. After collecting the pile of papers and cradling them in her arm, she turned to head for the door.

"Get some rest," Lana said as she exited the office, pausing briefly to look back at Gayle. "Call me if you need anything, okay?"

Gayle nodded. "Have a good weekend, Lana," she said with a tired smile. "I'll see you on Monday."

With that, Lana was gone, and Gayle was alone.

It had been a tough week, both physically and mentally. Her knee ached and she felt emotionally wrecked. The cadets would have a free study period on the Saturday morning, and while eventually they would be undertaking their specialist skills tuition on Saturday afternoons, for now they were free to pursue their own agendas over the weekends. Which meant the teachers were, too.

If Michael wanted to carry on working then so be it, but she was quitting the minute the hour hand hit five. Her smile grew as she watched the final few seconds tick away on her office clock.

She tossed her stylus onto the desk and put her feet up on its wooden surface, wriggling her toes in her boots. As comfortable as her CombatSkin was to wear, there was a limit to how long she wanted to spend in it. Originally, she had thought that she wouldn't be wearing it very much, but as every day involved some form of combat training, it had swiftly become the norm. Besides, the kids would be getting theirs soon and would need to learn how to operate in them, so it made sense she wear hers, too.

Maybe Lana had the right idea after all.

Perhaps a quiet night in was exactly the thing she needed right now. The tonic to cure all her ailments.

Closing her eyes, she took a deep breath and imagined the bliss of getting back to her apartment and changing out of the CombatSkin. Lounge pants, a baggy tee, no bra... Heaven.

Or maybe just pad around naked in the privacy of her own home, barefoot on the lush thick carpets...

"Two cents for them?"

There was a lightness to Michael's tone that made Gayle smile as she opened her eyes. He was leaning nonchalantly in the doorway with his arms folded across his broad chest.

"You *really* don't want to know," she laughed back. "What can I do for you, Tex?"

"I thought I told you never to call me that?" Again, his tone was more good-humored than annoyed. She decided to roll with it.

"Sorry. Couldn't resist," she chuckled. "The accent is pretty thick tonight."

"I was born in Lufkin, Texas," he smiled, a definite drawl in his voice. "Wasn't there long, though. My family moved north to Oklahoma just before the War, hence why the accent is pretty light. Usually comes out when I'm stressed, tired...or drunk."

"I'm voting for tired," she said softly.

"Long few weeks," he nodded. "It'll be nice to have some downtime."

An admission he probably wouldn't have made in front of Gayle a month ago, yet she was glad he was here now confessing to her.

Things had been a little awkward all week after she had warned him off her. It had been a gut reaction to being at a low ebb and feeling vulnerable. Another bad decision that, in hindsight, she regretted. She missed their evolving closeness, but maybe it wasn't too late to set things right.

"Interesting." Gayle smiled slyly at him.

"What's interesting?"

"That the perfect Captain Reynolds admits to getting drunk."

"Not often. Probably been a good five years since the last time."

"Fuck off!" she cursed.

"It's true," he said simply with a shrug.

Gayle was stunned. Surely, at the very least, he enjoyed a beer to unwind after a long day teaching. That was practically an American tradition... Wasn't it?

"By choice?" she asked, wondering if maybe it was something medical that prevented him from imbibing.

Another shrug. "Not so much. It just...happened."

Well, there's a cryptic answer.

But she also saw an opportunity to put things right between them.

"I feel like there's a story in there somewhere," she chided gently. "Care to share?"

"Maybe another time. I was just putting my head in to say goodnight."

Don't let him just walk away!

She thought about the run in the park. Their accidental kiss. That he had helped her when she was physically injured and cared about her when she was anguished. She thought about what Lana would tell her to do. What Allyson would say. She took a deep breath, made a spur of the moment decision, and nervously took the initiative.

"Goodnight? But the evening is young, Captain Reynolds, and I am in need of entertainment."

Bait dangled.

"Entertainment? What do you usually do for entertainment on a Friday night?"

Bait taken.

"Well…" Gayle grinned. "Usually I go home, change into something less military issue, and then settle down with a movie. But, with the right partner in crime, I could be easily persuaded to do something more fun…"

Michael cocked his head with an expression that implied curiosity. Hook, line, and sinker.

"I draw the line at crime. So, what d'ya have in mind?"

She spun her chair around and kicked her legs off the desk to stand up. Even at her full height in heels, he still stood a good three or four inches above her.

"Surprise me," she said coyly.

| 69 |

TEQUILA

– Michael Reynolds –
– Friday – London, England –

They sat on opposite sides of the table warily eyeing each other for a sign of weakness. It was, however, far too early in the game for that. The night was in its infancy, and the scruffy wooden surface of the table still held far more brim-full shot glasses than it did upside-down empty ones. And there were still plenty of limes, a full cellar of salt, and a ready supply of cheap tequila behind the bar.

"Okay, your turn. Make it good!" Gayle smiled across the table at him.

Michael sat back in his chair for a moment, deep in thought. Thus far, the questions had not been too probing or personal, but as he looked into her sparkling green eyes, he took her last statement as an invitation to up the ante.

"Okay, so... It's pretty obvious since I first met you that you hate bein' at the Academy..."

"Hate's a strong word," she interrupted. "It's not as bad as I thought it would be."

"I'll take that as a compliment," Michael laughed.

"It was meant as one."

Was she flirting? After what was said on the landing pad a few nights ago, he assumed that romance was off the table for them. Apparently not the case. He recognized that night had been a dip in the rollercoaster ride that was Gayle Knightley's moods. Obviously, she had bounced back somewhat.

He smiled back at her and leaned forward, tapping the table's surface thoughtfully with a finger.

"Was there a time when you loved being here?" he finished.

"Yes," she said without hesitation and pushed the shot glass at him.

The rules of the game.

Was the answer the truth? Or a lie? If she was telling the truth, then he had to drink the shot she had nudged in his direction. If he thought she was lying, then he pushed the shot glass back and called her on it. If he caught her in a lie, then she drank the shot. It was a trust exercise. You had no real choice but to believe the answer the other person gave. So far, it was four shots to zero, and not a drop of alcohol had thus far passed Gayle's lips.

Michael narrowed his eyes and looked at her carefully.

"You lie..." he said slowly, pushing the shot glass slowly back towards her. "You strike me as someone who was pushed to come here against their will when they were young. Rebel of the family. You made the most of it but were itching to get out of the Academy and into combat."

Gayle cast her eyes down to the table for a moment before pushing the shot glass back at him with a sad smile.

"No, it's true," she said. "I manifested when I was fifteen. Kind of a late bloomer by most hybrid standards. But when my abilities kicked in, boy, did they blossom fast. I was having real trouble controlling them and when my uncle suggested the Academy, I jumped at the chance. Do you know much about Fae powers in hybrids?"

"A little."

"A little?" Gayle laughed. "You're in charge of a class full of kids with these powers! You should know more than just 'a little.'"

"Teachin' them how to control their powers is *your* job, not mine," Michael laughed. "How 'bout you just give me the crib notes?"

"Okay, crash-course then." Gayle leaned in across the table, closing the distance between them. "Earth, air, fire, and water, blah blah blah, you know that stuff. The thing most people *don't* understand is how we control those powers."

"Through emotion. Your sister told me that much."

"Gold star, Captain Reynolds." She smiled. "Each of the elements is stronger when channeling a particular emotion. Air and Water respond better to positive emotion. Earth and Fire respond better to negative."

"What dictates which powers you get?" he asked, genuinely interested.

"Sometimes it's a natural affinity." She shrugged. "Sometimes it's hereditary."

"So, what was it for you?"

"Both. Fae are epically promiscuous, but they're also careful. Sometimes accidents happen, though, and hey, presto! You have a Fae-Human hybrid. When it happens, it tends to be a Fae father and a Human mother. But occasionally it's the other way around. What's even more rare is for the parents to stay together. Like my mum and dad. They met, fell in love, and wanted to have kids. Ally, Carrie, and I weren't accidents like most hybrid kids."

"So, what's the difference?"

"Well," Gayle sighed and continued. "It means that my sisters and I were conceived in love. That was the key. Then we spent nine wonderful months gestating in the womb of my Fae mother and percolating in her love-charged magical juices."

"Okay, that is just..." Michael winced and sat back in his seat. "Too much information!"

Gayle roared with laughter and spread her hands on the tabletop. "Sorry. But what it means is that I can control all four of the elements, and my power levels, by hybrid standards, are off the fucking charts."

"And your sisters?"

"Them, too," Gayle nodded. "But they're not trained like I am."

"Okay, so back up to the trouble part. Because I still need an explanation for why I'm drinkin' this shot and you're not."

"Well, the flipside of being a bad-ass with superpowers is

that, as a hybrid, I also got this hair and these eyes," she beckoned to her face and head.

"What's wrong with them?" His eyes locked with hers. "They look great."

Gayle held his gaze for a moment and then shyly averted it. An embarrassed smile flickered across her lips.

"Flattery will not get you out of drinking that shot," she laughed. "But shocking pink hair and bright green eyes makes you stand out as a freak at normal school. These were the early post-war days. Nobody trusted anyone who was different. Apart from Lana, no one wanted to be friends with the freak girl. I was teased. Relentlessly. I got angry...a lot. One day, I lost my temper and almost burned down my classroom. My parents removed me from school after that, but that just made things worse. The angrier I got, the more uncontrollable I got.

"Negative emotions are usually *much* easier to access. To this day I have occasional...anger issues."

"No shit..." Michael chuckled. "The first day we met, I thought you were gonna stalk me home and kill me in my sleep."

"Believe me, I was tempted. That was a particularly bad day." Gayle smiled. "But because of that anger, I also have the greatest affinity for fire powers. They're my most powerful weapon. The one I have the most...control over."

Her face changed, like a memory was passing through her mind. A bad memory. The smile that had been on her face faded and he could see an echo of pain in her eyes. Michael didn't say anything. He just let the silence lie between them for a moment and waited for Gayle to continue in her own time.

She sighed and shook herself gently from her reverie, her eyes changing to show a distinctly different emotion as she locked them with his again.

"It's easier to make yourself angry than it is to make yourself feel love," she said.

"You don't seem angry anymore," Michael said softly.

"I'm not," Gayle offered with a small smile. "At least not with you."

She held his gaze for a long moment.

"So, the Academy?"

"The Academy..." she hesitated, "was a place where I finally seemed to fit in. I was happy. For a while, anyway."

"So, what happened?"

Gayle paused for a moment and then smiled ruefully, shaking her head. "We grew up. But let's keep tonight light, shall we? No tales of misery and woe. Drink!"

Gayle plucked up the salt cellar and beckoned for Michael's hand. He licked the back of his hand to moisten the skin ready to receive the light sprinkling as Gayle shook out the contents. He quickly tasted the salt and then, with a grimace, necked the waiting shot of tequila. While Gayle laughed, he plucked up a slice of lime to suck on.

"Your turn. Go," he spluttered.

Sitting back in her chair again, she narrowed her eyes to look at him thoughtfully. Finally, she settled on a question.

"Have you ever been in love, Michael Reynolds?"

"Wow...you went to a *real* personal place."

"Shit just *got* real, son," Gayle laughed. "So..."

Michael started to shake his head, then tilted it before answering. There was a look of amusement on his face when he opened his mouth.

"Yup," he said simply.

Gayle looked him in the eye, squinting slightly. Finally, she nodded.

"Yeah, you definitely have been."

Michael picked up the glass. She had correctly judged his answer. The shot, therefore, was his to take.

"No explanation?" Gayle said with a twinkle of humor in her eye. "After *my* long-ass answer, that's all I get?"

To be honest, Michael wasn't sure how to answer her question. He might be drunk, or at least on the way to being drunk, but there were some secrets that should *stay* secret.

"It's a tough one to answer." He shrugged and swallowed the alcohol. "Story for another time maybe."

A flash of disappointment flared in Gayle's eyes, but to her credit she didn't push him.

"I'll hold you to that," she said softly. "Your turn."

He pointed to her hair. "Okay, the trademark pink..."

"Is your question going to be 'Does the carpet match the drapes?'" Gayle interrupted in mock offense.

Michael picked up his next shot, swilled it around the glass, and laughed. The thought hadn't crossed his mind till now, and suddenly it was all he could think about.

"No." he raised his hand in supplication. "I was simply gonna ask if you'd ever considered changin' it. Dyin' it or somethin'?"

"Of course I did. I *was* a teenage girl you know." She grabbed a handful of her hair and stared at it. "But for some magical Fae reason, hair-dye won't take. After a couple of days, it's back to pink again. I persevered for a while, but eventually gave up. I just learned to embrace it. Admit to myself that I look fucking cool."

"I'll drink to that," Michael said and knocked down another shot.

"My sisters made out better than I did. You met Ally, of course. Her hair is kinda deep blue, kinda dark. She likes to be professional, so diligently dyes it black. Even so, if you catch it in the light, it's still blue. The sister you haven't met yet is Carrie, the youngest. She's an investigative journalist, a *really* good one. Her hair is kind of lilac. Soft color. It looks good on her."

"The pink looks great on you. I'm not sure I could imagine you with another color now."

"Thanks," Gayle answered with a shy grin as she unconsciously tucked a long strand of pink behind her left ear. "You got siblings?"

Now, the ice was broken, the game was forgotten. Four weeks ago, he would never have entertained the idea that the two of them could have sat across from each other and just conversed like this. Yet Michael found her to be beguiling company, easy to confide in. In fact, he realized that the more time he spent with her, the more he found himself becoming attracted to her in a decidedly non-professional way.

"Twin," he said simply.

"Twins?" she echoed with interest. "Identical? Is there another tall, dark, and handsome out there?"

"No," Michael half smiled as he answered her. "Not identical."

"Shame," Gayle said, with a flirtatious tone. "What's that like? Being a twin?"

"Not what people think. Many assume that twins are psychically connected or somethin', but I've never experienced anything like that. We're not that close. Not anymore. Last time I saw Alex was maybe...two years ago."

He hadn't meant for his answer to sound so final, but it was clear from his tone that it was a subject he didn't really want to talk about. Once again, Gayle simply nodded and had the good grace not to press him for more details. A wave of guilt washed over him. She had unburdened to him on several occasions now. It felt only fair he gave her *something* in return.

"You know much about the US Marine Corps and the War?" he said quietly.

Gayle shook her head. Of course he knew she was lying; she knew her War history intimately. He appreciated this was simply her way of leaving the door open for him to keep talking. He refilled his glass and took another shot of tequila, steeling himself to talk about something he hadn't spoken about in years.

"I was seven when The Rising happened. Mom was career Army; she was lost in the early days of fightin'. As reports came in of the conflict approaching our home in Oklahoma, the rest of us were evacuated south to be picked up from the coast of Texas by the US North Atlantic Fleet."

"I've heard stories..." Her voice was full of empathy. "Tough life for a kid."

Michael shrugged. "Not ideal, but we had it better than most. Once it all settled down, we got a small room on the *Disney Fantasy*. The last of the big Disney cruise liners. It was never intended to house refugees for years, but basically became a floating community."

"How long were you there?"

"Eight years, give or take. Everybody pitched in. I was

workin' in the kitchens of the ship by the time I was eleven. Dad was drafted into the Army when I was barely twelve, leavin' us to fend for ourselves. At sixteen, I joined the Army myself. Partly because I wanted to do my bit to take back our country from the Vamps, but mostly I just wanted to get out of that tiny room and off that fuckin' ship."

"Just you?" Gayle asked.

"Me and Alex," he confirmed. "Both of us. Basic trainin' was...basic. Three months combat trainin' aboard the USS *Kitty Hawk* and then we were assigned to a unit. The 215th Recon. We fought all over...from South America to the Alaskan border. We were together when the US forces took back the west coast. By that time, I'd been promoted to first lieutenant."

Gayle raised what Michael would have sworn was an empty glass to her lips and took a drink.

"The Battle for Silicon Valley?" she asked as she put the glass back down.

Michael nodded slowly.

"I was there. Lot of good people were lost that day."

"Too many," Michael agreed. "You took down the monitorin' station on the Farallon Islands allowin' us the element of surprise when we retook San Francisco. That was the first time I heard of the 137th Hunters."

"We did our part." Gayle smiled, but there was a real sadness behind the expression.

He had seen the softer, more introspective side of her already. Had seen her hurting and vulnerable. Yet for all the bravado and cocksure attitude she usually exuded, this was the first time he had seen her really be a feeling, empathetic Human being. He had acknowledged the fact that she was beautiful a while back, but every time he uncovered a new facet to her character, he found himself increasingly attracted to her.

He stared into her stunning jade eyes and found her staring back at him.

"Why'd you join the HFA?" she asked quietly.

He wanted to tell her the whole story, but he couldn't. Not yet. Instead he went with a simple true statement.

"Norbel approached me. Offered me a job. I couldn't say no."

There was a pause in the conversation. Gayle played with the shot glass idly before eventually replying.

"I wasn't born till two years after The Rising," she said quietly. "This world...it's all I've ever known. You remember much from before?"

"Everything," Michael said without hesitation.

"Everything?" Gayle cocked her eyebrow. "How old are you?"

"I just told you how old I was at the Rising – can't you work it out?"

Gayle rolled her eyes. "I'm too lazy to do the math."

Michael laughed. "I thought you read my file?"

"I wasn't looking for birthdates."

"What *were* you lookin' for?"

"Just answer the fucking question," she said as her cheeks blushed the same color as her hair.

"Thirty-six," he said. "I'll be thirty-seven in January."

"January...that makes you Capricorn or Aquarius?"

He nodded and chuckled. "Aquarius. You believe in astrology?"

Gayle leaned forward. "Michael, we live in a world where I routinely manipulate the elements, where Vamps and Werewolves are real, and..." She shrugged. "Fuck knows what else. I can think of worse things to believe in, can't you?"

He paused to take a shot of his own before continuing. "Point taken," he admitted. "I remember bein' vaguely aware that the news reports had started talkin' about somethin' happenin' on the US Canadian border, but like most kids I wasn't much interested. It wasn't till things started to escalate that I paid attention, but by then everyone was tuned in.

"Problem was that we had no real news. No one really knew what was goin' on. News crews that went to the affected areas never came back. Then, about a week later, Mom was called back to service. I remember when it happened. My dad...he tried to put on a brave face, but..."

Memories flooded back, and emotions he hadn't shown in

decades started to well up within him.

"She left the next morning," he said somberly. "We never saw her again."

Gayle reached her hand out across the table and gently put it atop his. It felt warm and – for someone with so many years of combat under her belt – remarkably soft.

"That couldn't have been an easy time."

"It wasn't." He didn't elaborate any further.

"You don't need to talk about this stuff," she said quietly.

"Actually, I think maybe I do." Michael looked at her, staring into her emerald eyes. "I haven't spoken about any of this in a long time. As a soldier, you tend to push all this...all this emotion aside."

She nodded, understanding what he meant. This kind of emotional baggage was a distraction. In combat, distractions got you killed.

He extracted his hand and reached for the tequila bottle.

"I may need more of this to get me through the whole story, though."

"Well, I can certainly guarantee a healthy supply of that." Gayle smiled. "Plenty more where that came from."

"Anyways, you know the rest. The fall of America, yadda yadda."

Gayle spread her hands and laughed. "Babe, I am the daughter of the Diplomatic Envoy for the FSE and I studied for years at the Academy. I have been brought up around all this crap all my life. I could quote you the textbook history of this whole goddamn fucking war in my *sleep*."

Michael nodded. He knew his history, too.

"Thing is, as a kid it all seemed to happen so slowly. The evacuation to the coast seemed to take forever. Everybody was tryin' to move south. Everybody. There were huge traffic jams, long days on the road. The only food and drink we had was what we managed to take with us; all the shops on the route were inevitably looted. And then there was the paranoia...everywhere. A lack of real news and information meant everyone was lookin' over their shoulder.

"But when you look back at the history as an adult, you realize...it was just days. It shocks you when you see how fast the world fell apart. Perspective...it's a really fucked up thing.

"We were on the *Disney Fantasy* when news reports started to reach us that the battle in Europe had begun. I remember, even as a kid, thinkin' how fucked humanity was..."

"...and then the Fae stepped in and saved us all. Hoorah for them." Gayle giggled and lifted up her empty shot glass in a sarcastic toast.

Michael raised his own refilled glass and clinked it to hers in mock salute.

"You ever wonder?" Gayle furrowed her brow with thought.

"Wonder what?"

"Wonder who planned all that? The War, I mean. I never really bought that Sebastian StormHall was behind it all."

As a career soldier, the rhetoric Michael had always accepted was that StormHall had been the mastermind of The Rising. Yet, now he thought about it, he had to admit she had a point. Was StormHall, for all his bluster and political power, the kind of man who had the brains to plot such a coordinated worldwide assault? The more he considered it, the more he actually doubted it.

"You know, the worst thing was knowin' people were being killed," he mused. "Millions of people but havin' no idea how it was happening. We heard reports of fightin', but the death toll and the spread seemed more like a plague."

"Well..." Gayle interjected, "it kinda is...was... I mean, if you get bitten by a Vamp then you have three possible outcomes, but death is the most likely..."

She stopped mid-sentence as she realized what she was saying. His mother had gone to war with the very Vampyrii she was talking about so matter-of-factly. He knew she hadn't meant to infer that this was how his mother had been lost in battle, even if factually it was probably accurate. But he could see the look on her face, and he smiled to reassure her he wasn't hurt.

"Sometimes..." he began, then hesitated and looked at the

bottle on the table. It was almost empty now and he realized he had no idea how many shots he had taken. He wasn't drunk, not yet, but the alcohol had smoothed the edge off, allowing him to be more open than he knew he would usually be.

"Sometimes…" he started again, "I wonder what happened to our mother. She's likely dead, but sometimes I hope that I'll find her somewhere. Turned or in thrall. So that I could save her."

"There's no cure for a Vampyrii bite, Michael." Gayle squeezed his hand.

"Well, that…is where you're wrong." He tilted his head and smiled at her in an '*I know something you don't know*' way.

Her brow furrowed as she looked at him, puzzled.

"Do tell," Gayle said, her tone indicating a genuine curiosity about why he thought she was mistaken.

"Uh-uh. That's top secret. And I do believe it's my question."

"Oh? I thought we'd stopped playing games a while back."

"All part of my cunning plan!" Michael laughed.

"Bring it on," she said, winking at him coyly.

| **70** |

THIS KISS

– Gayle Knightley –
– Saturday – London, England –

As they sauntered together down the deserted street, Gayle found herself having quite the heated internal debate with the little voice inside her head that she referred to in private as 'Inner-Gayle.' 'Inner-Gayle' represented her gut instinct and was broadly responsible for many of Gayle's better decisions. Lately, however, 'Inner-Gayle' had been run over roughshod by the bad choices made by 'Emotional-Gayle.' This evening's deliberation concerned whether she was on the brink of making *another* awfully misguided, emotionally based decision.

Just admit it, 'Inner-Gayle' said pointedly. *You've been attracted to Michael practically since the start. Deny it all you like, but you know it's true.*

'Inner-Gayle' was a wise – and often sarcastic – bitch who generally had a better handle on things than Gayle herself did.

Very true, 'Inner-Gayle' agreed. *Remember Torbar?*

Yeah, like the Torbar mess. It was her vanity that had sent her spiraling into that disaster. She pursued the relationship despite 'Inner-Gayle's' warnings.

And Valletta, too?

Okay, okay. Point taken.

You really should listen to me more often.

"Oh, fuck you..." Gayle muttered to herself.

"Excuse me?" Michael looked at her with a furrowed brow. "Sorry. Just thinking out loud..."

The heavens had opened, and the streetlights reflected off the expanding puddles in a manner Gayle found improbably pretty. The bar seemed like a dim and distant memory, but her guilt was still fresh. Where Michael was perhaps a little worse for wear, she knew she couldn't blame the tequila for her own current state of mind. She hadn't sipped a drop. When the time had come for her to take a drink, she faked it. Child's play when you can conjure water out of thin air.

All of which led to the dilemma currently playing out in her head. This was not about *how* she felt about Michael Reynolds – on that point Gayle and 'Inner-Gayle' were singing from the same hymn sheet.

The more time she spent around Michael, the more confident she became that what she was feeling was...right. It had only been a short time – that much was true – but everything she understood about him led to the inevitable conclusion that he was a good man. Lana and Ally vouched for him, and they were generally far better judges of character than she was. By all accounts, he was kind, caring, generous of spirit...basically the anti-Torbar.

So, not the kind of man she was normally attracted to.

That would usually be the man with the deep, dark mysterious secret. The more mysterious or dangerous the better. Yet, in almost two months, she hadn't found a shred of evidence to suggest he was anything more than the man he presented to the world. Sure, there were things he didn't feel comfortable talking about right now, but didn't everyone have a few sore subjects? History that they'd rather not drag up?

That was normal, right?

So, if he's such a good man... 'Inner Gayle' chipped in, *then why are you lying to him?*

Was she lying to him? Or was she simply not revealing her own full story just yet?

Does that make a difference?

Did it? Was withholding the truth the same as lying?

It was her fear of his reaction that was compelling her to

keep her mouth zipped and play along with the ruse she had already started perpetrating. He would surely be angry at her if she told him the truth, that she was only play-acting at being drunk. She was afraid that revealing the little white lie would open the possibility of him asking why. And that was a truth she wasn't ready to expose right now. Gayle didn't want to potentially derail any progress they had made in their relationship.

'Inner-Gayle' naturally disagreed with this assessment and course of action.

Just tell him! 'Inner-Gayle' said. *Before it goes too far.*

Michael was strolling alongside her, talking about something and laughing. Gayle realized she had absolutely no idea what he was saying since her brain had changed frequency. She joined in with his laughter anyway, which caused her to genuinely start giggling at the absurdity of her laughing while having no idea what she was laughing at. She wanted to hold onto this feeling forever, which meant, annoyingly, that 'Inner-Gayle' was right. Again. She stopped laughing and took a deep breath.

"Michael," she started, "I need to tell you something..."

Good girl, 'Inner-Gayle' said happily.

Michael stopped walking, turning his attention to focus on her and what she was about to say, but that was as far as she got. As the rain beat down on them, she found herself lost in his eyes as he reached up and tucked her hair gently behind her ear, exposing the scar she usually kept hidden.

Caught up in the moment, she didn't care. All she could feel was her heart pounding in her chest. He was so close to her now. Those broad shoulders, powerful chest...and he was tall. She tried to recall how tall he was. Somewhere deep in her brain she knew that she had read it on his personnel file, but she couldn't remember. Six feet and then some...maybe six-three or six-four.

And those arms...

She pursed her lips, closed her eyes, and struggled to pull herself back from her biological impulse. Fighting with a side of herself that she had let rule for far too long. She tried to force herself to think about anything else but those arms, those lips...

Her home was right there; it would be elementary to let loose the pheromones and find out with absolute certainty just what Michael Reynolds was capable of. To feel his arms around her, his lips on hers.

No.

She tried to remember her steps. Or what her therapist had told her to do. Tried to focus. Attempted to re-discover the words that had been on the tip of her tongue mere moments before. But as she looked up at his handsome, square-jawed face, she couldn't find them. Lust and desire were terrible mistresses to deny, especially for her.

She was physically trembling, her breathing heavy, her chest rising and falling faster than normal. She could feel the inferno building within her and balled her fists tightly, squeezing her thighs together, clamping down on her impulses.

She wasn't sure whether that made things better or worse.

Michael was talking but she wasn't listening. She had no idea what he was saying. She was solely focused on the movement of his lips, not the sounds.

Compulsion took over.

She stood on her toes and placed her eager mouth on his.

Her hands flew up to his neck, arms encircling him and pulling his face to hers as she devoured him in passion, a desperate coming together of moist lips and inquisitive tongues. An endorphin surge of pure joy flooded her as she realized he was a willing partner in this dance.

His short hair felt soft in her fingers, and she groaned in desire as she felt one of those muscular arms encircle her waist. One hand gently gripped her hip, while the other slid up her spine and beneath her hair. She shivered as she felt his fingertips touch her naked skin at the nape of her neck. She had always been sensitive there, and now her mind was consumed with the thought of his mouth finding the spot, nibbling and nuzzling.

Driving her crazy.

Driving her upward.

That mouth was still locked to hers though, their tongues passionately searching and probing, becoming more urgent. His hold was loving and gentlemanly, his abstinence from lewd behavior was, she had to admit, making her even hornier.

Abstinence.

The word hit her brain like a sledgehammer, bringing her suddenly crashing back to the real world.

I can't!

The words were in her head as she breathlessly and reluctantly extricated herself from the kiss. Michael didn't try to force the issue. His arms still held her, strong and safe, but he let her lips detach from his. His breathing was as erratic as hers was, a tiny silver line of saliva linked their lips briefly as the separation was made.

"No. I can't," Gayle huskily whispered. "I'm sorry."

"It's okay," Michael said softly with a smile.

Fuck! Feels like my heart is going to beat out of my chest!

"No. It's...not you okay. I...." She leaned forward and put her forehead on his chest.

Tell him, 'Inner-Gayle' practically shouted at her. *Tell him!*

Her hands shook, and she wanted to cry. More than that, she desperately wanted to drag this man back into her apartment and spread herself wide for him and let him fuck her into oblivion. Her body felt like a live wire, charged with so much sexual energy.

Twelve months. Almost twelve months!

Was this her? Or was it her genetics?

How could she be sure? How could she know?

She gently but firmly pushed him away. He didn't resist.

"It's okay," he said softly. "I'm sorry if I... I'm a little tipsy, I think."

She shook her head vehemently and felt the tears welling in her eyes. Floods of emotion surging through her.

"It's not what you think...I...I have to go. But thank you...for a lovely night and for being...well...wonderful."

She bounced up to her tip toes again and placed her lips on his one more time. Gentle and not as urgent. A kiss goodbye;

not a kiss that sought more. As much as she really wanted the latter, she held herself to the former. Yet even with this revised agenda for locking lips, she lingered longer than was simply polite. She was trying to send him a message – this was a goodbye with meaning.

As she felt the moment slip away, she grabbed desperate hold of what limited mental faculties her biological impulses had left her with and turned away from Michael Reynolds, fleeing up the steps to her apartment building.

Don't look back! Don't look back!

She looked back with a bashful smile, reciprocated by the man who stood waiting for her to safely get inside.

Vaguely, she registered the sound of her front door slamming shut behind her as she ran to the bedroom, practically tearing off her clothes as she made for the bed. She was naked by the time she hit the sheets face down with her right hand buried between her thighs. She squeezed her legs together clamping it there, holding it as she rolled over onto her back and let it push her to the heights of sweet ecstasy.

Gayle Knightley had never been one to struggle sexually, never been one to hold back when she felt the need to scratch an itch, but the speed in which she brought herself to a shuddering climax surprised even her.

Well, fuck, I needed that.

She lay there bathed in the glow of the streetlights from outside, dimly realizing that she had neglected to pull the curtains closed in the haste to run headlong into her much-needed masturbation.

Was this cheating on her self-imposed vow of abstinence?

Staring at the ceiling she wondered whether this was allowed or not.

Am I just tempting myself?

How would she know when it was okay? When her therapist told her it was okay? Or is this a decision she could make for herself?

It'll be okay when you tell him the truth, 'Inner-Gayle' said wisely. *It's not rocket science.*

She closed her eyes and sighed, knowing once again that

the bitch was probably right.

| 71 |

BEING HONEST

– Michael Reynolds –
– Saturday – London, England –

Well. This is a right fine mess you've gotten yourself into.
Michael wasn't referring to the epic hangover he was nursing the next morning, though that certainly didn't help. It was more that the copious amounts of alcohol he had consumed the night before put him a state of mind where he was predisposed to take stock of his life as it currently stood.

Trouble was, the more he dissected it, the worse it looked.

He lay back, head propped on a double stack of soft pillows. The curtains were open just enough to send a sliver of sunlight across the crumpled black bedsheets that covered his nakedness from the waist down. His head continued to throb rhythmically as he stared at the ceiling, his cellphone lying on his chest. To call, or not to call...that was the quandary.

What are you doing, Mike?
He couldn't even begin to fathom the depths of Gayle's emotional troubles, or the root cause of them. Sigmund Freud he was not. Yet he did have a strong sense of empathy for her and what she was going through. He'd witnessed the death of friends and colleagues; it came with the territory as a soldier. To lose her whole team – her surrogate family – in one fellswoop had broken her. No. Bowed maybe, but she wasn't broken.

Gayle was made of sterner stuff that even she gave herself credit for. The tough exterior she projected lately was all for show; she had a reputation to uphold after all. But there were moments when the facade cracked, when she gave an honest insight into what was going on in her head. He suspected those glimpses were her subconscious forcing her to get the help it needed, but each time she recognized what she was doing, the armor went back on.

At least she was confronting her problems, however sporadic her progress might be. He knew, for instance, that she was reluctantly seeing a therapist, slowly processing her trauma bit by bit. Contrast that to his own method – the fine art of digging a deep mental hole and burying his issues in it. Followed by a strict regimen of ignoring the issue for as long as possible.

Gayle had hinted on more than one occasion that she was going to try and live to his standard. She had gone so far as to warn him off her. Not because she thought him unworthy of her, but because she considered herself to be damaged goods. She thought that made her unworthy of him. Which was bullshit. Her wounds, both mental and physical, had resulted in a splinter in her psyche, and splinters needed to be removed before they caused infection. She at least was trying to exorcise hers.

So why was he letting *his* splinter fester?

In truth, he was as damaged as she was. He simply hid it better.

Five weeks. It felt like so much longer. Her turnaround, while incomplete, had been remarkable. She had quickly migrated from the angry bitch who interrupted his class, to the vivacious but troubled soul who joined him in emptying two bottles of tequila and attracted his attention as a potential lover.

Two bottles...he shook his head at the memory.

The chemistry between them was undeniable and was only getting stronger. Was it irresponsible for them to be circling each other like this? Both were carrying the scars of a past from which they needed to move on. Was this potentially causing more harm to them both? Or were they a conduit to heal each other's wounds? And even if that was the case, was it healthy?

Maybe.

Could he honestly say that he had done *anything* about resolving his own issues up till now? He had run to London, a haven for him to escape the mess he left behind, the bridges he burned. None of it was his fault. At least that was what he told himself, but the truth was that he had handled things very poorly. He couldn't turn back the clock, but he did find himself wanting to follow the example Gayle was setting.

If she was trying hard to be a better person for him, then it was up to him to follow suit. To be worthy of her. So, yes, maybe this *was* healthy. Aren't partners supposed to bring out the best in each other? Encourage each other to be better?

He picked up the phone and unlocked it with a swipe of his thumb. The brightly colored screen stared back at him, but he made no effort to do anything with it. He gazed at it, locked in a state of indecision. He needed to fix things, needed to set things right, and that started with being honest. To everyone, including Gayle. He looked at his phone again and locked it. He needed to do this properly, and that was face-to-face.

The decision was made.

He untangled himself from the sheets and levered himself out of the bed, quickly dressing before he changed his mind. Within a few minutes, he was stepping out of his front door and into a pleasant London afternoon. A clear sky uncluttered by clouds and a bright sunshine that had raised the temperature to a level where he wouldn't need a jacket greeted him. Besides, he didn't have far to go.

He broke into a light jog, heading out with a renewed sense of purpose.

| 72 |

BLOOD TO EARTH

– Lyssa Balthazaar –
– Monday – Albany, New Victus –

Look at the stars, little sister. They came out for you.

Lyssa gazed wistfully upward. As a child, Vanessa had adored counting stars in a clear night sky, always responding with a playful giggle when she saw them.

Like sprinkles on a chocolate cake.

That was what she would call them. She dreamt about being an astronaut, fantasizing about what was up there beyond the range of her tiny telescope. Surely, she reasoned, if the Earth housed such a wide variety of life, then there *must* be more out there in the black?

Lyssa had never really considered it – her own belief system deeply rooted in the religious – but Vanessa was a dreamer who had never been one for the tenets of faith. She had no time for ethereal beings and musings on an afterlife. She wouldn't appreciate the funeral that was about to take place. She would, however, unquestionably have appreciated the view.

Maybe it was the succubus in her, but Vanessa had always felt emotions far more acutely than Lyssa. She fell in love easily and without reservation, a trait that made her childishly naïve and easily manipulated by someone who knew how to use that to his advantage.

She knew who.

440

What she didn't have yet was evidence.

Or know why.

Lyssa *would* uncover the truth and Storm would rue the day he decided to mess with her family. When that time came, Lyssa wouldn't hide behind lies and misdirection. She would confront and kill the man with her own bloodied fangs. He would know the face of his killer as she sank her vengeful teeth into his neck and tore out his throat.

Realizing her fist was clenched hard and her fingernails were in danger of drawing her own blood from the pressure, she tried to relax. Deep breaths. She glanced at her watch, an elegant timepiece in shiny silver with a black dial. Midnight was approaching.

It was time.

Traditionally the ritual should be done in the Sacred Hall of Balthazaar, on the ornate stone altar that lay above the sleeping place of their ancestors. Vanessa's illness and the circumstances of her death meant that to try it would have been controversial at best. Yet, in many ways, Lyssa knew that Vanessa would prefer it this way.

Just let me say goodbye somewhere beautiful, she would have said.

So here, in a field to the west of Albany near a small copse of trees, Lyssa would lay her troubled younger sibling to rest.

She reached down and gently picked up the edges of the elegant cloth that draped her sister and pulled them aside. Vanessa lay beneath the moon and the stars, just as her ancestors had when they were born. Lyssa made a mental note to thank Damian for putting her body in the life support pod for transport home. Vanessa looked at peace, like she was simply sleeping. The pod had kept her flesh soft, her blood fluid; preserving her for the ritual. She didn't know if that had been by luck or design. Either way, she was grateful for the chance to perform the ceremony unchanged.

There were only a few others present. Their other sister Nykola and a handful of close family members that Lyssa had entrusted with Vanessa's secret.

Nobody spoke as Lyssa knelt next to the low dais that she

abruptly realized wasn't as makeshift as it perhaps should have been. Mercy's doing of course. She had taken the time and effort to ensure that this low wooden alter wasn't merely a hastily assembled pile of wood. It was an ornately carved piece of *art*. Lyssa could make out the Vampyrii lettering etched into the edges, detailing the passages of their gods.

The scripture of the Blood to Earth ritual.

It had been a *long* time since she had spoken them.

"Our race was born of the holy union..."

A tremor shook her voice as she felt a conflict of emotion. Fear that she would forget these important words, and an overwhelming stab of grief. This was the beginning of the finality to her relationship with Vanessa. Was she truly ready to let go?

"When Solista, goddess of the Sun, turned away from Tellus, the Earth god, he and the goddess of the Moon, Nocturne, consummated their secret love and conceived Vampyrii."

She could hear the shaking in her voice as the recitation caught in her throat.

"Our father, Tellus, summoned the River of Blood, and fashioned for us bodies from the mud of its bed. We were molded, given physical form. Unseeing. Unthinking. Unknowing. As children of their union, we emerged as innocents. These bodies were his gift. Our eyes with which to appreciate his glory. Our legs with which to kneel before him. Our ears with which to behold his wisdom. Our hearts...to give home to our eternal devotion.

"As The Twelve crawled from the River, they cast their eyes to the heavens and the diamond stars at the neck of their mother, Nocturne. She, in return, looked benevolently upon them, finding them worthy of her gifts. One by one she placed a diamond in their hearts as she named them, bestowing upon each an aspect of her divine self.

Akhza. She of the Passion.

Haggari. He of the Faithful.

Izzicar. She of the Sea.

Khirion. He of the Land.

Jareb. She of the Confident.

Tarnhem. He of the Sky.
Lucasz. She of the Logic.
Vardan. He of the Courage.
Psyionicella. She of the Imagination
Yaznuma. He of the Strong.
Skarling. She of the Kind.
Balthazaar. He of the Wisdom."

As tradition dictated, the head of her own House was placed last on the list. Lyssa needed a moment to steady her voice as grief threatened to push an irresistible flood of tears to her eyes. When she was finally able to, she continued.

"Vanessa of House Balthazaar. Your mortal life has ended, your time has come. Tellus and Nocturne are waiting to welcome you home."

She carefully took the ceremonial blade from where it lay next to Vanessa and removed its sheath of snow-white silk. A double-ended dagger of mirror-finished steel, its blades gleaming in the moonlight that flashed crimson off the central ruby-studded grip. She gripped the black leather tightly, and it felt warm to her touch. Both the large main blade, and the smaller blade that protruded from the hilt, had been honed to an edge finer than the sharpest-cutthroat.

Tenderly, she took her sister's right wrist and, using the smaller blade, deftly sliced a line across her pale skin before leaving it to dangle off the altar's edge. Gravity would now do the work of Vanessa's unbeating heart. Blood started to slowly drip from the severed artery, pooling on the ground and sinking into the dirt.

"It is time for you to return to Tellus what was once given. To the Earth, we return your blood."

She walked around the altar slowly and performed the same delicate action on the left wrist.

"To the Earth, we return the life that was gifted to you."

She positioned herself above her sister and used the blade to deftly nick Vanessa's jugular, before gently turning her head to the side to allow the blood to drain more easily. As a trickle of dark crimson started to meander across her perfect pale skin, Lyssa bent down and kissed Vanessa's head softly before she embarked on the final part of the ritual.

She turned the knife around and positioned the larger, stiletto-type blade over her sister's heart. Its slender blade ended with a needle-like point that dimpled the skin of Vanessa's breast. Lyssa held her breath and concentrated on steadying her hand before pushing down hard. She felt the knife break the skin easily and slide between the ribs.

"And as your blood returns to the ground from whence it came," her voice broke, "Nocturne calls upon your soul."

Her thumb depressed one of the rubies embedded in the handle. The hidden button released a chemical from microscopic holes in the blade which reacted swiftly with Vampire physiology. Vanessa's body dissolved into the finest dust in front of her eyes, gently dispersing on the breeze into the night air.

"Go to her in peace, my sister."

Then she was gone. Leaving nothing on the alter but the silk of the burial shroud and the gleaming blade of the knife held tightly in Lyssa's hand. In the bloodied dirt, a ring of silver with sapphire stones glinted in the moonlight. Lyssa picked it up, holding it firmly in her grasp.

She looked up at the stars, the domain of Nocturne and the new home for her fallen sibling. She was safe now – there was nothing more this world or Sebastian Storm could do to hurt her. As Lyssa looked at the diamonds sparkling above her in the indigo sky, she swore an oath.

This all had to end.

She had much to do.

| 73 |

BEAUTIFUL STRANGER

– Mercy balthazaar –
– Monday – Nexus City, Iceland –

"Oh, my gods..." Mercy whispered under her breath as she took in every detail from behind her darkened glasses.

"Stunning, isn't it?"

"Like *nothing* I've ever seen before," she murmured, turning to see who had asked the question.

"Fae technology at its most sublime," he said with a warm smile.

She knew him from the video footage and photographs she had collated as part of her intelligence duties, but meeting him in the flesh gave Mercy a small thrill of excitement. He looked younger than his age on file; only the gentle peppering of grey in his hair and goatee betrayed him. He was handsome, with striking emerald eyes, just like his eldest daughter.

"Ambassador Knightley," she extended her hand. "Mercy balthazaar. I'm honored to meet you, sir."

"The honor is all mine, I assure you. Please, call me Jaymes." His hand firmly grasped hers. "At least while we're in the informal setting of the Atrium."

So, this is the Atrium.

Lyssa had told her about this place; it was everything she had described and more. The gentle waterfall drew your attention first. A crystal-clear cascade into a man-made lagoon of dazzling azure, where fish darted playfully beneath its rippling surface. It subtly dominated the room, providing both a picturesque backdrop, and unobtrusive ambient noise. It was the epitome of understated beauty.

The perfect place for a first kiss.

"Lyssa described this place..." Mercy whispered. "I didn't get the chance to see it the last time I was here. Is that real grass? Real sand?"

Jaymes nodded.

"Try removing your glasses," he said, and then noting her hesitation, "I promise you...it's safe."

The sun shone brightly in the sky above the transparent domed roof today, but she trusted him. She closed her eyes and slipped off her glasses, took a deep breath, and then tentatively cracked them open. What she saw made her open them wide.

Colors like she had never witnessed before.

"Oh, my..." She couldn't finish the sentence.

Around the lagoon, the floor transitioned from shimmering gold to a verdant green as it sloped up out of the water. Genuine trees and plants provided a refuge for brightly colored birds and insects that fluttered and flitted about, pursuing their own business. The Atrium was an explosion of vivid colors from every nook and cranny of the spectrum.

How is this possible?

Her eyes watered. Was it tears of joy or the heightened brightness? While surprisingly tolerable, the ambient light still stung her sensitive eyes, yet as the tears ran down her cheeks, she knew the truth. She gazed upward at the dome high above her, trying to figure out what made this miracle possible, and observed that the glass must be polarized. She moved her head back and forth while looking at the sun and noticed that the polarization seemed to follow her eyeline.

"Before you ask, I honestly don't know how it works," Jaymes laughed gently and shrugged. "Fae magic."

"Magic..." Mercy repeated, still staring upward.

"I hear you are here to proxy for Lyssa Balthazaar?"

"She has a personal matter to attend to," Mercy nodded,

forcing her attention back toward him.

"Such a shame. I was suitably impressed by her manner when we met at the gala evening. I was very much looking forward to her being here. Nothing too serious, I hope."

A statement. He wasn't fishing for information, simply expressing a sentiment. Even so, Mercy found herself unconsciously offering an honest response.

"A bereavement, unfortunately."

The ambassador bowed his head slightly and looked truly sympathetic.

"I'm sorry to hear that. Please, relay our condolences for her loss to your..." He paused for a moment, apparently unsure of the relationship between Lyssa and Mercy. "...sister?"

"Aunt," Mercy shook her head gently.

"Apologies. I assumed by your surname..."

"No, I'm a balthazaar with a lower case 'b,'" Mercy explained. "Technically, I'm a half-blood, born of Balthazaar's seventh daughter, Johanna...my father is Human. Some Houses wouldn't consider me 'pure,' and I would have been ostracized. Balthazaar is not so prejudiced. I was accepted as a half-blood granddaughter, hence the non-capitalization."

"Well, you have taught me something new today. I had no clue such tradition existed in New Victus."

"It's not a well-observed tradition. Other Houses, such as the Grand Chancellor's..." She paused trying to find the right diplomatic word, eventually settling on one. "...*frown* upon such an arrangement."

Jaymes regarded her, as if carefully weighing up his next statement.

"When Lyssa was here for the Gala it was evident that she has...strong feelings about the Grand Chancellor," he said diplomatically.

"That is somewhat of an understatement. It is fortunate that I've run into you, Ambassador..."

"Oh, there's nothing fortunate about it." Jaymes smiled warmly. "I saw the arrival of your flyer and came to greet who I assumed would be Lyssa."

"I'm sorry to disappoint," Mercy said with a smile.

"Good lord, no," Jaymes shook his head. "Your attendance is a surprise, certainly. Yet a most welcome one."

There was something effortlessly attractive about Jaymes Knightley. He had a manner that made you enjoy spending time in his presence. Mercy could see how that could easily translate into something more akin to romance under the right conditions. The ambassador was polite, charming, with not an ounce of pomp or prejudice. He was the type of man not often seen in the patriarchal society of New Victus since StormHall had come to power. It made for a refreshing change.

"I have documents," she said hesitantly. "Proposal documents for the NAA and Pack Nation delegations. I'm...not an experienced diplomat and Lyssa told me that if I needed help...then to ask you or your wife. That I could trust you. You made quite an impression on her, which isn't easy. Believe me."

"The opinion is mutual," he said quietly, his face sobering. "For all we talk about hope around here, it has been in short supply over recent years. Lyssa gave us a feeling of...optimism."

"You're not alone in that, Jaymes. I would be grateful for your advice. What we are proposing is...somewhat revolutionary in terms of New Victus thinking. Which is why the Grand Chancellor wanted Lyssa to pitch the proposal to the NAA and Pack Nation. As I said, I have no experience in diplomacy, so I was hoping that, as a neutral third party, you might be able to advise me."

"The Federation *does* have a military assistance pact in place with the NAA and a peace treaty in effect with Pack Nation...we have no such policy in place with New Victus. So, alas, we are hardly neutral."

"Ah, of course," Mercy nodded and laughed nervously trying to hide her disappointment. "You see...rookie mistake."

"However," Jaymes said with a conspiratorial raising of his eyebrow, "I wouldn't see anything wrong with inviting you for dinner tonight. As a way for us to establish a dialogue between our respective cultures. And if you felt like talking about where you'd like to see New Victus go in the future – hypothetically, of course – then I'm sure I could be forthcoming with my own opinions."

"Your 'hypothetical' opinions, of course."

"Of course."

"Dining with you and your wife sounds like the ideal way to spend my first evening in Nexus."

"Serlia is away currently, so it'll just be the two of us. I hope that doesn't make you uncomfortable?"

Mercy shook her head and smiled. "Not at all."

"Splendid. Shall we say eight o'clock? I shall prepare us dinner and we can talk while we eat. I'm unfamiliar with Vampyrii tastes – is there anything you don't eat?"

Mercy laughed. "Contrary to your popular myths, our diet is generally the same as yours. For myself, however, I'm vegetarian, so...no meat, thank you."

Jaymes nodded. "I shall send an invitation to the terminal in your quarters with a map detailing how to get to ours. I'll inform border control that you'll be crossing to our sector tonight."

"That would be helpful. Again, thank you."

He extended his hand to take Mercy's, and for a moment, she thought he was going to bend and gallantly kiss it. That was what Sebastian StormHall would have done, intending the gesture to be something grand and gentlemanly, yet actually coming across as creepy and sinister. Jaymes, however, gently shook it in a grip that was firm, but not overpowering.

"Until tonight then, Miss balthazaar."

"Ambassador," she replied, returning the handshake in kind.

| 74 |

FAMILY VISIT

– Allyson Knightley –
– Tuesday – London, England –

"General." Ally extended her hand. "Welcome to Nexus."

Norbel smiled at her as he descended the ramp of his personal flyer, moving from the dimly lit interior and out into the sunset shadows.

"No need for such formalities, Allyson."

"Simply extending you the courtesies, Uncle."

As he stepped onto the asphalt of the landing pad, he hugged her with his free arm. She returned his embrace tightly, using both of hers.

"It is good to see you," he said softly.

"You too. I didn't get word you were coming till your final approach. Business or pleasure?"

"A little of both." He responded to her question by patting the silver attaché case he was carrying. "I have documents to deliver to your parents that are ready for the conference, but also, it has been too long since I saw my nieces. I hear that Carrie-Anne is here, too?"

"She is," Ally nodded, leading her uncle toward the entrance to the main complex. "She's here trying to wangle a travel permit to visit NordScania for her next big story."

Norbel paused and gestured toward the Security Centre.

"Should we not—" he started before Ally shook her head

and cut him off.

"You've just landed behind the delegates from the NAA and there are dozens of them currently being checked through." She grinned. "Which is why it's your lucky day that you have a niece who is the Chief of Security and can sneak you in the back way. Come on."

Norbel smiled gratefully to her and they set off across the landing field. As they turned, Allyson paused. She thought she saw...something out of the corner of her eye. A fleeting impression of someone in the shadows below her uncle's ship. She hesitated, her eyes slowly scanning the landing pad and the airfield, not sure precisely what she was looking for.

Nothing stood out as suspicious, even though the hairs on the back of Allyson's neck were standing upright. Just the usual commotion of the SkyPort. Passengers heading for the terminal and the ground-crews fettling aircraft for a quick turnaround.

"Allyson?"

Her eyes flicked across the shadows beneath his flyer one last time. The ramp was finishing its ascent, closing with a gentle clunk and a hiss as it resealed the aircraft's interior. Pursing her lips slightly, she took a deep breath and turned back to face him, smiling reassuringly.

"It's nothing," she said. "Security has been on edge for a few weeks now. The Summit is a big deal at the best of times, but as this is the ten-year anniversary... It's got us all jumping at shadows a little."

"It never hurts to be vigilant, Allyson."

"Of course not," Ally said quietly.

She wondered what he would say if he knew she – the Nexus Security Chief – had slept with a New Victus ambassador.

Firmly pushing aside such thoughts, she led them to the main building. As the doors whispered open, they both displayed their ID cards to the security guards stationed there and were ushered in with little fuss or interest.

Ally tried to cajole her uncle into idle conversation as they walked, but Norbel had never been one for small talk. She loved her uncle, but the sooner she handed him over to her mother, the better. With that in mind she decided to lead them on a shortcut down the main concourse and through the Atrium.

The area was an immediate contradiction of themes, busy today with the hustle and bustle of diplomatic life contrasting sharply with the tranquility of nature. It shouldn't work, but oddly it did. There were a hundred different places to sit and talk, many of the most important diplomatic decisions of the last decade having been hashed out at the picnic tables that basked in the presence of this calmative beauty. Two opposing parties could have the bitterest of debates in any number of the conference or meeting rooms but bring them here and suddenly compromises were reached, and friendships forged. Allyson had long debated if the effect this area had on people was by design, or whether it was a purely a happy residual result.

"Such an exquisite place."

Allyson glanced at her uncle and smiled. He looked as if he were seeing the Atrium for the first time, his eyes flitting around and drinking in every marvelous detail, from brightly colored birds flitting between the trees, to the dragonflies skimming the surface of the rippling waters

"Probably my favorite place to be in Nexus City," Ally nodded. "It's all pretty spectacular here, but this place...this is really something else."

Glancing back to her uncle, she saw him regarding her with an odd look. She raised an eyebrow in a silent enquiry, and he laughed.

"I was just thinking how...pleasant it is to be here with you. I am looking forward to seeing Carrie, too. Things have been..." He paused for a second before continuing. "...less than pleasant dealing with your older sibling."

Allyson had wondered how long it would take before the conversation would turn to the subject of Gayle. She could understand what her uncle was trying to do by recruiting Gayle to the Academy. He was simultaneously trying to protect her, while also trying to keep her in the game, so to speak.

However, she also empathized with what her sister was going through. Gayle wanted to get back to work, to exact some retribution for what had happened to her friends. As a woman more prone to action than inaction, Gayle was always going to rail against Norbel's approach She wanted to work through her issues in a very *physical* manner. Yet she was not in the right place to pursue that agenda.

"All us Knightley girls have the same problem. We're headstrong, driven, and like doing things our own way. She's coming around, though. She's a whole lot better than she was after..." Allyson didn't need to complete the sentence. "She's going through a process. She'll be fine."

"You are confident of that?" Norbel asked oddly.

"Yes. I'm sure," Ally chuckled lightly. "Why?"

Norbel shook his head and gave an expression that indicated a shrug, yet his shoulders stayed exactly where they were.

"What she went through...losing her team, her friends. I would have thought it would break most people."

"Not Gayle," Allyson said confidently as they came to a halt outside her parents' suite. "She'll lick her wounds and come out swinging again. Trust me on that."

"I hope you are correct. Will you be joining us for dinner tonight?"

"I'll be there. I just have a few duties to attend to after I drop you off with Mum," Allyson nodded. "With today being Halloween, it adds an extra wrinkle to my responsibilities. You'd think in this day and age, kids would be discouraged from dressing as monsters...but the tradition persists."

"I can imagine the difficulties of policing Halloween in a mixed species community such as this," Norbel nodded.

"When is a Vampire not a Vampire?" Ally laughed.

"And your sister Carrie, will she be in attendance this evening?"

"Carrie is a law unto herself, so who knows?" Ally shrugged. "Most likely, though."

"Excellent." Norbel smiled as they arrived outside the door to Jaymes and Serlia's apartment. "Until tonight then."

Ally leaned in and gave her uncle a light peck on the cheek. "Until tonight."

| 75 |

LADIES NIGHT

– Gayle Knightley –
– Friday – London, England –

"You feeling okay, Sis?"

Gayle lifted her stare from the glass she was fiddling with, drawing patterns in the condensation, and cast a quizzical look at her sister.

"Yeah, fine. Why do you ask?"

"Because," Allyson said with a slight slur, "I've just spent three days having to sit through family dinners with Mum and Dad and Uncle Norbel, and I'm in need of conversation about a topic more exciting than politics. But you've barely said a word since you got here."

Gayle stared at her glass of decidedly non-alcoholic iced water again and sighed.

"Just...tired, I guess. Long week."

"Well, buck up." Ally swished the dregs of her vodka around the bottom of her glass before necking the rest of it in one gulp. "Because this is my *last* free couple of days before the Summit takes over my life, and I intend to enjoy them. And to assist me I need willing volunteers because it's no fun drinking alone."

"Well...Carrie should be here soon," Gayle muttered.

As if on cue, the door to the bar abruptly opened, admitting both a rush of frigid air and a sodden young woman in a long brown, woolen coat. Her head was covered down to her eyes in a cozy, black knit hat from which a few strands of her lilac hair could be seen escaping. She spotted them immediately and made a beeline for their table.

"Well, that was spooky..." Ally laughed.

"What was spooky?" Carrie asked as she shed her hat, coat, and scarf and sat down.

"Gayle predicting your arrival to the second," Ally said by way of explanation, pushing the spare water glass toward her and nodding in the direction of the bottle of wine that she was carrying. Carrie looked at the wine bottle and then at the tumbler with an arched eyebrow.

"What?" Ally snorted. "Like you're too good to drink wine from a tumbler?"

"I thought we'd be meeting at Barnun?" Carrie said, refusing to rise to her sister's bait. "And the wine was for later. At home."

"Well, unless you want vodka or beer or..." Ally paused for a moment to stare in disdain at Gayle's glass. "...tap water, then I suggest you pop your cork and get pouring."

Carrie looked at her bottle, then the tumbler, and finally glanced wistfully at the bar.

"Don't even think about it," Gayle laughed. "A classy establishment this is not."

"So, remind me why we're in this dive bar?"

"Because, Carrie, my dearest little sister, our other sibling—"

"That'll be me!" Ally interrupted.

"—disgraced herself at Barnun a couple of weeks ago."

"I was a *very* drunken monkey," Ally nodded.

"Anyway," Gayle continued, "I figured a change would be good for this evening. Plus, it's close to my place for when some of us stagger home later..."

"Me again!" Ally giggled.

"...and it's quiet here."

Carrie frowned and looked dubiously at the cleanliness of the glass she had been offered.

"For a good reason," Gayle muttered.

After a moment, Carrie's desire to drink wine won out, and she pulled the glass toward her, opened the bottle, and poured a generous helping. She threw back a large gulp of the claret liquid, closed her eyes, and sighed in pleasure.

Gayle chuckled at Carrie's blissful expression.

"By the way," she said, "I read your article on conditions in Alaska. Really thought-provoking piece, Sis. The hard winter and the food struggles. Gotta be tough out there."

"It is." Carrie grinned. "I'm glad you liked it."

"I loved it," Gayle nodded.

"Thanks. That means a lot."

"Hey, I read it, too," Ally slurred. "I also thought it was top-notch."

"Thanks." Carrie blushed and smiled proudly.

Regardless of where their lives had taken them, the Knightley sisters had always maintained an unbreakable sibling bond. It helped considerably that there were just four years separating the eldest, Gayle, from the youngest, Carrie. They diligently looked out for each other in all aspects of their lives. Gayle had earned Carrie's trust by critiquing some of her early, frankly substandard, work, so when she now said she liked something, Carrie knew it was not simply lip service. No bullshit. Honesty always.

That was *supposed* to be the long-standing sisterly pact.

"So, how's the knee?"

"S'fine," Gayle answered, immediately betraying the pact.

"Now tell Carrie the truth," Ally said, immediately calling her on it.

"Sore," Gayle sighed, remembering how futile it was trying to lie to Allyson.

Her younger sister had a compulsion to find truth, a character trait she backed up with a little pheromone trick of her own. Hers acted to compel people to tell the truth, a knack that came in extremely handy as a cop. Even without it, though, Ally had an uncanny intuition for knowing when somebody wasn't being truthful.

Gayle jokingly referred to her as a Human lie detector.

"Be patient. It'll heal," Carrie reassured her.

"It's already a lot better than it was. Despite me falling on my arse and bumping it the other morning."

"It's that bloody CombatSkin and your obsession with heels!" Ally rolled her eyes. "Just wear it in flats-mode, for fuck's sake!"

"I wasn't in heels," Gayle protested. "Or my CombatSkin for that matter. I was running in the park and tripped. End of story."

"Oh, how I've missed this bickering..." Carrie smiled. "It's been a while."

"It's been *too* long." Ally hugged her younger sister drunkenly.

"How many has she had already?" Carrie laughed.

Gayle smiled and gestured to the nearly empty bottle. "That much. I'm on water tonight. She was sober-ish for a while, but you're late."

"I have not drunken that much! Yet," Ally protested with a slur that told quite the opposite story. "I offered Gayle a glass, but she's obtaining..."

"Abstaining," Gayle corrected.

"Oh, my God, are you pregnant?" Allyson hissed, eyes suddenly very wide.

"What?" Gayle screwed up her face. "No! I'm...abstaining."

"Sex or alcohol?" Carrie asked.

"Both...I guess." Gayle slumped in her seat. "The latter because it usually leads to the former. And the former...well, you know why. Can we change the subject?"

"Hell, no!" Ally shook her head vehemently. "Carrie needs to know about your new love life!"

"I don't have a love life," Gayle protested.

"Yes, you do," Ally slurred.

"Ah, yes," Carrie laughed. "The mysterious...Malcolm?"

"Michael." Gayle smiled.

Carrie looked at Ally, who looked sideways back at Carrie with a knowing smile, a sly nod, and a raised eyebrow.

"See?"

"See what?" Gayle said.

"Well, just a month or so ago you called me to complain

about a number of things." Carrie started ticking off points on her fingers. "Firstly – to quote you – your stupid fucking therapist; Mum and Dad interfering in your life; Uncle Norbel; and finally, some stick-in-the-mud that you'd been paired up with at the Academy."

"Oh, come on!" Gayle protested. "Be fair. That was my first day back and I was having a really bad day."

"But now he's...Michael," Ally interjected.

"Michael, with a smile," Carrie finished breathlessly.

"Yeah," Allyson giggled. "And have you noticed the lack of swearing from our previously potty-mouthed older sister? That's 'The Michael Effect.'" Allyson made air quotes with her fingers as she said the last few words.

"Fuck. You," Gayle huffed as if to prove them wrong. She sat back in her seat to the raucous laughter of her sisters. "Fuck both of you."

She was still trying to deal with the feelings that the previous night had fostered within her. The situation was not a source of amusement for her. Evidently her sisters disagreed.

"Michael is *the* one," Ally purred.

Gayle shot her a look that could kill in an effort to stem the conversation before it started.

"Don't you dare, Ally," she said pointing an accusatory finger. "*You* did enough damage with the phone message."

Allyson just held her hands up to proclaim her innocence. Carrie laughed.

"What makes this different to that other guy you used to screw around with? Torbert?"

"Torbar," Gayle corrected.

"Yeah, him," Carrie nodded. "You went back to that well a number of times, if I recall."

Gayle shrugged. "Well, turned out he was a massive dick."

She realized what she had said a moment after the words left her lips. Ally burst out laughing, thumping the table with her hand, and Carrie started giggling uncontrollably.

"I thought that's what you were looking for?" Ally cackled, apparently proud of her own little double entendre.

"I don't do that anymore," Gayle said quietly.

Her cheeks blushed slightly, part annoyance and part embarrassment. Surprisingly, even in her drunken state, it was Ally who tipped to the reason for Gayle's reticence first.

"Oh, God...I'm so sorry. I totally spaced," she said sounding suddenly sober. "How long has it been now?"

"Ten months, give or take."

"Fuck." Carrie suddenly snapped into the same mind-set. "I'm...I honestly...I didn't mean to make light of it."

"I know you didn't." Gayle reached up to scratch her head, a gesture that morphed into her running her fingers back through her hair. "I'm sorry. My issues should *not* be causing a problem on girls' night. We used to be able to talk about this stuff all the time, and we still should. So...we had...a moment."

"You and Torbar?" Allyson looked confused.

"I'm assuming she means with Michael," Carrie clarified.

"That *would* make more sense," Ally nodded.

"I kissed him," Gayle said simply.

"Did he kiss you?" Ally clapped with barely contained glee.

Gayle nodded and grinned, much wider than she meant to. The memory was still fresh in her mind, vivid like a daydream. The touch of his hands, the soft press of his lips, the taste of tequila on his tongue as he...

"Hold on," Carrie broke her reverie. "Back up. I feel like you've buried the lead here. What's this Michael like?"

"I met him. He's a top bloke. Hot, too," Ally chipped in.

"Allyson!" Gayle hissed.

"What? I might be gay, but I'm not blind."

Gayle rolled her eyes, but the truth was she wouldn't have brought up the kiss if she truly didn't want to talk about this. Her sisters were her sounding board and their opinions mattered. She took a deep breath and launched herself into it.

"Anyway, I finished going through the first of the kids' assignments on Friday. It was late already. Michael popped his head in to see how I was, so...I took the leap and asked him if he wanted to hang out. So we went for drinks.

"Well, we grabbed a couple of bottles of tequila and started playing this game. One of us would ask a question, the other would answer either truthfully or not. The questioner would then guess whether the answer was true or false."

"Risky," mused Ally. "That game can lead to *many* a dark place."

"It was just to get to know each other. Things got serious, then they got...flirty. We left around three in the morning and he walked me home. That's when I kissed him. And that led to me feeling...something else..."

"I'll bet," Allyson snorted.

"Cryptic," Carrie said thoughtfully.

"Do I need to spell it out?" Gayle hissed as if her sisters should know what she was hinting at.

"She means it made her horny," Allyson shrugged.

Gayle nodded and buried her warm, blushing face in her hands.

"Well, isn't that kind of natural?" Carrie said quizzically. "A night out, a bottle of tequila, and a hot guy kissing you...who wouldn't feel horny?"

"That's not the point," Gayle growled in frustration. "And not that it matters, but I didn't actually drink a *drop* of tequila that night. I was stone-cold sober."

"I'm still not sure I see the problem..."

"I do," Allyson said softly.

"Does one of you want to explain it to me?" Carrie laughed.

"When do you know that you're falling in love," Allyson said while staring at Gayle, "and when it's just...biology?"

Despite her advanced level of inebriation, Allyson had just put into words the thoughts that were preying on Gayle's mind.

"I know I slept with Gabriel, and I loved him in a platonic way," she said. "And I know I was in love with Torbar—"

"You were *not* in love with Torbar," Carrie interrupted, shaking her head.

"I was with Torbar for almost a year...".

"That wasn't love. It was just fucking." Allyson confirmed her sister's opinion. "As I clarified for you last time I was here."

"I'm frankly surprised you remember that night."

"You were in a relationship which was nothing more than a power game," Allyson continued. "You two were the alpha-dogs of your respective teams. You never loved each other because you never respected each other."

Gayle sighed. She knew Allyson, drunk as she was, had a point; was being insightful, even. It was an observation that brought her full circle back to Michael, and her current feelings. It brought her to an epiphany.

"Oh, fuck," she whispered.

Once again, however, her inebriated sister was ahead of her on that particular train of thought, vocalizing the very thoughts that were now racing through Gayle's head unchecked.

"I'll tell you something else," Ally said wagging her finger, "this whole new you that we're seeing...the teaching, the lack of swearing, the non-drinking, the doubt...it's all because you *do* respect Michael. More than you'll admit."

Bullseye again. All Gayle could do was nod and confess.

"That first time we met...I honestly could *not* have made a worse impression. Now Torbar...he'd have held that over my head and used it as a bat to beat me with. Michael didn't, though. When I went to him, ass in hand, and offered my apology, he just accepted it. In fact, the more time we spent working together, the more I found that I actually *wanted* to be around him. Something inside me responds to him. He makes me want to be the best me. I'd swear that he's pulling some sort of Fae pheromone trick on me, but I know he's not."

Ally and Carrie were now just listening to her. It was absolutely what she needed, and she found herself profoundly grateful.

"Everyone else I've ever slept with...there's always been an ulterior motive. Sometimes for me, sometimes for them. Michael, though...he doesn't want anything. He sees me in a way I don't see *myself*. Past the hair, the eyes, the powers, the scars and injuries...he sees *me*. And he makes me feel...beautiful."

"You *are* beautiful," Carrie said, reaching her hand across the table to cover Gayle's.

"I don't mean physically beautiful," Gayle explained. "I mean..."

"We know what you mean." Ally smiled at her. "And it's

about fucking time someone made you feel good about your-self."

"You sound like you've fallen for him already," Carrie said softly.

"Maybe. But how do I know for sure?"

Carrie looked at Ally. Ally looked at Carrie. They were both grinning slyly at each other.

"Our recommendation is," Ally continued, "that you should just sleep with the Texan dreamboat."

"You know I can't do the sex thing."

"Why not?" Carrie said. "Make him an exception. Break your vow for one night. We guarantee...you fuck him, you'll know."

"Again with this? Could you two *be* any more cryptic?" Gayle said in annoyance.

Carrie and Ally looked at each other conspiratorially, revel-ing in the secret that they shared. This wasn't the first time this particular mystery had been mentioned, especially in re-cent conversations. Neither was it the first time their furtive-ness had grated on her nerves. It rankled a little to feel left out of their exclusive club.

All the sex I've had and these two know something I don't? How is that even remotely possible?

"No one can be told what the Matrix is..." Carrie giggled.

"...You have to see it for yourself," Allyson finished.

"Don't quote my favorite movies at me!" Gayle shot back with a hint of irritation.

"Just trust us," Carrie said reassuringly.

"Okay, now can we change the subject please?" Gayle pleaded.

"Sure," Carrie nodded. "What to?"

"Actually, since we're talking about sex," Ally whispered. "I have news! I may, or may not, have slept with Lyssa Baltha-zaar."

"*Lyssa Balthazaar?*" Gayle felt her jaw drop.

"Yeah." Ally grinned. "I *definitely* slept with Lyssa Baltha-zaar."

"Lyssa..." Carrie frowned at her sister's mention of the

name. "Oh, she was at the gala! You two were..."

Allyson nodded, the smile still plastered to her face. "We may have spent the night together..."

"Ally!" Carrie looked at her, gob smacked. "She's Vampyrii!"

"So?" Allyson shrugged.

"I mean...Vampyrii!" Carrie repeated as if that explained everything. "Gayle, you going to weigh in here?"

Gayle shook her head and leaned back in her seat deciding to sit this one out, content to watch her two younger siblings debate the finer points of interspecies relations.

"I have recently had an encounter with her niece, which has somewhat...changed my view on Vampyrii," she admitted.

"See?" Allyson thumped the tabletop. "Even Gayle can look past old prejudices."

"Thanks..." Gayle muttered. "I think..."

"Ally, you can't have a relationship with a Vampyrii!"

"Now, that sounds just a tad bit racist," Ally frowned.

"It's nothing to do with race," Carrie argued. "It's to do with practicality. It's not like you can take a booty-call trip to New Victus."

"She can come to Nexus!"

"Ally, she's practically Vampyrii royalty!" Carrie retorted.

"Is she?"

"Yes!" Carrie looked at Allyson in disbelief. "I can't believe you're the Security Chief at the most important diplomatic center in the world and you don't know the details of Vampyrii society!"

"Well, to be fair," Ally said, pursing her lips, "there's a fuck ton of stuff to learn. Mum and Dad have been mentoring me, but it's been so busy..."

"My point is that she's the current active head of House Balthazaar. She's not going to be able to slum it with you in Nexus City!"

"Excuse me, 'slum it?'"

"You know what I mean!"

It was at this point that Gayle decided to be the voice of reason.

"I think what Carrie is trying to say," she interjected, "is that there is a level of impracticality in pursuing a relationship with someone who can't be in the same place that you can."

"Well, it's not like we're *actually* having a relationship. It was just the one night," Ally sighed. "I'll probably never see her again. But fuck...it was good sex!"

"Okay, that's enough," Gayle said with a grimace.

"Actually," Carrie said, suddenly looking very thoughtful, "Lyssa can go to more than *just* Nexus..."

"Explain yourself, woman." Ally slumped forward, her chin resting on the palm of her hand, elbows on the table. With her other hand, she refilled her glass. Again.

"I..." Carrie started and then paused for effect, "...am going to Russia."

"In your dreams," Ally snorted. "Nobody goes beyond The Wall."

"It's not a wall," Gayle corrected. "It's a mountain range."

"Well they call it 'The Wall,'" Ally rebutted.

"Nobody calls it 'The Wall,'" Gayle rolled her eyes. "Only those who've watched too much '*Game of Thrones*.'"

"I thought you loved that show?" Ally shot back.

"I do. I wish they'd finished it before the War," Gayle sighed.

"Read the books! At least he finished those," Carrie interjected.

"You know I'm not much of a reader..."

"Unless it's comic books," Ally chuckled.

Gayle ignored her and continued. "Which is why I know that the Clypeus Mountains do *not* resemble—"

"Regardless..." Carrie interrupted her sisters. "I got permission to go."

"Holy shit! Really?" Gayle exclaimed.

"*That's* why you talked Dad into getting you a meeting with the NordScanians!" Allyson exclaimed as the penny dropped.

"Yup. I'm going to see what's happening in Eastern Europe. Why has nothing been heard out of Russia for almost thirty years? *That's* the next big untold story. I mean...why is travel into Russian airspace strictly forbidden? What's happened to the millions of people that live there? Or lived there? Did Zǔguó have anything to do with it? And what *about* the Clypeus Mountains? I mean, a new mountain range springs up overnight and no one asks why? What are they protecting? Or what are they protecting us from?"

"All very excellent questions!" Ally nodded a little too enthusiastically.

Journalists like Carrie worked mostly online, publishing their work on the NewNet. She had made a name for herself writing serious pieces, like 'The Alaskan Crisis,' or 'The New Gods Revealed.' The more offbeat the story, the better Carrie liked it. The fate of Russia had been her personal Holy Grail for years now.

"Even the HFA doesn't operate beyond the Clypeus range," Gayle mused. "To be honest, I think Command will be more than happy if it stays quiet on the Eastern side."

"I'm sure, but don't you think that's all a bit...strange? That we don't know what's happened over there? That no satellites survey east of the wall—"

"See," Ally interrupted. "She calls it 'The Wall,' too..."

Carrie cast a glance at her sister

"...and nobody will even talk about it," she finished.

"Maybe...now that I think about it." Gayle shrugged. "But the NordScanians were the ones who created the Clypeus range. We've always assumed they just deal with whatever lurks beyond. We rarely even venture over the NordScanian border."

"Well, Ambassador Alzim granted me permission to go to Dragontop Mount." Carrie grinned. "And from there...the world is my oyster."

"I'd love to come with you," Gayle sighed. "Always wanted to see Dragontop up close."

"Come with me!" Carrie said with barely contained enthusiasm. "It would be awesome. You and I adventuring into the unknown..."

Gayle laughed, shaking her head. "I can't. I have responsibilities. Kids aren't gonna teach themselves. Besides, I don't have a visa."

"Well, let me sweeten the deal..." Carrie added cryptically. "Ambassador Alzim gave us *all* permission to go."

"When you say all...?"

"I mean me, you, and Ally."

"Road trip!" Ally shouted with a fist pump.

Carrie ignored her. "Actually, Alzim said someone called Balent gave us permission."

"Balent?" Gayle shook her head slowly. "Not a name I'm familiar with."

"I searched NewNet." Carrie pursed her lips. "All I found was a vague reference to him also being known as *The Dragon King*."

"Fuck!" Ally stared at them wide eyed. "Do you think he's an *actual* dragon?"

"No idea, but there's literally *nothing* else about him anywhere. Oh, and that visa, it's not *just* for us. It includes two other names."

"Two others?" Allyson asked.

"Lyssa Balthazaar is on the list. As is her niece Mercy."

"Hey, isn't Mercy the one you met the other day, Gayle?" Ally interrupted.

"Yeah, she is," Gayle smiled at the memory of a very pleasant evening.

There was something very odd about Carrie's news though, and the smile turned into a frown as Gayle started to really think it through.

"Hold on," she said after a beat. "So, nobody has seen hide nor hair from anyone in Eastern Europe for over a quarter of a century, and no one has been allowed to pass beyond the Clypeus Mountains to find out what's happened..."

"Well, it's rumored the Fae sometimes travel beyond, but they're unsubstantiated rumors at best. That's one of the things I want to look into..." Carrie interjected.

"Ask Mum," Gayle suggested. "Or Uncle Norbel."

"You don't think I've already tried that? Both of them mysteriously change the subject whenever I bring it up. I once asked Unc' outright and he just said it was classified. Which, if it is, then I can't find any reference to it. Just makes me more curious as to what's being hidden from us."

"Okay, so maybe the Fae know, but they're obviously not telling. They won't even let us take a peek with that satellite network. But suddenly, you ask and they're all like, 'Yeah, come on over and bring all your friends!'"

"Well, yeah. I did think it was a bit weird," Carrie admitted.

"It's *a lot* weird," Gayle nodded.

"The other names were a surprise," Carrie agreed. "But when I saw it, I didn't know about your connections to Lyssa or Mercy. I wasn't sure why they'd been included, but now..."

"That connection is tentative at best and it does nothing to explain why of all the people in the world, suddenly we're the chosen ones," Gayle said. "The three Knightley sisters and two Vampyrii from House Balthazaar. It makes absolutely no sense."

"That may well be, but Ambassador Alzim assured me it was correct. He said, to quote, 'Balent sent word. The visa is for all. They are expected and welcome. Balent looks forward to meeting the Songbird.'"

"Am I the Songbird?" Gayle said, confused.

"I'm not sure who else fits the bill." Carrie shrugged. "And here's the other weird thing. The visa has a date on it. And it's not till the 19th January 2046."

"Next year?" Gayle muttered.

"A Friday..." Ally slurred from where she was still slumped on the table.

Both of her sisters looked at her, wondering how she knew the day of the week on which that date would fall.

"Don't ask," she said raising a hand. "It's a peculiar gift I have apparently..."

Gayle smiled and shook her head. "Well, regardless of the day of the week, why is it for that particular date?"

Carrie laughed and grinned at her sister.

"Welcome to the art of investigative journalism where the mysteries of the world are ours to uncover!" she said.

| 76 |

FAMILY

– Michael Reynolds –
– Saturday – London, England –

Synchronicity.

In psychoanalysis terms, it meant the simultaneous occurrence of causally unrelated events and the belief that the simultaneity had meaning beyond mere coincidence.

A little over a week ago, on their night of tequila-fueled self-reflection and flirtation, Gayle brought up the subject of his twin. While he hadn't wanted to talk about it, it *had* started the cogs turning in his brain. Maybe – after two years – it was past time to extend an olive branch, to try and repair their broken relationship. So, next day he headed into the Academy and accessed MercNet to find the contact details for his sister. Still, when he arrived at the moment to hit the '*send*' button on the email, he hesitated.

Am I ready for this? he had thought to himself.

He hit the send button...and waited.

A week later, there was still no response to his overture. Which was why when he opened his door to an unexpected evening visitor, he couldn't hide the look of shock on his face.

"Alexa?" he stammered.

"Hey, Mikey," Alexa replied with a sheepish smile. "Surprise?"

The last word was part statement, part question. He knew

why. She wasn't sure how he was going to react to her turning up on his doorstep unannounced two years after he had angrily told her to 'get the fuck out' of his life. Two years over which they hadn't exchanged so much as a phone call or an email. He'd been too angry, and he knew that she felt too guilty. This had been her way of making life as easy as possible on them both.

He knew all this because they were twins, and that was *exactly* what he would do if he were in the same position. Her fears were subtly etched onto her face.

She's wondering if I'll reject her...

He moved to wrap his arms tightly around her in a bear hug that she instantly – and gratefully – reciprocated.

"I've missed you, Lexy," Michael said with a tiny break in his voice.

"I've missed you, too," she whispered into his shoulder, her voice as broken as his. "I'm so sorry—"

He hushed her before she could say another word.

"I don't want to talk about it. It doesn't matter anymore. I'm the one who should be sorry for not reachin' out to you sooner. I'm so glad you got my email..."

She pushed back from him a little, staring at him with mild confusion.

"Your email?"

"Yeah. I sent a message to who I thought was you on MercNet..."

"Zarra Anderson?"

"Yeah," he shrugged. "Your call sign and mom's maiden name... I figured it was you. You...didn't get it?"

"No. I've not checked my messages since I left Pack Nation. I...I just thought that maybe after two years we might be able to..."

Synchronicity

"Well, I guess that proves the twin theory," he laughed. "My email...I was also thinkin' maybe it's time to put the past behind us."

"I'd really like that."

He let go of her and gestured for her to enter.

"Come on in. We have *a lot* of catchin' up to do. You still drink beer?"

He ushered her inside and closed the door. They walked down the short hallway, past the lounge and into the kitchen. Alexa's head panned around as she took in his home.

"Very nice..." she said under her breath.

"Never had my own house before." Michael grinned. "It takes some gettin' used to."

"Used to what?"

He gestured around the kitchen with his hand.

"The size. Remember how tiny our cabin on the *Fantasy* was? Here I got a kitchen, lounge, bathroom, bedroom, *and* a guest room."

She sighed. "I was actually thinking how much more comfortable this is compared to my quarters on my ship"

"Your ship?"

"My dropship."

"You have a dropship?"

Alexa nodded and laughed. "I imagine we have *a lot* to talk about."

Michael couldn't disagree. "We have time," he said softly.

There was an unspoken question implied in his tone. How long was she going to be there? He didn't want to ask overtly. These first few minutes of reconnection were going well, but still felt fragile. Alexa looked at him, her eyes softening. She nodded.

"We have time," she repeated.

His life had changed dramatically over the past two years, and he was sure she likewise lived a life unrecognizable from the sister he had known. As she followed him into the kitchen, he pulled open the refrigerator to grab them both a chilled beer. He popped the caps off the bottles and handed one to her.

"So, where do we start?"

"Well," Alexa perched herself on one of the tall barstools, "I just got finished with a hunt. You'll never guess for who."

Michael shook his head.

"Damian Dane."

"Holy shit!" Michael's eyes widened.

"Oh, and it gets worse," she laughed. "Alex was there, too."

"Lonewolf?"

She nodded and took a gentle swig from the top of the bottle, closing her eyes with a moment of bliss.

"Not had a beer for a while?" Michael chuckled.

"No beer in the forests of Pack Nation." She gave him a wry smile. "So, yeah, it's been a while."

"Well, I got plenty more. So, what was the job? Pack Nation is dangerous ground."

"Dane had Lonewolf on a trackin' job that got unexpectedly more difficult. He requested me for assistance."

"Why you?" Michael asked. "Surely Dane has a bunch of qualified spec-ops soldiers he could have put on it?"

"He found himself hunting a succubus," Alexa said matter-of-factly.

"A code eleven." Suddenly the pieces snapped together in his head. "Ah, of course... Three years ago. Seattle."

"Well remembered," Alexa laughed.

It struck Michael how easy it was to fall back into old patterns of sibling banter and he realized how much he had missed it. There was a pang of regret that he hadn't bridged the gap between them sooner. How many moments like this had they lost out on over the past two years because of his stubbornness?

"Difficult to forget," Michael sighed. "That was a hell of a day. She almost took down our entire squad."

"Well, you men anyway."

"True," Michael admitted. "So, how was it? Seeing Dane and Alex again?"

"It was...difficult at first. Especially Dane, for obvious reasons."

"Old flames...never easy."

"Yeah, it was awkward...so much history there. Alex, too. We bickered *a lot*. But then – after a while – things got easier."

She paused. Michael said nothing, not wanting to interrupt her train of thought.

"It's what led me here back to you," she said finally. "I figured if could mend fences with them, then it *must* be possible to do it with my brother. I mean… You and I… We're all the family we've got left."

The two siblings stared at each other in silence for a moment. Finally, Alexa broke the quiet between them.

"Mom and Dad would've been pissed if they'd known how we hadn't spoken for so long. We were supposed to support and look after each other. I'm sorry for my part in it all. For what it's worth, they'd be crazy proud of you for what you're doin.'"

"I think," Michael said as he leaned forward on the counter, "that we had an even share of the blame. We can't change what happened; just need to accept it and move on. I'm sorry it took so long."

He paused for a moment and then pursed his lips and smiled slyly. "So, do you think you can go back to usin' your proper name now?"

Alexa laughed. "Maybe. I'm considerin' it. I've made a professional name for myself as Zarra, though."

"Yeah, I gathered as much from your resume on MercNet. So, how much does a hunt in Pack Nation pay these days?"

"Three million credits," Alexa said with a sly smile.

"Fuck off!"

"I am officially now a rich bitch."

"So, you're saying…" Michael laughed, "that I picked *just* the right time to reunite with my older sister."

"Older by just thirteen minutes. Anyway, I have to share it with Becka, my partner, and pay a percentage to MercNet. Then I have the runnin' expenses for *Diana*. Still, I'll end up with enough left to be able to afford to take some time off.

"And technically, I never got your email. So, in actual fact, this is me reuniting with you."

As Alexa laughed, Michael shook his head in disbelief. His sister had made a life for herself that was good. Dangerous…but good. For not the first time in his life, but for the first time in a couple of years, he felt an odd surge of pride well up inside of him.

"Ask me again why I'm workin' for a pittance at the HFA?"

"You're doin' great work here, Michael. Teachin' those kids, it's a noble thing to do. Me? I just go out and catch and shoot things for money, but you...you're parlayin' your experience into something meaningful. I'm proud of you for that."

Alexa reclined against the low-slung backrest of the stool and swished the last dregs of beer around the bottom of the bottle. She spied his artist pad on the kitchen table and nodded toward it with her head.

"You still painting?"

Michael sighed and started to shake his head, before stopping and shrugging instead.

"No....yes... Just sketches mostly these days. I don't get much time to paint."

"Can I see?"

He was reluctant to show her his latest works because of what they would reveal. There was, however, a big part of himself that wanted to. He hadn't really had anyone to talk to about this and having Alexa back in his life gave him the perfect outlet. They had been close once, and this was the kind of thing they would discuss, but was it too soon in their renewed relationship?

With a nod, he stood straight and turned to the refrigerator to retrieve another couple of bottles to replace the ones they were both finishing off. He popped the caps off them and turned, handing a fresh one to Alexa. She plucked up the pad and started to flick through the pages slowly, perusing each picture as she went. She stopped in her page turning, and for a moment, regarded the image on which she had paused before looking up at him with a raised eyebrow and a cockeyed grin.

He knew which picture had caught her eye.

"Who is she?"

"Who is who?" he asked innocently.

"You know who I mean. You've always painted landscapes for as long as I've known you. You only start sketchin' portraits when you're into someone."

"That's not true."

"Really? You really want me to start listing them? There was Jenny Thompson when you were thirteen and we were livin'

on the *Fantasy*. Then there was Susan Cook when we were cadets in our first year. Oh, and then there was that Hawaiian
girl, Mililani—"

"Okay, okay, point made," he interrupted her flow of names
with growl of mock indignation. "It's... Okay, no judging, but
it's my fellow teacher at the Academy. Captain Knightley."

"Captain Gayle Knightley?" Alexa asked in a shocked tone.
He simply nodded his confirmation.

"Captain Gayle '*The Bitch of Bulgaria*' Knightley?"
He nodded again.

"The one the Vampyrii call '*Andrea Mors Est*?'"

"Yes, okay. '*The Pink Death*' herself."

Alexa placed the artist pad on the countertop, open to the
portrait sketched in shades of red, and regarded his clean lines
and pencil strokes while she supped on her beer direct from
the bottle.

"Wow," she said finally. "My little brother is hookin' up
with a legend."

"She's hardly a legend. And we're not hookin' up. We went
out once for drinks. Not even a proper date."

"Oh, she's famous in the right circles. Her and her team, till
Valletta, of course. She really this pretty?"

That last part Michael refused to answer on the grounds he
might further incriminate himself. He walked to the chair opposite and slumped into it, taking a swig from his bottle.

"She doesn't talk about Valletta. If you met her, you
wouldn't see her as this legend that everyone talks about.
She's...not what you'd expect. I learned that on day one; constantly full of surprises."

"I'd *like* to meet her."

"Come over to the Academy tomorrow," he said. "Gayle's
got the class for most of the day so I can show you around. You
can see the cadets goin' through their paces and I'll introduce
you to her."

He watched as his sister looked down at the sketch again,
regarding it in a manner that looked like she was evaluating
Gayle's suitability to have a relationship with her brother
simply from the pencil lines.

"I think I'd like that very much."

| 77 |

RETAKEN

– Kareena St. Claire –
– Sunday – Unknown –

She couldn't control it.

The fury that burned inside her.

She had never been one prone to anger; hers was a tranquil soul, something she had inherited from her parents. But since her change, she found untapped depths to this unfamiliar emotion. It was pure, unadulterated, and coursed powerfully through every molecule of her being. Shaking, she strained at her bonds, struggling to break free and exact a measure of vengeance on whoever it was that had bound her in these chains.

No. This is not me.

She didn't recognize this woman she had become. Not yet anyway. The last few weeks or so had been a whirlwind of confusion and self-discovery. She stopped struggling and forced herself to unclench her jaw. Deep breaths. It was time to stop giving in to her emotions and take stock of her current predicament.

Unlike her first bout of captivity, this one had no sexual component to it. In fact, it was almost the complete opposite in that respect. She had always been reserved; not a prude by any measure, but certainly reticent to show more skin than necessary. Her bathing suits were all one piece, her dresses long and flowing. There were no bikinis or miniskirts in her modest closet. Yet now she had been clothed in a form fitting bodysuit that left only her head, feet, and hands exposed. For the first time in weeks she wasn't naked, and it felt...unnatural. It felt like her senses were being dulled, suppressed somehow simply by the fabric's caress of her skin.

She also wasn't in the laboratory rat conditions of her last detention. Here, there were no two-way mirrors, no sterile environment, and no scientists making promises to her. This new prison felt like something very different; more like she had been boxed up, packaged. Was this new type of confinement some form of transport? Was she being shipped like cargo?

Or cattle?

While her current predicament was far more comfortable than when the monsters had taken her, it was considerably less forgiving. Ropes had been replaced with cold steel, this time holding her wrists inescapably behind her back. A solid strut of metal meant she could neither extend nor compress the distance between them. A wide post extended up from the floor adjacent to her spine, and a heavy chain snaked snugly around her midriff to hold her in-situ. The post ended at neck height where a band of padded steel was locked around her throat.

There was no escape. She had tried, struggling to use her enhanced strength to break free to no avail. Her bonds were unyielding.

The nature of her imprisonment was all supposition based on feel. The blindfold that hugged her face and let in not one photon of light saw to that. Once upon a time, being robbed of her eyesight would have terrified her, but Kareena had changed. Eyesight wasn't her only sense, and the others were now more attuned than they had ever been before.

"Where am I?" she shouted.

She didn't expect an answer, though one would have certainly been welcome. What she was really doing was proving a theory. There was no echo, no reverberation. Her voice just disappeared into the ether. This room was soundproofed. It felt like a bespoke prison, specifically tailored to hold her, and keep her suppressed.

Yes... Suppressed is the right word

No sight, no sounds... All she could smell was a clinical cleanliness. Even her new 'aura' sense detected nothing. It felt like her latest captors were trying to cocoon her in a bubble of seclusion, and she wanted to know why.

A subtle sound suddenly drew her attention. She felt a tiny change in the air pressure in her ear drums. A smell...reminding her of the lake back home. Water. Different though... Sea water.

Then it was gone, obscured...overpowered.

A new scent. A golden profile that reminded her of her father.

Kareena felt the movement of air as the stranger approached. Heard the rustle of clothes, the scuff of footsteps on the hard floor. The new arrival moved deliberately and with purpose, confidence coming off her in palpable waves.

"Kareena St. Claire," the stranger said slowly, her words a statement, not a question.

"Who are you?" Kareena whispered.

"A friend."

| 78 |

AND SO IT BEGINS...

– Jaymes Knightley –
– Monday – Nexus City, Iceland –

Oh, how I've looked forward to this!
Today was the first day of what was likely to be a fortnight of arguments, settlements, and late evenings of intense negotiation. The tediously frivolous pomp and circumstance of the opening ceremonies and introductions was now done, much to Jaymes' delight. With the gala dinners, pretty speeches, and polite conversation firmly in the rear-view mirror, *now* they could get down to the serious business of diplomacy.
This is where the rubber meets the road.
The background noise of dozens of impromptu conversations started to ebb away as each of the faction's delegates took to their seats. Jaymes almost rubbed his hands together in glee as the ceremonial bell rang, signifying a mere five minutes to the start of the day's session.
He had been sat in his comfortable chair for a little while now. This was his ritual. He liked to watch the room, trying to get a read on the body language of the other delegates. A sense of how the factions might be feeling today.
Was the AustralAsian ambassador looking pensive? Did the representatives from the Countries of South America look a little *too* smug when eyeing the delegates from the Independent State of Rio de Janeiro? And what shenanigans did the New

Victus diplomats look like they were planning?

At least he didn't have to worry about the latter today.

Serlia, sitting to his right, was doing likewise. Their aide, Narissa, entered the chamber carrying a pile of data tablets and papers. The computerized devices were for Serlia predominantly; Jaymes preferred the feel of paper between his fingers. Something on which he could scribble notes with his good old fashioned mechanical pencil.

A handful of moments later, a nervously excited looking Mercy balthazaar walked slowly into this modest amphitheater of international relations, her eyes wide and mouth agog. Jaymes smiled to himself.

They had shared a friendly, professional dinner together. The young woman had been delightfully enthusiastic company, quizzing him almost endlessly about the ins-and-outs of diplomacy in Nexus City. Questions he was more than willing to answer. It had truly given him a sense of joy to hear the verve in her voice when she spoke about her nervous anticipation for the Summit.

He thought back to the evening they had shared the week before. The conversation in which they had indulged over a bottle of wine and the empty plates of a delicious meal.

"I went to see the World Council Chambers after I spoke to you in the Atrium," she had said, her eyes shining with excitement. "It's beautiful. More so than it looks in pictures or on television. More...elegant. The wood and crystal...breathtaking. I just stood there for a while soaking it all in."

Jaymes had laughed gently.

"My dear, wait until you see it full of people," he said. "Wait until you see the Ice Giants and the Trolls. Till you hear a dozen different languages buzzing around the room. Till you're immersed in the verbal rough and tumble of diplomacy..."

He had let the sentence trail off, smiling at his memories.

"You truly love what you do, don't you Jaymes?" she had said with a sad smile.

"Yes," he nodded. "Yes, I do. I shall miss it when it's gone."

"Gone?" Mercy had queried.

He had shrugged. "I'm afraid I don't have your breadth of lifespan. I will no doubt need to consider retirement soon."

Mercy had said nothing, simply looked sad.

"How about yourself? Have you ever considered a life as an ambassador?" he had asked.

Her expression of sadness turned to one of disappointment as she looked down at the table, avoiding his eyes. Her voice held the hint of a sigh. "No...I'm a soldier, not a diplomat."

"From what I understand, Mercy, you have a gift for intelligence gathering. And from what I've seen, you also have a gift for making friends and allies. My eldest daughter, for example. Allyson told me that you made quite the impression on Gayle. Being a soldier is not all you are. Don't let it define you."

"Even if I wanted to—" she started.

"—Which I believe you do," he interrupted.

"Even if I wanted to..." she repeated, "it's not possible while StormHall is in power. My presence here is an exception to the rule, simply because StormHall *wants* something and is leveraging our family name to curry favor with you and your colleagues."

He had seen the look in her eyes that evening.

She was born to this profession. She had all the inherent traits that would make her a great ambassador. He also knew that what she was saying was true. While Sebastian StormHall was Grand Chancellor of New Victus, she would never be truly appointed to a role in Nexus City. She was a woman, a half-blood, and represented his closest rival. A quirk of circumstance was now giving Mercy an insight into a life she would never be able to truly have.

A glimpse of the path she couldn't take.

It pained him.

But to see her in the chamber today, her face lit with wonder, he smiled.

At least she will have this moment to shine.

Everyone was now in their seats, and the clock above the door chimed softly.

Midday.

The World Council Chamber slipped into silence, and

Jaymes slowly rose from his seat, pulling down on the front of his jacket in order to smooth out any creases. Once he was stood, he looked around the room. All eyes were now on him.

This was his moment.

"Delegates," he started, the tiny microphone he was wearing on his lapel amplifying his voice over the room's sound system. "Most of you know me by now, and will accept that I'm not one for big grandiose speeches. If the items you have all submitted to the agenda are accurate, we have much to discuss over the next fourteen days. I propose that we waste no more time than necessary and get stuck in. So...

"It is my great pleasure to announce the first item on the agenda of the Tenth Annual Nexus Peace Summit. Proposition six-twenty-five. A proposal for a lasting peace treaty between New Victus, Pack Nation, and the North American Alliance.

"I, therefore, call upon Ambassador Mercy balthazaar of New Victus, to open proceedings."

He gestured toward Mercy, smiling warmly before sitting down.

This may be the only time she would experience being there in this role. So, even though Vampyrii hated going out in the daylight...Jaymes was determined to give Mercy her moment in the metaphorical sun.

| 79 |

SURPRISED

– Gayle Knightley –
– Monday – London, England –

Class was in session and Gayle sighed, rubbing at her temples in an effort to massage away the inevitable headache that today's class was giving her.

It turned out that teaching these kids to harness their powers was not as easy as she had expected it to be. She had spent a long and difficult afternoon trying to communicate to them the concept of fueling their abilities using the *memories* of emotions, but not the emotions themselves. Anger, for instance. Yes, it might be the easiest way to manifest fire, but in battle, being angry could impact your decision making; a lesson she was trying to drill into the kids.

She had tried to explain how using their feelings in battle was a double-edged sword. While they wanted to gain access to their abilities as fast as possible and with as much potential destructive force as possible, feeling that emotion, rather than just using it, could be the difference between life and death.

It was a concept that they were obviously finding very confusing, and it was Dylan who voiced the question that she could see on all their faces.

"So," he had asked, "how do you *feel* angry without *being* angry?"

To be fair to the kids, Gayle herself had been struggling

with that very thing recently, hence her reluctance to use her powers. Valletta was always bubbling away just beneath the surface of her mind. Grief had become an almost constant companion, feeding a seething fury of which she was terrified she might lose control. Admittedly, though, lately she hadn't been feeling the intense depth of despair and its associated anger that she had a few weeks ago.

She suspected she knew why.

She had resorted to using movies as an analogy for how she wanted the class to control their abilities. Characters in films sometimes die, or bad things happen to them, and these scenes are intended to provoke an emotional response. Yet the watcher doesn't genuinely grieve for a movie character or feel righteous anger if something bad happens to them. They simply walk back out into the real world after the credits roll with a smile on their face having enjoyed the movie experience.

Finally, she seemed to find the comparison that flipped the switch in their tiny adolescent heads.

It is possible to feel the emotion of sadness, without being sad.

The problem – it was a tough skill to master.

"As repetitive as practice can be, you need to know this stuff instinctually because in the field, under combat situations, you don't get second chances. I don't want you to be angry, sad, or happy; I want you to remember what it *feels* like to be angry, sad, or happy...and then tap into that memory. It's a difficult distinction, I know, but while you're here, I'm going to..."

The knock on the door mid-sentence drew her irritation. If she was going to teach these kids, then people should at least leave her in peace while she did it. She glanced at the door.

Scratch that – some interruptions are more than welcome.

Michael gestured with a head movement for her to come out of the classroom. Just seeing him gave her a warm glow, soothing away the undercurrent of frustration she had been feeling all afternoon.

"...drill this stuff into you till you dream about it when you sleep. Now keep yourselves busy a moment while I see what Captain Reynolds wants."

She slid off the desk on which she'd been perched and headed to the door. As she exited into the corridor, she was a little taken aback to see Michael was not alone.

The initial surge of excitement ebbed as she found Lana and her uncle standing in the corridor behind him. Norbel's face was somehow more implacable than usual, while Michael's countenance suggested a somewhat sympathetic frown. So far, so worrying. But it was Lana's expressions that struck a chord of fear inside Gayle. Her best friend's eyes were puffy and bloodshot. She'd been crying. Her hand covered her mouth, as if she was trying to stifle a sob. Something was wrong.

Very, very wrong.

"What's going on?" she said slowly.

"Gayle..." Michael said softly, "there's been an explosion at the Nexus Summit... Your dad...he..."

She felt her chest tighten, and an icy grip squeezed at her heart. Her head started to spin, and her tongue seemed to swell in her mouth. Her throat was dry, and for someone who never had a problem talking, suddenly words wouldn't form.

No. Not Dad. Please no! Don't you fucking dare.

"Gayle," Lana said, her voice broken. "He's alive, but...it's pretty bad. He's been taken to Nexus ICU. I'm so sorry..."

If her best friend said anything more, Gayle didn't hear it. The corridor walls were closing in. The world felt off kilter, sliding to the side as she felt her breathing start to come in deeper gasps. She felt the gentle grasp of a hand on her arm. Her eyes flicked toward it. Gayle hadn't even noticed the close approach of her uncle, and it barely registered with her that it was his voice she heard next.

"There is an Air Force 'Banshee' coming in to landing pad three as we speak," Norbel said quietly. "It is the fastest ship I could source on short notice. It will have you in Nexus in a little over an hour."

"Mum?" Gayle's broken voice quivered. "Allyson?"

"Allyson and your mother are fine," Norbel reassured her.

"Cuts and bruises, nothing more. My staff tracked Carrie-Anne down to where she was working in Oslo. She is en route and will arrive twenty minutes before you."

"I got your classes covered," Michael said. "Now go."

Gayle felt tears welling. She gritted her teeth to prevent them, but one escaped to track down her left cheek. She ignored it. Without another word, she took off at a run toward the landing pad. She had everything she needed on her person.

She arrived just as the cacophony of the Banshee's howling engines informed her that her ride had arrived. The ground crew gave her the mandatory safety briefing while they helped her pull on a snug flight suit over her CombatSkin. Gayle wasn't listening, simply mechanically cycling through the motions of flight prep. This wasn't her first time riding in a Banshee.

Why?

Why did I have to be so fucking stubborn?

Six weeks ago, she walked out of her uncle's office fuming at the interference of her parents. Her ire focused mostly on her father, the parent she never thought would meddle in her life.

She was calmer now. Gayle had more or less accepted her new role at the Academy and was actually enjoying it. Yes, Michael had a lot to do with that, but she'd also simply started to come to terms with who she was now, post-Valletta.

The night Jaymes came to her house with Ally, she turned him away dismissively. She felt like a petulant child at the time and now, with this frightening turn of events, she was terrified that she had wasted her last chance to tell her father how much she loved him.

Her parting words to him that night had been a dismissive, "I know."

He had told her he loved her, and she had let pride rule her heart.

Fuck. You're so fucking stupid, Gayle.

Lost in personal recriminations, she simply stared blankly at the hornet-shaped aircraft as it dropped out of the grey London sky. The moment its wheels touched the landing pad, the ground crew sprang into well-rehearsed action, attaching the refueling hoses and rolling out the stairs that would allow Gayle access to the cockpit.

Her long legs made short work of the ascent, and in moments she was in the snug co-pilot's seat, making herself as comfortable as possible while the crew strapped her in tightly with practiced proficiency. As she pulled on her flight helmet, they plugged her into the internal communications port, instantly muting the screams of the engine. The voice of her pilot echoed professionally in Gayle's ears.

"Captain Knightley," he said, "I'm Flight Lieutenant Daniel Scott. The minute we're refueled, we'll be gear up and full throttle all the way to Nexus. I've already got pre-clearance to land at the hospital facility's pad, so this is a door-to-door service. I'll get you there as fast as I can."

"Thank you, Lieutenant," Gayle said flatly.

She leaned back against the headrest and closed her eyes.

And prayed.

| 80 |

AFTERSHOCK

– Allyson Knightley –
– Monday – Nexus City, Iceland –

Allyson Knightley knew that she had not passed out, nor had she been rendered unconscious. She knew that there was no missing time from her memory.

And yet, it *seemed* like there was.

A blink of the eye and the clock had skipped.

Skewing from one moment to the jarring next like the scratch of a record.

When she had arrived a quarter hour ago, she had taken up station a little way behind the New Victus delegation area. From there, she could carefully survey the World Council Chamber in her capacity as Security Chief, watching the double doors of the room's entrance. She had observed the delegates as they all filed in and took their seats. Watched with pride as her father had opened proceedings, inviting New Victus to get the ball rolling with the headline item on the agenda – a proposal to Pack Nation and the North American Alliance. Ally had witnessed an exuberant Mercy – dressed in a sharp black suit, her auburn hair plaited into a beautifully elaborate braid – barely contain her glee at being some part of this event, picking up the silver diplomatic attaché case and walking out to make the exchange with Ambassador Sabadini.

Her father had stood, Serlia and their aide, Narissa following suit. All bearing witness to what was supposed to be a historic moment.

Ambassador Sabadini had risen from his chair, rounded the Pack Nation delegate table, and walked toward Mercy, a warm smile on his face, his hand extended.

Then, Allyson had blinked.

The record had scratched.

And now the world was a *very* different place.

The acrid stench of smoke and the sound of panicked screams filled the room. The latter seemed hollow...distant. Her ears were ringing, a constant high-pitched dirge. Allyson flexed her fingers, curling them. She felt the wooden floor beneath her fingertips.

Everything hurt.

She felt the same smooth wood against her cheek and realized she was lying face down. She dug her fingernails into the floor in an effort to stop the pain and shut out the noise.

Neither abated.

Her eyes remained closed, her blink only half complete. In truth, she was deathly afraid to open them. If what they would see was anything like the image that her mind was conjuring from her other senses, then she wasn't sure she *wanted* to bear witness.

But this was her job. Her responsibility.

Ally forced herself to crack them open, slowly.

Mother of God...

The smell of smoke hung in the air like a fog, catching her throat as she inhaled sharply. She coughed. Coughing hurt. Her ribs and her back screamed in agony, it felt like someone had taken up a baseball bat and beaten her with it. With a groan, she slowly pushed herself up onto her hands and knees. Every muscle in her body cried in protestation, but she persevered staring at the polished wooden floor beneath her. It was smeared with blood...

Is that...mine?

Forcing herself upright, she sank back to rest her buttocks on her heels and, now kneeling, she stared at her shaking hands. There were minor injuries – small but numerous bloody cuts on both of her palms. A vague recollection of trying to reflexively shield her face popped into her memory, and she could see a number wooden splinters buried beneath her skin. Most were tiny, but a larger piece had pierced all the way through the webbing between the finger and thumb of her left hand. She tried to grasp it with the fingers of her right, but the trembling digits wouldn't cooperate.

Ally lifted the hand to her face and gripped it with her teeth, pulling it out. The clenching of her jaw sent a shooting pain to her forehead, making her grimace. As she spit the bloodied splinter onto the floor, she lifted the hand to her temple to tentatively check for injury. When she withdrew it, her fingers were crimson with her own blood. She could feel it matting her hair.

She stared at her hand, swaying slightly on her knees. Her head felt woolly, her eyes drowsy, struggling to focus. Her thoughts felt abstract, disconnected....

You have a concussion...

Turning slightly, she looked at the pillar behind her that formed one of the supports for the elegantly arched roof. A curved piece of wood that blended perfectly into the framework that held the stunning crystal windows, now marred with ugly cracks. Realization of what had happened was slowly coalescing in her mind.

An explosion.

She'd been violently thrown – back first – into the pillar.

A memory suddenly flashed through her head.

"Problem?" her mother had asked.

She'd felt uneasy, but lied... "No. No problem. A bomb threat..."

Fran didn't seem worried. "Warning," she had corrected.

Her father, likewise, had seemed unconcerned. "Ah, I see. Wouldn't be the first."

The explosion...

It was the case. The silver attaché case Mercy had been holding as she had passed the FSE delegate area.

Oh, no...

She stumbled to her feet, staggering on unsteady legs. She

reached for the toppled New Victus table, using the mahogany furniture to brace herself as she peered over toward where the bomb had gone off. There was debris everywhere. The crystal dome that covered the Authagraphic map was smashed, and the holographic projection itself was broken, stuttering through its animation. Papers lay strewn across the floor with the broken shards of crystal and wood.

And the bodies.

She couldn't tell if they were injured, unconscious...or worse.

But amongst them she could see the still form of a woman in black, with her beautifully elegant auburn braid.

Mercy was lying face down, her body in an unnatural position, near the shattered crystal dome. Pushing herself away from the table, Allyson staggered toward her.

Which was when, out of the corner of her eye, she saw her parents.

Serlia was moving, but Jaymes...

She tried to run, but her legs refused to cooperate. Her motion was a series of uncoordinated stumbles that eventually ended with her falling once more to her hands and knees next to her mother.

"Mum?" Her voice was a broken rasp, and she coughed again as the smoke stung her throat.

"I'm fine, I think..." Serlia answered as she sat up looking dazed and confused. "Where's Jaymes?"

Ally crawled along the floor to her father's unmoving form. She reached for his neck to check for a pulse. There was blood.

A *lot* of blood.

But there was also a heartbeat.

Oh, thank you, thank you, thank you!

It was weak, though. Her father needed help. He needed it fast.

Emergency services were now filtering into the room. She could see Francesca urgently looking around, directing security, firefighters, and medical staff. Ally waved toward her frantically.

"Medic!" Her voice was hoarse, but she forced it to shout as loud as she could. "I need a medic over here!"

There were tears in her eyes that were unrelated to the smoke. She grabbed her father's hand and clasped it tightly in her own. She felt the splinters of wood bite into her flesh, but she didn't care. The pain gave her an edge, kept her away from the oblivion of unconsciousness.

There was *so* much blood.

Ally couldn't tell what was her own and what was her father's, but suddenly she was praying under her breath to any god that would listen to spare his life.

Another record scratch moment.

The next thing of which she was aware was her mother pulling her away from him as the paramedics took over. So many paramedics.

Why so many?

They were kneeling around him, with wires and tubes and machines...

She looked around the room slowly, everything suddenly seemed in slow motion. So much damage, so many people lying injured or worse. Fran seemed to have everything under control, which was good because Allyson could barely think straight. And when she tried, two questions kept cycling through her mind over and over and over...

How did I let this happen?

What did I miss?

A PERSONAL WAR

– Sebastian StormHall –
– Monday – Nexus City, Iceland –

"At this time, it's difficult to ascertain exactly what has taken place at the 10th Annual Nexus Peace Summit. Nexus Security has not yet released a statement as to the nature of the attack, though we've been informed that a press conference is scheduled for this evening where Captain Allyson Knightley – Chief of Nexus Security – will address the media with an update. In the meantime, many difficult questions are already being asked about how this could have happened.

It is understood that Captain Knightley's father, FSE Diplomat Sir Jaymes Knightley, was amongst the wounded and was taken to Nexus City Hospital in what is being classified as 'critical condition.' The broadcast footage from the Summit has been taken offline, but prior to that, the video of the explosion seemed to indicate it originated at the Pack Nation delegates' table just as Ambassador Sabadini of Pack Nation was taking the floor to speak to the assembly.

There has been no word out of Pack Nation, but a strongly phrased statement from New Victus was issued earlier by Grand Chancellor StormHall..."

He muted the sound on the news channel. It was all unfolding just like she had said it would. Each chess piece being taken from the board in a precise, pre-determined order.

When she originally approached him half a century ago, he had spent a fair amount of time and effort trying to discover what her endgame was. Now, though...he really didn't care. Not anymore.

It truly didn't matter. His contract was complete, and now the power he had always craved was his. He was the ruler of a mighty nation, and he had his own plans to put into motion. Soon, they would all discover the hard way that Sebastian StormHall was *nobody's* pawn.

Now, everything would change.

Finally, he could bring vengeance down upon those who had wronged him.

Long before his benefactor had approached him to offer her aid, he had been quietly nurturing his own plans for greatness. Splintering away from the House into which he had been born, he had formed his own and never looked back. As Sebastian Storm, he made moves to solidify his own political ambition, forming convenient alliances and friendships to further his aims. To take the next step, though, required something more.

Money.

That was where Eloise Hall entered the picture.

The Halls were old money; old by Human standards, anyway. Real estate and hugely profitable investments had kept the family's bank balances climbing steadily, earning them money faster than they could spend it. With such riches, however, came spoiled children. Two sons and a daughter who had nothing better to contribute to society than buying fast cars, taking expensive holidays, and living decadent lives partying to luxurious excess. All while flaunting it like idiots on social media.

Malcolm Stephen Hall was not a man who appreciated what his children were doing with his money. His legacy. Were these overindulgent ingrates *really* his rightful heirs? They were just going to fritter away his hard-earned fortune from the moment he passed on and was laid to rest in an undoubtedly ridiculously overpriced coffin. Neither his children nor his latest trophy wife had even a modicum of taste; they would all be pretending to mourn his death while using it as an excuse for even more unnecessary excesses.

These were the lamentations that he had voiced in private to Sebastian after a few expensive glasses of scotch and a couple of even more expensive cigars.

What, ventured Sebastian in conversation, *if you could hypothetically* outlive *your children?*

What if he could offer Malcolm a way to control his fortune for the indefinite future?

What price immortality?

Of course, Malcolm was interested. Who wouldn't be? He enquired as to the details and Sebastian delivered his sales pitch. He extended Malcom the truth of the Vampyrii and what he could offer – immortality, for the small fee of his daughter's hand in marriage. Sebastian wished to unite their families, thereby creating a new House. Storm and Hall together with their combined wealth and power.

Turning the old man wouldn't rejuvenate him, but it would arrest the march of time and its effects going forward. Malcolm, of course, jumped enthusiastically at the opportunity and immediately gifted his daughter Eloise to Sebastian, despite her protestations. The threat of being cut off from the family fortune eventually brought about her compliance, and she reluctantly conceded to the union. House StormHall was born with the exchange of rings and an unhappy marriage of convenience.

But the truth was Eloise wasn't simply protesting the marriage on the grounds of being forced into it. She was protesting because she was in love with another. She hadn't ceded to her father's wishes due to the threat of being cut off – she was simply buying time to be rescued.

On their wedding night, she absconded with the Wolf King, Damian Dane. They fled north of the border into Canada, leaving a humiliated Sebastian apoplectic with rage. He vowed that taking down Damian Dane and his pack of dogs would be the very first thing he would focus on the moment he had the power he craved.

It was his silent declaration of a distinctly personal war.

Mere days later, he had received an anonymous message. It was his first contact with the woman who was to become his mysterious patron. She had a silver tongue, convincing him that he had to be harder, to inspire his kind to be ruthless. She told him the world was approaching a crossroads, that change was desperately needed, and Sebastian must be ready. He had to prepare the Vampyrii race, for he would be the leader they would rally behind. Maybe it was all playing to Sebastian's ego, but it didn't matter because it was precisely what he wanted to hear.

True to her promise, Sebastian StormHall soon thereafter became elected leader of the Vampyrii, and took his seat at the Head of the Council of Blood. A goal Sebastian had been working toward for so many years delivered practically overnight. He didn't know who this mysterious benefactor was, but he wasn't going to argue with her results.

The next stage of her plan surprised even him with its boldness. His role was to be the tip of the North American spear, part of a coordinated worldwide uprising. It was time to emerge from the shadows, to take their place...his place...on the world stage.

When the word was given, he had ordered his followers to strike. Her explicit instructions had been to attack the Human population; to kill, turn, or enslave them all, spreading out from his home in Colorado and proliferating quickly across the country. Take the United States from within by turning its own people against each other.

Sebastian had done just that, but at this juncture he had also subtly diverted from the plan. He couldn't simply forget about the affront afforded him by Damian Dane. He ordered House Balthazaar and House Taurus – who controlled the Vampyrii interests in Maine – to cross into Canada and attack Dane's stronghold.

House Taurus obeyed, sparking the escalation of the War along the Northern border, something he had specifically been told to avoid.

House Balthazaar, however, had politely declined. Lyssa Balthazaar wanted nothing to do with this War. What's more, she had set an example which the remaining Progenitor houses followed.

Neither Haggari, Jareb, nor Skarling rallied beneath Storm-Hall's banner. It was an embarrassment. Sebastian seethed, desperately wanting to make an example of them. But Vampyrii are deeply religious and punitively punishing any of the original twelve Houses would have been political suicide while his position was so tenuous.

As his forces swept across the United States, he diplomatically made no mention of the Houses that had refused to heed his call. His silence kept his allies onside, but forgiveness was not a virtue he was inclined to extend, especially when it came to Lyssa Balthazaar. He saw her as the ringleader in this little pseudo-rebellion. While it hadn't made a difference to the outcome of the War, it was yet another slight that could not to be forgotten. An affront that had earned her a place on his list of unfinished business.

Thirty years later, the shackles were off. He was finally free to pursue his own interests. His own plans.

It was time for a new, very personal war.

"Grand Chancellor?"

Disturbed from his reverie, he turned toward the door to his office.

"Doctor Shauston. I take it you have something for me?"

The doctor entered, a data tablet in his hand. Sebastian could tell by his body language that the news he was about to deliver was not good, but he had no time for the man to be hesitant. He raised an eyebrow, encouraging him to divulge the information without needless delay.

"We have the DNA and the blood test results from the female subject—" Shauston hesitated as Sebastian interrupted him to comment bitingly.

"It's about time."

"I'm sorry, Grand Chancellor. As you know, our facilities are not equipped to—"

Sebastian waved his hand dismissively; he didn't want excuses, simply answers.

"Her heritage is more complex than we imagined, Grand

Chancellor. We have identified her as…" There was a long pause as he geared himself up to deliver the bad news. "She is the daughter of Eloise Hall."

The information caught Sebastian off guard. Below the desk, his fists clenched in anger, but he kept the emotion out of his features as he stared at his chief scientist.

"You're sure?"

As Shauston nodded, he now understood why the man had been so apprehensive to reveal this detail to him. Now he understood what had made the girl so special, so unique.

For the first time in decades, he again wondered what his ex-benefactor was truly trying to accomplish.

| 82 |

THE ONCOMING STORM

– Damian Dane –
– Monday – Montreal, Pack Nation –

His lips drew a taut line across his tight jaw as he watched the horrifying news unfold on multiple channels. A feeling of dreadful inevitability settled into the pit of Damian's stomach. He thought of Lyssa and all their careful planning for the future. It was clear now that each passing second had simply been borrowed time. A clock that had finally run out.

War is coming, and we're not ready.

Media speculation was rife regarding finger-pointing for the atrocity, but thus far nobody had been blamed. Yet there had been too many high-profile casualties for this to be simply swept under the carpet without a scapegoat.

Video replays of the live newsfeed showed the explosion in distressing detail as it engulfed the FSE and Pack Nation delegations. The television analysts had already zeroed in on one of the silver diplomatic attaché cases as the source. Unconfirmed speculation suggested that it was the one given to the Pack Nation delegation by New Victus prior to the Summit.

New Victus was being uncharacteristically silent on the matter thus far, refusing to speculate without hard evidence. StormHall's only media comments had been to assure people that they were working closely with Nexus Security to find those responsible and punish them accordingly.

Damn you, Sebastian! Damn you to hell and back!

StormHall's fingerprints were all over this, but Damian knew that they would never find a trail leading anywhere close to the Grand Chancellor. Sebastian didn't need to do a damn thing to point the finger of blame; the media would do that job for him as the focus of investigations started to shift toward Pack Nation. Especially when details were inevitably leaked about what New Victus were about to propose at the Summit.

Public perception would be a powerful ally to StormHall. He was coming to the negotiating table in good faith to talk about a strategic withdrawal from certain contentious territories, and with a proposal to establish a continued ceasefire in conjunction with a global trade agreement.

The rhetoric would be that Pack Nation had responded with violence.

Fuck.

"Sir?" came the apologetic interruption from his aide, Kristoph. "Is there anything I can do for you?"

Damian took a deep breath. This fight was far from done. StormHall may have won round one, and the media was going to see him win round two on points, but Pack Nation wasn't down for the count. That said, what Damian did next was going to be critical to the future of not just his country, but his entire race.

"Clear my diary for the foreseeable future," he said decisively. "We have more important things to do. Set up a War Council meeting as soon as possible. I don't care where the generals are or what they're doing, I need them all here *tonight*."

Pack Nation was a large country and bringing in all the commanding officers from the various branches of their military would be a challenge on such short notice, but it needed to be done. If this was indeed StormHall's plan, then Damian was sure New Victus was *already* geared up for war. In the meantime, they needed both time and allies, because if full-scale war broke out again, Pack Nation was currently in no shape to fight it.

"And contact Nexus and arrange transport for me. I'll be

going there in person tomorrow."

"Are you sure that's wise?" Kristoph asked.

"Wise or not," Damian shrugged, "if there is any chance of defusing this situation, then I have to be seen there. Contact Federation Ambassador Serlia Knightley and set up a meeting with her as a matter of extreme urgency."

"Sir, her husband was one of those caught in the explosion. She may not be willing to—"

"I understand," Dane said sympathetically. "But she'll talk to me."

Sebastian StormHall was a clever adversary, a man with an extensive intelligence network, and a keeper of many secrets. But Dane had secrets, too. Serlia would know why he was coming to her. She would understand the importance and would also know that Pack Nation could not be responsible for this atrocity. It was his one trump card to play.

Kristoph nodded and turned to exit. He had been Damian's aide for many years and knew Damian's tone was his cue to leave. He recognized the dark clouds that were gathering over his leader's head, and he didn't want to be there for the inevitable storm that was to come.

With a voice command, Damian ordered the television off and slumped wearily into his chair, sighing heavily. His cellphone sat innocently on the desktop, taunting him.

When they had parted company after he delivered Vanessa's body to her, Lyssa had made it clear that she needed time and space away from him. Something had changed in her; he sensed it and silently vowed to respect her wishes to give her what she needed. This bomb had changed that. He didn't want to dial her number, yet he knew it was a call he *had* to make.

The bomb had been targeted at her as much as it had been at Pack Nation. Sebastian StormHall's clever plan to rid himself of two thorns in his side at the same time. Only she had opted to tend to her sister's funeral, sending Mercy in her stead. The price of her survival had been the death of her niece and best friend. She would be overwhelmed with grief, and Damian was about to call her with even more bad news.

She would know that this was not his doing, yet the fact remained it was his operatives who shot Vanessa, and it was an explosive device that had seemingly been aimed at the Pack Nation ambassador that killed Mercy. Even if there was no blood on his hands, he would not easily be able to wash the stain off.

Lyssa would *know* that this was StormHall's work, but she still wouldn't be eager to take his call. He knew her mind would be too crowded with grief and righteous fury to allow her to rationally reconcile the facts so soon.

But...if she had been as much of a target as Dane and his people were, it could mean only one thing – Sebastian Storm-Hall knew what she, what *they*, had been doing. He snatched up the phone and quickly dialed her number.

She *had* to answer. She needed to listen.

Lyssa Balthazaar was no longer safe in New Victus.

| 83 |

VENGEANCE

– Lyssa Balthazaar –
– Monday – Albany, New Victus –

Bastard.

Lyssa's knuckles were white, her fists balled up so tight they matched the knot in her stomach. Furious notions of retribution spun through her head as she stalked back and forth like a caged tiger. He had expertly maneuvered her into a trap of his own design by manipulating her optimism for a brighter future.

Storm played me like a fiddle. I should have seen this coming.

She *had* seen this coming.

The clues had all been there, and it wasn't like she could claim ignorance and say she missed them. Every step of the way she had been suspicious, wary of his long-term motives.

The meeting in Hearst Tower weeks ago had reeked of being played. His silken lies were promising Lyssa pretty much everything she had wanted for her people. Her questions had been many, and his answers had been convenient. Believable. So, despite her inherent mistrust she had listened to his plans, gone to Nexus, and done his business. More than that, she dragged Mercy into his web of lies, too. As the weeks passed, she became lax in her skepticism. Worse still, she had let her optimism and her night of passion in Allyson Knightley's bed temporarily blind her to the threat.

Oh gods, Allyson!

Lyssa ceased her pacing, her hand moving to cover her mouth. It may have only been one night, but she felt a connection with the young Knightley sister. Their time together seemed like so much longer than the sweeps the hour hand indicated. They had talked freely, laughed frequently, and Lyssa had felt a passion she had never experienced before. Sex with Damian had been scratching an itch. Sometimes she wished it was more than that, but she knew deep down it wasn't. Allyson, on the other hand, felt like the start of something very different.

Something that she was keen to explore to its fullest extent.

She knew the logistics of such a relationship would be difficult, but she had hoped that maybe her new diplomatic responsibilities would allow her opportunities. Especially since she had seemingly struck up a good rapport with Allyson's parents, Jaymes and Serlia. It had been another aspect of events that led to her eventual naivety regarding the Summit. While Storm preached the words of her own philosophy back to her so persuasively, it was the attitudes of Jaymes and Serlia that sealed the deal.

They had lit the flame of hope for the future within her.

A hope that had been cruelly blown out by the aftershocks of a terrorist bomb.

Lyssa wished that she could somehow reach out to her one-time lover. To extend her thoughts and prayers, and to assure her that, despite appearances to the contrary, Lyssa had no knowledge of how this happened. In one regard, she knew how Allyson must be feeling right now as her father lay in the hospital in critical condition, unsure of whether he would survive.

Afraid.

Lyssa felt an urge to be there. A need to be in Nexus. She knew that Allyson would be attempting to balance her personal feelings with her professional life. While there was obviously a conflict of interest in the investigation of this incident, Lyssa knew that Allyson would be determined to find the truth of what had happened. During their night together she had openly talked about her former career as a detective and her passion for seeking justice.

Why then, Lyssa had asked, *did you accept the job as Nexus Security Chief?*

Ally had shrugged and laughed. *Because London started to feel too small for my talents!*

And your ego apparently, Lyssa had responded as they lay in the aftermath of passion.

Seriously, though, Ally had then responded with a frown, *it just felt like I needed to be here. Like it's my destiny or something. I know that sounds crazy.*

Do you think tonight, this thing between us, is destiny, too? Lyssa remembered asking.

Y'know... Ally smiled bashfully. *I think it just might be.*

Lyssa resumed her pacing, the thoughts bubbling through her mind coming thick and fast. Allyson Knightley would find the truth about what happened in Nexus, and Lyssa wanted very much to be there to help. She knew the trail would lead to Sebastian. Somehow, in some way, she was certain of his culpability in these events. Lyssa wanted answers.

I want to know why.

Why would he *purposely* set a bomb that he knew would kill the New Victus delegates? She had to believe that Jaymes Knightley was collateral damage. There was no reason she could possibly think of that would make him the primary target. Which meant that the bomb was specifically targeted at Pack Nation Ambassador Sabadini. Was that his plan? To start a new war despite his protestations that New Victus were in no position to fight one?

Or was Mercy the target?

No...

Realization dawned.

Gods, I'm so stupid! Mercy was never the target.

Lyssa stopped pacing and slumped onto the sofa, running her fingers through her hair. Slowly the pieces of the puzzle came together in her head, one piece connecting neatly to the next. *She* was the one who was supposed to be at the Summit sitting next to Sabadini, showing the world a kinder, more diplomatic face than it was used to from New Victus. She, Lyssa, had always been the *real* target.

Had Storm known about Vanessa?

Lyssa had gone to great lengths to keep the details of her sister's condition a secret, but now doubts were creeping in. The hunt for her wayward sibling through the forests of Montreal and Vermont had been known only to a select few. Including Mercy, whose body was now lying in a life support-pod in the FSE sector morgue being preserved, ready for autopsy.

Was it worse than just being about Vanessa?

If he knew about her, then what else might he have uncovered the truth about? Did Storm know about Lyssa's regular forays north of the border? Did he know the nature of the visits? Or was it just enough that he knew where she'd been? Had she been targeted because of Vanessa or Dane, or both?

Did it even matter?

Pick your poison, Lyssa. The result is the same.

Obviously, Storm had been caught out by Lyssa's no-show at the Summit. He couldn't have known that Dane delivered Vanessa's body back to her. He wouldn't have had any idea that Lyssa would send Mercy as her proxy while she was performing the 'Blood to Earth' ritual for her departed sister. Lyssa had unwittingly put Mercy in the crosshairs of Storm's scheme.

This was all my fault.

She shook her head to clear out the negative thoughts.

No. This is NOT my fault.

This was all on Storm. The blame lay squarely at his feet. He had killed her niece and he would pay for what he had done to them. Lyssa would *not* allow this transgression to stand unavenged.

But how?

Storm lead the Night Quorum, who controlled the Council of Blood. He held all the power in New Victus, and unless she could sway more of the Council over to her side on the Earth Quorum, then the burden of proof was upon her to provide incontrovertible evidence of Storm's transgressions. Gaining such evidence would be next to impossible, especially now that it was clear that Storm was specifically gunning for her. He would have covered his tracks well; it was the inherent trait of the paranoid man.

She slumped back onto the comfy cushions and stared out into the room. It was a modest affair. Storm loved to bask in regal elegance; to lord it over his peers. Lyssa simply wanted to live a normal life, or as normal as it got for one of her station.

When Mercy returned from London and Nexus, Lyssa had listened to her stories. She had been enraptured by the possibility that this plan they were tabling at the Nexus Summit was their first effort toward getting a tiny piece of freedom back. A baby step down the road toward a world that accepted them and opened their borders once more. Travel was in Lyssa's blood, always had been, and she hated the way that Storm's actions had trapped her. A life of freedom and travel became one of confinement in a three million square mile cage called New Victus. She longed to see the world again.

She had let her guard down for a moment and been duped.

It would not happen again.

If taking him down took the last breath in her body, she would gladly sacrifice it to stop his evil from spreading. Before all this was over, he would feel her fangs on his neck. She swore it on her father's life and the name of her House.

On the coffee table, her cellphone started to ring.

She glanced at the caller ID and snatched it up immediately.

"Damian, you shouldn't be calling me, not now!" she hissed. "He knows. It's the only explanation."

"Lyssa, you have to get out of there," Damian growled.

"I know," she sighed. "Mercy contacted you, right? About the Exodus Initiative?"

"Yes, but Lyssa...we're not ready!"

"You have four days, Damian." Lyssa shook her head. "Dammit, I had a feeling something wasn't right. I knew it in my gut which is why I asked Mercy to talk to you. The Exodus Initiative is already underway from our end. Nykola is taking care of it. You *have* to be ready."

"Fine, I'll sort it. Fuck, somehow I'll sort it. But, Lyssa, you can't wait four days. You need to get out *now*! He'll be coming for you."

She closed her eyes and took a deep breath.

Damian was right, it was no longer safe for her in New Victus. Lyssa knew that Damian cared for her, was concerned for her life, but she found herself focused on something else. Her safety was secondary. Her needs weren't aligned to Damian's concerns right now, there were other things she wanted.

She wanted to talk to Serlia Knightley to express her sorrow.

She wanted to see Allyson and make sure that she was okay.

And she wanted answers.

There was only one place that she was going to get all those things.

"I'll be there...but first," she said resolutely, "I need to go to Nexus."

| Epilogue |

THE RIVER

– Norbel –
– Atlantis –

The city was as spectacular as he remembered. It represented the pinnacle of their achievements as a race, blending science, culture, and art into one cohesive, gleaming miracle. Its crystal towers stretched into the clear blue sky, reaching out like delicate fingers spun from gossamer strands of silken steel, framing diamond windows that reflected the sunlight as a thousand tiny rainbows. This was form and function blended with an aesthetic eye – architecture as art. Each structure didn't just complement the one next to it, but enhanced it in subtle ways, and all of it was rendered in a vibrancy of color that looked like it had come directly off an artist's palette.

It made even the most advanced cities of humankind seem so...primitive.

He meandered through the streets, absorbing the sounds and the smells of Fae society at work and play. It felt like a lifetime since he had been here, and in many ways it was. Norbel had valid reasons, of course, but for him to blame any one of them would be to simply persist in a lie. There was so much more to it than anyone else could – or would – understand.

Coming here, like this, would not have been his first choice. Yet he had to come. It was expected.

Today was the day Norbel had married Vaylur, and this was where they had been wed. Anniversaries were important, even for a race as long-lived as the Fae, and hence, they had always come back here to this place, on this day, to celebrate. This would be the first anniversary since Vaylur's death. To be absent today would be to raise unwanted attention.

Yet this city was a stark reminder of his greatest failure, one that he had spent much time and effort trying to correct. It had taken a lot of soul-searching to realize that it hadn't been his fault. Simply the whim of fate. Destiny making a mockery of the best laid plans. Over the centuries, it became clear that nothing would have changed the outcome that day; things had played out *exactly* the way they were supposed to.

Free choice was the ultimate illusion.

For now, anyway.

As he made his way through the city, he passed through each of its concentric rings. Each ring housed a different aspect of Fae culture and contained structures taller than the ring that preceded it. From the low-lying docks and landing pads on the outer ring, through the picturesque parks and residential areas, past the museums and galleries, the schools and universities, and then the ring that consisted of their science and industry. Finally, he reached the tower that stood at the heart of Atlantis.

The Spire.

The sunlight shimmered off its mirrored surface as it towered high above the city, the tallest man-made structure on Earth. It had always been a symbol. Of the need to reach upward; to strive for excellence. To expand knowledge past known boundaries and never be held back. It was a philosophy with which he passionately agreed.

In hindsight, there was a certain irony to this place that possibly no one else would understand. The Fae had fought for this city, fighting tooth and claw to preserve it and make sure it continued to exist in the future. While he respected the struggle, he also knew they had all fundamentally misunderstood that for which they were striving.

Today, though, the undeniable beauty of the city was not

his primary reason for visiting. He was here for something else, something to which none of the man-made elegance of the city could even *begin* to compare.

He entered the elevator in the Spire and used his security code to access the control panel that lit up and prompted him for a destination. He prodded the touchscreen, selecting the very lowest level. The view from the observation deck atop the Spire may have been one of the most astonishing things his eyes had ever seen, yet it paled in comparison with what lay almost five thousand meters beneath it.

The River.

He lost himself in the infinite depth and indescribable colors that ebbed and swirled below him. Looking into the River was the strangest of sensations. Not just for Norbel, but for anyone who had the profound experience of being in the presence of it.

Though it was *your* eyes that peered into its natural splendor, it felt more like the River was looking at *you*. Deep inside you. It overwhelmed you with a flood of conflicting emotion. It made you feel profoundly special, but also utterly insignificant. It made you realize your connection to life on this planet, yet also inspired introspection. It made you question everything you thought you knew and believed. Or didn't believe.

For all their advanced science and enlightened nature, even the Fae could neither prove nor disprove the notion of a deity. The one God or the many, depending on your belief system. The entity that played a guiding hand and coaxed life from lifelessness on this humble planet Earth. One either believed...or didn't. It was a matter of faith.

He was not a believer.

Actually, 'atheist' was the correct term. It wasn't that he disbelieved; he simply lacked belief.

All that said, though, standing there and looking into the River forced profound questions to surface from deep within. Questions that simply weren't possible to answer *without* faith and belief. Standing here was the only time that Norbel truly entertained the notion that there must be a supreme power. There had to be.

Otherwise, how could such a thing as this *possibly* exist?

This was the '*River of Time*,' and it only ever flowed in one direction.

It couldn't be dammed or diverted. It was immovable and immutable. It was a historian's dream, granting the viewer a window into the past. What the River *chose* to display for them was always seemingly random, however. For all their amazing technology, the most the Fae could do was skim its churning surface and witness what it deemed to show them. A flash here, a moment there.

Yet, it was not just history that the River could show you. It also gave tantalizing glimpses into the possibilities of the future.

Or at least it used to.

The River...was broken.

Norbel touched a control on the thick glass wall that separated him from its flow, scrolling his view forward in time as a million visions played out before him.

Somewhere in the world, a man buys flowers and smiles with anticipation. The picture dissolves into a woman driving a car while she's cursing and shouting. There are tears of frustration. A child is drinking from a soda can with a look of disgust. A father dies in a hospital bed; his daughter never makes it in time to say goodbye. Two young men share a tender first kiss, then look bashfully into each other's eyes.

Every moment a different picture. Always unique. Always unpredictable. Even scrolling to the same point of the River repeatedly simply gave you a different arbitrary image from a different random part of the world. Millions of different stories all playing out every moment of every day, from the spectacular to the mundane. The River had been a gift for scholars and historians, a window to the past. A glimpse of every era of the planet's evolution, a wealth of information through which to wade.

Then he reached it. The singularity. The one moment that was always the same. Never changing.

"It's been a while since I've seen you here," came the melodic voice from behind him.

He hadn't heard her approach, but he knew her presence. She had the unmistakable aura of her family line.

"Serlia."

"Brother." She took up station at the guard rail placing her hands on its warm surface next to his, following his gaze into the River. He slid his hand over hers in a loving, brotherly gesture.

"How are you?" he asked with tones of love and concern in equal measure.

She would ignore the question, but he knew it was his place to at least ask. Between the two of them, she had always been the strong one. It was she who truly carried the power of her family line, not Norbel. In truth, it was she who should have been the leader of the Fae. She had the skills, the demeanor, and was universally loved and respected in their community.

Yet she had never sought power. Serlia had made her choice, to pursue something greater. Something that was almost unique in their society. She had settled down, started a proper family. Fallen in love. He admired that more than she would ever know and regretted that the course of events had led her to this place of pain.

She deserved better.

"Loss haunts us both, Brother. It's been a while...but I still see your pain."

He knew to what she was referring and spoke the words she expected to hear.

"This location is the only place I can still feel him. Everywhere else is just static pictures and stale memories, not the smell or the feeling of him. But here... Maybe it is simply the memory of the fact that we met here. Maybe it is the River that somehow...perpetuates the feeling. There is much about it we still do not comprehend or understand. It is like Vaylur is still here somehow, just out of sight and touch. I apologize. I cannot explain it any clearer."

"I understand," she said simply.

"I am truly sorry for your loss, Sister. If I could have done anything..."

She did not acknowledge his sympathy openly, but he felt

her grateful acceptance. They stood quietly for a minute or so, both contemplating the silent flow of time for very different reasons.

"Still no change?" she asked, her voice tinged with hope. "I thought maybe after what has happened..."

He had checked prior to her arrival, as was his responsibility to do so. He continued to gaze into the River but shook his head slowly.

"I had the same hope, but no...there is no change. Do you wish to observe it?"

"No," she answered immediately, her voice a broken whisper. "No, I've seen it too many times before. I don't need...or wish to lay my eyes upon it again."

Norbel nodded in sympathy.

The River was protected now. Visible only beyond sandwiched layers of crystal glass and energy forcefields. There was no longer any way to directly access the River or its flow. That's how this had all started, after all.

Serlia slowly lifted her left hand and gently touched the surface of the barrier. Her fingertips pressed against it lightly, the crystal glass so transparent it was almost invisible, not even reflections gave its presence away.

"Whenever I see this...I wish that we had been as strict with our security back then. Closed it off as it is now. We paid a heavy price for our lack of vigilance. Our arrogance."

He remained silent.

"Do you think we can... Will it ever change?"

"I really do not know," he shrugged. "You may have to accept the fact that this simply may be inevitable, Serlia."

He didn't believe that. He wouldn't be here if he did. However, as Serlia's brother he needed to play Devil's advocate. The evidence suggested that the answer to his sister's question was never going to change. It was, therefore, his duty as her loving brother to prepare her for the worst.

"I can't accept that. I lost a husband this week...I will not lose any more. I'll never accept it, Brother." She looked at him with the welling of fresh tears in her hard eyes. "I can't...because she's my daughter.

"I won't lose her, too."

| COMING SOON BY JON FORD |

The Ballad of the Songbird – Book 2
Blood to Earth

The Femme Fatales – Book 1
THE BURNING SKY

| ACKNOWLEDGEMENTS |

I'd be remiss if I didn't acknowledge a few people, without whom this book would not have been possible. I give my heartfelt thanks to all those who supported me along this journey. Thank you!

Here are a few that deserve an extra special mention.

My Wonderful Wife
Right from the start, Jess has supported me in chasing my dream. Never wavering. She was the first person to tell me I could do this.
Love you always, little Bubba xxx

My Editor Supreme - Nikki Anderson
Hunters wouldn't exist today without her help and support. From her awesome edits, to helping me know WTF I'm doing. Meeting you on Twitter (@nikki_twisted) felt like fate!

Artist Extraordinaire – Marlena Mozgawa
What's a book without a kickass awesome cover?
I was referred to Marlena by Sylessae (*thanks Syl!*) and it was a masterstroke. I can't think of my books covered any other way.

My Beta-Reader Posse
Chell, Andy, Sarah, and Marisa. Your feedback made this a much better book. My eternal thanks. Hope you're up for the next six!

My Much-Loved Brother Matt
You always had my back Bro. Love ya, man.

The Inimitable Kevin Smith

"If you're alive, kick into drive. Chase whimsies.
See if you can turn dreams into a way to make a living,
if not an entire way of life." - Kevin Smith
That quote struck a chord for me, so I did it. I chased my
whimsy, and now you're holding it.

Special Thanks to:

Mercedes Lackey and Judith Tarr, who pointed me in the right
direction.

Finally, I'd be remiss if I didn't also shout out...

Katie Hagaman(@hagaman_kl), who created my amazing
book trailer. Now I want the TV show/movie!
Eaton Krone (@EatonKrone), who helped guide me through
the hair pulling exercise of formatting.

Easter Eggs Galore!

This book (*and the series as a whole*) has **LOADS** of little nods to
my influences, including:

My series title is an homage to **Alan Moore** and **Ian Gibson**'s
seminal *'The Ballad of Halo Jones'* which I fucking loved when I was
a kid!

The comic writing of **Simon Furman** was also a huge influence.
The title of *'Freelance Peacekeeping Agent'* is an homage to one of my
favorite characters of his creation, yes?

If you read the chapter titles, you may notice a few references to
song titles that I listened to while I was writing that particular
chapter. Go check out my website (*www.jonfordauthor.com*) for a
track listing of the songs that influenced me.

And to **Dan**... Yes. That is you piloting the Banshee at the end.
Best. Housemate. Ever!

| ABOUT THE AUTHOR |

Jon Ford lives in Worcestershire, UK with his awesome Wifey, their lovable puppy Vixen, and under the watchful gaze of their cat-overlords, Lana and Gale. He has far too many hobbies for one man to sensibly hold down.

In between his hobby-juggling, you'll find him working as an Implementation Consultant by day and burning the midnight oil to bring you **The Ballad of the Songbird** saga – an epic seven-book series.

To learn more about Jon and read his random musings, visit his website at:

http://jonfordauthor.com

He can also be found on:
Twitter at **@_Knightingale_**
Instagram at **@JonFordAuthor**
& on Facebook at **facebook.com/JonFordAuthor**

Made in the USA
Columbia, SC
29 June 2021

41043892R00317